DESA KINCAID

BOUNTY HUNTER

R.S. PENNEY

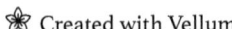

PART I

1

_____

Desa rode into town atop Midnight.

The large black stallion let out a snort of derision, his ears shifting this way and that as they entered a village where log houses stood on either side of the hard-packed dirt road. It was a primitive place by her standards, but she noted the presence of paraffin lanterns hanging unlit above every door. At this late afternoon hour, the sun still provided enough light despite a thick ceiling of clouds.

To her left and her right, tall pines rose up on the outskirts of town so that it seemed as if the only way out was along the east-west road. But Desa had studied maps, and she knew the area well. A smaller road branched off from the centre of town, heading south.

Midnight twisted his neck to give her a side-long glance with one eye. No doubt he felt the same disturbance she did. The Ether seemed distant. It was usually so in places where men's hearts were full of hate.

Closing her eyes, Desa nodded once in agreement. "I feel it too," she whispered, patting the horse. "Be at ease; we won't be staying long."

Midnight snorted again.

A petite woman in tan pants and a brown duster, Desa pulled the wide brim of her hat down to shade a face of olive skin. Her mother always told her that hers was a face that would inspire young men toward all sorts of trouble. Not that she cared very much about getting a man's attention. She had always fancied women, and that had remained true even through her brief marriage.

She urged Midnight up a side street where two women from neighbouring houses were gossiping on either side of a waist-high fence. One had her hair up in a thick, golden braid, and the other let dark-red tresses fall to her shoulders, but you might have thought them twins by the way they turned their heads in unison to stare at Desa.

A skinny man in a fine black coat and a bowler hat came walking past on the other side of the road. City fashion? Out here? Maybe he was the local banker. He paused just long enough to direct a sneer at Desa.

Puckering her lips, Desa blew out a breath. "It's going to be an interesting stay," she murmured to Midnight. The stallion whinnied in agreement.

A young boy in thick overalls that he wore over a white shirt came running out of one yard, dashing across the road. He was maybe eight or nine with a mop of yellow hair and a dimple in his chin.

"Boy!" Desa called out.

He stopped halfway across the road.

With a cheeky grin, Desa bowed slightly in her saddle. "Reckon a smart lad like you would know where a lady can find a hot meal," she said. "Where do travelers usually stay when they pass through town?"

He turned his head to look at her, squinting as he sized

her up, then gestured up the street. "Around the next bend," he said. "Place is called MacGregor's."

"Maybe you could show me?"

He shied away from her, backing up a few steps, glancing this way and that as if he thought his mother might come out and scold him for talking to a stranger. "I have to do my chores." Desa snorted. The boy didn't look as if he was very busy with chores at that particular moment. "You'll know it. It's taller than the other houses."

She nodded to him.

A squeeze of her thighs set Midnight in motion, and it wasn't long before the road curved slightly to her left. She passed more log houses, a tall man in a duster who led his horse by the reins and even a small village green.

The boy was true to his word; McGregor's was a large, two-story building made of wooden planks. Its gabled roof was still slick from a recent rainfall. A metal sign above the door depicted a man on the back of a rearing horse.

The very instant she arrived, a stable-girl came running out to meet her. A tiny slip of a lass with her body hidden under a poncho, she wore her bright red hair pulled back from a face as pale as snow. "Will you be needing a place for your horse, ma'am?"

Desa swung her leg over Midnight's flank and dropped to the ground with a loud *thump*. She straightened, reached up and tipped her hat. "Much obliged. Do you get many travelers here?"

"We're the biggest village between High Falls and Fengen's Wake," the girl replied. "Most folks stop here."

Desa stood before the child with hands shoved into her duster's pockets, nodding slowly as she considered the answer. "Lookin' for a fella as might have come through a few days ago," she said. "Maybe you've seen him. Thick dark mustache and a scar along his cheek."

The girl turned her head to study the inn's front door, then stepped back and scraped a knuckle across her brow. "Lots of folks stop here," she mumbled. "I'm sure I wouldn't recall if I did."

A moment of tense silence passed before the girl stepped forward and reached for Midnight's reins. The stallion nuzzled and licked her outstretched hand. "He's friendly!" Desa had to stifle the urge to laugh. The child didn't know the half of it! Once Midnight decided he liked you, he was your friend for life.

Taking him by the reins, the girl led him toward a stone path that went around the back of the inn. Really, it was Midnight who allowed himself to be led. That horse would not go anywhere he didn't want to go.

"Girl," Desa said.

She fished a coin out of her coat pocket and flicked it with her thumb. It tumbled end over end toward the girl, who whirled around to catch it with a deft hand. "For your trouble."

Inside, she found a saloon with sawdust on the wooden floorboards. Round tables were spread out beneath unlit lanterns that hung from the ceiling. For now, the light from the front window was enough.

A bar ran along the wall to her left, built against the side of a staircase that went up to the guest rooms. The man who stood behind the counter, wiping a glass with a rag, was tall with a barrel chest and a ring of dark hair. "Lookin' for a room?" he asked.

"And a drink," she said, removing her hat.

The barkeep wrinkled his nose at her, then shook his head. "Suppose you'll be wanting a Vinthen Red or something else they serve in the cities," he muttered. "Well, what'll it be?"

Desa hopped onto a stool, folding her hands on the counter and leaning in close. "Whiskey," she said. "Straight up."

His surprised grimace was almost enough to soothe Desa's annoyance. The man plunked a shot-glass down on the counter, then filled it with the contents of a brown jug and waited to see what she would do.

Desa picked up the glass, shut her eyes tight and downed it all in one gulp. The hot sting on her tongue and the warmth as it filled her belly were familiar companions, salves that soothed her many pains. "Now," she said. "Maybe you could answer my questions."

The bartender narrowed his eyes. "Maybe you could answer *mine,*" he shot back. "We don't trust strangers around here."

"That's funny, coming from a fella as runs an inn in a town where strange folks come through all the time."

"I may have to house 'em," he said. "I don't have to like 'em."

Pursing her lips, Desa held his gaze for a long moment, then nodded curtly. "Tell you what," she offered. "I'll answer one of your questions, and you answer one of mine. All square and even, no?"

"Why are you passing through?"

"I'm looking for a couple of lowlies as broke the law back in High Falls," Desa explained. "Figured they might have come this way."

The man looked her up and down, and his face tightened, his thick, black eyebrows drawn together. "I knew it!" he snapped, though his voice never rose much beyond a soft whisper. "You have the reek of a bounty hunter on you. Very few women hunters in these parts, and only one as looks like you. You're Desa Kincaid: the Widow."

Her mouth clicked shut, and her eyebrows climbed up her forehead. "I see you've heard of me," she said. "And unless the name of this establishment is entirely misleading, I presume you're McGregor. So...Where's Morley?"

"Don't know any Morley."

"I consider myself to be a woman of reason, sir," Desa said, her accent changing slightly now that she no longer had to effect the facade of a local dialect. "Surely, we can come to some kind of accommodation."

"There's nothing you have I want."

With care, Desa slid a gloved hand into her pants' pocket and retrieved a thick coin of pure Aladri silver. She held it up so the barkeep could see the sword embossed on one side. "Not even this?"

"I don't want witch silver."

Desa felt her lips curl, then bowed her head to him. "It's not what you think," she said. "There's no magic, simply a deeper understanding of nature. This could be a useful tool if you were willing to open your mind just a crack."

The man took it from her, squinting as he examined the coin. "How does it work?" he asked. "This...deeper understanding of nature."

"See the sword on one side?"

"Yeah..."

"Run your thumb along it from hilt to blade."

McGregor's cheeks puffed up as he let out a sigh, but he followed her instructions to the letter, clutching the coin in one hand and sliding his thumb across its surface. His eyes all but popped out. "It's cold."

A grin blossomed on Desa's face, and she nodded to him. "Indeed," she said. "Now, consider what you might do with it. You could put it in an icebox and use it to chill wine or keep food fresh. You could use it to bring down a child's fever, to provide some relief on a hot summer's day. Use that sparingly, and it should last months."

The coin would drain an enormous amount of heat energy before it was filled to capacity, but it would do so slowly. Desa had made sure of that when she created it. A person would have to hold that coin for quite a while before they were in danger of hypothermia, and frostbite would compel them to put it down first.

"For months?" McGregor spluttered. "How do I...make it stop?"

"Run your thumb over the sword from blade to hilt."

The very instant he did so, McGregor exhaled with relief. He set the coin down on the counter and bent forward, staring at her with beady eyes. "A treasure to be sure," he said. "But I'm of no mind to cross the man as passed through here two days ago."

"He made an impression, I take it."

"You might say that."

"Perhaps I should sweeten the pot."

She slid the coin toward McGregor, then reached into her pocket and retrieved its twin, setting the two down side by side. The bartender's eyes flicked down to the coins, then back up to her. "Two would be useful...But not enough to-"

"Just try this one. I think you'll be pleasantly surprised."

With a look of extreme annoyance, McGregor palmed the second coin and ran his thumb along it. This time, he gave a start and nearly dropped the thing. "It's hot!"

"Imagine a journey of several days in which you must sleep in a tent each night," Desa said. "Autumn's chill setting in, but that's of no concern to you. You'll be safe and warm all night long."

Silence stretched on for several moments in which McGregor seemed to consider the offer. Desa could see it in his face; he wasn't swayed. Finally, the man slid his thumb across the coin again and set it down next to its companion.

Standing up, Desa put her hat back on and pulled the brim down over her eyes. "If you're not interested..." She reached out, slapping a gloved hand down on the two coins, clawing them back toward herself.

"No, wait."

She looked up, arching one dark eyebrow. "I am in no mood to be trifled with, Mr. McGregor," she said coldly. "If you know something, then by all means share. Otherwise, I'll be on my way."

His mouth opened, and his eyes dropped shut. A shuddering breath forced its way through his lips. "This Morley you speak of," McGregor said. "He came through here a few days ago. Darkness seemed to follow his every step."

"The light dimmed?"

McGregor winced, shaking his head so quickly he might have made himself dizzy. "Nothing so obvious...It was more...a feeling you got when you were near the man. Folks were happy to see his back."

"Do you know where he went?"

Before McGregor could answer, the door banged open, allowing a young man to stumble into the saloon, trailed by several of his friends. The leader of this group was tall and lean with short, black hair and fuzz on his upper lip that might have been an attempt at a mustache.

The two louts who shuffled in behind him were at most a few years younger, both skinny lads with pale faces, though one had obviously suffered a broken nose some time ago. Desa tried to ignore them, but it seemed they were unwilling to allow her any peace.

"Who might this be?" the leader asked.

Desa had her elbows on the counter, her mouth covered by the tips of her fingers. Aside from a quick glance when they had made their entrance, she made it a point not to look. That would only encourage them.

The leader seemed not to notice her disinterest. Desa heard his boots thumping on the floorboards, and she could practically *feel* the air stirring on the back of her neck. He would be within arm's reach in seconds.

"My dear," the man said. "You are-"

Desa's hand snapped up, seizing the fellow's wrist before he could tap her on the shoulder, holding him tight in an iron grip. "Utterly disinterested," she said. "Now would be a good time to move along."

She released him, and the man staggered away, his feet scuffing across the floor. "By the Almighty's left nut, girl!" he barked. "Who do ya think you are? In these parts, women know better than to-"

Desa turned around.

Lifting her chin, she stared him down without a single word, her eyebrows slowly rising. "Reckon you meant to apologize and wish me safe journeys," she said, assuming a local accent once again. "I thank you for your kindness, sir."

The man was bent over and rubbing one wrist with the other hand. When his eyes fell upon her, she saw hatred there. He reached for the holstered revolver on his hip.

"Ducane!" McGregor called out. "Not in here!"

With his hand hovering over the grip of his pistol, Ducane stiffened, then looked away and spat on the floor. "Another time then, Missy," he whispered. "'Less, of course, you're smart enough to leave town before I find ya."

Desa said nothing more.

Defeated for the moment, Ducane jerked his head

toward the door and then left without even checking to see if his two lackeys bothered to follow him. Of course, they did, and then Desa had a little peace again.

"He'll make good on that threat," McGregor said. "This Morley you're after? He went south. I suggest you do the same. Keep your witch coins; leave us honest folk alone. Just get on your horse and ride."

SEVERAL HOURS LATER, Desa was walking down a street of hard-packed dirt with her hands in her coat pockets. Full night had come on, and the houses on either side were just square shadows, silhouettes against the blackness, made visible only by the wan light of a crescent moon. She saw an orange glow in some windows – light from a fire that hadn't been doused – but most of this sleepy little town had turned in.

She had completed two circuits of the village and was well into her third, thoughts of Morley tumbling through her head. The man was a rabid animal, but it was his master that Desa feared most. Bendarian's experiments with Field Binding had killed six people and wounded several others. He was to have been incarcerated in Aladar, but of course, the man escaped.

The Synod had been willing to just let him go – someone else's problem – but not Desa Nin Leean. No...At nineteen years old, Desa had been certain that she could bring the man to justice; so she hopped onto a horse and rode off in pursuit. That was ten years ago, and Bendarian's power had become monstrous in the decade since.

She rounded a corner and winced when the lantern above McGregor's door made her eyes smart. The small inn kept a light shining for anyone who might want to avail themselves of its services after dark, as did the sheriff's station and the local physician's office. She had passed all three several times on her walk.

Desa stepped into the light with her head down, sighing softly. "What did you do to these people, Morley?" she wondered aloud. "What-"

Her ears picked up a crunching sound.

Shadows on an intersecting street resolved into Ducane, who came into the light with a hand on his pistol. The other two were right behind him, both sneering, especially Mr. Broken-Nose. That one seemed to be itching for a little violence.

"Well now," Ducane said. "I believe we have a score to settle."

Desa shut her eyes and tried to remain calm. "I have no time for this." Her voice was ice. "Leave me to my business, and I'll be gone by noon tomorrow. You can go back to lording over this small town and thank your Almighty that I have larger concerns."

The grin on Ducane's face promised pain. He chuckled, no doubt convinced that he had control of this situation, and shook his head. "I made you a promise, Missy," he said. "What kind of man would I be if I didn't keep it?"

"A wiser man than most."

"No one embarrasses me like that, Missy."

What to do? The man was about two seconds away from drawing his gun, and if he got too close, he would certainly want to pummel her. Why kill a woman when you could just put her in her place? More satisfying when you could force her to acknowledge your superiority. Perhaps the time had come to drive her point home.

With a thought, Desa ordered the stone on her necklace to drain light energy. The lantern above McGregor's went out, as did the glow in every nearby window. In truth, all of those fires were still burning, but they would provide no illumination so long as Desa's necklace was nearby.

With so little light to take, they were left in total darkness. Even the crescent moon had vanished from the sky. It was still there, of course, but someone would have to get at least a hundred paces away from Desa to see it.

"What the-" Ducane spluttered.

The man was incredibly loud, stomping around with feet scuffing in the dirt, giving away his position with every step. His two lackeys were no better, both shuffling about. One drew his pistol with the distinctive *click* of a hammer being cocked.

Desa moved silently through the darkness, pacing a circle around the group. "You will leave this place now." Her voice spooked them, and one jumped, startled to find that she was no longer where she had been. "You will not trouble me again. And if you do...I will turn you into a toad."

She had no such power, but the superstitions of backward-thinking men were often more useful tools than any feat she might actually produce.

She ordered her necklace to stop feasting on light.

The lantern above McGregor's door flared to life once again, revealing three men standing with their backs to the saloon, all frantic and looking about as if they expected a demon to leap from every shadow.

Desa stood in the intersecting street with fists on her hips, her chin thrust out as she watched them scramble. "Have I made my point?" she asked. "Or must I do something even more...drastic?"

The two lackeys bolted down the street without looking back. Any loyalty they had for Ducane would only last until they encountered someone more frightening than he was. That was the price of employing such men.

Ducane, however, was not cowed. His face reddened, and he yanked his pistol free of its holster. "Witch!" he shouted. "Witch!" In the blink of an eye, he had the gun aimed at her, his thumb pulling back the hammer.

Desa raised her left arm up to shield herself, her bracelet feasting on kinetic energy just before the gun went off with a *CRACK! CRACK!* Two bullets jerked to a halt right in front of her and hovered there, the bracelet holding them suspended in midair.

She let her arm drop.

The bullets fell with it, landing at her feet an instant before she stepped over them. "I did warn you," she said, beginning a slow, inexorable march toward Ducane. "But that was attempted murder. I only wanted to pass through this village without incident. I was even willing to turn a blind eye to your destructive tendencies. I'm afraid that is no longer an option."

Ducane stumbled backward, lifting the gun in a shaky hand.

Once again, the street went dark, and Desa stepped aside to get out of the line of fire. Her bracelet might stop a third bullet, but not a fourth. Not until she replenished its power. Thankfully, Ducane did not shoot.

He did shuffle about, making noise, breathing hard as though he feared for his life. "Where are you?" he shouted into the darkness. "Show yourself, witch!"

Desa moved slowly, deliberately, closing the distance with barely any sound. Years of training had given her the instincts of a huntress. She could be as quiet as a spider on the ceiling when she wanted to be. Ducane panted. When the light finally returned, Desa was right next to him.

Ducane rounded on her.

Desa kicked the gun out of his hand. She spun and back-kicked, her boot slamming into the man's chest, driving him backward. A wheeze exploded from Ducane as he lost his balance and fell against the side of a log house.

The man drew his knife and held it with the tip pointed at Desa's heart. He watched her over the length of a trembling arm. "I'll send you back to the Inferno, witch! Tell your demon masters that you failed. You won't take my soul!"

He rushed her, intending to drive the blade through her chest.

Stepping aside, Desa twirled on the spot and seized the man's arm as he passed. She forced Ducane to bend double, then brought her knee up to strike his nose. That knocked the fight out of him.

When she released him, he collapsed to the ground, moaning in pain. Idiot. There were days when she regretted her decision to leave Aladar in pursuit of Bendarian. The people out here were savages.

Desa squatted down next to him, shaking her head. "Had enough?" she asked. "Are you ready to come with me to the sheriff's station?"

Ducane groaned.

"Yes, I imagine it is quite painful." Grabbing a clump of his hair, Desa pulled his head back to reveal a bloody nose. "I abhor violence, but I will not suffer a murderer to go free. On your feet, sir!"

There were faces in nearby windows, watching her. Some of them would have seen the lights of their lamps go out. Her necklace would drain light from any source that was close enough; walls were no impediment to its power.

Desa mopped a hand over her sweat-slick face, then

blinked several times. "Get up, Ducane," she growled. "We have a long walk ahead of us."

WITH THE BARREL of her pistol pressed against Ducane's back, Desa nudged the man through the door to the sheriff's office. Inside, she found a simple room of wooden walls, illuminated by a paraffin lantern on the desk.

The young man who sat behind that desk – a deputy, by his badge – stood up and flinched when he saw them. "What's all this?" He was lean and slim with a pale face and short blonde hair that he parted to one side. "Bringing Mr. Ducane in? Who are you?"

Ducane spared her the trouble of answering.

The man turned his head to show clenched teeth and hissed at Desa. "A witch," he rasped. "She used her magic on me."

"Men in these parts are a superstitious lot," Desa said. "Weren't no magic at play. I'm just a bounty hunter passin' through, and this one tried to kill me. You'll find plenty of witnesses as can testify to the gunshots."

"I shot at her!" Ducane shouted. "She made the bullets stop!"

Closing her eyes, Desa touched two fingers to her forehead. "Aye, he shot at me all right," she agreed. "Though, I can't be blamed if he couldn't hit the broad side of a barn at ten paces. A smart-lookin' fella like you don't believe in magic, do ya?"

The young deputy gripped his belt in both hands, then looked down at his feet. "No, ma'am, I do not." When he leveled his gaze on her, his face was stern. "Mr. Ducane has a reputation for causing trouble."

"Lenny," Ducane said. "You know me."

"Aye, I do," Lenny replied. "And I know you're as like to start a fight as you are to drink every drop in McGregor's storehouse. Many have warned you that it would bring you to a bad end, Charles."

Snatching up a ring of keys from the corner of the desk, Lenny moved to a door in the wall to Desa's left. He glanced over his shoulder, frowning at them. "I'd just as soon have you in a cell until this matter is sorted," he added. "But ma'am, I'll have to ask that you remain in town to testify before a magistrate."

"Won't be possible, sir," Desa said. "A girl has to earn her living."

"That's as may be, but the law is the law."

Once again, Desa found herself regretting the decision to come to this benighted little town. How much time would she lose waiting for a magistrate to arrive? How far away would Morley get? She had lost the man's trail several times over the last five years; sniffing him out again had felt like a miracle.

But what could she do? She was the only one who *could* testify against Ducane, and if she left, the man would go free to terrorize some other young woman. There were days when she hated her lot in life.

Lenny jiggled the keys several times and finally forced the door open. "This way," he said. "And make no trouble, mind."

Desa poked Ducane with her gun.

Reluctantly, he started forward, passing through the door to a narrow corridor of white bricks with cells in both walls. They were all empty except for one at the very end where two young men sat side by side.

One on the left, in tan pants and a blue shirt, had his hands on his knees as he stared into his lap. By the look of him, he might have been Lenny's twin. In fact, Desa was quite certain that he was.

The other one had thick black hair that he wore parted in the middle and pale skin that was marked by a single blemish on his cheek. A three-pointed star from a branding iron. It must have been done recently because the flesh was still raw and red.

"You're selling him into slavery?"

Lenny shrugged. "His choice. It was that or the gallows."

Whirling around to face the young deputy, Desa looked up to stare into his eyes. "What was his crime?" she inquired. "Something monstrous, I would hope, to merit such punishment."

Lenny flinched at the change in her voice – she had let her accent slip – then shook his head and recovered his wits. "Fornication." His mouth twisted as if speaking the word left a bad taste. "With each other. My brother was man enough to choose the noose."

Before Desa could offer a scathing reply, yet another man appeared in the doorway. This one was tall with gray hair and a sheriff's star on his barrel chest. "What's going on here, Lenny?" he demanded. "I heard gunshots in the night."

"That would be Mr. Ducane's doing,"

Twisting around to shove a finger in Desa's face, Ducane backed up until he almost hit the cell at the end of the corridor. "She's a witch!" he cried out. "She used her magics. No wonder young Tommy and Sebastian here have turned to sin. With degenerates like this woman in our town..."

"Enough!" the sheriff snapped. "You finally gone and stepped over that line you been skirtin' eh, Charles? Throw him in a cell, Lenny."

The deputy did as he was ordered, turning his back,

sliding a key into the lock and pulling the barred door open. Ducane shuffled through without protest and dropped onto the wooden bench inside. Once he was safely tucked away behind bars, Desa holstered her weapon.

Lenny slammed the door shut with a *clang.*

"Now," the sheriff said, blocking the exit with his arms crossed, frowning as he looked Desa up and down. "Who might you be, and what exactly happened between you and Mr. Ducane?"

Ignoring him, Desa turned her back and went to the cell at the end of the corridor. The two men inside both looked up. Like frightened animals. It sickened her to see that brand on the dark-haired boy's face.

Desa licked her lips, took a deep breath and nodded once. "Sheriff, you will release these two men immediately," she said. "What they've done is no crime, and slavery is an affront to all that is good and decent in this world."

"Release them?" the sheriff spluttered. "On whose authority?"

"On the authority of Desa nin Leean," she said. "Prime Field Binder of Aladar. If you are so eager to be rid of these young men, then I will happily take them away. They can come with me to Aladar and live in peace."

"Witch," Ducane muttered from behind the bars of his cell.

The sheriff blinked, surprised by her declaration, and stepped back to brace a hand against the door-frame. Lenny positioned himself between Desa and the other man with his hands raised defensively. "Wait, hold on!" he said. "I don't want to see my brother die, but the Almighty's laws are clear."

"Not everyone believes in your Almighty, sir."

Lenny narrowed his eyes, trying to stare through her.

"Ducane was right," he said, nodding. "You *are* a witch. Sheriff Cromwell, maybe we should be arresting her as well. Before she corrupts the townsfolk."

"Lenny," the sheriff said. "Enough. And you, madame. I thank you for bringing a known troublemaker in, but I do believe it's time that you be on your way."

"Not without Tommy and Sebastian," Desa insisted.

Lenny drew his revolver, thrust his arm out and aimed for Desa's chest. His thumb rested on the hammer, but he didn't cock it. "Shut your mouth, witch," he whispered. "Be thankful that Sheriff Cromwell is willing to let you go."

Desa stretched a hand out, the knuckles of her closed fist mere inches from Lenny's nose, and then her ring began to glow with a brief flare of light. The young man squeezed his eyes shut, stumbling back in shock.

Desa kicked him in the belly, forcing the lad to double over. She punched Lenny's face with one fist, then the other, a ferocious pair of blows that knocked the wits right out of him. He bent low, practically touching his forehead to the floor.

Desa reacted without thought, one hand deftly pulling a throwing knife from her belt and hurling it over the young man's back. It tumbled end over end toward the sheriff, who drew his gun just in time for Desa's knife to nick his hand.

His fingers uncurled.

The pistol fell to the floor.

With a growl, Desa jumped and rolled across Lenny's exposed back, popping up to land just behind him. She rushed the sheriff before the man could recover from his shock.

Cromwell looked up at her with wide eyes.

Desa leaped and kicked high, slamming her boot into the man's chest, driving him backward into the small office that fronted the building. He staggered across the wooden floor, hit the wall and collapsed.

Nimble as a cat, Desa landed right in front of the desk, then whirled around to find Lenny on his knees in the middle of the cell-block. The young man snatched up his fallen pistol, stood on shaky legs and cocked the hammer as he turned.

Desa pulled another throwing knife.

Her hand came up, the knife flying from her fingertips, tumbling end over end on course for its target. Lenny spun around just in time for the blade to sink half an inch into the soft skin of his thigh.

He fell over backward, his arm flailing as he pulled the trigger. The gun went off with a roar like thunder, and chunks of wood rained down upon Lenny an instant after two bullets punched through the ceiling.

Squatting down just inside the cell-block, Desa retrieved the sheriff's revolver and held it up in front of her face, the barrel pointed upward. "Now," she said. "I assume you don't want any more trouble."

Lenny was clutching his wounded leg.

A glance over her shoulder revealed Sheriff Cromwell leaning against the wall with a hand over his heart, his every breath a ragged gasp. "This was only a small taste of my power," Desa assured them. "I'd rather not have to do anything drastic."

"Witch..." Ducane whispered in his cell.

"We-" Cromwell puffed out a wheeze before he could finish that sentence. "We will release the young men to your care."

Moaning in pain, Lenny tried to sit up, but he had to steady himself with one hand on the floor. His head lolled.

"Ducane was right..." he whispered. "You're an affront to all that's holy."

Desa cocked the hammer on the sheriff's pistol and pointed the weapon at Lenny. "Put your weapon down, son," she pleaded. "Don't make me kill you."

Mercy be praised, the boy actually did as he was told, setting his gun down on the floor. Then he stood up woozily, turned around and shuffled to the cell and the end of the corridor. "You want my worthless brother?" he mumbled, shoving the key into the lock. The door swung open with a *clang*. "Take him."

Tommy and Sebastian stood side by side in the cell, both slack-jawed and staring at her like she was some kind of demon. Neither one moved. Maybe they didn't believe their own eyes.

"Well?" Desa said. "Do you want to stay here and wait for the gallows, or do you want to come with me?"

There was a long moment of silence in which both lads were still. Desa suddenly felt very nervous. If she had just gone to all this trouble to free a pair of lads who were determined to remain here and accept their fate, well...That would be embarrassing. And dangerous. She had made a few enemies tonight. It was likely she wouldn't ever be able to come back this way. To have done all that to save a pair of primitive boys who were so inculcated with this backward little culture that they would die before-

Finally, Tommy stepped forward, cleared his throat and nodded to her. "Thank you, ma'am," he said. "Let's be on our way."

It took Sebastian a few more seconds to decide that he would rather ride off with his lover than allow the lowlies of this town to sell him into slavery. Desa made a vexed sound.

She would have to do something about that brand on his cheek. "I..." Sebastian began. "I want to go too."

"Hope you boys have horses," Desa said, glancing back at the sheriff who would no doubt bring a mob of angry townsfolk down on her the very instant she let him out of her sight. "We have a long ride ahead of us."

2

_____

Tommy's eyes flew open.

His mouth became a gaping hole as he yawned and sat up. "Where am I?" The sky was still a deep twilight blue and covered with clouds, and there were trees everywhere. Memories of everything came back to him.

For half a moment, he wondered why he wasn't in his bed, but then he remembered the events in the sheriff's office and their hasty escape from Sorla. The townsfolk were all roused by the commotion, but most were too confused, and McGregor had advised them all to avoid doing anything foolish. By the time they found Lenny and Sheriff Cromwell tending their wounds, Tommy had already saddled his father's horse and followed Desa Kincaid into the night. His heart ached when he realized that he would probably never see Sorla again.

"Wake up, lazy bones."

He looked and saw Desa striding between two elms with a smile on her face. The woman nodded once. "It's breakfast time," she said. "Come join me. Tell me a bit about yourself."

Reluctantly, Tommy stood up. Though he was still fully clothed – pants, shirt and a duster – he felt strangely exposed. He set a wide-brimmed hat on his head and shuffled over to a spot where Desa had a pot of boiling water...on the ground...with no fire.

Desa seated herself on a log with her hands folded over her knees, staring wistfully at something in the far distance. "Come on then," she said. "It won't stay hot forever, and you need something to take the chill away."

Tommy squatted by the pot and lifted it to reveal a penny underneath. Was that the source of the heat? For the fourth time since departing the village last night, he began to wonder if trusting this woman was a good idea.

Desa handed him a pewter cup.

He filled it with mint tea that sent steam wafting up toward his face. Tommy shut his eyes and breathed it in. "Thank you." He took a sip, surprised to find that it was really quite tasty. "How..."

"How what?"

Tommy felt his brow furrow, then shook his head. "How were you able to heat it without a fire?" It occurred to him that the question might offend Desa. "That is...if you want to tell me."

Desa looked up, and her smile returned. "It's called Field Binding," she explained. "A way of manipulating energy. I can teach you if you like."

Tommy forced his eyes shut, a shiver passing through him at the thought of doing magic. "You can teach me?" His voice was hesitant. Really, he shouldn't even be asking this question, but this woman *had* used her powers to save him and Sebastian. "How...Not that I want to, but how..."

"To Field Bind, you must learn to commune with the Ether. That is the first step on your journey. And the hardest.

Some people need years of practice just to sense the Ether. Others pick it up in a matter of weeks, but anyone can if they try."

"What is this...Ether?"

Desa pressed her lips together, her eyebrows slowly climbing up her forehead. "No one really knows," she admitted. "Some say it's a vestige of the goddesses who made this world, a piece of their power."

"Goddesses...But...The Almighty..."

"Yes. Of course."

Desa stood up and tramped over mucky ground with a thick carpet of leaves to the spot where her horse waited. Unlike Tommy's mount, the large black stallion was not tied up. He just waited by the dirt path that cut through the forest, watching them chat with an idle curiosity. Or so it seemed, anyway.

Sebastian was still in his bedroll, curled up on his side and shivering under the thick blankets. It was cold, but Tommy suspected that his love's desire to remain abed had more to do with an aversion to Desa's company than a need to stay warm. Sebastian had been quiet through most of last night's ride, breaking his silence only to voice his apprehension about riding off with a witch.

It seemed an Aladri sorceress was fine company when you needed a way to avoid the gallows, but now that Sebastian was free, he seemed to think that he and Tommy should ride off on their own and leave Desa to whatever she was about.

Tommy leaned his back against a tree trunk, closed his eyes and breathed in the cool air. *What have I gotten myself into?* he wondered. *Does the woman want to make a warlock out of me?*

Desa strode past, shoving some crusty bread and a bit of

cheese into his hands. "Eat up," she said. "We'll be on our way soon."

It was a slow and dreary ride, southward through the forest. The trees had sprouted thick green leaves, but even though spring had finally asserted itself, bits of winters chill still clung to the wee hours of the night. The dampness didn't help.

Tommy buttoned his duster and shivered in the saddle.

Behind him, Sebastian's body provided some amount of warmth as the man sat with his arms wrapped around Tommy's midsection. "I've seen the maps," he whispered. "The forest ends in about twenty miles. We can be on our way."

"No!" Tommy hissed.

Apparently, his reaction was loud enough to make Desa glance over her shoulder with a frown. Did the woman know what he and Sebastian were discussing? Would she be offended if he rejected her help now after accepting it last night?

"We can be free," Sebastian urged.

Tommy winced, then reached up with one hand and pulled the brim of his hat down over his eyes. "We've never been more than a few miles out of the village," he whispered. "We know nothing about the world out there. We need her."

Sebastian grumbled.

The hours passed with very little talk and even less to stave off the boredom. Every now and then, Tommy caught sight of a chipmunk or a squirrel scampering through the forest on either side of that path. But there were no people. Desa seemed content to let them ride without intruding on their privacy, and Sebastian was unwilling to say anything more with a witch in earshot.

Every now and then, she took off at a gallop, and without fail, Sebastian seized the opportunity to recite his litany of reasons why they would be better off without the aid of an Aladri. Desa always returned within a few minutes, assuring them that the path ahead was clear and that they would be fine.

It was hard to get a sense of time with gray clouds blanketing the sky from horizon to horizon, but Tommy figured that it was just past midday when Desa reined up and shot a glance in their direction. "We would cover more ground if one of you rode with me," she said. "Midnight is stronger and can bear another rider more easily."

Tommy watched her with his lips pursed, blinking slowly. "Thank you, ma'am," he said, nodding to her. "But I think we'd rather stay together."

"I'm afraid I must insist."

"But-"

Desa turned Midnight to bar their path and frowned as she shook her head. "I'm in pursuit of a very dangerous man," she said. "I need to cover as much ground as possible. So, I'm sorry, but one of you rides with me."

Five minutes later, it was Tommy sitting behind Desa with his arms around her, and *that* made for an even more awkward ride.

WITH THE ONSET OF TWILIGHT, the gray sky began to fade to a somber blue, and Tommy found himself standing at the edge of a clearing that Desa had chosen for their campsite. Oak and ash trees formed a haphazard ring around them with roots all digging into the mucky earth so that it would be hard to find a comfortable place to lie down. Their leaves were not yet in full bloom, and water dropped from every one.

A light drizzle fell upon them, not enough to leave them soaked but enough to make for a very uncomfortable night. Tommy shivered despite himself. He knew perfectly well what would happen if he even glanced in Sebastian's direction, but he did so anyway and found the other man glaring at him. Somehow, this was all Tommy's fault.

Desa stood in front of him with her back turned, planting her fists on her hips and nodding as she inspected their campsite. "Well...It will have to do," she said, tapping the springy earth with her foot.

Tommy shut his eyes as cold raindrops pelted his face. Some of them dripped from his chin. "Begging your pardon, ma'am," he said, stepping forward. "But we'll catch our death out here."

Desa turned to him.

Her bright smile almost did away with his anxieties. "Not to worry, boys," she said. "I've been doing this a long while, and I promise that I won't let you die from exposure."

"How would you prevent it?" Sebastian asked.

He had his shoulder pressed to the trunk of a tall oak, his arms folded as he watched Desa with obvious misgivings. "More of your witchcraft?" The disdain in his voice made Tommy groan.

Looking him up and down, Desa smiled again and then tapped the leather pouch on her belt. "Not witchcraft," she said. "Technology."

"Technology?"

In answer to Sebastian's question, Desa hopped over a root and went to her large, black stallion. The animal twisted its head around to watch as she took a small pot from her saddlebags.

With a flick of her thumb, she sent a coin tumbling through the air, then reached up and caught it. "You'll see." She delivered the pot to Tommy with a grin and a request that he fill it with some water from the nearby stream.

Sebastian's nostrils flared as he snorted. "I suppose you'll be wanting me to start a fire," he said. "I can gather some wood."

"Did we have a fire this morning?"

For the first time since leaving Sorla, Sebastian's ever-present sneer faded to a look of confusion. "No," he stammered. "How did you heat the tea."

"You'll see," Desa replied. "Why don't you go help Tommy?"

Tommy stalked off through the woods, twigs snapping under his boots as he went toward the sound of babbling water. It wasn't long before he found a stream curving its way around the base of a hill, roughly parallel to the road.

Crouching down beside it, Tommy frowned and scraped a knuckle across his brow. "Gather water, she says," he muttered under his breath. "Well, I suppose we will need to drink something."

He dipped the pot in and filled it. The water he retrieved was mostly clear, but he didn't want to think much about those few dark flecks. Besides, Desa was clearly going to boil it, and that would make it safer to drink.

"You don't have to do what she says," Sebastian said as he came up behind Tommy. "You're not her slave."

Twisting slightly, Tommy looked over his shoulder and squinted at the other man. "That woman saved me from a trip to the gallows," he said. "She saved you from a much worse fate. Show some respect."

Sebastian was leaning against a tree with his hands folded over his stomach, staring wistfully at the darkening sky. "Oh, I'm grateful," he replied. "Doesn't mean I want to bed down next to a witch."

"She's not a witch."

"You saw what she can do."

"Aye," Tommy grumbled, scratching his chin. "I saw. And I also heard when she told me that it ain't no witchcraft."

"And you believe her?"

Tommy stood and, in one smooth motion, spun around to face his lover. He thrust out his chin. "I believe that people who'll kill a man just for loving another man ain't the kind to be trusted," he said. "I believe that any lady who risks her life to save a stranger deserves better than to be called a witch."

Tommy stepped forward, shoving his hands into the pockets of his duster and then turning his head to spit on the ground. "You wanna go, you can go," he said. "I won't try to stop you. But Mrs. Kincaid has seen a thing or two of this world, and I feel safer with her than I would on my own."

That put an end to Sebastian's protests.

Tommy carried the water back to camp.

ALONE IN A SMALL THICKET, Desa stood with her head tilted back. Rain dribbled over her face, streaming over her skin in thin rivulets. She breathed deeply. And then she got to work.

Desa punched the air with one fist then the other. She spun and kicked out behind herself, striking nothing at all. The rain gave her chills. Sinking into a rhythm she knew by rote, Desa moved without thought.

She jumped, curled up into a ball and backflipped. Seconds later, she dropped to the ground with her hands up in a defensive posture. It all felt natural. Every kick, every pivot, every breath of cold air that filled her lungs. Since childhood, Desa had been very proficient with *Shian Kaji,* a form of self-defense that was common among her people. It had become a part of her Field Binding...just as Field Binding had become a part of how she fought.

Falling backward, she dug her hands into the mud and rose into a handstand. Desa flipped upright, then jumped and kicked the empty air. She lost herself in the simple joy of movement, pushing conscious thought aside, becoming completely immersed in the task. And when her mind was empty, she felt it.

The Ether.

The instant she welcomed it into her mind, her perception of everything changed. She no longer saw trees or mud or sky. Instead, it seemed as though she was looking at galaxies of tiny swirling flecks Too may to count. Her own body was not a single object but billions and billions of tiny specs, smaller than dust and yet more vibrant to her mind, all spinning in an elegant dance.

She gathered the Ether into herself, and then she focused on the coins in her pouch. She Infused each one with a connection to the Ether, granting them an affinity for heat. It took time; minutes passed while she built a lattice, using strands of Ether to connect the molecules that made up each coin.

Each one would release heat when triggered.

Some people called it a surplus of heat, but while that phrasing got the point across, it was technically inaccurate. The coins did not store heat; they merely provided a conduit through which the Ether could release heat into the physical world.

Energy could flow in either direction. If she reversed the pattern of her lattice, the coins would drain heat instead of releasing it. The Ether was infinite. It could release or absorb any amount of energy. But to create enough warmth for three people. Desa would need to spend a few minutes on each coin.

Time passed, and she was dimly aware of the chill in her body. When she finished with the coins, she moved on to her bracelet. It had been Infused with the ability to drain kinetic energy from the physical world. But it had absorbed almost all the energy it could handle when Desa had used it to stop Ducane's bullets.

She renewed its connection to the Ether, and once again, she was forced to work for several minutes before the bracelet could drain enough energy to stop six shots. Desa let out a breath; she was getting tired. Working with the Ether in this way was exhausting.

Despite her fatigue, she moved on to her belt buckle.

She might need to fly soon.

WHEN DESA RETURNED to the clearing, she found her two companions squatting by a pile of wood they had gathered while Sebastian tried to light it with a match and some sandpaper he had taken from a metal container. There was very little daylight remaining; they would soon need fire to see.

Desa clicked her tongue. Matches were still a new technology throughout most of the Eradian continent. Though she supposed traders were passing through Sebastian's village, and he had probably bought some there.

"No," she said.

Sebastian looked up, and his face twisted with hate. He stood, gestured impotently to the pile of wood and said, "Be my guest."

"No fire," she insisted.

"And how do you expect us to see?"

Removing her ring, Desa tossed it to the ground, and with a thought, she ordered it to release light energy. Just a little. Enough for them to make out the shapes of trees and roots but not much more. The small golden band began to glow with orange light.

Tommy's eyebrows went up when he saw it, and then his face lit up with a grin. He seemed to be curious about Desa's abilities.

Sebastian, on the other hand, jumped back as if the ring were a viper that could bite at any moment. "You expect us to use...that?" he demanded. "Curse my soul! I'm already damned as it is!"

Blowing out a breath, Desa shook her head. "Fire creates an awful lot of light," she said, striding over to the boy. "And in case you've forgotten, I am chasing a pair of very dangerous men."

Tommy swallowed visibly, grabbed the brim of his hat and pulled it down over his eyes. "You..." His body trembled as he forced the words out. "You think they might find us, ma'am?"

"They should be at least two days ride from here," Desa clarified. "But it's possible. Morley has doubled back and tried to kill me before. I'd just as soon not light a signal for him, you understand?"

"Who is this Morley?"

Desa crouched near the would-be firepit and cleared the wood away. When it was gone, she set one of the coins down on a flat rock and triggered it with a thought. The air grew warmer in seconds. "The water, Tommy," she said.

He did as he was bid, bringing her a full pot. She set it directly on top of the coin. It wasn't much; that pot would provide enough water for one person. She would have to get a bigger one if she planned on traveling with companions. But for now, they would have to make multiple trips to the stream. Desa would go herself. Her legs could use a little stretching after a day in the saddle.

Frowning as the ring cast orange light on her face, Desa blinked and considered Tommy's question. "A very dangerous man," she said. "The worst kind of killer. Morley takes pleasure in his victim's pain."

"Why are you chasing him?"

That came from Sebastian.

Desa was quite aware of the young man standing a few paces behind her. She paid attention to the sound of his breathing. Slow and even. Unless he was far more dangerous than she had surmised, Sebastian wasn't planning to do anything rash.

Rubbing the back of one fist over her nose, Desa grunted. "Morley is a servant of Radharal Bendarian," she said. "I've been pursuing him for a long time...A long time."

Tommy's feet made a squishing sound in the muck as he paced around the pot. He looked over his shoulder with those sharp, inquisitive eyes. "And who is this Radharal Bendarian...if you don't mind my asking."

"He was a Field Binder of Aladar."

"*He* was?"

"Yes."

Tommy stood across from her with his hands in his pockets, nodding slowly as he pondered that. "So, men can be Field Binders too," he mumbled as if speaking to himself. "Interesting..."

"I did offer to teach you this very morning, did I not?" Desa offered. "One would think you might infer from my offer that men can be Field Binders."

"Yes...I suppose you did."

"Tommy..." Sebastian muttered in a dangerous voice.

Desa ignored him, checking the water instead. It was beginning to bubble. A minute or two at a good boil should be enough to deal with any pathogens. "Of course, men can be Field Binders," she said. "The man who taught me was one of our best."

"So, men live in Aladar."

Tilting her head back with a grin, Desa rolled her eyes. "Yes, Tommy," she replied. "One hundred and seven women founded the colony, but they had been on their own less than five years before the Wrath Wars came to Eradia."

"And that brought men?"

"Men bring war, and war brings men," Desa muttered. "A vicious cycle if ever there was one."

Tommy looked crestfallen, standing with his shoulders slumped, his eyes fixed on the muck beneath his feet. Like a sad little puppy dog. Normally, she would leave him to sulk, but Desa actually felt pity for the lad. True, she had saved him, but she was also the one responsible for dragging him out of his home. "Don't mind me, Tommy," she said. "My eyes have seen too much in thirty short years."

He seemed to accept that.

Tossing the lad a coin, she watched as Tommy stumbled backward to catch it. "Run your finger along the edge clockwise," she said. "The coin will emit heat. You can use it to stay warm tonight."

"And if I want it to *stop* emitting heat?"

"Run your finger along the edge anticlockwise." She gave another coin to Sebastian and suffered his sigh of disapproval. When she Infused an object with a connection to the Ether, she could decide how that connection was accessed.

A Simple Infusion would tie the coins to Desa herself, allowing her to "trigger" and "kill" each one with a thought. However, if she wanted a Heat-Source that anybody could use, tweaking the shape of the lattice would provide a physical mechanism to activate and deactivate the coins. "Sebastian," she said. "You'll find some bread, salted meat and a tin of tea leaves among the supplies. Please fetch them for me. My cups as well. I only have two. You boys will have to share. We should eat something and then get some sleep."

3

After two days of riding and three nights of sleeping rough, they came to a village of tile-roofed houses. The clouds had parted, and though strips of gray still crossed the blue sky, the sun was bright and strong.

A dirt road with houses on one side and lush green grass on the other was filled with people going about their daily tasks: boys painting whitewash on a fence, women carrying laundry baskets. A carriage came rumbling toward Desa and her companions, and when it passed, the driver tipped his cap.

Desa walked with Midnight's reins in hand, smiling as she took in the sight. "You know, I don't think I've ever been through this town before," she said softly. "It's nice."

Tommy was at her side, shuffling along with his hands in his pockets and offering a wan smile whenever she glanced in his direction. "It is," he mumbled. "Kind of reminds me of Sorla."

"Was that the name of your little town?" Desa asked.

"Aye, ma'am."

Behind them, Sebastian had the reins of the brown

gelding that Tommy had taken from his father's stable. Desa made it a point to keep an eye on that one. When someone looked at you with malice in their eyes, it was generally a good idea to avoid letting them out of your sight. But more than that, she didn't trust Sebastian to avoid doing anything that might earn them unwanted attention. "And you?" she asked the lad. "Have you ever been this far south?"

Sebastian's mouth was a thin line as he nodded slowly. "This is Glad Meadows," he answered. "My father took me here once when I was ten."

"Did you like it?"

The lad just snorted.

Glancing up toward the open sky, Desa rolled her eyes. "Remember," she told them both. "We're just passing through. We'll be leaving early tomorrow morning; so, we keep to ourselves and try to avoid notice."

No sooner had she said that than three men stepped into the road to bar their path. Each one wore a silver star that marked him as a deputy in the sheriff's office, but it was the one in the middle who got her attention.

He was tall and well-muscled, tanned with a scraggly beard, and he nodded when Desa got close. "That's far enough," he said, stepping forward. "You will forgive our lack of hospitality, but this town has no love for strangers at the moment."

Releasing Midnight's reins – the stallion would remain where she left him without having to be minded – Desa strode forward at a measured pace and looked up to gaze into the man's eyes. "You've had problems with strangers?"

"Some."

Her face was split by an impish grin, and she laughed softly as she nodded. "Let me guess," Desa began. "A big man with a mustache came through here a few days ago, and he caused all sorts of trouble."

Her suspicions were confirmed when the deputy stepped back with a hand on his holstered pistol. His face was haggard. "Madame, the fact that you know that doesn't fill me with confidence."

"You needn't worry, sir," Desa assured him. "I'm no friend of Morley's."

"Be that as it may, best you just pass through."

"I will," Desa agreed, "as soon as I've had a chance to purchase some supplies and learn as much as I can about where Morley might have gone."

The lead deputy stepped back, glanced to the man on his left and then the man on his right. They all looked uneasy, and Desa was worried that she might be stepping into a precarious situation.

Finally, the lead man closed his eyes, bowed his head and scrubbed a hand across his brow. "The Silver Fox Tavern," he mumbled. "If there's anything worth knowing, you'll learn it there. Don't plan on staying the night."

"I won't."

She had to lead the others off the main road, down a smaller street lined with even smaller houses. With the midday sun in the sky, the town was abuzz with activity, and it was slow-going as they waded through the crowds.

"Begging your pardon, ma'am," Tommy said as he fell in at her side. "But I thought we were trying to avoid attracting notice. Why go ahead and tell those deputies that we're chasing this Morley?"

Desa shut her eyes, breathing deeply and then letting it out again. "They'll find out what I'm up to as soon as I start asking questions," she said. "May as well ask somebody who might have a useful answer."

"Aye."

The inn was a large, white-bricked building black tiles on its slanted roof and large rectangular windows in the front wall. It was a quaint little place, and despite her promise to the deputy, Desa found herself tempted by the prospect of one good night's sleep in an actual bed. Her muscles ached.

A young man who was even skinnier than Tommy came scrambling up in a wide-brimmed hat. Huffing and puffing as he took those final steps, he stopped in front of Desa and said, "Do your horses need stabling, ma'am?"

"Yes, thank you."

"It's twenty-five cents a night per horse."

She retrieved a small purse from her saddlebags and paid the lad with coins that she hadn't Infused with a connection to the Ether. Desa could tell which were which. A Field Binder could sense any object that she herself Infused even if someone carried that object to the other side of the world.

Inside, she found a saloon that was not at all dissimilar from McGregor's: sawdust on the floor and round wooden tables. Paraffin lamps up on the walls – none were lit at this time of day – and few decorative fixtures.

Someone had stuffed and mounted the head of a moose over the bar where it could gaze down imperiously on any guest who approached the barkeep. The scent of beef stew filled the air.

Tommy stepped up beside her, frowning as he took in the sight. He seemed to be feeling uneasy, as well he should. They were only a few days south of his town. Though it was unlikely that word of his escape had reached Glad Meadows, you could never be too careful.

"Get something to drink," Desa murmured with just

enough volume for Tommy to hear. "Keep to yourselves and don't make too much noise."

He nodded.

Removing her hat, Desa paced across the room to the bar. The man who stood behind it – a fair-haired fellow with a neat goatee – was caught off guard by her arrival.

He looked up when he sensed her approach, sized her up in half a second and then nodded. "Looking for a bite to eat?" he asked. "Or is it a room you want?"

With a friendly grin, Desa shook her head. "'Fraid I won't be able to stay the night," she said. "Just passin' through. Need to make good time, you understand."

"Where you headed?"

"South, toward Ofalla."

That brought a grimace to the bartender's face, and he looked away as if he felt put off by her destination. Curious. "It's five cents for a bowl of stew," he said. "If you won't be staying, then we'd best get you on your way."

Desa let her eyebrows climb as she studied the man. "You look tense," she said. "Is there something wrong with going south?"

"Not a thing, ma'am."

She set a coin down on the counter and slid it toward the barkeep. He looked at it, frowned and then met her eyes with a quizzical expression. "For the stew," Desa said. "I could use a hot meal."

STEAM ROSE to fill Tommy's nose with a delicious scent as he stared forlornly into a bowl of stew. With his pewter spoon, he stirred up chunks of meat, some chopped celery and carrots. It looked delicious. It *tasted* delicious.

He just wasn't hungry.

"So that's the plan, then?"

When he looked up, Sebastian was leaning over the table and squinting at him. "We just follow her until she decides she's done with us?" The other man glanced toward Desa as if he were afraid that she might overhear. The Almighty smile down on him, she very well might. Tommy didn't know the limits of Field Binding.

Lifting a spoonful of meat out of the bowl, Tommy blew on it and then shoved it into his mouth. He chewed thoroughly, swallowed and then fixed his love with a steely gaze. "We've been over this."

"But I'm not done talking 'bout it."

Tommy felt his brow furrow, then shook his head in exasperation. "You really are that dumb, ain't ya?" he spat. "We leave Mrs. Kincaid, and I give it two days until we die from exposure."

"We could stay here."

"Until one of Sheriff Cromwell's men comes to visit Glad Meadows and discovers us? Nah...I'll take my chances with Desa Kincaid."

Sebastian had the sullen look of a child who knew he was wrong but who refused to apologize. Well, let him sulk. After two days of this, Tommy was bloody well fed up, and he had no inclination to argue further. The question of what precisely he should do with himself had been on his mind of late.

In Sorla, his father had been the tanner, and Tommy had always thought he would do the same. In truth, Tommy had never really found any vocation particularly appealing. He would just do what he had to do to get by. Sooner or later, they would stop in a town where he could settle down. Perhaps Tommy could be a tanner there.

"Well, my word!"

The newcomer's intrusion made Tommy jump.

He looked up from his stew to find a girl about his own age standing over the table. Tall and willowy in a pair of dungarees and a short brown coat, she greeted them with a warm smile. "What are a pair of handsome fellows like you doing in a town like this?"

Her face was lovely, with high cheekbones, dark skin and black hair that she wore tied back. "Here I thought nothing interesting ever happened in Glad Meadows." Without an invitation, she took a seat, spit in her palm and extended her hand. "The name's Miri. Miri Fontane."

Tommy took her hand, shuddering at the slimy texture of her saliva. "Tommy," he said. "That's Sebastian."

"Ooh, a sophisticated name!"

Sebastian glowered at her.

If Miri noticed, she offered no reaction. She just sat back with a great big smile on her face and studied Tommy for a very long moment. "So, I've been in town 'bout a week. My horse broke his leg, you see. Been working for Mrs. Miller to raise enough to buy me a new one."

Slouching until it seemed like she might fall out of her chair, Miri put a toothpick in her mouth – of all things – and then waggled it around. "Now, the missus, she's getting on in years. Still has a family to feed! And her husband, bless his heart. He caught himself a nasty case of the influenza on a trip up to High Falls. Ain't never been the same since."

"That's awful."

"Now, what you need to understand," Miri went on, "is that folks 'round here ain't got much to spare. Which means they pay less, but also everything costs less, you know? It has a kind of equalizing effect." Abruptly, she leaned in close and swatted his leg. "You listenin' to all this, Lommy?"

Tommy's mouth worked silently for a few seconds. He

blinked and gave his head a shake. "It...It's Tommy," he stammered. "My name is-"

"Uh uh," Miri insisted. "Met a Tommy once. Broke my heart. Swore to myself I ain't never gonna be friends with no Tommy no more. So, you gon' be Lommy, and I'm gonna be Miri, and we're gonna be the best of friends."

"I don't think-"

"And you..." Miri twisted around to face Sebastian with a finger pointed in his face. Her jaw dropped. "My word, I ain't never seen anybody look so miserable when the sun is shining bright. What's got you so unhappy, precious?"

Sebastian flinched away from her finger as if he thought her touch might burn him. "I'm fine," he said. "We were just enjoying a quiet meal together, that's all. And we'd like to get back to it."

"Almighty be praised, I ain't stoppin' you," Miri said. "Eat your stew."

Tommy was almost relieved when he saw Desa striding toward them. She paused a few feet away, took in the sight of Miri and raised an eyebrow. "I see you've made a new friend, Tommy. Care to introduce me?"

Tommy went red, then shut his eyes and scrubbed a hand over his face. "Her name is Miri," he explained with some roughness in his voice. "She came by and thought she would join us for-"

With two fingers, Miri removed the toothpick from her mouth and blinked as if she didn't quite believe her eyes. "Oh stars above," she whispered. "Pray tell me, which one of y'all is married to this fine specimen of femininity?"

A cool stare was Desa's only response to that compliment, but just when the silence became tense, she favoured Miri with a smile. "Neither one of these good gentlemen can claim that honour," she said. "My husband died five years ago."

"Did he now?"

Desa sat across from Miri, plunked her elbow down on the table and rested her chin in the palm of her hand. "He did," she said. "So, I must ask you, Miri, what brings you to our table...other than an appreciation for a 'fine specimen of femininity?'"

"Actually, I prefer the menfolk," Miri said. "But a girl can admire her competition, don't you think? And as I was telling Lommy here, I've been in town for about a week."

"For what purpose?"

"Why, I need a new horse, of course." Miri's face lit up with a grin. "Goodness me, that rhymed, didn't it?"

Desa leaned back with her arms crossed, nodding slowly as she assessed the other woman. "I see," she said at last. "Well, if you've been in town for about a week, perhaps you could tell me about some travelers that passed through a few days ago. One of them had a very distinctive mustache."

Tommy had been stuck in his cell when this Morley fellow passed through Sorla, but he remembered the way Sheriff Cromwell's deputies kept whispering to each other. Whoever this stranger was, he was dangerous.

To his surprise, Miri propped her booted feet up on the table and folded her hands behind her head. "Well now," she murmured. "Just what would a lady like you be wantin' with a villain like him?"

"That's not your concern."

"Oh, you don't wanna be runnin' afoul of that one, darlin'," Miri said. "He ain't no ordinary street tough."

Sebastian had been spooning stew into his mouth all this time, but he paused just long enough to look up and sneer at Miri. "Sounds like you're afraid of him…Darlin,'" he said. "What's so terrifying about this Morley?"

Miri got out of her chair.

Then she crouched next to Sebastian with a hand on his shoulder and smiled as she gazed into his eyes. "You ever seen pure evil?" she asked. "If you have a mind to, all you have to do is spend five minutes alone with Morley."

Desa stood up with a sigh and nodded to the other woman. "Thank you kindly for your advice," she said. "But my friends and I must plan our trip. If you would excuse us please, Miri."

When she was gone, Desa sat down again and scraped her chair across the floor as she moved closer to the table. "What little I've learned from the bartender isn't good," she began in hushed tones. "Morley killed a young woman when he came through here two days ago."

Sebastian closed his eyes, his nostrils flaring as he exhaled. "And you want to go after him," he mumbled. "What's this man done to make capturing him so important that you'll risk our lives to do it?"

"Sebastian!" Tommy snapped.

"Have you heard nothing of what Miri said?" Desa hissed.

"I try not to listen to what Miri says."

It might have been Tommy's imagination, but the room seemed to be a tad darker when Desa turned her glare upon Sebastian. "Then perhaps you will listen to what I tell you," she whispered. "Morley is a killer who serves a Field Binder of Aladar."

"Yes, but-"

"As dangerous as he is," Desa went on, "his master is far worse. And Bendarian is the one I want."

"Be that as it-"

Desa lifted a hand, and her ring began to glow. Sebastian flinched away from it. "I've grown exceptionally weary of your constant complaints," she said. "Come with me, or stay behind. Frankly, I don't care. But from this point onward, you will keep silent."

"Then I suppose I'll be staying here."

Desa said nothing.

She simply got up and walked out of the tavern. When she was gone, Sebastian gave Tommy one of those pleading looks. Oh, this was bad...Every instinct toward good sense told Tommy that he should stay with Desa Kincaid, but if he did that, he would lose the man he loved.

Before he had a chance to second guess himself, Tommy was out of his chair and chasing Desa out the door. "Mrs. Kincaid!" he called out. "Mrs. Kincaid, wait!"

He found her in the narrow lane of brick houses just outside the inn. Slowly, she turned and raised an eyebrow.

Closing his eyes, Tommy gulped air into his lungs. "I want to stay with you," he panted. "I'm not like him. I don't..."

When he realized that people might overhear, Tommy stepped closed and lowered his voice. "I don't think what you do is wrong," he said. "In fact, I want to learn. There is nothing for me back home, and if you'll still have me-"

It shocked him when Desa smiled and let out a peal of musical laughter. "You can come with me, Tommy," she replied. "And I would be happy to teach you Field Binding. Now, we'll need supplies-"

She cut off at the sound of some hubbub in the street.

A crowd of people had gathered together in the nearest intersection, all talking in frenzied voices. The sight of it made Tommy uneasy. Whenever people got agitated like that, misery usually followed.

The crowd parted, allowing three men in blue uniforms to emerge. A wave of panic hit Tommy like a punch to the gut. He recognized those uniforms and the badges on each man's chest. Those were Sheriff Cromwell's deputies.

And one was his brother.

Lenny stepped forward and thrust out his chin, removing his hat so that everyone could see his black eye. "We're looking for two fugitives who escaped custody in Sorla!" he shouted. "And a witch!"

People started muttering the word witch.

"What will you do with this witch?"

The wicked grin on Lenny's face gave Tommy chills. "What does anyone do with a witch?" he shouted. "I'm going to execute her."

4

The people of this region were becoming quite a nuisance.

Desa watched as the smug little toad she had knocked around in Sheriff Cromwell's office strode through the street. People backed away from him, making room for Lenny and his fellow deputies, and he nodded to them. "Good upstanding folk," he said. "Who dwell in the light of the Almighty. You won't suffer witches among you."

"Fools never grow tired of her foolishness." Desa became aware of Tommy's rapid breathing. The boy was frightened. "Go to the stable," she told him. "Saddle the horses."

At her side, Tommy was slumped over with a hand on his stomach, panting as he took in the sight of his brother. "Sebastian?" he whispered. "What about Sebastian?"

"He's made his choice."

For an instant, Desa thought that Tommy would protest, but the lad seemed willing to follow her lead. Quietly, he ducked around the side of the inn and vanished from sight. Now, Desa would have to give him enough time to ready their mounts.

She stepped out into the open with hands in the pockets of her duster, smiling and shaking her head. "You wanted a witch, Lenny?" she shouted. "Well, here she is!"

The young deputy looked up, and his eyes widened when he noticed her. His shock was quickly replaced by a mocking grin. "Now, this is brazen," he said. "Sinners usually prefer the shadows to the light of day."

Murmurs rippled through the crowd.

The townspeople had formed two lines, one on each side of the street, and they watched the scene play out with a mix of fascination and trepidation. Lenny and his two deputies came forward with hands on their holstered pistols.

Pursing her lips as she studied the man, Desa narrowed her eyes. "And fools prefer violence to talk," she said. "I have no quarrel with you, Lenny, but if you draw those guns and put these people in danger, you will regret it."

"Where's my brother?" Lenny demanded.

"Safe."

"You'd deny him the chance to repent? Lead him deeper into decadence and vice?" Lenny's hand tightened on the grip of his pistol. "Even witches die when you fill 'em with bullets. So, what's it gon' be, woman? You wanna come quietly and avoid the fires of Hell a few days longer? Or shall I send you to your master now?"

"Don't force my hand, Lenny."

In response, he drew his gun.

Desa jumped and, with a thought, she ordered her belt buckle to drain gravitational energy. Untethered to the Earth, she floated upward gracefully until she could see the top of every roof.

The people in the street all gasped. Lenny's deputies looked up at her with gaping mouths. She would have only a moment before the shock wore off and they decided to start using those guns.

Drawing her own pistol, Desa popped out the cylinder and spun it until the bullet she wanted was next in line. She slapped it back into place, cocked the hammer and fired down at the street.

Her bullet went straight into the ground.

She ordered it to release gravitational energy, and suddenly every single gawker in that crowd and every object that wasn't tied down was pulled into the middle of the road. Loose stones gathered together over her bullet. Bodies piled up on top of each other as people cried out in surprise. A few would have bumps and bruises, but for most of them, it would be no worse than stumbling and falling to the ground.

With more gravitational energy to drain, Desa's belt buckle was filling itself at an accelerated rate. She pointed her gun out to the side and fired again. The recoil sent her flying sideways over the roof of the inn.

Once she was over the stableyard, she allowed gravity to reassert its hold on her for half a second. Only half a second, but that gave her enough downward momentum to fall lazily to the Earth like a leaf on the wind.

She landed just outside the paddock, where horses were whinnying at the strange sensation of being pulled forward by something they could not see. This far away from her bullet, it would feel like nothing more than a slight tug – easily resisted with a little effort – but it was still enough to frighten them.

Squeezing her eyes shut, Desa concentrated and released her belt buckle's hold on gravity. She left the bullet active. It would expend its supply of energy in just a few more minutes anyway.

Inside the stable, she found Tommy opening the door to Midnight's stall. Desa's horse seemed to pay no mind to the unseen force that tried to pull on him, but the others were all stamping about and making noise. The brown gelding that Tommy had taken from his father was wide-eyed, with his ears slanted back, and he refused to come out into the open.

Gasping, Tommy turned to face her and nearly jumped back in surprise. He pulled off his hat and shook his head. "I won't get him out of there," he muttered. "Whatever it is you did, the horse is spooked."

"We'll ride on Midnight," Desa said. "Get your bedroll."

He did as he was bid without protest.

"In there!"

Desa whirled around, one hand on the grip of her holstered pistol as she squinted at the door. "It never ends," she whispered to herself. "Mercy shelter me from men and their foolish superstitions."

Three men in deputy's uniforms came barging into the stable. Not the same three that Desa had faced in the street. In fact, the slight difference in cut and colour suggested that these men were from the Glad Meadow's sheriff's office.

The one in the middle was tanned with a scraggly beard; she recognized him as the deputy who had stopped her on her way into town. "What did you do to them, witch?" he demanded. "I knew you were trouble when I saw you."

"They'll be fine," Desa promised him. "I sincerely doubt that anyone was seriously injured; allow me to leave without incident, and I promise that your people will be free as soon as I'm gone."

Of course, the man drew his weapon.

His two lackeys did the same.

In a blink, Desa triggered the Light-Sink in her necklace,

draining light energy until the stable was pitch black. She stepped aside to avoid being where they had last seen her. The vicious *CRACK, CRACK* of gunfire and the feeling of bullets whizzing past told her it was a good move.

Estimating the deputy's position wasn't hard.

Desa kicked the gun out of his hand, producing a grunt as the weapon dropped to the floor. That done, she allowed the light to return, and the deputy stood empty-handed, blinking at her. His two companions were both petrified.

Desa spun and back-kicked, driving a foot into the man's stomach, propelling him backward into one of his companions. Both men fell to the floor, one landing on top of the other. The third deputy managed to aim his weapon.

Reacting by instinct, Desa raised her left hand to shield herself, and her bracelet drank deeply of kinetic energy. The deputy fired with another loud thunderclap, and his bullet stopped dead in midair, mere inches away from Desa.

"Almighty shelter us!" he whispered.

Desa let her arm drop, the bullet falling to the floor, then leaped and kicked the fool square in his chest. That forced him down onto his back, and he landed with a grunt. The other two were rising.

The momentary distraction gave her time to shove her hand into her duster's pocket and slip on a set of brass knuckles. These, too, had been Infused with a connection to the Ether.

Scraggly-Beard was glaring at her with bared teeth.

He came forward.

Dancing backward through the aisle between stalls, Desa suddenly became aware of the frightened horses. Every last one was whinnying. Except Midnight, of course; he was waiting in his stall and watching the whole scene play out with a kind of halfhearted curiosity. She heard

Tommy in the next stall over, desperately trying to quiet his father's gelding.

Red-faced and fuming, Scraggly-Beard came forward as if he meant to squeeze the life out of Desa with his own bare hands. He probably thought that she had used up all of her "magic," and now, she was helpless.

Desa let him get close, and then, when he reached for her, she dropped to a crouch and drove her fist into his chest. The brass knuckles released a powerful burst of kinetic energy on contact.

Her enemy was thrown backward like a rock kicked up by a twister. He crashed through the stable doors, knocking one off its hinges, and landed in the yard outside. The other two men gasped.

With a growl, Desa slammed her fist down on the floor.

A tremor shook the stable, and cracks spread through the hard-packed dirt. Horses screeched in terror. The two remaining deputies both stumbled as they lost their balance. Each man fell to the floor.

"Tommy!" Desa barked. "Let's move!"

She felt it when her bullet let out its last sputtering gasp of gravitational energy. In less than half a second, the fearful moans that she had been tuning out became screams as people on the street ran in all directions. Now that they were free of its gravitational pull, they would want to flee.

Tommy led Midnight out of his stall by the bridle. His face was bone-white as he looked around, but to his credit, he steadied himself. "I'm ready," he said. "Let's go before we run into more trouble."

The men on the stable floor were groaning.

Putting one foot in the stirrup, Desa swung her other leg over Midnight's flanks and settled herself in the saddle. She extended a hand to Tommy and then pulled him up to sit behind her. "Go!" she told Midnight.

The horse bolted out of the stable.

With a whinny, he leaped over Scraggly-Beard and took off at a gallop through the yard. He was following a path that would take him around the front of the inn. Desa still heard people screaming in the street.

Wincing as she shook her head, Desa let out a huff. "I am expending far too much energy for you boys." She drew her gun, popped out the cylinder again and spun it until she had the bullet she wanted.

As expected, Lenny and his two subordinates came running around the side of the inn, skidding to a stop when they saw Midnight headed their way. Growling, Lenny drew his weapon.

Desa extended her hand and fired.

CRACK!

Her bullet struck the ground at Lenny's feet, and the instant it did, she triggered its connection to the Ether. A wave of kinetic energy hurled the three men backwards. One landed in a line of rose bushes at the edge of the property. Another ended up face-down in the grass.

Midnight reared as he felt an invisible force trying to throw him backward, hooves kicking as he whinnied. The stallion was used to this sort of thing; his front feet slammed down on the grass, and then he was galloping around the inn.

Once they were on the street, Midnight took off at full speed, his hooves kicking up dust as they rushed down a narrow road lined with small houses and whitewashed fences. People jumped out of their way, some of them screaming.

"Wait!"

Desa looked back to find Sebastian on the roadside with his arms around a bundle of all his possessions. He was running at full speed, sweat glistening on his face. "Please wait! I'm coming with you!"

Gritting her teeth with a hiss, Desa shook her head. "Idiot boy," she muttered. With a gentle squeeze of her thighs, she ordered Midnight to keep running. There was no way Sebastian could keep up without a horse, and stopping would mean death.

"Wait!"

"Mrs. Kincaid," Tommy pleaded.

"We can't," she said. "I'm sorry. He made his choice."

THE SOFT SCUFF of shoes on dry dirt was the only sound as Marcus moved cautiously under the night sky. A tall man in dungarees and a long, brown duster, his dark-skinned face marked by a neat, square beard, he inspected the scene of the latest fiasco that Desa Nin Leean had created.

He crouched down near the bullet that she had used as a Gravity-Source, nodding to himself. "I don't like it," he muttered. "This is the second time in as many weeks that she has openly displayed her abilities. She's usually more subtle than this."

"Circumstances forced her hand."

Marcus looked up, squinting at his sister. "I do not believe what I'm hearing," he said. "You almost sound sympathetic."

Leaning against a wooden pillar that supported the overhanging roof of the general store, Miri gave him a dismissive glance and then sniffed. "You know what happened in Sorla," she replied. "These primitives would have killed those two boys for something as benign as their sexual preferences."

"How is that our problem?"

Miri stifled a yawn with her fist, then scratched her back against the pillar. "There are days when I find myself amazed by your capacity for apathy," she said. "I would not have left those boys to await execution."

"You're not a Field Binder of Aladar."

"No," she agreed. "I'm not."

Standing up with a sigh, Marcus dusted his hands and then turned to face his sister. "The last time the primitives attacked Aladar, we barely fended them off," he said. "Even the most advanced technology can only do so much against overwhelming numbers."

"True."

"And now, Desa Nin Leean threatens to bring those hordes down on us once again. So long as she kept a low profile, the Synod was content to let her pursue her foolish crusade, but every time she brazenly displays the power of Field Binding, she puts Aladar at risk. You know our orders."

Miri nodded. "I do."

"Desa Nin Leean will come back to Aladar to answer for her actions." Marcus drew aside his coat, revealing a holstered revolver on his hip. "Or she will die."

5

The small, golden ring glowed with a soft orange light, casting shadows over the trees of this small glade. Wind sighed through fluttering leaves, and every now and then, he heard the skitter of some animal moving through the underbrush.

Tommy sat on a log with his hands on his knees, frowning into his lap. "Everything is going wrong," he whispered. "No matter how hard I try, I can't keep it together."

Sebastian was gone. Less than a week ago, Tommy had been prepared to die for the man he loved, and now that man had abandoned him. He was hunted by his own brother. He would never see his home again.

Was he really such a terrible man? Was loving another man so great a sin that the Almighty himself would turn all of his wrath upon Tommy? Something deep inside of him wanted to say no, but he felt broken.

He had felt a brief flicker of hope when Sebastian came running to join them, but that had died when Desa Kincaid refused to stop for him. Maybe it was wrong to say that Sebastian had abandoned him.

No, *he* had abandoned Sebastian.

There was barely a sound as Desa stepped into the light of the glowing ring. She had removed her duster, revealing a sleeveless shirt beneath, and a sheen of sweat coated her face and upper arms. "It's done," she declared. "I've Infused my supplies with a new connection to the Ether."

Pressing his lips together, Tommy nodded. He felt numb inside. Just a few hours ago, the prospect of learning Field Binding had seemed enticing, but now...Well, he had committed himself to the path of sin. There was no sense in being squeamish now.

Desa stood before him with fists on her hips, a stern expression on her face. "What is it?" she asked, raising an eyebrow. "You look uneasy."

"It's nothing."

"I doubt that."

Hunching over, Tommy set his elbows on his thighs and then buried his face in his hands. He split his fingers apart to look at her. "Did we really have to leave Sebastian to the mercy of that crowd?"

Desa eased herself onto the log across from him, folding her arms and letting out a breath. "The alternative would have been to put *ourselves* at the mercy of that crowd," she replied. "Field Binding can only do so much to protect us."

"But Sebastian-"

"Would have left at the earliest opportunity," Desa insisted. "I know that you want to trust him, Tommy, but I've seen his kind before."

Tommy felt his mouth tighten, but he said nothing. A tear slid over his cheek in a hot, sticky trail. Maybe Desa was right. Sebastian had been kicking up a fuss during their journey to Glad Meadows. Just a few days ago, Tommy had proclaimed that Sebastian could go if he wanted to go, but he would stay with Desa Kincaid. How could he have been so certain then and so full of doubt now? "How does it work?" he said at last.

"Field Binding?"

Tommy nodded.

Sitting up straight with hands gripping the surface of her log, Desa turned her face up to the starry sky. "The Ether is part of the very fabric of reality," she said. "You might say it's a holdover from Creation itself."

"Left by the Almighty?"

Desa grimaced, shaking her head. "The Almighty's a myth," she said. "As I told you, this world was created by two goddesses: Mercy, and Vengeance. Mercy to give energy and Vengeance to take it, and Field Binding a balance between them."

Clasping his chin in one hand, Tommy shut his eyes and considered that. "So, this Ether you speak of...It's..."

"No one knows for sure exactly *what* it is," Desa explained. "You might think of it as a remnant of the goddesses. But it connects the souls of all humankind. With enough discipline, anyone can learn to commune with the Ether."

"Anyone?"

"Anyone."

"Even me?"

Desa's smile was kindly. Maybe even fond. Either way, it was enough to take the edge of Tommy's pain. "Yes, even you," she said. "I would not have offered to teach you if I did not know that you could do it. But it won't be easy. Yes, some people learn Field Binding very quickly, but for others, it takes years of practice."

"How do I begin?"

Desa stood up with a grunt, as if her bones ached, then

stretched and finally strode over to him. "You must begin by training your mind," she said. "You will meditate for at least half an hour at night before sleep."

Tommy looked up with uncertainty plain on his face. "How should I do that?" he asked. "I don't really know what meditation is or how I should go about doing it, but I'm willing to try if-"

"It's fairly simple," Desa cut in. "Repeat a mantra quietly to your yourself. Make it something simple. One, two, three, four, five should suffice."

So, he tried.

One, two, three, four, five. Was he supposed to feel something? One, two, three, four, five. Goodness, this was painfully dull. Was he really supposed to sit here for half an hour, just repeating numbers like a toddler? One, two, three, four, five. It was so hard to keep his mind focused on the task.

He powered through it as best he could, but when he finally gave up in frustration after what must have been, at most, ten minutes, he only felt exasperated and annoyed. A cynical thought occurred to him. Was this *really* the way to learn Field Binding? Or was Desa just stringing him along?

He curled up in his bedroll and fell into a fitful sleep.

COME MORNING, Tommy woke to find the glade teaming with life. In the last week or so, the trees had sprouted thick green leaves, and now they fluttered in the breeze of a warm spring morning. The sky was a bright, vibrant blue.

Desa was crouching with her back turned, but he could see steam rising from the pot she tended. So, there would be tea, at least. His stomach was aching with hunger, but hot tea might settle it a little and...Did he smell roasted rabbit?

He looked around to find that there was indeed a rabbit roasting on a spit that Desa had set up over a...Well, not a fire. She appeared to be using three of her Infused coins to cook their breakfast. Tommy could feel the heat from here.

He felt his mouth stretch into a yawn, then winced and sat up with a hand pressed to his forehead. Gently, he massaged the fog out of his brain.

"Good morning," Desa said without looking.

"Morning."

Without having to be told, he got up, stretched and then made his way over to the spot where Midnight waited patiently. The stallion gave him a nonchalant glance and then remained still while Tommy fetched cups and ground tea leaves from the saddlebags.

He delivered them to Desa.

Her lips curled into a small smile as she filled one cup with leaves and then lifted the pot to carefully pour water on top. "Let that steep a moment," she said, handing the cup to Tommy. "It seems you made a good start last night."

Tommy wrinkled his nose, then shook his head in distaste. "A good start?" he said. "I barely managed ten minutes, and the whole time I felt like an idiot reciting lessons that his mother taught him as a child."

Desa filled the other cup, inhaling the aroma that wafted upward. "That, my friend, is how everyone begins," she said. "Meditation is a difficult skill to master. But if you're feeling bored, it probably means you're doing well."

"Rabbit for breakfast?"

"I had hoped to purchase some supplies in Glad Meadows," Desa explained. "But your brother robbed us of that opportunity."

"I'm sorry."

Lifting the cup to her lips, Desa sipped her tea with a

satisfied murmur. "And why should you feel sorry?" she asked. "You are not responsible for what he does, Tommy."

"I know."

"Do try to remember it."

The rabbit was crispy and juicy and delicious. Tommy savoured every last bite and licked his fingers clean afterward. With a full belly, he was tempted to just rest his head against a tree trunk and sleep a little longer. He briefly entertained the idea of giving up on civilization altogether and living peacefully in these woods. It was pure foolishness, of course, but civilization seemed to despise him...And Desa could teach him to hunt rabbit.

He put such notions out of his head and began packing their things to continue their journey southward. Another week or so on the road, and they would reach the grand city of Ofalla. Tommy had always wanted to see it.

But he missed Sebastian.

TAKING one last look at their campsite, Desa nodded to herself. "All right," she said. "Let's get-"

Something was wrong.

Drawing her pistol in a flash, she whirled around and pointed its barrel at a small thicket of trees. Leafy branches drooped low, making it hard to see anything beyond the two elms that grew so close together, they were almost twined around one another. But someone was in there. "Come out."

The branches rustled, and the woman from the inn stepped out into the open. It took a moment for Desa to remember her name. Miri. Tall and slim, she wore her dungarees, her duster and that wide-brimmed hat. And she glared at Desa with all the indignation of a woman who had caught some fool boy peeping on her bath. "Well, now, ain't this just a fine coincidence: me finding you out here?"

Tommy was adjusting Midnight's bridle when he heard Miri's voice. The poor lad spun around with a start and reached for his belt knife. A moment later, he let out a deep breath of air.

Desa holstered her weapon.

Crossing her arms, she stepped forward and looked up to meet the other woman's eyes. "Why are you following us?" she asked. "More importantly, why are you skulking in the bushes instead of announcing yourself?"

"My word, I ain't never been so insulted!" Miri protested. "You think a lady such as myself is in the habit of skulking?"

"You *were* in the bushes."

Miri shrugged her shoulders. "Out for a simple morning stroll, is all," she insisted. "I can't help it if I wandered through the woods and got lost. Heard a man talkin', and I thought I'd head that way."

Desa covered her face with one hand, gently massaging her eyelids. "We don't have time for this," she muttered into her palm. "If you wish to skulk, by all means, do so. But you will leave my companion and me to our business."

"Speaking of your companions, maybe you'd like to have the other one back?"

Tommy perked up at that.

Jerking a thumb back over her shoulder, Miri grunted in disapproval. "He's about a half mile up the road with our horse," she explained. "Town didn't seem quite so friendly after all that noise you kicked up; so we both headed south. Figured, we'd walk together for a spell."

"I thought you said your horse broke its leg."

"Actually, it ain't my horse," Miri replied. "It's Lommy's."

Turning her back on the other woman, Desa shook her

head as she stomped across the campsite. She paused with her fists on her hips. "We do not have time for this," she said. "Tommy, let's go."

Of course, that wasn't the end of the discussion. Getting Tommy into the saddle was next to impossible now that he knew that his lover was just a short ride away. Or thought he knew. Desa was not willing to trust anything this Miri said. Honest people didn't skulk and spy.

After five minutes of whimpered protests from her young companion, they were finally on their way. Miri just stood at the edge of the campsite with a curious expression, watching them go. Somehow, Desa knew that she hadn't seen the last of that woman.

She tried to help Tommy with Field Binding. She encouraged him to meditate on their long ride south – it wasn't as if they had anything better to do – but the lad seemed to be hopelessly distracted. It almost broke her heart, and more than once, she considered going back to fetch Sebastian. But for all she knew, that was a trap.

She explained as much to Tommy, and he seemed to accept her reasoning. But that did nothing to ease his sorrow. It took everything Desa had to resist the urge to groan in frustration. Just what she needed! A lovesick young man slowing her down! Any hope of catching Morley was dwindling with every passing second.

She sighed as Midnight continued his slow plod southward.

6

_____

The forest gave way to fields of tall grass growing strong under the clear blue sky. Warm sunlight made Desa smile as Midnight continued along the meandering dirt road. Aside from a few trees that dotted the landscape here and there, there was nothing to see all the way to the southern horizon.

They rode until the sun began to dip. Sensing Midnight's fatigue, Desa decided that this was as good a place as any to settle in for the night. Tallgrass would make it hard to move without making noise – which meant catching another rabbit would be difficult – but it also limited the potential for enemies to sneak up on her.

A tall oak by the roadside grew with its limbs spreading wide and its green leaves catching the light of the setting sun. As soon as he got out of the saddle, Tommy seated himself with his back against the massive trunk and stared wistfully into the distance.

Desa stood just a few feet away, scratching her forehead with the knuckle of one fist. "You should meditate," she told him. "If you want to learn Field Binding, you must practice as much as possible."

He nodded numbly.

Letting her arms drop, Desa turned to face him and removed her hat. A fierce wind teased her short brown hair. "I know that you wanted to go back for him," she said. "But Sebastian is probably still in Glad Meadows."

"Or dead..." Tommy mumbled.

Desa squatted in front of him with her hands on her knees, holding the young man's gaze. "Possibly," she admitted. "Tommy, I wish I could have-"

"You made your position clear, Mrs. Kincaid." Tommy spoke with a firmness that she had never heard from him before. It frightened her. "Going back for Sebastian would have cost us our own lives."

"That's true," she said. "But I want you to understand-"

"I understand perfectly well."

Accepting discretion as the better part of valour, Desa chose to end the discussion there. What more could she say? Tommy probably thought there was some vindictiveness in her decision to leave Sebastian behind – and she had to admit that she was glad to be free of that young man's endless scorn – but she would not leave anyone to the whims of a mob. Not even a loathsome creature like Sebastian.

But it seemed her decision had soured Tommy's good opinion of her. Perhaps he too would abandon Desa at his next opportunity. It irked her to realize she was actually a little sad about that.

Desa had no interest in men as lovers – her marriage to Martin Kincaid had been a matter of simple necessity – but she had grown to enjoy Tommy's company. Most places she went, people greeted her with fear and suspicion. But not Tommy. His curiosity about her abilities was refreshing.

An hour of quiet solitude passed while Desa searched

for a suitable dinner. By the eyes of Vengeance, she was beginning to wonder if she had been cursed. Years of passing through town after town without incident, and suddenly trouble was lurking around every corner.

The sun was a red disk on the western horizon, the sky a deep twilight blue when she heard the steady *clip-clop* of hooves on dirt. Desa looked around to find the silhouette of a horse coming up the road. A horse with two riders.

Desa reached for her gun but thought better of it when she recognized one of them. A good thing too. After all the trouble she had encountered lately, she was down to eight bullets. She did not want to have to use ammunition unless it was absolutely necessary.

The woman in front was obviously Miri; even in the dark, Desa would recognize *that* woman's silhouette. But the other rider...It was hard to tell since he sat behind Miri, but Desa was fairly certain she knew the man's identity. Her suspicions were confirmed when he spoke.

"Tommy?" Sebastian called out.

At the sound of his lover's voice, Tommy leaped to his feet. He peered around the trunk of the tree, clearly unwilling to believe his ears. "Sebastian?" he mumbled. "Is...Is it really you?"

Sebastian hopped out of the saddle and ran to seize his love in a tight embrace. "Oh, thank the Almighty!" he shouted. "I didn't think I'd see you again."

"I didn't think I'd see *you* again."

Closing her eyes, Desa breathed slowly through her nose. Let those two boys have their reunion. She had other concerns to deal with. In three quick strides, she put herself in front of Miri. This close, she could tell that the horse was indeed Tommy's dark brown gelding. "Why are you following us?" she demanded.

"My word," Miri said, swinging one leg over the horse's flanks. She dropped to the ground with the scuff of boots on dust, then rounded on Desa. "I have never been treated so rudely in my life."

"Drop the act."

Thrusting her fist out, Desa summoned light from her ring and took satisfaction in Miri's surprised blink. The other woman backed away with her hands raised defensively. "I ain't lookin' to get into a fight," she said. "Or to anger a witch."

"I'm not a witch."

Licking her lips, Miri let her head drop. "Like I told you," she began. "I wanted to get out of that town after the commotion you caused. Sebastian had a horse; I knew a bit about the land. So, we helped each other. I *reckoned* you'd be happy to have your friend back. Suppose I was wrong about that."

"We appreciate you returning Sebastian to us, however-"

"I brought food!" Miri broke in. "Snagged a couple rabbits at the edge of the forest. Sebastian wanted to stop and cook 'em, but I said we had to keep riding if we were gonna find you. At least let a girl stay and eat the food she caught. Even a witch oughtta have enough manners for that."

With a thought, Desa killed the light from her ring.

Heaving out a sigh, she trudged through the grass to a spot where the silhouettes of Tommy and Sebastian stood holding hands and gazing into each other's eyes. "Boys," she said. "It seems Miri brought us some food. Help her prepare it."

. . .

THEY ATE in the wan light of Desa's ring, all sitting in a circle under the branches of the oak tree. It had taken every last drop of heat from her three coins to cook both rabbits; Desa would have to Infuse them with fresh connections to the Ether. Tomorrow. She was too tired to bother with it now.

Miri dabbed her mouth with a handkerchief, then looked up to direct a warm smile toward Sebastian. "Told ya it would be worth the wait," she said. "Promised ya we'd find your friends, and here we are."

He sat cross-legged across from her, smiling as he popped the last bit of meat into his mouth. "You were right," he said. "I shouldn't have doubted you."

Amazing how readily he listens to her when he resisted me at every turn. Desa bit back a curse. Was she really feeling jealous because Sebastian respected Miri more than he did her?

Tommy was next to his love and holding Sebastian's hand. The huge grin that split his face made it all but impossible to believe he had been so forlorn just a short time ago. "I'm glad you came back," he murmured.

"I couldn't leave you," Sebastian replied.

With her arms crossed, Desa leaned back against the trunk of the tree. She looked up toward the heavens, lost in thought. What was she to do with this troop of fools she had gathered? Somehow, she suspected that Miri would be traveling with them no matter what she did to prevent it.

Her mouth opened in a yawn that she covered with one hand. "We need to sleep," she muttered. "We'll need to have an early start tomorrow if we hope to gain any ground on Morley."

"You're still set on chasin' down that devil," Miri grumbled.

Desa turned her head to study the woman through

narrowed eyes. "Indeed I am," she said. "If that troubles you, you're more than welcome to part company with us at any time. I have no intention of dragging you into danger."

The dim light cast shadows over Miri's face, but it was clear that the woman was scowling. "It ain't me I'm worried about, darlin'," she said. "Any woman fool enough to tangle with him is askin' for trouble."

"I think you've seen that I can handle myself."

"This ain't no ordinary man."

Sebastian offered a limp shrug of his shoulders. The young man's face was white. "Can't we just...let him go?" he inquired. "Let him be someone else's problem?"

"You're also welcome to part ways with us, Sebastian," Desa said. "I will not keep you against your will."

"I think I'll stay."

Of course he would. Well, at least the young man seemed more agreeable than he had before Glad Meadows. Perhaps fearing for his life had taught him some manners. At least she wouldn't have to deal with his sneers. For a little while.

Sleep came fitfully that night; Desa did not feel comfortable drifting off with Miri just a few feet away. Every noise woke her, and each time, she expected to find Miri with a knife to her throat. What *was* that woman up to?

There were many possibilities, of course, but the one Desa feared most involved Miri working for Bendarian. That bastard had sent assassins after her before. None had tried to ingratiate themselves with her, but there was a first time for everything.

The next day brought very little change in scenery. Just open road and grassy fields with the odd tree here and there. Desa had tried to persuade Miri that it would be best for her to move on and find opportunities elsewhere, but the woman was determined to stay with them a while longer.

They began their ride with Desa and Tommy on Midnight while Sebastian and Miri took Tommy's old brown gelding. But that poor beast lacked Midnight's strength, and he required frequent stops. More than once, they had to dismount and walk for an hour to let the poor creature recover.

Eventually, Miri suggested that Tommy's horse would have an easier time carrying the women, as they were both smaller and lighter. Desa didn't like that one bit – Midnight was *her* steed – but she could hardly argue the point when she had been the one to insist that speed was of the essence. So, she rode the gelding while Midnight gave her sidelong glances and snorted at the strangers on his back.

On any other day, having a lovely woman's arms wrapped around her would leave Desa feeling content, but she did not trust Miri. Every time the woman squirmed behind her, Desa flinched at the fear that she might find a knife in her back.

"So," Miri asked, tightening her grip on Desa's belly. "Why is it you're so keen to find this Morley?"

Sitting in the saddle with the reins in hand, Desa shut her eyes and tried to remain calm. "He's a murderer," she answered. "And a servant of a much more dangerous man. It is that man I hunt."

"Who might that man be?"

Desa chose not to answer – the less Miri knew about her business, the better – but Sebastian took the opportunity to fill the silence in the most unhelpful way possible. Why oh why did she tell these boys her secret? "His name is Radharal Bendarian," Sebastian said. "He's a Field Binder of Aladar."

"Like you," Miri said.

Desa blew air through puckered lips. Her patience was growing thinner and thinner by the second. "Yes, like me," she answered. "That's why I'm the one who must stop him. I'm the only one who can."

"So, witches take responsibility for other witches? Huh?" Miri poked Desa between the shoulder blades. "Well, now, bless my soul! What exactly do you call a man witch? A warlock?"

Sebastian laughed with just a bit too much enthusiasm. He leaned in close, brought his lips to Tommy's ear and murmured, "Would you like to be a warlock, my love?" That was followed by a fit of giggles.

Desa felt heat in her face and sweat on her brow. Hard as it was, she forced herself to remain quiet. She was beginning to suspect that Sebastian might have told Miri a great deal about her in their time together. Perhaps this was an attempt to provoke her.

"Well?" Sebastian prodded after a moment. "You didn't answer, my love."

Tommy growled and shook his head, which produced another outburst of laughter from Sebastian. Desa sighed. It was going to be a long journey, that was for sure.

TOMMY KNEW they were close to Ofalla when he spotted the first farmhouse. It was nothing special – just a small house of gray stone with a gabled roof – but the sight of it soothed his troubled mind. It had been four days since their flight from Glad Meadows, and in all that time, he had not seen another human soul outside of their small party. He was beginning to worry that they had reached the edge of the world.

Two tall apple trees grew in front of the farmhouse, and he could hear the mooing of cows who grazed in the field. A shaggy mare stood just outside a barn of whitewashed wood, munching on some grass.

Shading his eyes with one hand, Tommy squinted as he stared down the road. "We must be getting close now," he said. "I hope we get there by nightfall; I could use some rest in a decent bed."

Next to him, Desa sat her horse with the reins in hand, smiling fondly as she shook her head. "You won't be sleeping in a bed tonight," she informed him. "Or tomorrow, for that matter. We still have a long way to go."

Tommy felt his mouth drop open, then lowered his eyes and grumbled to himself. "But the farm!" he insisted when he worked up the nerve to speak. "How can there be...I mean who lives this far away from the city?"

Miri was behind Desa with her arms around the other woman's waist, and she gave him a look that called him an idiot. "Ain't you never been more than two steps outside of your little town, Lommy?"

"It's Tommy."

He knew for a fact that Miri heard him, but she ignored his protests as she always did. "Well, Lommy," she went on. "Big cities like Ofalla have villages surrounding them on all sides. We'll pass through a few of those."

"Maybe we could find an inn?" Sebastian suggested.

Desa wrinkled her nose at that, but she kept her gaze focused straight ahead as if she expected to find trouble behind the next hill. "We don't have enough money for that," she said. "If we find an inn, we'll stop for a hot meal, but we're sleeping rough tonight."

Tommy felt it when Sebastian shifted in Midnight's saddle, and the stallion snorted in protest. He didn't seem to like it when one of his riders squirmed. Or maybe it was just this particular rider that he didn't like. Midnight was as friendly as an excited puppy when Lommy approached him, but he glared daggers at Sebastian.

Tommy felt a spike of alarm.

Did...Did he just think of himself as Lommy? May the Almighty have mercy on his soul, that damnable woman was actually training him to answer to that ridiculous name! He liked Miri just fine – most of the time, anyway – but he was beginning to understand why Desa found her so vexing.

Sebastian leaned toward Desa, and Tommy cringed at the thought of what he might say. "What do you mean 'we don't have enough money?'" Sebastian began. "You seemed to have plenty in Sorla."

She gave him a cool stare beneath the brim of her hat. "I spent years traveling alone and living off the money I made hunting fugitives," she said. "Which was always enough to get me to the next town. Now, there are four of us."

Sebastian muttered but he made no further protest.

Tommy was glad for that small mercy. When his love had returned to him, all he could think about was how happy he was. Happy and relieved. But now Sebastian had resumed his habit of challenging Desa at every opportunity. Now, Tommy could remember why he had been willing to watch the man he loved walk out of his life. A year ago, he would have never imagined that Sebastian could be capable of such ignorant hatred. In fact, he almost wished that Sebastian *had* stayed behind in Glad Meadows. It was so confusing. Why couldn't his fool brain just make up its mind?

The afternoon grew warm as they continued their south-ward journey, passing one farmhouse after another. Every now and then, they saw a man tending to his cows or a woman hanging laundry on a line. No one paid them any mind. Perhaps these people had grown used to the sight of travelers.

Tommy kept his mind busy by enjoying the scenery: the lush green grass, the clear blue sky full of puffy clouds, the occasional field of wildflowers. Only, it seemed to him, after a while, that the scenery was losing some of its luster. As the day wore on, the grass seemed less green. Maybe it was just his imagination.

The others were talking, but he paid them no mind. His thoughts were focused on sorting out his feelings for Sebastian, and the harder he tried to avoid that task, the more urgent it became. Perhaps he should try to meditate

One, two, three, four, five.

One, two, three, four, five.

It wasn't working.

Tommy held the reins in a tight grip, anxiety clawing at him as he frowned down at the pommel of his saddle. "You said there would be towns," he muttered. "I thought we'd have seen one by now."

When he shot a glance in her direction, Desa offered a reassuring smile. "We will," she promised him. "We're still a good ways out. Towns tend to spring up around cities. Less so in the countryside."

He nodded.

When his mind refused to quiet down, he went back to looking at the scenery, but that did nothing to soothe him. The grass *had* changed, and now he knew it wasn't just his imagination. Something had taken the colour from every blade. Not all of it, but enough for him to notice. It wasn't just that the grass was turning brown the way it sometimes did in a prolonged drought. No, it was more of a gray. There was still a hint of green, but not much. More like a memory of green.

Come to think of it, the dirt beneath Midnight's hooves wasn't quite so brown. The sky was still a vibrant blue – so, they had that – but something was wrong here. When he looked at the trees, he didn't see green leaves but gray ones that hung limp from each and every branch.

Tommy lifted his hands up and flexed his fingers. His skin still retained its pinkish hue, and his clothes were also unaffected. Trousers as brown as the day his mother made them and scuffed booths with black visible beneath: *he* looked perfectly normal. As did all of his companions. The horses were fine too.

But the land...

The land was fading.

He looked toward Desa for some indication that this was all perfectly normal and found her riding with a hand pressed to her stomach. She was grimacing, and she looked about ready to empty her belly.

Tommy felt his lip quiver, then steeled himself and sucked in a breath of air. That too felt wrong, somehow. It was almost imperceptible, but the day's heat seemed to have faded. It wasn't *cold;* it was just...nothing. The air felt stale and motionless. There was no breeze. "What's going on?" Tommy mumbled.

"Something is very wrong," Desa said. "We need to stop."

7

Ignoring the churning of her stomach – the Ether was out of sorts, somehow – Desa dropped from her horse and landed in a crouch. She straightened, reached up and pulled the brim of her hat down low over her eyes.

Grass and road alike had faded to a dark, somber gray, both so muted that she could hardly tell one from the other. The sky overhead was normal, but the landscape had died. Or worse. She wasn't sure that she had a word for this.

Desa paced a short ways up the road, then knelt and grabbed a tuft of grass that had sprouted from the dirt. The stuff was dry and rough as if something had sucked the life out of it. "By the eyes of Vengeance..."

She turned back to the others.

Her three companions stood side by side between the horses, all watching her with fearful expressions, hoping that she would have some answer for all this. Sebastian was the first to step forward. "Should we...Should we go back?"

Desa strode toward him, shutting her eyes and shaking her head. "No, we must go forward," she insisted. "This is

Bendarian's doing, I'm sure of it. I can *feel* a wrongness in the Ether."

"But...But how?" Tommy stammered.

Crossing her arms with a sigh, Desa felt her mouth tighten. Her head sank as she tried to put it all together. "I wish I knew," she said. "When I began pursuing him, it was because he had begun conducting experiments with the Ether."

"Experiments?" Miri asked.

"Bendarian claimed that we had only scratched the surface of Field Binding's true potential. He believed that we could Infuse the Ether directly into a human body, and he was cast out of the order for his refusal to relent on this point. Any skilled Field Binder can tell you that living tissue will not accept an Infusion, but Bendarian insisted on trying anyway. His experiments resulted in the deaths of thirteen people."

Tommy swallowed visibly.

Sebastian was deathly pale as he stood with one hand inside his coat pocket, staring down at his boots. "But you said that he was Infusing people," he mumbled. "Why would doing that change the land?"

"I don't know."

She scanned her surroundings and found a small farmhouse just a short way up the road. It couldn't be more than a quarter mile distant, and it too was gray. She had to know more about this phenomenon.

Desa stood in the road with her arms hanging limp, her eyes downcast as she took those first few steps forward. "We need to know more," she said. "So, let's see if anyone survived...whatever this was."

Ordinarily, she would have gone alone, but there were two people in this party she didn't trust, and she had no inclination to leave the horses in their care. Midnight would resist any underhanded attempt to steal him, but Tommy's gelding might not.

On the other hand, she wasn't thrilled about going into a dangerous situation with Miri at her side. The woman might decide to pull a knife at the worst possible time. And while she trusted Tommy, the young man was susceptible to Sebastian's influence. That left her with one option.

They all went in together.

The house was a small, squat building with a gabled roof and a window on either side of the door. It was pleasant, homey. Or rather, it would have been if not for whatever had destroyed everything within a square mile.

There should have been noise; a farm was never this deathly quiet. She should have heard the lowing of cows or the braying of sheep. Or even just a goodwife chastising her husband! Instead, all she heard was silence.

Squeezing her eyes shut, Desa drew in a breath and then nodded. "As I suspected," she said, turning back to the others. "They're either dead themselves or gone. I pray it is the latter, but we cannot be certain until we search the grounds."

Tommy watched her with a gaping mouth, blinking slowly. "Begging your pardon, Mrs. Kincaid," he began, "but shouldn't we be gone ourselves. What if whatever this was is...What if it's catching?"

"I suspect you would have caught it already if that were the case."

"But-"

With an exasperated sigh, Desa looked up toward the heavens and rolled her eyes. "If you would rather wait with the horses, that will be acceptable," she said. "But I must search the house."

Gray grass crunched beneath her boots as she stepped off the road. The sound of it only served to intensify her uneasiness. The air was so painfully still it was a miracle she could even breathe it.

"Hello!" Desa called out.

No one answered.

Briefly, she considered drawing her pistol but thought better of it. She didn't want to frighten anyone who might have survived this tragedy. If indeed anyone had survived. So, she crept through the grass as quietly as she could.

When she neared the door, Desa knocked. The wood sounded hollow somehow, but it resisted her repeated blows. She waited several moments for someone to answer, but no one did. Finally, she decided to try the door.

At first, she was pleased to find it unlocked, but the implications of that became all too clear before she could thank Mercy for good luck. If the door was unlocked, it likely meant that the family had been present to witness whatever had caused this catastrophe.

Thrusting out her fist, she triggered the Light-Source in her ring and breathed out a sigh of relief when it projected a cone of radiance into the small house. Field Binding still worked in spite of what Bendarian had done to the Ether. She let the ring go dark. There was no sense in wasting energy when natural light was so abundant.

Desa stepped through the door with a hand on the grip of her pistol, scanning left and right for any sign of trouble. "Hello?" she shouted, moving deeper into the house. "Is anyone here?"

She saw a wooden rocking chair next to the fireplace and a small table with four chairs: all gray. There was no sign of life. This place felt more like a tomb than a house; so, if the family had been present when their world turned gray, what had happened to them? She would have imagined that they would be as dead as the grass outside, but that would mean corpses. And she saw none.

In the back of the house, she found a kitchen where copper pots hung from a bar above the stove, though they looked more silver without their colour. Suddenly, a thought occurred to her.

Bracing her hands on the windowsill, Desa leaned forward to peer into the backyard. "I wonder if you have any ammunition to spare," she muttered, her eyebrows rising. "Mercy knows I need it."

She began a search of the house, opening drawers and cupboards. Stealing from the dead left her with an unsavory feeling, but there was no telling what kind of trouble she would find over the next hill, and she wanted more than eight bullets.

Climbing the stairs with one hand on the wall, Desa cringed at every creak of the floorboards. "The Goddess smiles upon me," she whispered, reciting a prayer her mother had taught her. "I shall not fear."

On the second floor, she found a single room with four beds underneath a triangular roof and a square window on the wall that provided enough light to see. Once, it would have saddened her to see people living like this. No running water, no antibiotics. And no electricity either – she couldn't even begin to describe how hard it had been to get used to *that* – but the people she had met on her journeys seemed content with their simple life.

There were no bodies in any of those beds. For all Desa could tell, this house had been abandoned years ago. It sickened her to realize that she would have been relieved to find corpses. Desa went to a chest of drawers.

Pulling one open, she began rummaging inside, casting

aside plaid shirts and folded-up socks. Clearly, these were the husband's garments. Her fingers closed around a small wooden box, and she was fairly certain of what she would find inside.

"What have we here?"

She opened to find about two dozen bullets inside, bullets that were made to fit a Lessenger-22. There was a reason why Desa carried the most common pistol available. It wasn't the most reliable weapon, but you could always find ammunition.

Picking one up, she held it in front of her face and squinted. "Hmm..." she said. "I wonder if you'll actually fire."

These bullets were as gray as everything else in the house. Aside from the lack of colour, everything else seemed unaffected; doors still opened, floorboards still supported her weight. But she was dealing with something entirely unnatural. There was no telling how inanimate objects might have been affected.

She slipped the box into her pocket and moved silently down the stairs. Despite her fears, the sitting room was still empty, and when she glanced through the open front door, she saw her companions waiting on the road with the horses. They looked so strange, all of them in full colour against a landscape of unrelenting gray.

Desa stepped out into the open, rubbing her forehead with the back of one hand. "I found no one inside," she said, pacing through the grass toward them. "Something about this feels incongruent."

Sebastian was standing with his arms folded, shaking his head at what he obviously believed to be a stupid remark. "You don't say!" he spat. "The world turned gray around us, and something feels incongruent."

Desa ignored him.

"The door was unlocked," she explained, "which would imply that this strangeness happened when the family was at home and busy with their daily tasks, and yet I saw no bodies. So, where did they go?"

"Maybe they fled after the grayness came," Miri suggested.

Desa shrugged. "I doubt that," she said, moving slowly toward her friends. She was careful to make sure they heard the *crunch-crunch* of dead grass beneath her feet. "Look around you. All the plants are dead, and we don't hear the sounds of livestock. So, if the family was present when the grayness came..."

"There should be corpses," Tommy muttered.

"Exactly."

Frowning as she turned her head to inspect the landscape, Miri offered a sniff of disdain. "Begging your pardon, ma'am," she said, "But your reasoning's hardly iron-clad. Maybe the grayness didn't come all at once, and the family had time to run."

"Perhaps."

Tommy had two fingers over his mouth as he nodded slowly. "What interests me," he began, "is how we seem unaffected. If the grayness was lethal, we should have died as soon as we were exposed to it."

"So, what does that mean?" Sebastian asked.

"It means," Tommy broke in before Desa could answer, "that whatever caused the grayness also killed all the plants and animals. All we're looking at are the after effects of...something."

Desa strode over to him, looked up to meet his gaze and then nodded once. "I am pleased to see that one of you is thinking clearly," she said. "I would remain here to learn more, if I could, but we must catch Bendar-"

Her ears picked up something.

A growling sound.

She turned around in time to see a man coming around the side of the house. This fellow was shorter than average, with a barrel chest, a bald head and a thick beard, and he was gray from head to toe.

He stood there in a pair of trousers and a simple work shirt, both utterly stripped of colour, and he salivated from his open mouth like a hungry wolf that had just laid eyes on a rabbit. If there was an intelligence behind that dull stare, he didn't show it.

Desa faced the man with a hand on her weapon, remaining still in case he was the sort to react to sudden movement. "Hello," she said. "My name is Desa Kincaid. Can you tell me what happened here?"

The gray man said nothing.

"We'd like to help if-"

Before she could finish that sentence, the stranger growled and ran toward them at full speed. Desa moved to draw her pistol, but Miri was faster. The other woman stepped forward, pulling aside her coat to reveal an assortment of weapons on her belt.

Her hands were a blur as she drew throwing knives. One blade landed in the gray man's chest. And then another. And then *another*. Only then did he take notice. He paused just long enough to look down at himself, surprised by the sight of metal protruding from his flesh. Then he was charging them again.

"Damnation take this," Sebastian said, stepping forward. He drew his revolver and thumbed the hammer with a *click*. Extending his hand, he pointed the gun at the charging man, who was now just a few paces away.

"No!" Desa shouted.

Sebastian fired anyway.

The stranger faltered as a bullet ripped through his chest, stumbling backward with a shriek. Inky black ichor leaked from the wound. When the stranger looked up, his teeth were bared, and his eyes were as dark as obsidian.

He charged again.

Another thunderclap filled the air as Sebastian fired again, and this time, the bullet pierced the stranger's forehead. That did the trick. The gray man dropped to his knees and then fell flat on his face, revealing a hole in the back of his skull.

Rounding on Sebastian, Desa seized the young man's shirt and pulled him close so they were almost nose to nose. "Idiot child," she said, her voice as smooth as silk and as hard as steel. "Always reacting without thinking!"

"I saved us!"

"You saved us?" Desa protested. "You saved us? You may have-"

She cut off at the sound of more low, throaty growls, and when she worked up the nerve to look, she found five more gray people coming around the house. There was a tall woman in her middle years who wore a tattered white dress and a youth about Tommy's age with a mop of hair that might have been sandy-blonde once.

There was an old bald man with a thick beard and a young slip of a woman with a braid that fell to her shoulder-blades. There was even a child, a boy of about eight or nine who stared at her like a rabid dog. All were as gray as a tombstone, and every last one of them had dead, black eyes.

"Run," Desa whispered. "All of you, run."

"But-" Tommy stammered.

"Run!"

Without allowing any further protest, Desa stepped over

the dead man's corpse and drew a pair of knives from sheaths on her belt. If these creatures wanted to slaughter her companions, they would have to go through her. She heard the distinct sound of Midnight snorting as Tommy mounted him. "Hurry," he said.

Desa spread her arms wide, pointing the tip of each blade out to the side, and bent her knees to brace herself. "Well, come on then," she goaded the gray people. "Let's see how well you fare against a Field Binder of Aladar."

Old Graybeard was the first to accept her challenge.

He came rushing toward her with inhuman speed, and the others all followed him. Slobbering like a dog, Graybeard smacked his lips and dark saliva dripped from his chin. *Patience...Let him get close...Three, two, one, now!*

Desa pulsed the Gravity-Sink in her belt – triggering it for only half a second – and this allowed her to jump over Graybeard's head. She flipped through the air and dropped to the ground behind him.

The girl with the braid was next in line.

Desa rammed both knives into the young woman's chest, and when she pulled them free, the blades were coated in thick, black ichor. Her enemy was unfazed by what should have been a lethal wound.

The young woman responded with a back-hand blow that almost knocked Desa into the next life. Everything went dark, and pain consumed her reality. Desa barely even felt the touch of dry grass beneath her or the sensation of rolling across the ground.

She flopped onto her back.

When her vision cleared, she saw Graybeard running toward her with teeth bared. A shot to the head: that was how Sebastian had done in that first one. Discarding one knife, Desa pulled her gun free of its holster.

She thumbed the hammer, took aim and fired.

Graybeard's hand snapped up, closing around something, and smoke rose through the cracks between his fingers. Did he...Did he actually manage to catch the slug? How fast were these creatures?

"Not smart."

Desa triggered the Force-Source she had Infused into the bullet, and Graybeard's hand exploded in a spray of ichor. The kinetic blast sent him flying backward with enough force to knock down two of his companions.

The youth with the mop of gray hair had managed to avoid the collision. He came forward with his hands out, fingers bunched up as if he intended to claw Desa's face. And he seethed with every breath.

Snatching up her daggers, Desa somersaulted backward over the rough ground and came up in a crouch. Slowly, she rose to stand at full height. "Come, boy," she said. "It's past time we ended this."

He swiped at Desa's head.

She ducked and felt a claw-like hand pass over her, then drove one knife hilt-deep into the young man's gut. That produced a screech of pain. Desa popped up and slashed the other blade across his neck, opening his jugular vein. Black blood spilled out.

Desa kicked him, and the youth fell onto his backside, lying in an expanding puddle of dark fluid. Three more of these creatures stood behind him: both women and the child. Graybeard was on his knees as blood fountained from the stump where his hand should have been.

The child surprised her.

He leaped with incredible strength and flew toward her with his hands outstretched, ready to choke her. Desa reacted by instinct.

Bending her knees, she raised her left arm to shield herself and triggered the Force-Sink in her bracelet. The Infusion she had placed within the metal would only take kinetic energy from objects that were coming toward her.

The boy stopped dead in midair.

When Desa let her arm drop, he fell to the ground as well, landing flat on his face. Both women were scrambling toward her in a mad dash. They seemed to be unaware of their dying companions. Unaware or apathetic.

With a single thought, Desa ordered her belt-buckle to take in gravitational energy, and she leaped. Free of the Earth's pull, she soared high into the air and twisted around to see the two black-eyed women staring up at her.

She let gravity reassert itself just enough for her to float gently to the ground and land in front of the house. "That's right," she said with a nod. "You face one who controls the very forces of nature itself."

The two women began a mad sprint toward her.

Desa ran to meet them.

She chose the older woman in the tattered dress as her first target, and when she got near, that woman jumped up for a fierce kick. Desa fell to her knees, allowing her enemy to pass by overhead.

She rose and spun to find the younger woman right in front of her. That one clawed at Desa's face, and only a quick flinch saved her from blindness. Seizing the opportunity, Desa plunged her knife into the other woman's belly.

It did no good.

The black-eyed demon grabbed two fistfuls of Desa's coat, lifted her off the ground and threw her with devastating force. Dizziness set in as Desa went shoulder-first into the farmhouse's front door.

Wood splintered, and when she landed, she was in the

dimly-lit sitting room. The pain made it hard to think, but she had to focus, had to keep her wits. Desa got up and looked through the open doorway.

The young woman with the braid was running toward her, snarling as black tears streamed over her cheeks. And she still had a knife sticking out of her belly!

Wiping her bloody mouth with the back of one hand, Desa winced. "I must congratulate you," she said in a hoarse voice. "It's not often that an enemy can truly surprise me."

Desa triggered the Heat-Sink she had Infused into the knife. Halfway through her next step, the gray woman froze in place with the crunching sound of blood crystallizing. Frost spread over her body, a wave of white that began in her core and went all the way to the tips of her fingers.

Desa leaped through the door. She spun in mid-flight and kicked out behind herself, slamming a boot into the frozen woman's chest with enough force to shatter her. Chunks of frozen flesh fell to the ground as Desa landed.

That left only the older woman.

And the child...

The child who was standing off to the side, near the corpses of his fallen friends, and watching this conflict unfold with a kind of morbid curiosity. He cocked his head to the side and blinked at Desa. Those black eyes reflected the sun. "Interesting," he said in a voice much too deep for one so young, a voice that seemed to echo. Almost as if there were many people speaking in unison. "They told me that you would be dangerous, but I would never have imagined that your kind would master the secrets of the Ether."

He began to pace back and forth, nudging the corpse of Graybeard with his foot. "It is not as I would have imagined it," he went on. "Soft flesh, given form and substance. So unlike what came before."

"What are you?" Desa whispered.

The child turned his head to fix dark eyes upon her, and his lips parted in a rictus grin. "Something more," he said. "Have they walked among you? Guided your steps? Or do they still hold to the old covenant?"

Desa sank to a crouch, head hanging as she let out a breath. "I do not understand." She looked up to study the child. "Whom do you speak of?"

He waved away her question with a dismissive hand. "It is immaterial." Suddenly, he stared into his palm as if transfixed by the sight of his own flesh. "This form cannot contain me. A substitution is required."

"This form is also insufficient."

Desa's head whipped around when she heard the older woman speak. Or perhaps it was not the woman herself. She spoke in the same multitude of voices that came out of the child's mouth.

Desa braced herself for another attack, but the woman just stood there with hands clasped in front of herself, staring dully at nothing at all. "You have destroyed my other vessels, but they would not have served."

A droplet of sweat formed on Desa's forehead and slid downward in a warm, sticky trail. "Why did you attack us?" she whispered. "We did nothing to antagonize you."

"To understand," the woman answered.

"To understand what?"

"This realm," the child replied. "And the rules that govern it. Specific and highly arbitrary." He blinked once, and when his eyes opened, the blackness was gone. Aside from the lack of colour, he looked as normal as any other little boy. For a second, Desa thought he had been restored to his true self, but the child collapsed to the ground. Dead.

Her mouth dropped open as she watched him fall. "No," Desa mumbled, shaking her head. "No, you can't do that!"

She turned to the other woman.

"You state a falsehood," the strange voice said. "Clearly I can, for I already have. Or is truth fluid in this realm?" Desa wanted to protest, but the blackness retreated from the other woman's eyes. Like the child, she collapsed to the ground.

Desa ran to her.

Dropping to one knee, she gasped as she felt sweat rolling over her face. "No, no, no..." She rolled the other woman onto her back and found a corpse staring blankly up at the sky.

Reluctantly, Desa stood up and shuffled away from the body. Finding Bendarian was now more important than ever.

8
———————

When Desa caught up to her traveling companions, she found them sitting around a crackling fire that sent sparks drifting up toward the stars. She wasn't inclined to chastise them for it; none of them could Field Bind, and they had to produce light *somehow*. And it pleased her to see orange flames casting warm light on trees with lush green leaves.

Desa stumbled into their campsite with her arms hanging limp, her head drooping with fatigue. "It's done," she whispered. "The creatures have been destroyed."

When she looked up, she saw Tommy sitting on the other side of the fire, staring up at her with horror on his face. "We didn't..." he began. "We didn't know if we should have gone back for you or-"

Desa scrunched up her face. "You were right not to try," she said, pacing a circle around the fire. Midnight stood at the edge of the campsite, watching her approach.

She laid a hand on his long nose, and he licked her fingers. "Those things were not human; if you had come back, you would have been killed."

She wanted sleep more than anything else, but that

would have to wait. Fighting the gray people alone had forced her to deplete her supply of Infused weapons, and there was no guarantee that they would not face something as bad or worse before they made it to Ofalla. She would have to make more.

It took some effort, but she forced herself to return to the fire. Miri was crouching there with the flames casting orange light on one side of her face. "Well, I dare say you've gone and had yourself an adventure," she said. "So, what happens next?"

Desa knelt in the soft grass and nearly fell forward with exhaustion. "I must find Radharal Bendarian," she said. "He is responsible for what happened today."

"How can you be sure?"

Stifling her frustration, Desa looked up to glare at the other woman. She narrowed her eyes to slits. "I am sure." That was all she could bring herself to say at the moment. It was all she owed Miri. In fact, saying that much may have been too much.

Tommy had gone to fetch something from their supplies.

He returned now with a waterskin in hand, squatted down next to her and offered it to Desa. "Mrs. Kincaid," he said. "Here."

Desa took the skin, brought the spout to her lips and drank deeply. Only then did she realize the depth of her thirst. Her muscles ached and her body felt like a rug that had been beaten too many times.

Wiping her mouth with the back of one hand, she exhaled and then slumped over with her head hanging. "We continue to Ofalla." Her voice was a breathy rasp. "It's most likely that we'll find Bendarian there."

She looked up, expecting to hear a challenge from

Sebastian, but the young man was a lump in his bedroll. If he had heard their conversation, he opted to remain blessedly silent on the matter.

"Rest," Desa said. "We must get an early start tomorrow."

SHE FLOATED in the sense the sense of calm that came whenever her mind touched the Ether. To her eyes, everything was different. The trees and the grass were spiraling bits of matter held together in a loose configuration. Her companions were close enough that she could sense them effortlessly. She was aware of almost *everything* within about a hundred paces of her body.

She focused on the duster that she had left folded over a rock, not so much a coat but a galaxy of particles all buzzing like busy bees. The box in her pocket still contained bullets she had taken from the farmhouse. She directed tendrils of the Ether toward it and gasped. There was no box.

Moving her body when her mind was in this state was next to impossible, but she forced herself to do so anyway. She nudged the coat with her foot and felt the box in her pocket. It was there, but she could not sense it with the Ether.

That should have been impossible.

Nothing was beyond the reach of the Ether!

She fed those tendrils of energy into the space where the box should have been, searching for the bullets inside, but they were gone too! So far as the Ether was concerned, neither box nor bullets existed. Was that a consequence of the Grayness?

Desa came back to her waking self.

Her vision snapped back to normal and she saw the

branches of a massive elm tree extending over her head, barely visible in the light of the fire. Her duster was there on the rock. She nudged it again with her foot.

Dropping to a crouch next to it, Desa closed her eyes and breathed out slowly. "So, how did you do this, Bendarian?" she wondered aloud. "What can separate an object from the Ether?"

She retrieved the box from her pocket and opened it to find gray bullets inside. All perfectly normal except for their lack of colour. What to do now? Could she still use them as ordinary bullets?"

Lifting one between her thumb and forefinger, Desa squinted at it. "Did Bendarian do this?" she whispered. "Or was it that *thing* at the farmhouse?"

She pulled her revolver, popped open the cylinder and fed the bullet into an empty slot. That done, she spun the cylinder so that the gray round was next in line, closed it and thumbed the hammer.

She chose a thin tree about fifty feet away.

CRACK!

"Almighty have mercy!" Tommy shouted, sitting up and clutching his blanket to his body. The poor lad was frightened, glancing this way and that, probably expecting to find himself under attack.

The shot landed true, leaving a big hole of splintered wood in the tree trunk. These bullets still obeyed the laws of physics – so far as Desa could tell, anyway – but they did not respond to the Ether. Well, normal ammunition was better than no ammunition, but not by much in her estimation.

"Will it never end?" Tommy groaned.

Desa strode toward him. "I'm sorry for waking you," she said. "I had to find out if the bullets I took from the farmhouse were usable."

The young man looked up at her with an expression that said his patience was wearing thin. "And are they?" he asked. "I bloody well hope so, since you decided to test them in the middle of the night."

"They can be used as ordinary ammunition."

"But..."

Desa folded her arms and hunched over. She puckered her lips and blew air through them. "But they will not accept an Infusion," she said reluctantly. "In fact, the Ether does not seem to recognize them. I cannot use them to Field Bind."

"Lovely," Sebastian grumbled. The young man was turned away on his side with a blanket pulled up over his head. "At least there is something in this world that is immune to your witchcraft."

"It occurs to me that perhaps you will take the gray bullets, Sebastian," Desa said. "And give me some of yours instead." Exactly when did the fool get his hands on a pistol anyway? Both boys had been unarmed when she took them from Sorla, which meant that Sebastian must have purchased a weapon after they were separated in Glad Meadows. Or perhaps...perhaps Miri had given it to him.

Miri.

That woman was dangerous.

Pursing her lips, Desa looked up toward the heavens and blinked. "After all," she went on. "It's of no difference to you. The gray bullets will fire as readily as any other."

"Cursed bullets," Sebastian muttered. "Just what I need."

From the corner of her eye, Desa saw Miri lying on her back with her eyes closed, seemingly asleep. That one was trouble. And it was past time that Desa dealt with her.

. . .

Desa's eyes popped open.

She was lying on her back with hands folded over her chest, gazing up at a predawn sky. Carefully, she sat up and noted the dark figure of Miri moving off toward some trees by the roadside.

Desa stood slowly with one hand on her holstered weapon and pursued her strange new companion. The grass was soft and moist from recent rainfall, but it still made more noise underfoot than she would have liked. Not that there was any chance of Miri hearing it at this distance, but years as a bounty hunter had taught her the value of silence.

Her companions had made their campsite in an open field that was dotted with trees here and there. It was a wise enough choice; there was little chance that anyone would be able to sneak up on them unnoticed. That said, there were copses thick enough to hide at least two or three people. Miri had chosen one of those.

As Desa neared, she became painfully aware of the silence. Miri was around here somewhere, and anyone struggling to avoid roots and branches in the dark would make a fair bit of noise. The only people who didn't were-

Desa spun around in time to see a shadowy figure looming over her, the silhouette of a tall, slender woman in a duster. Before she could even speak, that silhouette tried to punch her.

Desa ducked and felt a closed fist pass over her head. She threw a pair of jabs into Miri's stomach, then rose to slug the fool woman's nose. That had an effect. Miri gasped and stumbled away.

The woman was surprisingly quick, moving with lightning speed as she drew one of her throwing knives and flung it at Desa. Instinct pushed all thought aside.

With a ferocious growl, Desa raised her left forearm and

used her bracelet to drain kinetic energy. The knife froze in place mere inches away from her, hanging in midair. A spike of alarm went through Desa when she realized that Miri had just tried to kill her.

She drew her gun and pointed it at Miri's chest. "Why?" she demanded. "Why are you trying to kill me?"

Miri backed away.

"Why?"

"You frightened me!"

Desa let her arm drop to glare at the other woman. Her face was burning, her brow slick with sweat, and she was in no mood for games. "I frightened you? No, I don't think so. People with your skills don't frighten easily."

The silhouette shook her head, then backed up with her hands in the air. "I thought it might have been a bandit," Miri said in that same twangy accent. "Or one of those gray things come to kill us."

Yes, the accent remained, but Miri's speech was more formal than it should have been. Her mask was slipping. "I'm disappointed," Desa said. "Your lies aren't usually so transparent. Tell me why I shouldn't end you now."

"Mrs. Kincaid-"

Thrusting her pistol forward, Desa cocked the hammer with the distinctive *click*. If that frightened Miri, the woman showed no sign of it. But her presence in the group was becoming a problem.

Desa had been living with a fear of betrayal ever since this woman showed up with Sebastian on her heels. Enough was enough. Sebastian, she could deal with – that fool of a boy was harmless – but Miri? Miri was trained and deadly. "Who are you?" she asked. "You have one chance to answer, and if I don't like what I hear, I will pull this trigger."

"She is Miri Nin Valia," a man said, emerging from the trees. "One of the Ka'adri and a servant of Synod."

Tall and broad-shouldered, this newcomer would have been imposing in his long coat, but Desa had met more than her fair share of imposing men, and whatever smidge of respect she might have felt once upon a time was long gone. Besides, she would know that voice anyway.

Her lips writhed, showing clenched teeth as she turned her gaze on him. "Marcus," she said. "What brings you all the way out here? I didn't think anything could make you leave Aladar."

Marcus reached up and tipped his hat to her. "A pleasure to see you as well," he said. "You are, after all, the reason why I'm here."

"I am?" A thought occurred to her. "Wait...Isn't Valia your mother's name? Are you telling me that Miri is your *sister?*"

The other woman stalked off toward the campsite where Tommy and Sebastian had been roused by all the noise. Desa could only imagine the questions that she would have to answer after this. Perhaps it was for the best.

"The Synod will no longer tolerate your...escapades," Marcus replied in a voice dripping with disdain. "You are ordered to return to Aladar at once."

Holstering her revolver with a sigh, Desa shook her head. "I can't do that, and you know why," she said. "If Miri has been sneaking off to meet with you, it stands to reason you've been following us. Which means you saw what happened back there."

Marcus crossed his arms and thrust his chin out. The approaching dawn provided just enough light for her to see his scowl. "Yes, I saw," he spat. "All the more reason for you to return."

"And how have you come to that conclusion."

He began to pace a circle around Desa, grunting as he stamped one foot down in the grass. "You must have felt the Ether in that place," he said. "The wrongness. Aladar needs its best Field Binders."

"What we need," Desa insisted, "is to catch Bendarian before he repeats whatever he did on that farm."

"What makes you so certain this is Bendarian's doing?"

Desa blew out a breath, strode forward and put herself right in front of the man. She looked up to meet his eyes. "You know what happened," she said firmly. "Bendarian tried to directly Infuse the Ether into living people."

"What does that have to do with anything?"

"Those creatures that I fought," Desa began. "They were possessed by something. An intelligence of some kind."

"And you think Bendarian put it there?"

Craning her neck to hold his gaze, Desa felt her eyebrows rise. "That makes more sense to me than any other explanation," she said. "If you're here, you can help me. Two Field Binders will stand a better chance against Bendarian than one alone."

Marcus grimaced, turning his face away from her. For a brief moment, he stiffened. "That is not my mission," he mumbled. "I was sent to bring you home."

"Then set aside your mission for the time being."

His eyes fell upon her like bullets trying to pierce her flesh, and his cheeks flushed to a deep crimson. "Who do you think I am?" Marcus snarled. "I cannot simply abandon a mission without the blessing of the Synod."

"We don't have time for that," Desa groaned. "Even if you penned a letter today, it would take months to reach Aladar."

To her surprise, Marcus answered that with a wry grin

that almost made her want to punch him. The fool of a man had always known how to rile her. "You have lived among primitives too long," he said. "There are other options. When was the last time you even bothered to make an Electric-Source?"

It had been years. Electricity was a dangerous form of energy to harness. Trigger an Electric-Source, and it would lash out at anything that got too close. Electric-Sinks could be even worse, condemning those caught in their fields to a painful death of convulsions. "Why?" Desa asked. "Are you planning to kill someone with lightning?"

"I have a radio."

"You *what?*"

Had the technology improved so much in just a decade? When Desa had left Aladar eleven years ago, radios were heavy and bulky contraptions with circuitry that would not do well when exposed to the elements. Not the sort of thing that one could easily take on a long journey, especially if travel by horseback was required.

Marcus raised his hands to forestall her and took a careful step backward. "I don't have it with me," he said. "I left it in safekeeping at a bank in Ofalla. We could journey there and learn the will of the Synod in less than two days."

"I suppose that's something," Desa said. "Perhaps someone will get a good look at the device and learn a thing or two."

Marcus grimaced at that. "You know we don't share technology," he countered. "It would invite invasion."

"And *you* know I've never agreed with that policy. We were already on our way to Ofalla. If you wish to accompany us, I have no objections." It would make things easier. She could be fairly certain that Miri would not try to kill her again so long as Marcus was intent on bringing her home. Mercy knew there was no getting rid of the woman.

"We will go," Marcus said, "and speak to the Synod. After that, it will be a simple matter of booking passage on a ship."

"We'll see..." Desa muttered.

9

It took another day and a half of riding to reach Ofalla, and by the end of it, Tommy was worn out. He would have expected to see something grandiose upon their arrival – a large, stone wall encircling the city, perhaps – but there was nothing like that.

The city seemed to almost grow naturally out of the surrounding countryside. Small buildings appeared almost haphazardly on the roadside, growing more and more frequent the closer they got to the centre of town.

Eventually, dirt roads became cobblestone streets with tall, black lampposts on each raised sidewalk. Narrow townhouses with black-tiled rooftops were packed so closely together that there wasn't an inch of space between them. And the noise! Oh, the noise! Every street was bustling with people.

They traveled side by side on horseback with Desa and Miri riding Midnight while Tommy and Sebastian shared his father's gelding. Mrs. Kincaid had been eager to reclaim her mount, and she had insisted that they switch places this morning.

Marcus, the newcomer to their group, rode his own horse, a proud beast the colour of a summer storm cloud. How fitting that he had named the creature "Thunder." Tommy thought it fit well, but Desa snorted every time Marcus called the horse by name.

At one point, they were shouldered out of the way by a horse-drawn carriage that came up behind them and rumbled past without so much as an apology from the driver. Some aristocrat was late to some function, or so Tommy reckoned. No time to spare any notice for the little people.

"So, this is city life," Sebastian muttered behind him. "I could do without it."

Tommy frowned into his lap and gripped the reins a little tighter. He felt no desire to engage in more verbal sparring with the man he loved. Best to just leave Sebastian to his endless litany of complaints.

They rounded a corner...

And Tommy gasped.

Before him, a massive stone bridge stretched over a river that must have been at least a mile across. "The Vinrella," Desa said when she caught him gaping. "It flows all the way from the Molarin Mountains to the eastern coast."

Tommy forced his mouth shut with a click, then gave his head a shake. "Why, it's magnificent," he whispered. "Mrs. Kincaid, I must thank you for bringing us with you on this journey."

Sebastian snorted.

To his delight, Desa turned her head and favoured him with a smile. "You may call me Desa, Tommy," she said. "My husband is dead, and I've never felt much claim to his family's name."

They started across the bridge with Marcus in the lead,

riding his tall, lean gray and occasionally looking back to cast a glare at the rest of the group. Tommy wasn't sure what made the man so cantankerous, but he suspected it was something between Marcus and Desa, and so he wanted no part of it.

It occurred to him that the bridge was not high enough to let tall ships pass beneath it, which meant...Which meant that the Ofallans had created a wonderful trading port for themselves. Ships from upriver would have to unload their cargo and transfer it to other vessels. The crews who did the work almost certainly made a tidy profit, and Tommy was willing to bet that the city put tariffs on cargo that changed hands. Yes, a wonderful, little trading port, indeed.

On the other side of the river, Ofalla looked much the same: tall townhouses and cobblestone streets, fruit carts on the roadside where men promised the best peaches and plums in the county. Tommy could do with a peach himself. It had been a steady diet of rabbit and duck the whole way down, munching on leftovers in the saddle and going hungry as often as not.

Soon, they turned up a side street and stopped in front of a building that stood three stories high with black tiles on its slanted roof. The sign out front named it the Golden Horseshoe Hotel.

Marcus swung one leg over the back of his horse and dropped to the ground with a grunt. "Mr. Jackson offered me a discount rate the last time I stayed at his place," he said. "I'm sure he'll do the same again."

Pressing his lips into a frown, Tommy looked up toward the sky. He blinked as he considered their predicament. *Everything here is so big,* he thought to himself. *Why, there must be at least ten thousand people in this city. How can we find this Bendarian in all of that bustle?*

Sebastian poked him.

Tommy forced his eyes shut, trembling as the spike of alarm that made him want to jump out of the saddle faded away. That didn't seem right. Why was he uncomfortable around the man he loved. "Please don't do that."

"Lighten up," Sebastian muttered, dropping out of the saddle. He dusted his hands and turned his attention to the Golden Horseshoe. "Finally, a decent night's sleep in a real bed. I didn't think we'd ever manage that again."

Desa was sitting atop Midnight and glowering at Marcus. "I trust we can rely on Mr. Jackson's discretion?" she asked. "If Bendarian is still in this city, I would prefer not to alert him to our presence."

Marcus replied with a cheeky grin and a nod so slight it was almost imperceptible. "You needn't worry about that," he promised. "The man respects his guests' privacy."

"You can be sure of that?"

"He caught me in the middle of Infusing some bullets," Marcus explained. "Said he had no interest in what I did with myself so long as I didn't trouble the other guests."

"I suppose it will do," Desa mumbled.

AN HOUR LATER, Tommy was stretched out on a soft feather mattress with hands folded behind his head, smiling as he stared vacantly up at the ceiling. It was good to get off his feet for a while. Aches that he had forgotten about were now leaping to the forefront of his mind.

Sebastian was at the window with his chin clasped in one hand, stroking his jaw as he peered through the glass. "We should go exploring," he said. "I bet we could stay here a month and still not see all of this city."

"I don't think Mrs. Kincaid would like that."

Sebastian's head whipped around, and his gray eyes were like hot pokers stabbing through Tommy's chest. "Do you let that harridan make every decision for you?" he spat. "I thought you had a mind of your own."

"Desa saved our lives."

"No, she saved *your* life. You were the one stupid enough to choose the gallows."

Tommy sat up and became very much aware of the dull ache in his shoulder that he had been ignoring. "And what was the alternative?" he asked. "Let my brother sell me into slavery. A day of that life would have destroyed you, Sebastian. I know that much."

"I wouldn't have gotten that far," Sebastian muttered. "My plan was to escape."

"You're a fool."

Their fight was interrupted by a knock at the door, and before either of them gave him leave, Marcus poked his head into the room. "We'll be having dinner in ten minutes," he said. "I suggest you join us."

Tommy supposed the man didn't need permission to enter the room – after all, he was sleeping here as well – but Marcus knew about him and Sebastian. The man probably wanted to respect their privacy.

"We'll be down shortly," Tommy assured him. He gestured to Sebastian but the other man seemed intent on pretending that he hadn't heard one word of that exchange. Well, let him sit up here with his hunger if he was so inclined.

It wasn't very long before Tommy found himself sitting at one of the long wooden tables in the hotel's saloon. Daylight through the two front windows provided more than enough illumination for him to see the serving girls bringing food and mugs of ale to the various guests.

One set a mug down in front of him.

Tommy looked up with a shy smile and nodded to her, "Thank you," he said. The girl – a pretty young lass with waves of long blonde hair – blushed and then moved on to the next table.

Miri was across from him with her elbow on the table, her chin resting on the back of her hand. "I do believe that she likes you." Her twangy accent was gone, replaced by crisp, clear enunciation. In fact, she sounded a lot like Desa.

Now, it was Tommy who blushed and lowered his eyes, nervously scratching his head. "I'm spoken for," he mumbled.

"And I suppose you don't like girls."

The question left him feeling a bit taken aback. He supposed he had never given it much thought. *Did* he like girls? He remembered being smitten with Darcy Miller, back home, when he was twelve, but he had never found the courage to talk to her. And after that, he had become infatuated with Robert McGregor. "I suppose," Tommy said, "that I wouldn't be averse to it."

"Then maybe you should go talk to that girl."

Tommy grimaced, shaking his head. "I couldn't." He sat forward with his elbows on the table and laced his fingers over the top of his head. "Besides, I love Sebastian. I could never betray him."

When he looked up, Miri was watching him with pursed lips and a stern expression. "That's a shame, Lommy." Her ridiculous nickname was even worse without the twang. "Because Sebastian will betray you."

"What are you talking about?"

"That boy is trouble."

"No...He's just angry at the world."

"Well, I can understand why," Miri said. "Life isn't easy

when the world hates you simply for being who you are. But there is a difference between you and Sebastian."

"And...And what's that?"

"When the world told you that you were despicable," Miri began, "you looked deep within yourself and realized that they were wrong. But Sebastian believed them. He hates himself. But more than that, he hates that the rest of us don't."

"Hate ourselves?"

The grim resignation in Miri's eyes made him shiver. "Indeed," she said. "Look at the way he treats Desa."

Clamping a hand over his mouth, Tommy shut his eyes and breathed in through his nose. "Why does he hate Desa?" The question had vexed him for some time. "I've never seen someone with so much animosity toward someone who saved his life."

"It's simple," Miri said. "Desa Nin Leean is a woman with power, and everything Sebastian believes about the world tells him that shouldn't be possible. So, he calls her a witch. If he can explain away her power as something evil, it will no longer threaten his manhood."

The serving girls brought them a meal of roast duck, buttered carrots and broccoli, and Lommy wolfed it down...*Tommy!* His name was Tommy! It was a good meal, but he hardly took time to savour it. Eating was mechanical for him, done out of necessity and nothing more.

Miri said nothing more on the subject of Sebastian's impending betrayal, and she tried to engage him in friendly conversation on other topics, but he wasn't feeling all that talkative. He just wanted to eat and sleep and forget everything that had happened since Desa took him away from his little village.

No, that didn't go back far enough. What Tommy really

wanted was to forget every day that had passed since his father caught him and Sebastian in the hayloft. What a fool he had been to think the world would allow him even a morsel of happiness.

The meal ended with a mug of beer, and he was about to slink back to his room, but a man with a thick dark beard came in to play guitar, and Miri seized the opportunity to pull him into a dance. At first, Tommy resisted, but when others started dancing, he chose to just go along with it. The alternative was resuming his fight with Sebastian.

They twirled around in circles, and Miri laughed at his fumbling attempts to recall the steps to *any* dance he had been taught. Eventually, she patted him on the cheek and said, "You're a fine man, Lommy. Don't waste yourself on a wretch like Sebastian."

Shoving his hands into his pockets, Tommy turned around and shuffled away from her with a smile on his face. *Maybe this wasn't so bad,* he thought. *It did me well to get a few moments away from-*

He looked up to find Sebastian standing at the foot of the stairs and watching him. That cold stare made Tommy want to groan. How long had the other man been there?

And how much did he hear?

10
———

Morning sunlight through the window made Desa feel uneasy. Normally, she liked mornings, but this dawn brought with it the prospect of following Marcus to his bank and using the radio to contact the Synod. She stood before a rectangular pane lined with dark brown muntin, watching silver rays bounce off the slanted black roof across the street.

A knock at the door startled her.

Desa stood with her hands clasped behind herself, hanging her head at the sound. "You may come in," she called out. "I am the only one here."

She turned in time to see the door swing inward, allowing Marcus to step into the room. He was dressed in brown trousers and his long duster, and he carried his hat in one hand. "I trust you're ready to go."

Desa shut her eyes, breathing deeply to calm herself. "I would remind you that this is a terrible idea," she protested. "The Synod cannot hope to fathom the danger without seeing Bendarian's atrocities with their own eyes."

"You agreed to speak with them."

"But *not* to abide by their decision," Desa said raising a

single finger. She felt her eyebrows climb as she studied him. "And the only reason I agreed to that much was the faint hope of enlisting other Field Binders to our cause."

Marcus leaned against the door-frame, folding his arms, and scowled as he shook his head. "Aladar cannot spare more Field Binders," he said. "Losing you was a blow to the economy."

"Perhaps we should train others."

"Blasphemy," Marcus spat. "These primitives wouldn't even be able to grasp the most basic principles."

Cocking her head to one side, Desa blinked at him. "I disagree," she said. "I have begun instructing young Tommy in the art. He shows considerable potential."

Marcus stood up straight, and his face became as grim as a rumbling thundercloud. He took two cautious steps forward. "You revealed the secrets of Field Binding? That is a capital crime, Desa."

"I've never agreed with that law," Desa countered. "Field Binding does not belong to Aladar. It is the birthright of every human being."

"You would empower our enemies?" Marcus bellowed. "Give them the means to destroy Aladar?"

Desa looked up to match him stare for stare, then narrowed her eyes. "They are not our enemies," she insisted. "And I am not the one who left advanced technology in their care."

It disappointed her when Marcus rested a hand on the grip of his pistol and glared at her like a sheriff who expected a criminal to run. "You will come with me to speak to the Synod." It wasn't a question or even a demand. From Marcus, it was just a statement of fact. "And you will answer for your...decisions."

She went without protest, though she wasn't sure how

long she could do so. It was all too likely that the Synod would demand her immediate return to Aladar, and if they did, Marcus would not relent. A cold feeling settled over Desa when she realized that she might have to kill him and Miri as well. The woman would not take it kindly if Desa killed her brother.

Though it took longer, Marcus decided to walk and leave their horses stabled. Desa wasn't sure what to make of that. Did the man believe that she would have an easier time escaping with Midnight? Still, a longer journey meant more time to consider her options.

The bank was on the other side of the Vinrella, which meant crossing a bridge that was full of people even at this early hour. A group of young women in colourful dresses strolled toward them; several of them eyed Marcus, and when they passed Desa heard soft giggling.

The steady clip-clop of horse hooves told her that a carriage was coming up behind them, and when it rumbled past, the coachman – a spindly fellow in a gray coat – actually lifted his top hat in greeting. It was a beautiful morning with a clear blue sky and the sun hovering just above the eastern horizon. Even now, the day was beginning to grow warm.

In tan pants and her brown duster, Desa walked with hands in her pockets and kept her eyes focused on the ground. "You realize that if we decide to go," she began, "we will be leaving these people to Bendarian's machinations."

Marcus was on her right and staring grimly into the distance. Was he deciding what to do if Desa decided not to follow the Synod's directives? "They are not our people," he said. "We have other concerns."

"That seems callous."

"It is the simple truth."

Desa looked over her shoulder, squinting at him. "You were never interested in the world beyond our borders," she said. "But now you seem eager to watch it burn. Tell me, did something happen while I was away?"

It made her uneasy when Marcus put a hand on his gun, but he seemed to be doing it without thinking. His chest expanded as he took a breath, and then he nodded once in confirmation. "Too much has happened."

That felt ominous, but Desa chose not to press the point. Her mind was filled with images of Eradian troops laying siege to Aladar, of Field Binders tearing through armies of men on horseback, of the roar of cannons.

It made her sick to her stomach.

WHEN THEY FINALLY ARRIVED, the bank was just opening. A gray, stone building with an arch-shaped overhang framing the wooden front door, the place looked very imposing to Desa's eyes. Almost more like a church than a bank. Perhaps, that was the building's original purpose before new management purchased the property.

An older man in a long black coat with silver buttons on the cuff of each sleeve slid a key into the lock with a shaky hand. He jiggled it several times and then grunted as he pushed the door open.

Finally, the man turned around.

Tall and reed-slim, he was more than presentable with a cravat around the collar of his white shirt. His leathery face was lined with creases, but his silver hair remained thick and full. "Mr. Von...Von..."

"Von Tayros," Marcus corrected.

The banker closed his eyes, exhaling through his nose, and then nodded to Marcus. "I assume you wish to retrieve your equipment," he said. "A pity. Two dollars a day is as much as most guests pay at a fine hotel. I'm loath to part with the income."

Baring his teeth with a hissing breath, Marcus stepped forward and tried to skin the other man alive with his glare. "I pay you for discretion," he said. "I trust that you haven't gone poking around my property."

"No need for such theatrics," the banker assured him. "A contract is a contract, and if I wished it, I could have the City Watch here in minutes. Your thinly-veiled threats may intimidate the ruffians that you hunt for bounty, but I can assure you that they shall have no such effect on me."

Marcus hesitated as if he were surprised by his own display of hostility. Desa was certainly startled by it. The young man she had known in Aladar had been grim, but this Marcus was a stick of dynamite just waiting for a spark. Twice now, he had reached for his pistol while in the grip of anger, and Desa was becoming more and more afraid of what he might do if she refused to go back to Aladar.

"Just take us to the vault," Marcus grumbled.

"As you wish."

The banker shambled through the open door, and when they followed, Desa found herself in a large room with a vaulted ceiling of gray bricks. A clerk's desk was placed just inside the front entrance, and a man in his shirtsleeves worked in the light that came in through an arch-shaped window.

He was a portly, bespectacled fellow who looked up just long enough to squint and then grunt when he recognized Marcus. "Mr. Von Tayros," he mumbled, opening one of his books and leafing through pages of ledgers. "You're paid up to the end of the month, sir. Do you wish to retrieve your equipment today?"

"I do."

"And may I inquire as to the identity of your companion?"

Marcus shot a glance in her direction, and for some reason, his lips curled into the thinnest smile. "This is Desa Nin Leean," he said. "She will be accompanying me."

The heavyset man stood up and fished a ring of keys out of his desk drawer. That done, he moved off toward a metal door built into the back wall. "If you'll please come with me," he said without bothering to see if they were indeed following.

Marcus turned to Desa.

She offered an apathetic shrug and then gestured to the fleeing clerk. "Don't look at me," she said. "You're the one who insisted on coming here. If I must endure the Synod's condemnation, I would just as soon be done with it."

They walked through a central aisle with thick stone pillars on either side, passing desks where bookkeepers worked diligently. Most didn't even bother to look. Everything about this place seemed designed to evoke thoughts of religion. The architecture included all the visual motifs that she had seen in the few churches she had visited, and yet there was no pulpit. Churches generally didn't have vaults built into them.

Pressing her lips together, Desa felt creases lining her brow. "This place," she said. "Was it always a bank?"

The portly clerk halted in mid-step and looked back toward her. "You are no doubt referring to the architecture," he said. "Mr. Phillips commissioned the great Jian Castelli to design this building. He said that he wanted something awe-inspiring, and this is what he got."

Desa resisted the urge to make a comment about men and their seemingly endless need to command respect through the construction of large, obtrusive monuments to their power. Only a money lender would choose to imbue a place of commerce with religious significance.

The clerk slid one key into a hole in the vault door, and with a forceful twist of his wrist, he unlocked it. The door groaned as it swung outward to reveal a place that looked very much like a cell-block inside.

Desa stepped through with lips pursed, shaking her head. "Cages for people," she said. "Cages for money. Funny how they should look so very similar."

On either side of a narrow corridor, barred doors looked in on stacks of gold bullion or piles of bank notes tied with thin ribbons. The fortune contained here could probably feed a city for at least a year.

Marcus followed her into the vault, then shut his eyes and exhaled. "It was the most secure place I could find to store the radio," he said. "If you please, Mr. Hatch, I'd like to inspect the equipment I left in your care."

The portly clerk made no complaint as he pushed through the tight space between Desa and Marcus and stalked off down the corridor. He led them to a smaller door at the very end, then unlocked it.

Inside, they found a simple table that supported an ornately-carved wooden box with a grill in the front and two antennae sticking out of the top. There was some other device attached to it by wires.

"Thank you, Mr. Hatch," Marcus said. "That will be all."

The clerk folded his arms and gave Marcus a disapproving stare. "I am required to supervise your movements so long as you remain in the vault," he said. "But if you wish privacy, I'm sure Mr. Kent's office will suffice."

"No, thank you," Marcus said. "You may remain."

He strode to the table and retrieved something from his

pocket. It looked very much like a small metal button with three prongs sticking out of it. Lifting the radio to expose its underside, he plugged those prongs into slots made to fit them. "An Electric-Source," he said. "Infused with enough energy to last for nearly a day of continuous use. This should only take a moment."

Marcus began fiddling with dials, producing a crackling sound from the grill on the radio, and the clerk jumped back in surprise. "Sorcery," he whispered as the colour faded from his face. "What kind of devilry is this?"

"Not devilry," Marcus said. "Technology."

With a small smile, Desa bowed her head to the poor man. "It's a device," she said. "No different than a steam engine."

"But how..." the Clerk stammered.

Desa only patted the man's arm and hoped that would suffice to calm him. A decade of traveling the Eradian continent had given her some small measure of sympathy for the peoples of this land. Marcus would need to learn such patience if he intended to join her on her mission.

It was easy to call these people primitive, but that did not make them inferior. There was nothing special about Aladri citizens beyond the good fortune of having been born in a society with a more advanced understanding of physics.

The clerk jumped again when a voice issued from the radio's grill, using the Aladri language. That was why Marcus had allowed the clerk to remain; he knew that there was very little chance the man would understand what he overheard.

"Marcus Von Tayros," a woman said through the radio. "You've been out of contact for quite some time."

Planting fists on his hips, Marcus stood with his back

turned and nodded as if the speaker could see him as well as hear him. "Apologies, Prelate," he said in Aladri. "But I have Desa Nin Leean with me."

"You found her?"

"I did."

"Well then..." That haughty voice could only belong to Daresina Nin Drialla, the woman who had led the Synod when Desa fled Aladar in pursuit of Bendarian. It seemed she had retained her position through the intervening years. "What precisely do you have to say for yourself, Desa? Abandoning your people?"

"My loyalty is not just to Aladar but to every living soul on this Earth," Desa replied. "*We* abandoned *them* when we allowed Bendarian to enter their lands uncontested."

"And yet, ten years later, their world remains intact."

"Don't be so sure," Desa countered. "Marcus and I have seen things that put paid to any notion that Bendarian was at worst a minor threat. He has twisted the Ether in some way and unleashed...something."

"Something?"

Desa scowled as the memory of what she had seen on that farm sent a chill down her spine. "I don't know what it was," she explained. "An entity of some kind, but vastly intelligent, and I get the sense that it has been looking for a way into our world for quite some time now."

"Has she gone mad, Marcus?" Daresina inquired. "Perhaps exposure to the locals has infected her with their superstitions."

Marcus set his jaw in stubborn defiance, and Desa braced herself for the worst. The way things were going, it wouldn't surprise her if he chose to deny seeing anything out of the ordinary. Perhaps he thought that would make her more inclined to return to Aladar with him. "Desa Nin

Leean speaks the truth," he said to her shock. "Something stripped the life and the colour from the land."

"What do you mean, 'stripped the colour?'"

"He means that the land was gray," Desa cut in. "And the trees, and the people. It was all gray: every stone, every leaf, every blade of grass. I found bullets that had turned gray, and they resist any attempt to Infuse them with a connection to the Ether. Whatever this was, it seemed to destroy the natural order."

"You can confirm this, Marcus?"

He folded his hands behind his back, and his lips parted to show clenched teeth. "I just did," he said forcefully. "The threat is real."

"We need Field Binders," Desa added.

"Field Binders?" Daresina exclaimed. "Are you mad or just foolish? I cannot spare such a precious resource on a rumor. In fact, this city needs its most skilled Field Binder to return home."

Desa stood with her hands in the pockets of her duster, her head hanging as she let out a breath. "I can't come home," she said. "What Bendarian has done may threaten the whole world."

"I am uninterested in your excuses, Desa."

She looked up slowly, then narrowed her eyes. "Those aren't excuses," she said, her voice as cold as winter frost. "If you will not aid me in protecting these people, then there is nothing left to say."

"Marcus," Daresina said. "You will take Desa Nin Leean into custody and return her to Aladar by the fastest ship you can find."

Unwilling to defy the Synod, Marcus turned to her and looked her up and down. "Don't make this harder than it has to be." His hand settled once again onto his gun. Was the fool really going to force the issue?

"I'm not going back with you," Desa said.

"How can you defy the Synod?"

"Do it long enough, and it becomes remarkably easy."

"Marcus," Daresina said. "You will-"

Before she could finish that sentence, Desa picked up the radio and extracted the Electric-Source from its bottom. The transmission ended with a fizzling sound, and then Desa thrust the device toward Marcus.

He stumbled backward as it fell into his hands, then turned his head to stare at the wall. The change that followed was quite visible. His expression hardened with resolve. "You're going to make me take you in."

"You won't be able to take me in."

Spinning around with a flourish, her coat flaring with the motion, Desa marched out of the cell. The clerk hopped back in surprise, blinking at her, but she was already halfway down the corridor and making her way toward the vault door.

She heard the sound of footsteps behind her, and it was clear by Marcus's pace that he intended to catch up with her. Perhaps he meant to restrain her before she could leave the bank. Or maybe he would try to reason with her again. Either way, she was prepared to do what was necessary.

She could feel her trinkets like little bundles of awareness in the back of her mind. The Gravity-Sink in her belt, the Light-Sink in her necklace. Her daggers which could fry or freeze anything she stabbed, her bracelet that could stop seven or eight bullets before it had taken all the kinetic energy it could handle: they were all with her, but that did little to ease her fear. It had been years since the last time she had been forced to fight another Field Binder.

She pushed open the vault door and froze.

Five men in dark-blue uniforms and billed caps stood side by side at the end of the aisle. The one in the middle – a sergeant, by the epaulettes on his shoulders – took a step forward and said, "By order of the City Watch, you are under arrest."

11

Desa looked up with a grim expression and felt a surge of warmth in her face. "On what charge?" she asked, striding through the aisle between the pillars. "We are just travelers passing through the city. We've broken no law."

In the middle of a line of five men, the sergeant stood defiant with his back straight and his shoulders square. He looked about ready to stare down a tidal wave. "The charge is witchcraft and practice of the dark arts."

She grimaced, shaking her head as she closed more than half the distance. "That is foolish," she said. "As I've told Mr. Hatch, the device that my friend is keeping inside the vault is nothing but a piece of machinery."

In seconds, Marcus was coming up to stand beside her and directing a hard stare at the men in his path. "You are ordered to depart," he said. "On the authority of the Synod of Aladar."

Folding her arms across her chest, Desa turned to him and looked up to meet his gaze. Her brow furrowed. "You do realize that I was *just* trying to convince them we're nothing but simple travelers, right?"

"Remove yourselves from our path," Marcus insisted.

In unison, the five men drew their sidearms. The sergeant stepped forward, shaking his head. "Don't make us resort to the use of force," he pleaded. "Come to the Magistrate, and we will get this sorted out."

"There is no need for this," Desa began. "We-"

Marcus reached into his pocket and flung a coin at them, glittering metal catching the light as it tumbled through the air. In that instant of surprise, all five men were blown off their feet as if by a strong wind, hurled to the floor.

When the kinetic wave hit her, Desa didn't resist. She just fell backwards, slapped her hands down on the floor and flipped upright. She took the opportunity to run to the nearest pillar and hide behind it before the watchmen started opening fire.

Closing her eyes as she took a deep breath, Desa rested her head against the stone pillar. "Five men," she whispered to herself. "All in a line...Attack from the side where they can't all fire at once."

She opened her eyes to find Marcus leaning against a pillar on the other side of the aisle, peering around the corner to get a good look at the watchmen. "They're winded," he said, cocking the hammer on his pistol. "Strike now before they recover."

"Wait!" Desa hissed.

She yanked her necklace up over her head and closed her fist so tightly around it the metal pendant dug into her skin. "Fool of a man," she growled, tossing the necklace around the pillar. It skittered across the floor, and she didn't have to look to know that it had landed right where she wanted it. "There are other ways to solve problems."

Desa drew her knives.

With a thought, she triggered the Light-Sink and

listened for the gasps of men who had found themselves in darkness. A quick glance around the pillar showed her a strange dark patch in the middle of the bank, as if all the gloom in the world had decided to come together in one spot.

Her necklace took only enough light to reduce each man to a shadowy silhouette. She could see the shapes of their bodies, but there was no colour, and from the way that they stumbled about, it was clear they were petrified.

Desa ran toward them.

One man got his pistol up, but he didn't know quite where to aim. "Almighty help us!" another bellowed. "Help us!"

With a knife in each hand, Desa leaped into the blackness, choosing one man at the end of the line as the first target. He heard the scuff of her boots on the tiles, turned to face her and tried to lift his pistol.

Desa slashed with one knife, striking the gun and tearing it out of the man's hand. She used the other to draw a thin, shallow cut across the man's neck, producing a yelp as her enemy stumbled backward.

Desa kicked him in the chest.

Thrown off his feet, he toppled backward onto the next man in line, and they both fell to the floor. The third man in line – the sergeant - seemed to realize that there was just enough light to make out the shape of each body. He swung his arm around, pointing his gun at Desa.

Falling backwards, Desa caught herself by slamming both hands down on the tiles. There was a clap of thunder, and bullets zipped past above her, each one burying itself in the wall.

She let the light return.

The sergeant shut his eyes, unprepared for the sudden brightness, and he staggered. That gave Desa the opening she needed. In a heartbeat, she was upright and throwing one dagger.

It tumbled end over end, struck the man's gun and knocked the weapon out of his grip. He gasped and shook his hand frantically at the sting of shallow cuts. Now that they could see again, the final two men were spreading out so as not to be in a line.

"Don't even think it!" Marcus snarled.

He was standing in the aisle between pillars with one hand extended, pointing his gun at one of the two remaining watchmen. The look on his face – the grim resignation in his eyes – made it clear: he didn't want to pull that trigger, but he would.

In that brief pause, the first two men that Desa had knocked down got to their feet and cast nervous glances around the room. "She's a demon," one stammered. "A bloody demon. We can't let her get away."

"You've seen our power," Marcus said. "Don't force us to fight you."

The sergeant was still looking down at the cut on his hand, and when he turned his gaze upon his men, the fear in his voice spoke volumes. "These two have power unlike anything we've seen," he said. "We might take them, but several of us will die."

"I'm willing," one man said.

Hissing air through her teeth, Desa shook her head. "This is beyond foolish," she said. "Does the fact that we have made every effort to avoid harming you mean nothing? Killing you would have been much easier."

The sergeant turned his cold stare on her, and he

nodded reluctantly. "That's true," he said. "But you're guilty of a crime, madame. Witchcraft is expressly forbidden under the law."

"What we do is not witchcraft."

"What I've seen here says otherwise."

"Well now!" a twangy force boomed through the room. Desa cringed as soon as she heard it. She knew that voice all too well.

The five city watchmen parted to reveal a barrel-chested man in black pants and a white shirt standing in the doorway. He was pale, with a thick dark mustache that showed more than a few flecks of silver, and his eyes were shaded by the wide brim of his black hat. "You want something done right," he said. "How does the rest of that go?"

"Morley!" Desa hissed.

Without thinking, she drew her revolver, cocked the hammer and pointed it straight at the vile man's chest. She fired once, twice, three times, filling the church with furious thunder, and Morley stumbled as bullets chewed through his body. Black blood soaked into his lily-white shirt.

The son of a bitch closed his eyes, and when he opened them again, they were as black as those she had seen on the gray people. As if someone had filled the inside of his skull with tar. But this wasn't the same. Aside from his eyes, Morley was in full colour, and he didn't seem to be under the control of that creature. "Something the matter, Desa?" he asked. "Not quite what you were expecting, is it?"

Morley ripped open his shirt, sending his buttons flying, and exposed three holes in his chest. Holes from which black slime oozed. In mere seconds, they closed themselves, leaving only unblemished skin.

Morley looked up to show her a beatific grin, then shook

his head ever so slowly. "It's a part of me now, darlin'," he said. "You can't kill me."

Desa screamed.

She ran toward him, leaped and drew back her fist to punch his vile face. When she got close enough, Morley's hand snapped up to catch her shirt and hold her with her boots dangling several feet off the floor.

She punched him anyway.

The man smiled up at her with black blood dripping from his nostrils, droplets of it sliding over his chin. "Lord Bendarian has given me new life," he declared. "And you, my dear, are nothing but an insect!"

He threw Desa with incredible force, sending her flying backward through the aisle. Ignoring her dread, Desa used her belt buckle to free herself from gravity's pull. That way she would fly all the way back to the vault.

When she neared it, she backflipped, pressed her feet against the metal door and pushed off to launch herself back toward her enemy. Morley was pulling a revolver from his holster and taking aim.

Desa let gravity reassert itself.

She landed in the aisle and ran at full speed, raising her left hand to shield herself. There was a deafening *CRACK, CRACK,* and then two bullets stopped dead right in front of her. She ran for the nearest pillar.

Desa slammed her shoulder against it, taking refuge in the safety of cover. And not a second too soon! Bullets grazed the side of the pillar, breaking chunks of stone off. Her ears were ringing from the noise.

Lifting her gun up in front of her face, its barrel pointed at the ceiling, Desa gasped for breath. "Bullets," she panted. "Bullets."

She flicked open the cylinder and quickly loaded three

more of the gray bullets she had taken from the farmhouse. None were Infused, of course, but they would do. Oh yes, they would do.

Desa threw herself sideways, rolling across the width of the aisle, and came up on one knee. She extended her arm and fired.

Another slug pierced Morley's chest, forcing him to stagger backward with his arms flailing. That gave her a second to get up and run for the next pillar, taking cover behind it and catching her breath.

"You can't win, bitch!" Morley's voice echoed through the bank. "Ain't nothin' you got can kill me! Understand?"

There was a mournful bellow as Marcus went flying backward to land atop one of the bookkeepers' wooden desk. The entire structure gave way beneath his weight, and he dropped to the floor.

She spun around the pillar to find Morley striding through the aisle with his teeth bared. "What can you do against me?"

"Something like this."

Raising the gun in both hands, Desa squinted as she took aim. She fired again and again, burning through all five rounds. With each hit, Morley stumbled and black blood drenched his clothing.

He was off balance.

Desa ran to him, jumped and drove her shoulder into the man's face, throwing him down onto his back. She unsheathed her only remaining dagger and plunged it hilt-deep into Morley's stomach.

He tossed his head back and screamed. So, the man could still feel pain. Well, that was certainly welcome news. Before she could celebrate, however, Morley seized two fist-fuls of her shirt and flung her upward.

Which was exactly what she wanted.

Desa triggered the Gravity-Sink inside her belt buckle so that she wouldn't fall, and when her back hit the ceiling, she grunted. Twisting around to hang upright, she grabbed one beam of the vaulted ceiling and swung herself like a pendulum. Then she triggered the Heat-Source that she had Infused into the knife. Morley's screams filled her ears.

At the apex of her arc, she let go, curled up into a ball and somersaulted through the air. When she was far enough away, she let gravity resume its pull and dropped to land in the aisle.

She turned around.

Morley was on the floor, writhing in pain as his skin turned a deep, blistering red. His clothes caught fire, and within seconds, dark spots of charred flesh appeared all over his body. He was burning alive.

Desa slumped over, her head drooping with fatigue. Sweat drenched her hair, fat droplets sliding down her forehead. "It's over," she whispered. "Five long years hunting you, and you're finally-"

The charred and blackened Morley sat up with a gasp. Then, to her shock, he got up and turned around to face her with a smile. "That all you got, bitch?" His voice sounded like cracking ice. "Aren't you listening? You *can't* kill me!"

It only got worse when his burns began to heal. Scorched flesh turned red and then pink, and then finally resumed a pale flesh tone. Blisters shrank and shrank until they all vanished, leaving smooth flesh behind. Most of his clothing, now only blackened ashes, crumbled away, leaving only the top of his pants as a pair of ragged shorts.

His mustache was gone, his eyebrows and hair as well, but he remained healthy and strong. "Come on then!" Morley said. "Let's finish it."

When she looked past Morley, she saw Marcus standing in the aisle behind him. It was clear that they could not win this fight. The same force that Bendarian had unleashed on the world had transformed Morley into something inhuman.

Desa looked back at the city watchmen.

They were clustered together near the bank's front entrance, all pale, all sweating, and one of them was praying for his life. "Run!" she screamed. "This is beyond you!"

Desa used her Gravity-Sink.

She jumped and kicked Morley's face, then twirled in the air and kicked him again with the other leg. The harsh crunch of a broken nose gave her a sense of satisfaction as Morley backed away.

She landed in a crouch, reached into her pocket and slipped on the brass knuckles. "You want to fight me?" she hissed. "Come, then! Taste oblivion!"

Morley snapped himself upright, blood dripping from his chin, and she was treated to the sickening sight of his nose literally snapping back into place. "I'll rip you to pieces, bitch!" And then he was charging toward her.

He threw a wicked punch.

Desa ducked and felt a whoosh of air passing over her head. She slammed her own fist into Morley's chest, and the brass knuckles released a dreadful blast of kinetic energy that lifted him off his feet.

He was propelled backward through the aisle, flailing as he reached impotently for her. Seconds later, he dropped to the floor and skidded a few more paces, stopping just in front of Marcus.

As expected, Marcus jumped and shot straight upward, unrestrained by the pull of gravity. He drew his pistol, spun the cylinder and then pointed his gun straight down at his enemy.

The air split with the sound of thunder.

Marcus's bullet didn't strike Morley but instead landed just in front of him. He roared with laughter. "Your aim is terrible, Field-Bind-" Morley cut off suddenly as streams of crackling blue lightning lashed out from the bullet. Some struck the pillars; some struck the ceiling, and some struck Morley.

He screamed as electric current raced through his newly-healed flesh, scorching it all over again. It was the howl of a damned soul, the mournful wail of a man who felt a pain beyond words.

Miraculously, none of the lightning hit Marcus, who hovered just a few short paces above Morley's head. The Infusion that he had crafted must have been designed to release electric energy at any nearby object *but* him, in much the same way that Desa's bracelet only took kinetic energy from objects that were coming toward her. That was some truly remarkable Field Binding. She would have to learn that trick.

Thrusting his pistol out behind himself, Marcus fired one bullet into the wall. The kickback propelled him forward, over Morley and down the aisle toward Desa. When he got close, he dropped to the floor.

Marcus stiffened. "That won't subdue him."

"We should run," Desa agreed.

They were rushing through the door without another word of discussion, bursting out onto a street with squat gray buildings on the other side. One or two had chimneys belching smoke into the sky.

Desa and Marcus ran across the street, and with near-perfect synchronicity, they triggered their Gravity-Sinks and leaped. Free of the Earth's pull, they rose to the rooftop of the nearest building and landed there.

Desa shut her eyes, sweat oozing from her pores. Her breath came in ragged gasps. "Do you believe me now?" she panted. "Do you see the danger Bendarian represents?"

Marcus was bent over with his hands on his knees, grunting in irritation. "This isn't the time," he said. "If we stay here, we die."

No sooner did he issue that warning then the sound of doors flying off their hinges startled them into turning around. In nothing but a tattered pair of shorts, Morley stood under the arch-shaped entryway of the bank. "You!" he shouted, thrusting a finger toward Desa. "This ends now!"

Suddenly, he was bounding across the street.

Desa broke into a sprint across the flat rooftop, trying to ignore the icy dread that squeezed her heart. When she neared the edge, she triggered her Gravity-Sink and leaped, flying across the gap in one long arc. Marcus followed a second later.

She landed on the slanted roof of a townhouse and scrambled up its surface to the peak. There, she paused just long enough to look back. Morley was charging across the rooftop she had just left behind.

Down the other side of the roof then. She half-fell, half-ran until she reached the ledge, and then she jumped. Once again, her belt buckle protected her from what would have been a nasty fall and carried her like a soaring falcon to the house across the street. She landed there and released her hold on gravity. Her buckle had nearly taken all the energy it could. A few more minutes of this, and she would be unable to leap from roof to roof. "We need a new plan."

Gasping on the edge of the slanted roof, Marcus looked back over his shoulder. "I do believe you're correct."

They ran to the peak, and Desa fished a bullet out of her coat's inner pocket. When she turned, she saw Morley rushing down the slope of the roof across the street, his bare feet leaving cracks in the tiles with every step. "Trigger your Gravity-Sink," Desa said. "And leave it on until I tell you otherwise."

She did the same.

Morley leaped from the roof's ledge without the aid of any Field Binding and flew across the street at blinding speed. He landed atop this new townhouse with enough force to send chunks of black tiles flying, then threw his head back and roared.

"Men and their endless displays of aggression," Desa muttered.

She tossed the bullet and watched it pass over Morley's head to land in the street behind him. Then she triggered the Gravity-Source she had Infused into it. Morley was yanked backward by invisible hands, pulled down off the rooftop. He landed in the street with an ear-splitting bellow.

"Time to go," Desa said.

They ran down the other side of the roof and leaped off, allowing gravity to reassert a sliver of its power and pull them to the ground. It also slowed their forward motion. The bullet was still pulling them backward.

When they landed in the street, Marcus quickly pulled Desa into an alley. "Come," he said. "We can't defeat him with force. Our only option is to hide and pray that he does not find us."

Once they were out of sight, Desa extinguished the Gravity-Source she had Infused into that bullet. Leaving it active was dangerous. It would pull on anything within range. Knives would fly off tables; people in nearby houses would be thrown into walls. Using a Gravity-Source was only a shade less risky than using an Electric-Source, but Morley had left her with no option. The man would have killed them both if she hadn't subdued him.

They ran for the better part of an hour before Desa was convinced that Morley was no longer chasing them.

12

The instant she passed through the door to the room she shared with Miri, Desa took off her hat and tossed it onto her bed. She strode to the window, put her fists on her hips and shook her head. "Now, what do we do?" she muttered. "Morley has never had that much power before."

When she turned, Marcus was hunched over in the doorway with one hand on his stomach, breathing hard. "It was more than just raw power," he said. "You must have felt it: the wrongness about him."

Desa sat down on the windowsill, crossed her arms and scowled at the floorboards. "I did indeed," she muttered. "It was the same thing I felt on that farm."

"This man must die."

"And we can't kill him."

There was a scuffing sound as Marcus walked into the room, thrust out his chin and gave her what might have been a conciliatory glare. The man seemed to have a glare for every occasion. "I was wrong to oppose you," he said. "This Morley must die before we can even entertain the idea of returning to Aladar."

"Thank you."

"So how do we go about it?"

With an elbow on her knee, Desa covered her mouth with one hand. She closed her eyes and considered the question. "The entity that I encountered on the farm seems to be keeping Morley alive."

Marcus seated himself on the edge of her bed and then stared intently at something on the wall. "So, if we can sever his connection to it," he began, "That might take away his strange powers."

"Or kill him outright."

They were cut off by the sound of someone knocking on the door, and when Desa gave permission to enter, Lommy came stumbling into the room...Tommy! Damn it, but Miri's strange nickname for the boy was becoming infectious.

Tommy was panting, his face flushed and glistening as if he had just run up the four flights of stairs between this room and the saloon. "Did you hear?" he stammered. "Some hubbub in the market district."

"I'm afraid we did more than just hear of it," Desa said.

"We caused it," Marcus added.

For some reason, Tommy was ghostly pale after hearing that, but to his credit, the lad shut his eyes, caught his breath and took control of himself. "I should have reckoned as much," he said. "So, what happened?"

"We encountered Morley."

"And you killed him?"

Grunting at the ache in her legs and back, Desa rose and marched forward to stand in front of him. She shook her head. "I'm afraid not. It seems that Morley cannot be killed by any means at your disposal."

"What do you mean, 'cannot be killed?'"

She explained briefly about Morley being in contact

with whatever had animated the gray people on the farm and watched the horror in Tommy's eyes swell to the point of outright panic. This time, the lad had to work a little harder to push down the fear, but he managed it.

When he asked what they should do next, Desa was at a loss. If Morley had simply been invulnerable to most things that would kill an ordinary man, that would have been one thing. You could throw a man like that into a cell and leave him to rot. But Morley had also displayed feats of incredible strength. Could stone walls hold him?

Desa would have said that they needed more Field Binders, but what good would that do when her best Infusions had only slowed Morley down. They had to find a way to cut him off from the entity.

She and Marcus spent the better part of half an hour debating how to do that while Tommy listened without comment. The poor lad was probably wishing that he had stayed in his sleepy little village. For some people, a death sentence would be preferable to the horrors Tommy had seen.

"Bendarian tried to Infuse people with the Ether," Marcus said.

"Yes."

"Do we know how he managed it?"

Desa scrunched her eyes tight, then drew in a shuddering breath. "I don't think he did manage it," she said. "This thing...whatever it is...It seemed to imply that it was not of our world."

"What does that mean?"

"It means-"

Before she could finish that sentence, the door swung inward to reveal a tall and slender woman standing in the hallway. This one was painfully beautiful in a white dress that left her shoulders bare. Her face was immaculate with a dimpled chin, hollow cheeks and deep blue eyes, and golden hair fell to the small of her back. "You are Desa Kincaid, I presume?"

Desa felt rather foolish, sitting on the floor with her back to the wall and her legs stretched out. "Yes, and who might you be?" she asked with a raised eyebrow. "More to the point, how did you know to find me here?"

The woman glided into the room with the haughty air of someone who assumed that an invitation was a foregone conclusion. "My name is Adele Delarac," she began. "I know what you did this morning."

"What I did?"

"Let's not be coy, Mrs. Kincaid," Adele said. "I am well aware of your skirmish with Morley. I knew the man *before* he was transformed into...whatever it is that he has become, and I found him odious then. Now, he is a threat to everyone in this city, and I can think no one better qualified to end that threat than you."

Marcus was on his feet in an instant, standing just behind Adele and glowering at the back of her head. "The relevant question," he said, "is *how* you know so much. And why we should trust you."

A light touch of crimson flooded Adele's cheeks, but she nodded as if she had been expecting that question. "I am a Sensitive," she said. "I have been in communion with the Ether since I was a little girl, and I have used it to keep watch on events in this city. Desa Kincaid, you are the only one who can stop Morley before he does more damage."

"A Sensitive?" Tommy inquired. No one bothered to answer his query.

Desa stood up.

In two quick strides, she was toe to toe with the other

woman and looking up with a disapproving frown. "You seem to be very well informed, Miss Delarac," she said. "What makes you think I can destroy Morley?"

Adele closed her eyes and wilted like a dying flower. "I know that you are a Field Binder," she answered. "I have watched you through the Ether."

"Then you know that my best efforts had no lasting effect on Morley. So, I will ask you again: why do you come to me?"

"I have seen it in the Ether. You *will* destroy him."

Turning away from the other woman, Desa crossed her arms as she paced over to the wall. "You will forgive me if I don't take you at your word," she said. "For all I know, you were sent here by Radharal Bendarian. There is nothing you have said that he could not have told you."

"No one despises Bendarian more than I do."

"How do you even know Bendarian?" Marcus demanded.

That was a very good question indeed. Curiosity made Desa turn around, and when she did so, she was surprised to find that Adele was quite flustered. The woman shuffled about as if she wasn't entirely sure what to do with herself. "Perhaps you have noticed my surname," she said at last. "Delarac. As in Mayor Timothy Delarac. I am his niece."

"That doesn't answer my question," Marcus insisted.

In the corner of her eye, Desa saw Tommy standing by the window and scratching his chin as he considered Adele's story. The boy seemed to have formed an opinion, but he wasn't willing to share it.

Adele just stood there with her arms hanging and her eyes fixed upon the pointed toes of her leather boots. "My uncle frequently hosts parties for the city's aristocracy," she said. "Bendarian is often in attendance."

Well...It was a start. At least, now, Desa had some idea of where she might find the man, but the fact that Bendarian had been ingratiating himself with the city's elites did not bode well. It suggested that his plans were large enough in scope to necessitate a sizable financial backing.

"So, we ambush him outside one of these parties," Marcus suggested.

"No," Desa cut in before anyone else could speak. "The probability that innocent people will get caught in the cross-fire is much too high. Our goal should be to discover Bendarian's current place of residence."

"And confront him there?"

"Perhaps."

Adele popped open her handbag, retrieved a small slip of paper and handed it to Desa. The note was only an address written in smooth, flowing script, an address in the city's northwestern quarter unless Desa missed her guess. "My uncle has sent Bendarian no small amount of corre-spondence," she said. "I was able to procure that easily."

Desa looked up to study the woman, then narrowed her eyes. "How convenient," she said. "I suppose that if I were to go to this place, I would find Bendarian completely unpre-pared for my arrival?"

"What do you mean?"

"She means it's a trap," Marcus said bluntly. The man stepped up behind Adele and brought his lips to her ear. "Desa is correct; this is too convenient."

Adele shuddered when she felt his breath on her cheek. "I only want to help," she said. "Please, you must believe me."

"I think, Miss Delarac, that you should be on your way now." Desa's voice wasn't just cold; it was a blast of frigid air. "My friends and I have much to discuss."

· · ·

"Do you think she'll go?" Sebastian asked.

Bathed in sunlight that came through the window, Tommy sat on the edge of his bed with his hands on his knees. He shook his head and grunted in response. Who could say what Desa Kincaid would do? Or why she would do it?

Sebastian was leaning against the wall next to the window, tapping his pant leg and staring vacantly at nothing at all. "That is what she wants to do, isn't it?" he went on. "Go off to kill this Bendarian character?"

"I don't know what she wants."

"You were there."

Tommy flopped back onto the feather mattress and blinked at the ceiling. "Indeed I was," he said. "For all the bloody good it did. There were several points where I was sure they had forgotten about me."

Sebastian turned his back, braced his hands upon the windowsill and bent forward to peer through the glass. "Is that such a bad thing?" he muttered. "Let her forget us. We can be on our way."

"We've been over this..."

"Yes, but-"

The door opened to admit Marcus, and the man showed no concern for having interrupted their conversation. He paced across the room with boots that thumped on the wooden floor, tossed a slip of paper onto the small table in the corner and sighed.

A moment later, he turned, looked over his shoulder and watched Tommy with all the suspicion of a wolf who expected his prey to bolt. "What are you two discussing?" he grumbled. "Still trying to decide whether to abandon Desa Nin Leean?"

"We would never do such a thing," Tommy protested.

"You should."

Tommy sat upright and felt his jaw drop. It took a moment to regain his composure, but he pushed the anxiety down into the pit of his stomach. "I don't understand. Why do you want us to betray her?"

"Betray her?" Marcus scoffed. "Boy, you would free her from the burden of having to keep you alive. We've traveled far enough. There's little chance that you will encounter anyone from your sleepy little village. Take your horse, set off down the south road and don't look back! I will even provide you with enough money to book passage on a ship if you're so inclined."

Each word was like a punch to the gut. It was all Tommy could do to avoid tearing up. He hated feeling like a burden. Almighty have mercy, he had felt that way all his life – with his brother, his father, with most of the village – and he was bloody tired of it.

Sebastian turned away from the window with a sly smile, then offered a sad little shrug of his shoulders. "Isn't that what I've been saying?" he asked. "We should go."

"Listen to your lover, boy," Marcus grated. "If you know what's best for you, you'll be on your way within the hour."

Tommy wanted to argue, but what could he say? When you saw it one way, and the rest of the world told you that you were wrong, well...One person's opinion didn't amount to a whole lot when stacked against all that. He was being selfish by remaining here and forcing Desa to look after him.

But he was afraid to go...

He wanted to say as much, but Marcus stomped out of the room without another word and slammed the door so hard it made the frame rattle. That left Tommy alone with a very smug Sebastian.

The other man was sitting on the windowsill with hands clasped together, smiling down at the floor. "We should go," he said again. "There's nothing for us here."

"And nothing for us out there."

"Tommy..."

"It's true."

With a groan, Sebastian got up and paced over to the table in the corner. He picked up the slip of paper and scanned its contents. "Now, what do you suppose this is?"

"Bendarian's address," Tommy muttered.

The other man spun around to face him with a raised eyebrow. "Are you telling me that this is what Desa Kincaid has been looking for?" Sebastian inquired. "Well, then she must be halfway to the man's house by now. I wager he'll be dead by sundown."

"Desa thinks it's a trap," Tommy explained. "She doesn't trust the woman who gave that to us, and I can't say that I blame her."

Sebastian grinned as he held the paper up to the light. Then he crumpled it up and tossed it to the floor. "Excellent!" he said. "While she and Marcus are busy deliberating, you and I can slip away."

"I'm not leaving."

"You heard what Marcus said. My love, I mean you no offense, but in a fight, you are less than useless. In fact, you're actually a hindrance. The best thing you can do is get away from Desa Kincaid so that she doesn't have to waste energy protecting you."

Fury propelled Tommy to his feet and made him tower over the other man. The heat in his face was rivaled only by the inferno burning in his chest. "I don't care what Marcus says!" he insisted. "Desa would not have offered to teach me

Field Binding if she did not think I could be of use! I refuse to see myself as a burden!"

"You're still set on learning her vile magics," Sebastian muttered. "I do swear it by all that's holy: meeting Desa Kincaid is the worst thing that ever happened to us."

"She sav-"

"You tell me again about how she saved us, and I might just have to slap your face. I want nothing to do with a witch, Tommy."

Sebastian was marching across the room and pulling the door open before Tommy could even think to protest. He paused briefly, offered one last withering glare and then stepped out into the hallway. "It's time that you faced facts, Tommy," he said. "This is no place for either of us."

13

Miri flowed through the crowds of people with ease, maneuvering past men in dark coats and bowler hats, women in colourful dresses and the odd horse-drawn carriage that pushed its way through the narrow street. Ofalla was a cosmopolitan city with all sorts of different people. Some were light, others dark. Some had the features of men from the far south. No one noticed her; in a crowd like this, she wouldn't stand out.

A small group of people parted, allowing her a glimpse of her prey. Sebastian was shuffling up the street with his coat wrapped tightly around himself, moving with the haste of a man with someplace important to be.

Grinding her teeth, Miri looked up at him. Her mouth twitched. *What are you up to, boy?* she wondered. *Desa and Marcus both focus so intently on this Morley character that they completely ignore you.*

Sebastian turned.

Miri let the crowd flow around her like water over a rock in a river. In seconds, a dozen people blocked her view of the boy and his view of her. Did he see her? Only one way to find out.

She started forward again, slipping around two well-dressed men who stood at the foot of stairs that led to a townhouse and then rounded a corner onto yet another narrow street. This one had fewer people.

Sebastian was just a short ways off with his back turned and his shoulders hunched. The way he clutched his coat despite the warm morning sunlight only added to the cloud of unease that radiated from him. Fool boy. Walking around like that was a good way to convince a lawman that you were a thief...or worse.

Miri started up the street with a swagger in her step and a grin on her face, nodding to several people that she passed. They all replied with friendly smiles.

On her left, she saw a fruit cart by the roadside where a copper-skinned man in his middle years proclaimed that he had the best apples anyone had ever tasted. Well...You couldn't just let a claim like that go unanswered.

When she passed the cart, she set a few pennies on the edge and palmed an apple before the man could even offer his nod of approval. "Don't you want your change?" he called after her. She ignored him.

Tossing the apple up, Miri threw her head back and caught it with her teeth. Her incisors ripped off a piece of skin, and when the apple fell, it landed in her waiting palm. Practice was a good way to maintain her coordination.

Sebastian was about thirty paces ahead of her, still huddled up and still moving at a brisk pace. The sad little boy didn't even bother to look back. Which could only mean one of two things. Either he really was as useless as he appeared...

Or he was a master at feigning such ineptitude.

She followed.

Their journey took them around two more corners and down a sloping hill toward the riverbank. Then Sebastian went over one of the smaller bridges that stretched across the Vinrella. Naturally, she followed him.

Miri shuffled along with both hands in her coat pockets, shaking her head as she studied the cobblestones. "Maybe he's had enough. Perhaps he's finally decided to leave us all behind," she muttered. "It would certainly make things easier."

On the other side of the river, they went up another sloping hill where men in rough clothing went rushing down toward the docs. Sailors, unless she missed her guess. Well, they certainly spooked Sebastian. He jumped and then looked around.

Miri ducked out of sight behind a set of stairs that led up to the front door of a gray townhouse. Peeking through the metal bars that supported the banister, she saw Sebastian take off down a side street.

Shutting her eyes tight, Miri felt a bead of sweat on her forehead. A sigh escaped her. "Of course..." she whispered. "It was too much to hope the boy was headed toward the edge of town."

She followed him.

A few more twists brought them to an unassuming street with houses that looked uniformly similar to all the others she had seen thus far. By the eyes of Vengeance, this town was a dreary place. What she wouldn't give to see something with just a little flair. A yellow house with green shutters! Was that too much to ask?

Sebastian chose one unit in the middle of the street, climbed the steps to the porch and pounded on the door. A moment later, it was answered by a serving maid with dark, olive skin and ringlets of brown hair that framed her face.

Miri was too far off to hear what was said, but Sebastian was admitted without very much protest.

This couldn't be good.

THE FRONT HALL of Radharal Bendarian's townhouse was dimly lit, but the little round window on the door provided enough illumination for Sebastian to see a staircase leading up to the second level and dark red carpets in the narrow hallway that stretched on to the back of the building.

A man appeared at the head of the stairs, and Sebastian jumped back with enough force to make the door rattle when he hit it. This fellow looked like something out of a fairytale. One glance, and it was clear that it must have been Bendarian.

The man was tall and slender, handsome in a well-made blue coat. His face could have been chiseled by a sculptor, and hair so blonde it was almost white fell to the small of his back. "I must congratulate you," he said, descending the first few steps. "Very few people could have talked their way into my home. But then very few people have heard the name Desa Nin Leean."

Closing his eyes, Sebastian let his head drop. "She has been a traveling companion of mine for some time now," he said, taking a hesitant step forward. "And I would be rid of her if I could."

"Truer words were never spoken."

Sebastian looked up at the man with wide eyes and felt a twitch in the corner of his mouth. "You seem to be the one person she fears," he began. "You and that monstrosity of a servant of yours."

A smile lit up Bendarian's face, and he shook his head as he descended to the foot of the stairs. "And what would you know of the men in my employ?" The chill in the man's voice made Sebastian uneasy.

"Only what my lover tells me," he insisted. "Desa Kincaid...That is, Desa Nin Leean, fought your man this morning."

"That she did."

"And lost."

"Lost? She still lives, doesn't she?" There was bitterness in that question. "I would hardly call it a loss...What are you doing here, boy?"

It was all Sebastian could do to keep his voice from shaking, but he steeled himself, stepped forward and held the other man's gaze. "I wish to propose a trade," he said. "I tell you where to find Desa Kincaid-"

"The Golden Horseshoe."

Sebastian flinched.

That brought another smile to Bendarian's face, this one colder and crueler than the last. "How do you think my people found Desa Nin Leean this morning?" he asked. "Mr. Jarvis, at the bank, ran to gather the City Watch while Desa was busy in his vault. It pays to have allies in the right places."

"I...Well..." Forcing his eyes shut, Sebastian swallowed and then took in a ragged breath. "I suppose you don't need me then."

"Nonsense," Bendarian replied. "Only a fool passes up an opportunity to make a potential enemy into an ally. But much will depend on your price."

"I just want to leave," Sebastian whispered. "I'll tell you anything that you want to know about Desa Kincaid, and in exchange, my lover and I depart. No questions asked."

Bendarian gestured to the staircase and then proceeded up to the second floor as if Sebastian following were a foregone conclusion. Of course, it was. Sebastian had come this far; there was no point in turning back now.

On the second floor, he found another narrow hallway with deep burgundy carpets and doors in one wall. One led into what appeared to be a sitting room with two chairs in the light of a window that looked out on the street below.

Bendarian went to a small table, uncapped a decanter and poured dark red wine into two glasses. He turned and strode toward Sebastian with a glass in each palm, the stems between his middle two fingers. That cold smile had returned.

Sebastian took a glass without hesitation, brought it to his lips and sipped the wine. "Quite good," he mumbled. "Better than anything my father had, anyway."

"So," Bendarian began. "You only want to leave. To be free of Desa Nin Leean and her foolhardy vendetta. A rather modest goal, if I do say so myself."

"It's what I want," Sebastian insisted.

Lifting his glass with exquisite poise, Bendarian smiled again and then took a drink. "Are you sure that's *all* you want?" he asked. "A man in my position could be a valuable friend to you."

The blood drained from Sebastian's face as he recalled the things he had seen on the journey to this wretched city. "I saw what you did," he whispered. "Those gray creatures. I...I want no part of that."

"How little you understand," Bendarian said, turning to the window. Warm sunlight on his face almost made him appear beautiful. Angelic. Not at all like the man who could summon such horrors as Sebastian had seen. "My goal is nothing less than the perfection of humanity."

"You turned those people into feral beasts."

"And what I learned from doing so allowed me to gift my associate Mr. Morley with power such as you could never imagine. *You* can have that power too, my boy."

"I want no such power."

Sebastian felt a strange flutter in his belly, a sensation similar to what he had once experienced when dropping from a very high branch of an oak at the edge of his father's property. But what startled him was the way that Bendarian let go of his glass... and it did not fall. "Power," the man said, "should not be casually cast aside."

Hugging himself, Sebastian rubbed his arms and stepped back. "I don't want to be a Field Binder," he said. "My soul is already stained without indulging in witchcraft."

"Field Binding," Bendarian scoffed. "You have spent too much time with Desa Nin Leean. She has trained you to think small."

"What else is there?"

A lump of ice settled into Sebastian's stomach as Bendarian stepped forward with a mocking grin. "Come with me, boy," he said. "See for yourself."

CLIMBING the final few steps up to the second floor of the Golden Horseshoe, Miri sighed when she found Tommy standing in the middle of a hallway with wood paneling on the walls and paraffin lanterns to supplement the light that came in through windows at either end of the corridor.

The young man was standing there like a statue that was just begging for pigeons to perch on its shoulders. His unwavering gaze was fixed on the wall, and she could tell that he was ruminating on the same worries that had plagued him from the moment they had set out from Glad Meadows.

Now, she had to make that worse.

Miri strode through the corridor at a brisk pace, shaking her head in frustration. "I think we should talk, Lommy," she said. "Things have just gotten worse."

He turned to her, looked up and then set his jaw. Good. The lad had some fire in his belly. "It's Tommy," he insisted. "We've been over this time and again, and I've grown so tired of your little pet name for-"

"Sebastian has betrayed us."

Tommy blinked and then stepped back. Any semblance of confidence vanished as he slumped against the wall. "What happened?" No protests. No vehement declarations that his lover would never do such a thing. Perhaps he was starting to believe her.

Miri stepped forward with her fists clenched, unable to lift her gaze from the dusty hardwood floor. "He went to a house in the city's north-west quarter," she replied. "And since he doesn't know anyone outside of our group-"

"He went to see Bendarian," Tommy grumbled.

"You don't seem surprised."

The lad made the kind of face one might see on a five-year-old who had been forced to swallow cod liver oil and then shook his head. "He's been talking about leaving for days now," Tommy said. "And he *hates* Desa."

Leaning against the wall across from him, Miri let out a breath. "Yes...You're right about that," she said softly. "Pack your things; we must leave at once. I'll tell the others."

"Maybe you should just leave me behind."

"Nonsense."

Tommy looked up, and his face hardened. The anger in his stare actually made her a little uneasy. "Your brother didn't think so," he snapped. "How did he put it? 'Take your horse and go, boy. You're nothing but a liability.'"

"Marcus is wrong about a great many things."

"Not about this."

"Now, you listen to me, Lommy...Lommy...What is your last name, anyway?"

"Smith."

"No, that's no good." Miri wrinkled her nose in distaste at such a commonplace surname. "Anyway, we'll work on making you more interesting later. The point is that of all the backward-thinking men on this benighted little continent, you were not threatened by a woman like Desa Nin Leean. In fact, you were willing to learn from her. If you ask me, that counts for something."

"Thank you..."

"Pack your things," Miri said. "I'll go find the others."

14

————

Desa floated in a world of tiny swirling particles, each one infinitely smaller than a spec of dust and yet distinct to her mind. It was breathtaking. In this state, she could see a world that remained hidden from her waking eyes. She could sense almost everything within a few blocks of the Moonlight Traveler, the hotel Marcus had chosen after they had been forced to flee the Golden Horseshoe.

She saw clusters of particles that represented men walking up the street outside the hotel. She could see every lamppost on the sidewalk. She could sense the young maid in the hallway outside her room. It didn't matter that there were walls between her and the things she wished to view.

She could even sense the swirling galaxy of particles that made up her own body, sitting on the edge of her bed. She could sense it but nothing more. Something as simple as trying to lift her hand was nearly impossible in this state; to be one with the Ether was to surrender almost all control of your physical form. Almost as if she had separated her mind from her body.

Carefully, she built a lattice between the particles that

comprised her bracelet. Bit by bit and piece by piece, she Infused a connection that would allow it to drain even more kinetic energy. She was nearly finished when she sensed a new form in the hallway. With a little reluctance, Desa let her mind drift away from the Ether.

The world snapped back into a realm of solid objects. She saw wood-paneled walls and a paraffin lamp on a small round table in the corner. The square window that looked out on the stableyard showed a sky that had darkened to a deep blue.

With the calming presence of the Ether gone, her anger returned. Miri had told her about Sebastian's journey to the address Adele had scribbled onto that piece of paper. By the eyes of Vengeance, she should have been rid of that boy sooner. Or perhaps she should have killed him. It was not an option she would take lightly, but she would not discount it either.

Desa closed her eyes, breathing deeply to relax her body. "You can come in, Miss Delarac," she called out before the other woman knocked. "I've completed my work for the time being."

The door opened.

When Desa twisted around on the mattress, she saw the other woman striding into the room in a dark red dress with sheer sleeves that revealed her arms to her shoulders. Once again, Adele's swooping neckline drew the eye. The woman had braided her hair and changed her earrings to thin silver hoops. All that since the last time Desa had seen her earlier this afternoon.

"I came to tell you you're not safe here," Adele said.

Desa rose with a grunt, crossed her arms and rounded the foot of the bed. "So long as Bendarian lives, none of us are safe," she said, approaching the other woman. "Though I suspect I don't have to tell you that."

Adele lowered her eyes, took a breath and then nodded. "You do not," she agreed. "I came here to tell you that Bendarian has contacts within the City Watch. It will not be long before he discovers where you've gone."

"And how did you discover this?"

"I told you; I'm a Sensitive."

"Indeed you did," Desa said. "And you will forgive me, but I still have considerable difficulty believing it. When I connect with the Ether, I can sense everything within about half a mile, but perceiving the entire city? That is beyond me."

Adele's face hardened, but her gaze never wavered. Not for an instant. "It is a very rare talent," she muttered. "Though I must inquire, Miss...Nin Leean? How do *you* think I found you?"

Grinning sheepishly, Desa took a step back and shook her head. "It means 'daughter of Leean,'" she explained. "There is no 'Miss.' Aladri do not use such titles."

"Then what should I call you?"

"'Desa' will suffice."

That produced an uncomfortable silence that seemed to last for an eternity. By the look on Adele's face, it was clear that the woman was straining for something to say, for words that would turn this conversation in her favour.

"To your other question," Desa said, "How could you have known how to find me if not through your connection to the Ether? It seems to me that the most logical answer is also the most obvious: Bendarian told you where to find me."

A wave of crimson flooded Adele's face, and her eyes cut

like daggers. "What must I do to convince you?" she spat. "I've come here to help you!"

"And how exactly do you plan to do that?" Desa was marching forward before she even realized it, each step forcing the other woman to retreat. "You must think me a fool if you believe that I will simply walk to the address you gave me and challenge Bendarian to a duel."

Adele bumped into the wall next to the door, and her lips quivered as she searched for words. Desa did not allow her the opportunity to speak. "You should know," she went on, "that your gift provided one of my companions with the opportunity to betray me."

"I did not intend that!"

Pressing her lips into a thin line, Desa looked up and held the other woman pinned by the force of her stare. "I am unconcerned with what you intended," she grated. "Slink back to Bendarian and see if he will spare you for failing to lure me into his trap."

Of all things, Adele began to cry. Fat tears slid over her cheeks, and she sniffled as her body trembled. "I don't know why you won't believe me!" she whimpered. "It should not be this hard!"

"To deceive me?"

Adele opened her mouth but no sound came out. Her tears ruined the light coating of rouge she had used on her cheeks. Finally, the woman found enough courage to squeak out, "To earn the trust of your soulmate!"

"I beg your pardon..."

"I've watched you through the Ether," Adele whispered. "I've known for some time that you would come to Ofalla, that our fates would be connected. I've dreamed of you. My father tried to arrange a match with the son of a man who owns a shipping company, but I put him off because I didn't want him. I didn't want any man! I wanted *you!*"

This was beyond ludicrous. It was all Desa could do not to laugh. Still, there was a part of her that couldn't help but wonder...If this was some attempt to maneuver her into one of Bendarian's traps, it was a remarkably sloppy one. Which meant that either Adele was a master in the art of manipulation...or she really was what she claimed to be.

Desa backed away with her arms folded, looked the other woman up and down and then snorted. "First, you try to gain my trust with a ludicrous story," she said. "When that fails, you resort to tears. And now you attempt *seduction?* Miss Delarac, has anyone ever told you that you are exceedingly bad at-"

Adele surged forward like a pouncing cat, took Desa's face in both hands and then kissed her on the mouth. Every nerve in Desa's body responded. Rational thought fled; it was all she could do to hold onto some scrap of suspicion. *This is wrong,* she told herself. *You're letting yourself fall under her spell.*

It didn't matter.

Perhaps this *was* a trap – perhaps she would regret it later – but it had been months since she had felt the comforting touch of another woman, and right now it just felt too damn good. She would deal with the consequences when they presented themselves.

Desa drew one of her daggers, and with one quick slice, she cut a slit in the back of Adele's dress. The other woman squeaked, but Desa's practiced hand was skilled enough to cut fabric without marring the soft, supple skin beneath it.

The garment fell away, and Desa pushed the other woman down onto the bed. After that, she stopped thinking and let instinct take over.

. . .

As she caught her breath, Desa stared open-mouthed at the ceiling and felt sweat matting dark hair to her forehead. "Wow..." she said, her eyebrows rising. "That was...a unique experience."

Adele snuggled up with her head on Desa's chest, squeezing her tight. "It was," she agreed. "Have you...Have you ever done that before? With a woman, I mean."

Desa kissed the other woman's forehead, then flopped back with her head on the pillow and smiled lazily at the ceiling. "Of course I have," she murmured. "But I get the distinct impression that you can't say the same."

Adele giggled.

By instinct, Desa ran her fingers through the other woman's hair. This felt strange to her; she was not inclined to trust easily, and there was still a chance that Adele was one of Bendarian's agents. But when she looked at Adele, she did not see a killer. The girl would probably faint at the thought of holding a gun. And despite her twenty-three years, there were times when Adele seemed quite girlish.

Now, for instance. She cuddled up to Desa like a moon-struck youth in her lover's embrace for the very first time. And why not? If what the woman said was to be believed, this *was* her very first time.

"So," Desa said. "How do you plan to help me?"

Another fit of giggles bubbled from Adele's mouth as she sat up and watched Desa with lovely blue eyes. "I'd like to think I already have." She leaned down and kissed Desa again. For a brief moment, Desa allowed it.

Then she broke the kiss and turned her head to press her cheek into the pillow. Her brow furrowed. "I'm serious," she said. "How do you plan to help me stop Bendarian?"

"I've told you where to find him."

"Yes," Desa agreed. "And even if your intentions were pure, Sebastian's betrayal has almost certainly made approaching the man's house a foolhardy plan."

The other woman sat up with the sheets held to her chest, then grimaced and shook her head. "I don't know what else I can do," she said. "I'm not a Field Binder like you."

"Have you ever tried?"

"What? Of course not!"

"Why not?"

Adele's scowl deepened, and she turned her face away as if the question brought her shame. "Everything I've read on the subject suggests that it's extremely dangerous," she muttered. "I was afraid."

Interesting; so the woman had read something on the subject. Books on the theory of Field Binding were rare outside of Aladar, but it was not impossible that someone in a city as large as this might have had one. Especially a member of the mayor's family.

Chuckling softly, Desa shook her head. "Those are lies told by powerful men who would prevent you from discovering your full potential," she said. "Field Binding can be dangerous if you don't know what you're doing, but those dangers are minimized in the presence of a good teacher."

"Are you offering to teach me?"

"Are you willing to learn?"

Instead of answering, Adele just kissed Desa again. Sweet Mercy, the woman was eager! One taste of passion, and now she couldn't get enough. Perhaps this really was her first time.

Adele pulled back, blinking, and strands of golden hair

fell over her face. "From you," she said, "I'd be willing to learn anything."

When Desa looked out the window, she saw only a black sky. Full night had fallen. She pulled Adele close and smiled when the woman snuggled up with her head on Desa's chest. "For now," Desa said, "the only thing you need to learn is sleep. It's late."

She held Adele close and waited for her to fall asleep. Then she gently slipped away, pulled the covers up to Adele's shoulders and got dressed.

DESA EMERGED from her room in tan pants, a blue shirt and her long, brown duster, the wide-brimmed hat sitting firmly on her head. The familiar weight of her revolver and her daggers on her belt was a comfort to her. She had Infused all of her weapons with a new connection to the Ether.

She was ready.

The wood-paneled hallway was dark, lit only by wall-mounted candles under glass covers, but that was enough for her. It did not surprise her in the slightest to find Marcus leaning against the wall.

The man turned his head to direct a tight-lipped frown her way. "I take it that you enjoyed your dalliance with that fool woman?" he asked. His disdainful tone made Desa want to punch him.

She closed her eyes, stuffed the anger down into the pit of her stomach and then shook her head forcefully. "Tell me," she said, stepping forward. "Are you incapable of expressing any emotion besides scorn?"

Of course, he didn't answer.

Desa strode past him without a second thought, making her way to the stairs at the end of the corridor. She paused on the top step, looked back over her shoulder and raised an eyebrow.

Marcus stood in the middle of the corridor with his fists clenched, his lips parting in a contemptuous sneer. "And where are we going now?" he asked. "To find the girls father and beg her hand in marriage."

"We're going to kill Bendarian," Desa said. "Are you coming?"

15

Desa landed on a slanted rooftop, then crouched on the edge, leaning forward and squinting into the distance. The cool, damp wind assaulted her face. "This is it," she said. "Now, we decide what to do next."

She ordered her belt-buckle to stop draining gravitational energy and just like that, her arms and legs felt oddly heavy. You could get used to the feeling of weightlessness. It only took a few minutes of being free to make the Earth's natural pull feel wrong.

On the other side of the street, she saw a line of townhouses with dim lights in their windows. The one belonging to Bendarian was dark except for one round window on the third floor that watched her like the eye of a cyclops.

Marcus landed beside her and dropped to one knee, shaking his head with a grunt. "Killing Bendarian is one thing," he said. "But if we have to fight that beast again, there is little chance we will survive."

Desa winced at the thought of another confrontation with Morley, then scraped the knuckle of a fist across her forehead. "You are correct," she admitted with a great deal of reluctance. "One of us will have to keep him distracted."

"One of us," Marcus scoffed. "You mean me."

Perched upon the ledge with her arms crossed, Desa sniffed in disdain. "You seem to pride yourself on your ability to intimidate people," she said. "Do you mean to tell me that you're afraid of Morley?"

Marcus showed his teeth in a vicious snarl, then turned his head to glare at her. She could feel his eyes trying to drill holes in her skull. "I would be a fool if I did not fear that man!" he spat. "And you are doubly so if you do not!"

Desa nodded.

She stood up on the ledge, and the wind made her duster flare out behind her. "Go in first," she said with a curt nod. "You can get through the window on the second floor. I wager Morley is in that house."

"And what would you have me do?"

"Lead him away from here."

With a sigh of frustration, Marcus stood up, and then his body grew tense. "By the eyes of Vengeance," he cursed. "From our first meeting, you have caused me nothing but trouble, Desa Nin Leean. We should fight this Morley together."

"One of us has to stay to kill Bendarian."

"And you reserve that pleasure for yourself?"

Glancing over her shoulder, Desa felt her eyebrows try to climb up her forehead. "I don't consider it to be a pleasure, Marcus," she said. "That is why it should be me."

He made no further protest; he just leaped from the rooftop, and whatever he used as a Gravity-Sink carried him across the street. Watching him go twisted Desa's stomach in knots. Marcus was right about one thing; condemning him to face Morley alone after what they had seen this morning was reprehensible. But Morley wasn't the biggest threat. Without his master, the man could be contained.

But Bendarian...

Left to his own devices, Bendarian would destroy this world and every living soul in it. If he could transform Morley into a monster, there was no telling how powerful he had become. Much as she hated doing it, Desa would send Marcus to deal with Morley because she would be the one to face the greater threat.

MARCUS CRASHED through the window in a shower of glass, landing in a room that was pitch black to his eyes. He didn't bother using his ring for light; having been outside with only moonlight and the odd lamp, his eyes would adjust faster than those of anyone who had been upstairs. The very instant his feet touched the floor, he heard the distinct thumping sound of people rushing to meet him.

Marcus huffed air through his open mouth, then shut his eyes and tried to ignore the beads of sweat on his brow. "Come on then," he mumbled. "Let's be done with it."

He drew his pistol and held it up beside his head with the barrel pointed up at the ceiling. Then he took two steps forward. A gasp escaped him when two glass plates on the walls began to glow with intense light. No doubt Bendarian had Infused them.

This was a simple room with burgundy carpets, dark-red walls and two chairs that faced the window. A small bookshelf in the corner was filled with leather-bound texts on the theory of Field Binding; each one had Aladri script on the spine.

Baring his teeth, Marcus sucked air into his lungs and then shook his head. "Well, at least we know this is the right address." He itched to put a bullet through Bendarian's skull. The bastard had earned a death sentence from the Synod.

A man burst into the room.

No...Not a man but a beast in a brown coat and a wide-brimmed hat. His grizzled face was marked by a small scar on the cheek and thick gray mustache. "You!" Morley spat. "I would have thought you would have more sense than to come here."

In less than a second, the man was striding across the room and kicking one of the chairs, sending it flying toward Marcus. A thought was all it took to trigger the Force-Sink that he had infused into the pendant beneath his shirt.

The chair came to a halt in mid-flight.

Then it fell to the floor.

Without waiting, Marcus thrust his arm out, cocked the hammer on his pistol and fired several times. Gray bullets that Desa had stolen from that farmhouse pierced Morley's flesh and made him stumble backward.

Marcus turned with a flourish of his coat, then leaped through the open window. A fraction of a second to let gravity pull him downward, and then he triggered the Sinks he had Infused into metal studs in his shoes.

Marcus landed on the sidewalk, then dropped to one knee, grunting in displeasure. He looked back, then quickly got to his feet and ran. There were lights in some windows and people poking their heads out to see the commotion.

Marcus kept running.

His lips writhed as he panted, and thick droplets of sweat slid down his forehead. "Come on," he choked out. "Follow me you bastard!"

His wish was granted when he heard the smacking sound of shoes on cobblestones behind him. A quick glance revealed that Morley had jumped out the window. The man was slowly rising from a crouch.

He turned hateful eyes on Marcus.

Without warning, Morley jumped and flew in a high arc that took him right over Marcus's head. The man collided with the front wall of a neighbouring townhouse and then dug his fingers into the stone. He clung to the building like a spider on a wall.

Morley leaped off, grabbed one of the black lampposts with both hands and ripped the damn thing off its mountings as he fell to the ground. He spun around and around in circles, swinging the lamppost and then finally threw it at Marcus.

Pulsing his Gravity-Sinks, Marcus jumped and let the metal pole pass beneath him. He landed with a grunt, raised his weapon and fired.

More bullets tore through Morley's body, each producing a spray of black blood as the man stumbled backward. That sight alone would have been unnerving, but Morley's soft laughter made it even worse.

A wicked grin split the man's face in two. "Fool," he spat, shaking his head. "You never learn, do you?"

"No," Marcus said. "*You* never learn!"

He retrieved a penny from his coat pocket and tossed it down on the cobblestones just in time to watch Morley step over it. The other man was charging like a raging bull, ready to tackle Marcus to the ground.

Marcus triggered the Gravity-Sinks in his shoes along with the Gravity-Source that he had placed within the coin. Without warning, Morley was yanked backwards, thrown to the ground.

Killing his Source but leaving the Sinks active, Marcus ran forward at full speed. He leaped, flipped upside down in midair and extended his arm to fire his very last bullet down at his enemy.

It pierced Morley's forehead.

With a bellow of triumph, Marcus turned upright and killed his Sinks. He landed in a crouch, grunted and then slowly got to his feet. "Well then," he said, turning around. "I suppose that puts an end to-"

The hole in Morley's forehead sealed itself, and the man groaned as he sat up. "You really don't learn," he panted. "I must have said it a dozen times now. You can't kill me!"

WHEN SHE SAW Morley follow Marcus up the street, Desa made her move. She took a deep breath, triggered her Gravity-Sink and then leaped from the rooftop. In seconds, she was passing through the shattered window in Bendarian's front wall and then landing in what appeared to be a sitting room.

Releasing her hold on gravity, Desa bit her lip and nodded. "No time to waste," she whispered. "Let's be done with this."

She drew aside her coat, pulled her gun from its holster and thumbed the hammer. Glass crunched beneath her feet as she made her way slowly across the room, but Desa figured that with all the commotion outside, no one would notice. All she had to do was get upstairs and then-

Bendarian stepped into the open doorway.

The man looked very much as she remembered him: tall and lean, dressed in a fine coat with golden lions embroidered on the sleeves. His face was immaculate and framed by long blonde hair that fell to the small of his back. "Good to see you again, Des-"

Desa was yanked backwards and sideways by some unseen force.

Her shoulder went right into the wall, and she grimaced on impact, one tear rolling over her cheek. "Marcus," she hissed. "You never were careful." It lasted only a moment, but that surge of gravity could have seriously injured any number of people on this street. The sound of gunfire outside made her flinch.

Bendarian had braced himself against the door-frame, and the shock of it had taken most of the colour from his face. "Your friend Marcus is something of a blunt instrument, it seems." He regained his balance with little difficulty and faced her as the very image of stately poise. "Crude but effective."

Desa looked up to fix her gaze on him, then narrowed her eyes. "You would know something about that, wouldn't you?" she breathed. "I have had the pleasure of tangling with your favourite blunt instrument many times."

The smile on Bendarian's face only widened as he took a few graceful steps into the room. "Indeed," he said. "You couldn't even kill Morley when he was nothing more than an ordinary man. And now...Now, he is something else entirely."

"What did you do to him?"

Bendarian shrugged, then tittered as he shook his head. "I did only what he asked me to do." Somehow, Desa had a difficult time believing that even a bastard like Morley would ask to become an abomination. "I made him immortal."

"You don't have that kind of power."

"Don't I?"

Red-hot anger flared to life within Desa when she remembered the things she had seen on the road to Ofalla.

"The people you killed at that farmhouse," she began. "They were possessed by something. What is it?"

Bendarian spread his arms wide, threw his head back and roared with self-satisfied laughter. "The future!" he exclaimed. "The end of one world! The beginning of another!"

She was about to sneer at Bendarian's grandiose claims when he surprised her by stepping aside and revealing Sebastian in the hallway. The treacherous young man was deathly pale as he watched Desa with wide eyes. "Your friend here has seen the wisdom of cooperation," Bendarian said. "Like many his age, he is unwilling to let humanity be constrained by outdated ideas and-"

CRACK!

Sebastian flinched when a bullet ripped through his body, his arms flailing as he fell to the floor. Blood pooled around him, soaking into the thick red carpets.

Desa stood with one arm extended, smoke rising from the barrel of her gun. Even *she* was surprised by how readily she had killed the boy. Perhaps Tommy would hate her, but she could deal with that later. Sebastian had caused enough trouble. She wasn't about to risk her safety by leaving him alive.

By the fear in Bendarian's eyes, it was clear that the man had not expected her to kill one of her former companions. "You've grown ruthless, Desa," he whispered. "A pity. The boy had potential."

"This ends now," she whispered.

"Indeed."

The room went dark, and Desa threw herself to the floor just before she heard the *thunk* of a knife landing in the wall. There were muffled footsteps on the carpet, and then

Bendarian's shadowy silhouette was leaping through the window, sailing across the street.

Clenching her teeth with a throaty growl, Desa shook her head. "So, escape is your game, is it?" she muttered, getting to her feet. "Sadly, Bendarian, it won't be that easy."

She spun around and ran for the window, then leaped and ordered her belt buckle to suppress gravity's power. Flying across the street, she stopped herself by bracing her hand against the wall of a townhouse.

Without gravity to pull her downward, it was easy to scale that wall and climb to the roof. There, she found Bendarian leaping from the peak and crossing the next street over. He landed lightly on a rooftop and ran.

"You won't elude me this time," Desa rasped. "This ends tonight."

Up the slanted roof and down the other side; she didn't even bother to extinguish her Gravity-Sink. Running while weightless made it easy to avoid damaging the tiles or slipping and falling to her death.

She leaped from the ledge and flew across the street with her arms stretched out before her. Wind caressed her face and blew her hat off. She didn't try to catch it. All that mattered was ending Bendarian once and for all.

Desa hit the next roof and then somersaulted across the tiles. In a heartbeat, she was crouched and then rising to her feet.

She ran in hot pursuit.

At this rate, she would expend her Gravity-Sink's power in about five minutes. She had to be cautious. Forcing her to use up her Infused arsenal might have been Bendarian's plan all along. It was time to change tactics.

Desa killed her Gravity-Sink every time she landed. Doing so forced her to move at a slower pace – it was all too possible to lose her footing on these precarious rooftops – but she had to conserve her power for the fight to come. Keeping up with Bendarian was not *that* difficult.

He was headed for the river, bouncing from rooftop to rooftop.

She followed.

Eventually, the man settled on the flat rooftop of a small warehouse by the docks. He chose that place to stand his ground, spinning to face Desa and drawing his own gun. So, it seemed the man was capable of something other than rampant cowardice.

Desa landed on one knee near the ledge, then slowly rose to face her enemy. Gusts of wind pummeled her as she strode forward. "Tonight, you're going to answer for all the people you killed," she said. "For all the lives you destroyed."

From up here, she could see the dark river snaking its way through the city and beyond it, more buildings, some with lights in their windows The gibbous moon allowed her to make out wooden ships moored along the riverbank.

Bendarian chuckled softly and moved toward her with his eyes fixed on the stone under his feet. "Your talent for severity never ceases to amaze, Desa Nin Leean," he said. "If you truly wish to kill me, by all means, try."

With lightning-quick reflexes, she drew her pistol, thrust her arm out and fired twice. Each squeeze of the trigger produced a flash from the barrel of her gun, and gray bullets jerked to a halt in front of Benwoth.

The man raised his own weapon.

Desa triggered her Gravity-Sink and jumped.

The roaring thunderclap of gunfire filled her ears as bullets sped past beneath her. Letting gravity reassert some of its power, she flew over Bendarian's head in a wide arc and then descended to land on the rooftop behind him. Quickly, she spun around to aim her weapon.

Bendarian was faster.

He was already facing her and throwing a golden coin that glittered as it caught the moonlight. A powerful wave of kinetic energy hit Desa like a gale-force wind. She was propelled backward off the rooftop.

Her Gravity-Sink prevented her from falling, but now she was stuck in an uncontrolled flight over the neighbouring buildings. Humans were not built to ride on air currents. She could not easily adjust her trajectory.

And Bendarian was taking aim.

Letting herself drop a few feet, Desa flinched when she felt bullets passing over her head. She pointed her own gun into the distance behind her, aiming slightly downward, and fired several times. The recoil sent a jolt of pain through her arm, but it was enough to push her back toward the warehouse. It also used up the last of her ammunition, and there was no telling when she would get a chance to reload.

Desa grabbed the lip of the roof, planted her feet against the warehouse wall and then launched herself upward without gravity to slow her. Killing her Sink, she flipped over Bendarian's head and dropped to the rooftop behind him.

She turned to face him, tossed her gun aside and took a few steps forward. "For ten long years, I have pursued you across this continent," she said. "I must admit that ending this with a bullet would be far less satisfying."

Bendarian whirled around, hissing softly, then dropped his pistol and drew aside his coat to reveal the rapier on his hip. "You speak truth, woman." He drew the sword with a menacing rasp. "We always knew it would end this way."

Desa removed the ring from her finger and then threw it

down in the middle of the rooftop. With a thought, she made it glow, producing enough light to see Bendarian as he adopted a battle stance.

He flowed toward her with exquisite grace, moving across the rooftop like a ribbon on the wind. There was no fear, no trepidation as Desa waited for his approach. She drew her daggers, focused on her breathing, and let her instincts take over. Bendarian raised his sword and swung downward in a vertical arc.

Desa hopped to the left, the blade whistling past her right shoulder. She stepped forward, kicked the back of Bendarian's leg and forced the man down onto his knees. She swung her dagger out to the side, trying to cut the back of his neck.

Bendarian threw himself forward, somersaulting across the rough rooftop. He rose with graceful elegance, then spun to face her.

When she turned, she found the man striding toward her with his teeth bared in a mocking sneer. Light glinted off the curved blade of that rapier as he raised it in a salute.

He performed another downward cut.

Desa crossed her knives above her head, catching his sword in the *x* of her blades. She kicked the man's stomach with all the strength she could muster, producing a wheeze of pain as Bendarian stumbled away.

Desa jumped, then twirled in midair, one foot lashing out for a spinning kick that took Bendarian across the cheek. Blood flew from the man's mouth as he went sideways toward the ledge.

Desa landed.

Rounding on him, she sprinted across the roof at full speed. It surprised her when Bendarian reached into his coat pocket, pulled out a coin and then tossed it down in front of her. She tried to stop, but it was too late.

Frost spread across the rooftop in a wave, and the air turned bitter cold. Desa's ears burned from the chill. Her feet slipped on the ice, and then she was falling, sliding on her backside toward Bendarian.

The man lifted his sword as if he meant to hack her to pieces.

Skidding to a stop next to him, Desa used her daggers to catch his blade before it carved her up. Bendarian used that opportunity to deliver a quick kick to the ribs. Sharp pain flared through her body.

Desa rolled like a log across the roof, trying to put some distance between them. She got up slowly and forced herself to ignore the agony in her middle, a fierce ache that made her want to double over.

Bendarian was coming toward her in a slow, inexorable march, the tip of his blade bobby and weaving with every step. He was smiling, showing bloodstained teeth.

Clenching her teeth and seething with every breath, Desa shut her eyes. "All right," she whispered. "Let's end this."

She slid one dagger back into its sheath. Then she reached into her duster's pocket and slipped on the brass knuckles. With a bellow, she slammed her fist down on the roof.

Kinetic energy spread through the stone with a rumbling sound. She kept her fist in place, draining the Force-Source of every last scrap of energy. Thick cracks spread across the rooftop and Bendarian stumbled.

Stone fell away beneath him as the roof collapsed, but Bendarian did not fall. His Gravity-Sink allowed him to float gracefully on nothing at all, and his smile never faded. Not for an instant. Clearly, the man didn't understand his predicament. He couldn't move, and Desa was lucky in that a small lip of rooftop remained beneath her.

She jumped and slammed into him, wrapping her arms and legs around Bendarian as her momentum propelled them downward. Without gravity, the fall seemed to last forever and a day.

Desa punched him with the brass knuckles, striking his nose again and again. At full strength, they would have shattered his skull, but she had drained them of every last drop of kinetic energy. That didn't make it any less satisfying.

They landed, and Bendarian brought his knee up to force Desa off him. She rolled away over a pile of smashed wooden crates. Her clothes were covered in dust when she finally stood to find herself in a narrow trench between mountains of stone fragments.

Bendarian was at the other end of that trench with the sword in hand. His hair was in a state of disarray, and there was an ugly gash across his forehead. Desa imagined that she didn't look much better. Her ring had fallen with them, and now it cast a fierce glow upon the both of them.

Removing the brass knuckles, Desa flung them to the floor. She looked up to fix her gaze upon her enemy. "What was it?" she asked again. "The thing that you unleashed upon this world."

"A power such as you could never imagine."

She drew her daggers, crouched down and faced the man with her blades pointed out to the sides. "And yet you rely on Field Binding to defeat me," she said. "This power you speak of must exact a terrible cost."

Bendarian said nothing.

He just came forward with the grace of a master swordsman. No longer toying with her, he moved with serpentine grace and surprising speed, closing the distance in a matter of seconds.

He swung at her neck.

Desa ducked, allowing the sword to pass over her head. She moved in close to slash at his leg, drawing a red gash across his thigh. That brought a hiss of pain to Bendarian's lips and forced the man to bend double.

Desa rammed her blade upward into his stomach, producing a croaking sound as Bendarian shuffled backward. Blood spilled from his mouth and dribbled over his chin. He tried to speak, but a fit of coughing overtook him.

It was over.

MARCUS RAN AS FAST as he could across rooftop after rooftop, then down into the city streets. His Gravity-Sinks were nearly filled to capacity. He would not be able to evade Morley much longer.

His teeth were bared, his face slick with sweat as he sprinted up a street lined with squat, stone buildings on either side. There was no one in sight, nowhere to turn for help. He was alone. And the thudding of Morley's heavy footsteps filled his ears.

He turned around to find that demon of a man a mere twenty feet away and loping up the street without the smallest sign of exhaustion. Morley pulled a stop in front of him, and a grin split the man's face. "Finally decided to stop running and take what's coming to you, huh?"

Marcus backed away.

"Oh, don't be shy now," Morley said, shaking his head. He came forward with the cautious movements of a predator could all but taste its cornered prey. "Ain't nobody here to see your shame. Might as well get it over with."

Marcus shut his eyes, a single tear rolling over his cheek. "May the blessed light of Mercy welcome me home," he whispered. "Let my sins be forgiven. Let my failings be absolved. I walk into this new life clean."

"Your heathen god can't save you, son," Morley said. "No one can-"

The man shrieked as he folded up with a hand on his belly, and black blood slipped through the cracks between his fingers. But how? Marcus didn't stab him or shoot him.

Morley began to cough, and each spasm of his body produced a stream of black blood from his lips. The man sank to his knees, gasping. What was going on here? Had Mercy decided to intervene? Did she hear Marcus's prayer?

BENDARIAN WAS on his knees and clutching his stomach. He ripped the knife out of his flesh and then shrieked from the pain of it. "You stupid woman," he whispered. "You have no idea what I am."

"I know precisely what you are," she countered. "A man whose wrath upon this world is over."

Bendarian looked up at her. His face was pale, his eyes glassy. The man was dying, and yet, he somehow maintained a show of defiance. "I told you," he choked out, "I have found a power unlike any you could imagine."

He closed his eyes, and when he opened them again, they were pitch-black from corner to corner. It was all Desa could do not to jump back in horror. The entity that she had seen on the road to Ofalla, the one that had made Morley impervious to every one of her attacks: it had possessed Bendarian as well.

Despite his wounds, Bendarian stood up. In fact, he didn't seem to be at all troubled by the hole in his stomach.

"You thought you understood power," he said. "You and your little trinkets."

By instinct, Desa backed away from him.

He thrust a hand out toward her.

Something lifted Desa off the floor and slammed her into the warehouse wall. She croaked as invisible fingers closed around her neck and began to squeeze the life out of her. Her feet kicked.

With a dismissive flick of his wrist, Bendarian strode forward. Desa went sideways until her shoulder hit a pile of rubble, and chunks of stone fell upon her head. Just as she was overcoming the pain of that, she went flying in the other direction and hit yet another pile. *By the eyes of Vengeance...*

Bendarian raised his hand.

Desa went flying up toward the massive hole in the ceiling. The man brought his hand down, and she was thrown to the floor. She hit hard, lying face-down on her belly. Her body ached from head to toe.

Summoning all her strength, Desa looked up at him with tears streaming over her face. "What is it?" she rasped. "What did you let in, Radharal?"

Bendarian's sickening grin was even more horrifying than those dead, black eyes. "That which lies beyond the Ether," he replied in a husky voice. "The primordial essence that existed before your precious Mercy created this universe."

With hands on his knees, he crouched down and smiled at her. "The antithesis of the Ether," he said. "The Nether."

"It will destroy us," Desa squeaked.

"It will free us!"

Desa felt her lips writhe, felt hot blood dripping from the corner of her mouth. She shook her head. "The Ether is natural," she wheezed. "A part of this universe. What you let in will unravel the natural order."

"It will liberate us from the natural order!" Bendarian exclaimed. "Think of it, Desa. We create technology, we refine our Infusions. We exploit nature to better ourselves, to improve our lives! Imagine what we could accomplish if we could *write* those laws!"

"No," Desa pleaded. "We were never meant to have that power."

"You're a fool," Bendarian said. "Trapped by outmoded thinking You-"

He staggered backward with a hand over his heart, throwing his head back as he shrieked in pain. Bendarian fell to his knees, and suddenly Desa was no longer certain that she was going to die tonight. That would have been a relief if not for the nightmare playing out before her eyes.

Bendarian's skin shriveled; his cheeks became hollow, and liver spots appeared on his face. His hair grew, turned gray and then fell out. It was like watching a man live out his adult life in a matter of seconds.

Desa forced herself to stand.

With a gaping mouth, she blinked at him and then shook her head. "Radharal, what did you do?" she whispered. "Sweet Mercy..."

She ran to him, ignoring her pains, dropped to her knees and then took his face in both hands. Glassy eyes stared back at her. His mouth moved, but he could not seem to form words.

"The Nether," he finally whimpered. "The Nether."

Marcus watched his enemy tremble.

Morley was on his knees in the middle of the road,

hugging himself and shivering. Every ragged gasp sounded like the man's last breath. Marcus wasn't sure what he ought to do? If he saw any other man in such pain, he would try to help. Perhaps the best thing to do for Morley was to put the bastard out of his misery. Except every previous attempt to kill the man had failed.

Liver spots appeared on Morley's cheeks. His mustache went from dark with flecks of gray to pure white, and wrinkles lined his brow. He seemed to have aged thirty years in a matter of seconds. What was going on here?

DESA FELT as if someone had stabbed her through the chest with an icicle. Watching Bendarian's pain was surreal. The man was trembling, reaching for her with a hand that showed long, curved nails. "The Nether," he whispered. "The Nether."

The Nether...Antithesis of the Ether. While the Ether was orderly and predictable, the Nether was chaos made manifest. Bendarian had said so himself. The Nether would allow him to rewrite the natural laws that governed the universe. Which meant it quite literally destroyed the natural order with results that no one could anticipate.

Gray people, unkillable men, rapid aging: who could say what horrors this force would unleash? Bendarian thought he could control it, but for all the power it offered, the Nether was beyond anyone's control.

Desa closed her eyes, her head drooping as she let out a breath. "You have to listen to me, Radharal," she began. "I can take you back to Aladar. We might be able to help-"

"No!"

"You can't remain like this."

He seized her shoulders with gnarled fingers and shoved

her backwards. Exhausted as she was, Desa fell to the floor with a grunt. When she sat up, Bendarian was trying to stand. He managed to rise slowly.

The face that looked down upon her might have been dignified – the kindly visage of a loving grandfather – if not for its hateful sneer. "I will never...go back...with you," Bendarian whispered. "Never."

He vanished.

There was no warning, no preamble; one moment he was there, and the next he was gone with only the slight whoosh of air filling the space he had vacated to announce his departure. It was over. After a decade of chasing this man, she had lost.

Because now he could be anywhere.

PART II

16

Tommy woke up to the sound of his door banging open as Desa Kincaid marched into his room, illuminated by the glowing ring on her left fist. Its fierce white light cast shadows on the wood-paneled walls and the empty bed with its covers undisturbed. So, Marcus was still out.

Tommy sat up.

His mouth dropped open, and he blinked at her. "What's going on, Desa?" he asked, shaking his head. "Where's Marcus."

"Dead," she answered. "We have to leave."

Gritting his teeth, Tommy winced and pressed the heel of his hand to his forehead. "What do you mean, 'dead'?" he whispered, rubbing the fog out of his brain. "We just saw him a few hours ago."

Desa stopped at the foot of his bed, planted her fists on her hips and then shook her head. "We went to confront Bendarian," she explained. "I told Marcus to distract Morley, and I haven't seen him since."

"Did you...Did you find Sebastian?"

For some reason, Desa's lip quivered, and then her face

crumpled with the kind of anguish you only saw on someone who had been punched in the stomach. "I'm so sorry," she said. "Sebastian is dead too."

That felt like a blade in Tommy's chest. He had cried himself to sleep, thinking about the implications of Sebastian's betrayal. He was not naive; he knew there was very little chance of ever seeing his love again. But now...now there was no chance. As angry as he was over what Sebastian had done, it pained him to know the other man was dead. "You saw his body?" Tommy inquired.

"I did."

Tommy got out of bed, undaunted by the prospect of Desa seeing him in his smallclothes, and quickly pulled on a set of brown trousers. His shirt came next; he buttoned it with considerable speed.

Looking up to meet the woman's eyes, Tommy felt his mouth tighten. He nodded once. "I assume then that Bendarian is coming here," he said. "Will we be moving to yet another hotel?"

"Bendarian is the least of our problems," Desa began. "In fact, I don't think we will ever have to worry about him again." Tommy was just itching to figure out what *that* was supposed to mean, but he kept his mouth shut. He had grown used to keeping quiet and following Desa's lead. "But Morley might be on his way here as we speak, and even if he isn't, the City Watch will be looking for us."

"So, where are we going?"

"We're going to leave Ofalla and-"

Marcus came rushing through the door, took two steps into the room he shared with Tommy and then froze. "You survived," he barked when he saw Desa bathed in the fierce light of her glowing ring.

She closed her eyes and then bowed her head to him.

"As did you," she said. "May I presume then that Morley is dead?"

"I don't think anything can kill that man."

Desa stiffened at his response. Bracing one hand on the bedpost to steady herself, she let out a breath. "No, I suppose not." The fear in her voice left Tommy feeling uneasy. "How did you elude him?"

A grimace twisted Marcus's features, and then he shook his head in disgust. "It was like nothing I've ever seen before," he replied. "The man...The man aged right in front of me. Consumed by the ravages of time."

Rapid aging? What could cause something like that? The little that Desa had told him about the Ether left Tommy feeling certain that Field Binding was not at play. Even taking his scant knowledge of the subject into account, it was clear that if the Ether could do something like that, Marcus would not be reacting with such fear and-

Why was Desa so quiet?

Tommy forced himself to look at the woman and found her backing away from Marcus at a slow pace. The fear in her eyes told him everything he needed to know. This was something out of the ordinary.

Desa sat down on the windowsill, set her hands upon her knees and huddled in on herself with her shoulders hunched up. "It happened to Bendarian too," she whispered. "I saw it. Right after I stabbed him in the stomach."

"You stabbed him in the stomach?" Marcus exclaimed.

"Yes...Why?"

Gaping at her in disbelief, Marcus shook his head slowly. "Morley was chasing me through the northwest quarter when he suddenly collapsed from a gut wound." So, the two men mirrored each other. But what could-

No, that was wrong.

The pieces snapped together in Tommy's head. Desa had inflicted a gut wound on Bendarian, but Morley's wound was spontaneous. If their relationship was bidirectional, then Bendarian should have displayed wounds from all the gunfire that Desa had inflicted on Morley, and she would have mentioned something like that. "That's how you kill him. It's so simple."

They both looked at him.

With his shirt untucked and half-buttoned, Tommy came around the foot of his bed and positioned himself between the two of them. "Don't you see?" he spluttered. "Wounding Bendarian hurts Morley."

Desa's mouth dropped open, and her eyes widened. "Of course..." She paced over to him, clapping Tommy on the shoulder. "Brilliant!"

Tommy shut his eyes, his cheeks suddenly very warm. "It's nothing," he said. "But you might be able to eliminate two problems at once."

"First we have to find Bendarian."

The door banged opened to admit Miri. Tall and imposing in her faded dungarees and weather-worn coat, she strode into the room with a snarl that made Tommy flinch. "No," she said. "The first thing you have to do is leave."

Miri stepped up to Desa with fists on her hips, shaking her head. "Whatever you did out there," she began, "it earned you more attention than you would like, I think. The City Watch is on high alert."

Tommy noticed Adele in the doorway.

The woman looked somewhat out of place in a pair of tan pants and an old work shirt that she left untucked. Her long blonde tresses were a mess of flyaway strands as if she had been tossing and turning through a fitful night's sleep.

"My uncle has no love for troublemakers," she said. "You destroyed a warehouse."

It shocked him to see Desa blush – he didn't think the woman was capable of it – but there she was, pink-cheeked and averting her gaze. "It couldn't be helped, and...Wait, how do *you* know about that? Word could not have traveled so fast."

"I told you," Adele replied. "I'm a Sensitive."

Desa muttered something under her breath.

Dropping onto the edge of his mattress, Tommy scrubbed both hands over his face and then ran fingers through his hair. "We have to leave," he said. "We should be out of the city by dawn."

"Glad you caught up to us, Tommy," Desa muttered. That stung, but he chose not to make an issue of it. "If there are no further objections, perhaps we could be on our way."

"I'm going with you!" Adele insisted.

"No!" Desa snapped.

The venom in that reaction was a bit more than Tommy would have expected. And it seemed that Adele shared his reaction. The woman seemed hurt. There was something going on beneath the surface, but he wasn't about to pry into that. Not his business. What Tommy wanted was to be away from here. If Desa wanted to dally with the mayor's niece-

Almighty have mercy...

Sebastian...

Tommy had been so fixated on the news of Desa's skirmish with Bendarian that he had not really taken a moment to note the passing of his love. Sebastian had betrayed them all, but...But Tommy still loved him.

He closed his eyes as hot tears streamed over his cheeks and dripped from his chin. "Sebastian..." he whimpered. No one seemed to hear him. They were all too busy arguing with each other. He let them.

Right then, he just wanted to mourn.

THE NETHER EMBRACED BENDARIAN.

He floated in a storm of endless darkness, not a void but something else entirely, blacker than the Pits of Despair and more violent than a tempest. It felt as though he were being torn apart molecule by molecule. He didn't think he could stand it.

A vertical seam appeared before him, a jagged crack through which brilliant light spilled. The darkness split apart, leaving him bathed in radiance, a soft glow that slowly faded to reveal the wrecked sitting room of his townhouse.

Bendarian fell to one knee atop shards of glass, gasping for breath. His head hung, and the few remaining strands of silver hair that dangled from his bald scalp caressed the floor. Every breath was a labour.

"What did you do?"

He looked up to see an aged Morley with his shoulder pressed to the door-frame. The man was scowling as he pressed one hand to his belly. Almost as if he were trying to hold his guts in. Unsurprisingly, the knife wound that Desa had inflicted on Benwrth had translated through their bond. But Bendarian had healed himself with the Nether. Which meant that Morley should have been...Well, out of mortal danger at least.

Bendarian narrowed his eyes, hissing as he drew in a breath. "She is stronger than I gave her credit for," he whispered. "We must end her."

"You're in no shape to fight her." Morley lifted trembling

hands up in front of his face, gnarled hands with liver spots and bony fingers. "And neither am I? What did you do, Radharal?"

"A minor setback."

"A minor setback?" Morley boomed. "You promised me immortality, but instead you take the life from me!"

Clenching his teeth, Bendarian growled as he shook his head. "I have yet to learn all of the Nether's secrets," he wheezed. "When I do, I will reverse this...accident and restore us both to full health."

Morley turned away from him and began shuffling through the hallway with one hand on the wall. He froze in place after only a few steps. "Be sure you hurry," the man said without looking back. "Because if killing you is the only way to end my pain, you can be sure that I will do it."

Radharal...

Bendarian's mouth dropped open as a low, painful groan erupted from his throat. "No..." he pleaded. "Not now."

You aren't holding up your end of the bargain.

"Please! I must destroy Desa Nin Leean."

She is irrelevant. Free me!

"I..."

FREE ME! the voice demanded. *FREE ME!*

THEY MOVED through the city streets under the dark of night, two to a horse, except for Marcus who sat his gray alone. Tommy suspected that was because no one else felt inclined to suffer the man's company; he certainly did not. The process of packing their things and fetching their horses had been hindered by Adele's constant insistence that she *would* be coming with them and Desa's refusal to budge on that point. The mayor's niece kept blathering on about destiny or some such; Tommy wasn't sure he believed in all that. Deep down, he wasn't entirely sure that he believed in the Almighty, but for all of Desa's protests about not bringing a pampered aristocrat on this journey, Adele had somehow managed to join their group.

She sat behind Tommy on his father's old brown gelding. From the way she kept fidgeting – and the way she kept looking at Desa and Miri on Midnight – it was clear that she would have preferred other arrangements.

They were moving quietly down a narrow street lined with small shops on either side. Tommy saw a bakery, a butcher shop, a tailor's shop. Or at least that was what he thought they were. It was difficult to read the signs with so few lamps lit. All were closed up for the night, but he still had this odd feeling as if someone was watching them from the windows.

"You need me," Adele whispered behind him.

On their right, Desa sat atop Midnight with the reins in hand. She turned her head, glowered at the other woman and hissed, "Be quiet! You're no good to us if you wake the whole damn town."

"As if anyone can hear me," Adele muttered.

Tommy grimaced.

A moment later, Marcus emerged from one of the intersecting streets, reined up and nodded once. "Another group of watchmen two streets over," he said softly. "We'll have to adjust our route."

Desa took the news in stride.

Tommy, however, slumped forward in the saddle, exhaustion making his head so heavy he thought it might fall off. "How much further," he asked. "To the edge of town, I mean..."

How long before I can sleep?

No one answered him, but Adele swatted him between the shoulder blades hard enough to make him jump. "Keep your wits, boy!" she snapped. "I won't have you riding us into the river."

"Be quiet!" Desa snarled. "Both of you!"

She was not in good spirits.

Throughout their whole ride south, Desa had displayed an outward calm that had set Tommy's mind at ease. Now, she was frazzled. Perhaps she was disturbed by what she had seen while confronting Bendarian, but Tommy suspected that Adele's presence had a lot to do with it.

They turned onto a wider street that ran all the way to the southern edge of town. It was empty, so far as Tommy could see. There were a few lamps lit but no sign of anyone nearby. He did hear horses hooves in the distance, which meant the nearest patrol of City Watchmen could probably hear them as well. Hopefully, they would just assume that it was another patrol.

After the incident at the bank and then the destruction of the warehouse, those men would certainly be looking for a small woman who met Desa's description. They might not recognize her on sight, but they would take in anyone they found out and about at this hour. *Just a little longer,* Tommy assured himself. *We're almost out of this city.*

He pulled his horse up alongside Midnight and leaned sideways to speak to Desa. "About Sebastian," he whispered. "Did you see how he died?"

Desa's face hardened.

"Mrs. Kincaid?"

"No...I didn't."

Tommy swallowed, then shut his eyes and felt a single tear on his cheek. "I guess I'll just have to settle for knowing that you'll put the man who did it in the ground." A chill went through him. "Once we find him."

"Once we find him," Desa agreed.

Tommy could feel Adele pulling away from him. The woman was uneasy; he could not say why. But then it should have been fairly obvious. Anyone would be uneasy riding off into the night and trying to avoid the lawmen. He just hoped that Desa had more of her Infused weapons.

He kept his mouth shut for the rest of the journey. It was probably only about ten minutes – fifteen at the most – but it felt like an eternity. Tommy kept looking back over his shoulder, expecting to see City Watchmen on their tail. All he got was the odd glare from Adele, which was almost as bad.

Once they were safely beyond the city limits, he let out a sigh of relief. Of course, Ofalla didn't end in open country-side. There were farms along the roadside, and he could even see the lights of a village in the distance. Which meant they had to keep going. The sun was well above the horizon when they finally stopped to rest in a small glade.

Tommy wanted nothing more than to curl up with his coat for a pillow and sleep at least a few hours, but he was fairly certain that once they had taken some food, they would be riding until nightfall.

17

"He's going west," Adele said while standing on a small rock in the middle of a glade about half a mile south-east of Ofalla. Rays of bright sunlight streaked through the trees, and the wind sighed as it made the leave flutter.

The mayor's niece was straining and squinting into the distance as if those few extra inches of height would somehow let her glimpse Bendarian, whom she claimed was miles away from here. Perhaps she really could. The woman was in communion with the Ether; Desa could feel it as a kind of resonance. That Adele could even move or speak while in such a state of mind was...remarkable.

Desa was leaning against the trunk of an elm with her arms folded and the brim of her hat pulled down over her eyes. "So you've said," she mumbled. "Many times now, in fact. You'll forgive me if I don't take your word for it."

Adele broke contact with the Ether.

She hopped off of her rock, then strode over to Desa with her fists clenched and her arms swinging. "I have been on your side from the beginning," she said. "I am growing weary of your constant insinuations to the contrary."

Tommy was sitting cross-legged with his back to a tree trunk. His eyes were closed, and it was clear that he was trying to meditate. Trying and failing. Desa's heart went out to the boy. Her argument with Adele certainly wasn't helping matters.

Tommy cracked an eye when he heard the woman's approach, then resumed his focus. It would work for him eventually. Desa could already feel the faintest whispers of the resonance she had felt in Adele.

In tan pants and a tattered coat, the mayor's niece stood with her fists on her hips, frowning and shaking her head. "I led you directly to Bendarian's townhouse," she added. "It wasn't a trap."

"No, it wasn't," Desa agreed.

"Well?"

Removing her hat, Desa blinked at the other woman. "I'm not sure what you want from me," she said. "You're here despite my protests. Perhaps it would be best to accept your victories graciously."

"Accept my victories-"

They were cut off by the sound of trees rustling as Marcus stepped into the glade with Miri on his heels. The man drew himself up to full height, scowled and then nodded to Desa. "I made some discreet inquiries," he said. "Athrin is about two miles south of the city, but so far they haven't been visited by any Watchmen. No one knows anything about what happened last night."

"So, it's safe to pass through?"

"As safe as can be hoped for."

Miri removed a large knapsack that she carried on her back, set it down on Adele's rock and then opened it to reveal a loaf of bread and cheese inside, all carefully wrapped up in cotton. "Supplies," she said. "Enough to last a few days. Though, I suppose whether we'll need more depends a great deal on where we're going."

"West!" Adele insisted.

"There's nothing west of here," Marcus grumbled. "You can follow the river for about two hundred miles before it bends northward. You'll find Thrasa on its northern bank but not much on this side. And getting across won't be easy. After that, it's open country all the way to Fool's Edge."

"Fool's Edge?" Tommy inquired.

Pressing her back to the tree trunk, Desa slid downward until her bottom hit the ground. Then she drew her legs up and hugged them. "The last outpost along the edge of the Gatharan Desert," she explained. "Venture out beyond that point, and you can expect a painful journey that ends with you dying of thirst."

Marcus showed his teeth in something that was halfway between a smile and a snarl. "There are oases along the way," he protested. "Traders have made the journey to Relanoth on the other side. Some have even gone all the way to the western shore of this continent and lived to tell about it."

"Crossing the desert and then the Molarin Mountains?" Desa said. "Possible but not wise. And why would Bendarian go that way?"

"I don't know," Adele insisted. "But he is."

Craning her neck to stare at Marcus, Desa felt creases forming in her brow. "You see what I've had to deal with all morning?" she mumbled. "This one has been a fount of supposedly useful information."

Marcus slipped his hands into his coat pockets, his face twisting into the kind of grimace that belonged on a man who was ready to empty his stomach. "If we're going to go west, then we exited the city on the wrong side," he said.

"Roads extend from Ofalla like spokes on a wheel. We'll have to hike across country to move between them, and that will take us right through several farms."

"What about the outlying villages?" Tommy suggested. "Surely, there are roads connecting them."

"There are," Marcus replied. "But going that way means chancing an encounter with the City Watch. They will eventually expand their search beyond the city limits, and many will be on the lookout for a small woman who fits Desa's description."

"I don't think we have a choice," Desa said. "Let's move. The sooner we're on our way, the better our chances of passing through a town before the Watch does."

THE SUN WAS SINKING FAST, and the sky was a deep blue fading to a band of pink on the horizon. A warm wind blew through a town of wooden buildings and dusty streets, the third they had passed through today.

At this hour, most people were finishing dinner or having tea, but there were still a few out on the streets, going about their business. One man with a leathery face and white hair gave Desa a nasty glare as she passed.

She led Midnight by his bridle, keeping her head down so that the brim of her hat could shield her face. "Folks don't like strangers," she murmured to the horse. "Doesn't matter where you go."

Adele was trudging along on Desa's right and fussing with the hat that Miri had lent her. The woman let out a huff. "I don't see why I should have to wear this ridiculous thing," she said for the fourteenth time.

"So that no one will recognize you."

"I've never even been to Shovan," Adele said, gesturing

to the wooden buildings all around them. She tripped over a rock, stumbled a few steps and then cursed. "How could anyone recognize me?"

Drawing her pistol, Desa spun it around her index finger, then caught the grip and held the gun up in front of her face, its barrel pointed at the sky. "The first rule you need to learn, girl," she said. "Someone is always doing what no one should be able to do."

On her left, Miri was walking arm and arm with Tommy and filling his ears with constant chatter as he led his father's gelding. The boy looked positively mortified, which made the infectious grin on Miri's face that much more amusing.

"Now, listen carefully, Lommy," she said. "There's a few things you need to know about this region. Its two principal exports are cotton and tobacco, though peaches do grow well in this climate, and a farmer can make a tidy profit selling them to traders who ship them downriver. You listening, Lommy?"

Desa laughed.

Marcus was in front, leading that massive gray of his and no doubt glaring daggers at everyone who passed. Perhaps that was why the old man had glowered at her. It might have been wiser to let Marcus take up the rear – Desa's senses were as sharp as his after a decade wandering the wilderness; she would spot trouble as easily as he did – but the man did what all men do.

If there was trouble headed their way, then Marcus wanted to be the first one to meet it. Or some such nonsense. Desa might have protested under other circumstances, but she was tired, and they still had a way to go.

"Why would Bendarian go west?" Adele muttered.

"You're the one who insisted that he did."

The young woman removed her hat again, much to Desa's annoyance, and the soft breeze made those golden tresses flutter. "Yes, but I can only see *where* he is," she said. "I have no idea why he went there. When last I checked, he was about ten miles upriver."

Pressing her lips together, Desa squinted into the distance. "I might be able to catch up with him," she said. "Midnight and I should be able to cover that distance in less than an hour."

"Bendarian is not alone," Adele said. "That Morley character is with him and half a dozen other men I don't know. And correct me if I'm wrong, but you haven't had time to replenish your arsenal of Infused weapons."

The girl was right, though Desa hated to admit it. Bendarian was a dangerous enemy before he acquired his new powers. Attacking him while she was exhausted and lacking Infused weapons was a death sentence. So, she did the only thing she could.

She kept walking.

DESA FLOATED in the Ether's embrace, barely aware of her own fatigued body. All she saw was a tempest of particles all swirling about. The exhaustion was a faint ache in the back of her mind, easily ignored, and the other pains throughout her body quickly faded away as the injuries she had acquired fighting Bendarian healed themselves. Communing with the Ether accelerated the body's natural healing process.

She Infused the brass knuckles with a new connection to the Ether, structuring a lattice of energy that would have them release a wave of kinetic force when two physical conditions were met. Her fingers had to be pressed against the inside of all four rings, and the outward face of all four rings would have to come into direct contact with a solid object. Since she had given them a physical mechanism to trigger the release of energy, anyone could use those brass knuckles to full effect.

She had Infused several bullets, both of her daggers and her belt buckle with fresh connections to the Ether. Her bracelet still contained a Force-Sink that would be able to drain the energy of at least six bullets. That was the best she could manage. There were limits to just how much energy a Field Binder could manipulate, though Desa suspected that Adele could make even more powerful weapons if she set her mind to it.

Adele...

The young woman had a natural talent for manipulating the Ether, a talent unlike anything Desa had ever seen before. In fact, Adele was communing with the Ether at this very moment. Desa could feel the woman's scrutiny.

She let herself drift back into her body.

She was sitting on a log, her eyes shut as a cool breeze blew strands of hair back from her face. This tiny patch of woodland they had discovered about half a mile southwest of Ofalla was the best campsite they were likely to find. Desa could hear the singing of cicadas all around her.

She opened her eyes.

Tommy was curled up in his bedroll with the shadowy figure of Miri sitting just a few feet away. She turned her head as if she could sense a change in Desa, and though it was too dark to see, Desa could swear she felt the other woman's eyes on her.

Marcus was standing between two trees at the edge of this grove, staring out at the vast open field beyond them. The fool of a man would probably insist on staying awake all bloody night to keep watch despite the fact that he must have been as exhausted as she was. Men!

That left Adele.

Foolishness was by no means limited to males. The mayor's niece sat primly on a rock, lost in a trance. The slow rhythm of her breathing was unmistakable to anyone with a keen ear.

Desa got up and trudged over to her. "Enough," she said, putting herself right in front of the woman. "Why are you watching me?"

Marcus spared them a glance but quickly decided that this was none of his concern and returned to his "duty" as a sentry. Well then, at least he wasn't a total idiot.

Adele rose slowly – she was really quite tall – took a deep breath and then shook her head. "I commune with the Ether every night," she said. "I was watching Bendarian, but your Field Binding is rather distracting, and I must admit I was curious."

"I would prefer it-"

"*I* would prefer it," Miri cut in, "if we could all get some sleep. Perhaps you could save your petty bickering for the long ride westward? I'm sure that it will do wonders to alleviate the boredom."

Desa wanted to snap at the woman, but she chose to keep silent. Miri had a point; they did need rest. As she settled into her bedroll, she gave in to the urge to sigh. She was hoping for at least one more night in a real bed. But then, the life of the bounty hunter did not offer much in the way of comfort. She would kill Bendarian soon. She could almost feel it. And then...And then who could say where her life would take her?

18

Miri took in the sights.

The dirt road that cut through a field of lush green grass, running parallel to a river of sparkling black waters. The sky overhead was a lovely shade of blue, with fluffy clouds drifting past.

She sat upon Tommy's old brown horse with the reins in a loose grip. The young man's hands were on her hips, and she had to admit that she didn't mind. Somehow, Adele had managed to trade places with her over Desa Nin Leean's objections. Miri didn't mind that either. Desa had been dreadful company since Ofalla.

She smiled, then let her eyes drop to the pommel of her saddle. "So, Lommy," she began. "I notice you're a little less shy...Or at least a little more familiar with me." Miri wiggled her hips to emphasize the placement of his hands.

She ventured a peek over her shoulder.

He was wincing at her comment, his body suddenly as stiff as a board. "Look, um, Miss...Nin...Miri!" Now, *there* was the uncertain lad that she couldn't resist teasing. "I do not mean to be rude, but-"

"Relax. I'm only joking."

"That's good."

It was hard to force these next words out of her mouth – this was a difficult subject that she had been avoiding – but sooner or later, you had to address the painful realities you would rather hide away in the closet. "You must be in a lot of pain," she said. "After losing Sebastian."

"I thought you hated Sebastian."

With her lips pressed together, Miri looked up toward the heavens, then shrugged her shoulders. "I didn't hate him," she explained. "I just saw him for what he was. A sad man and a dangerous fool...But I didn't want him dead."

Tommy's grip on her hips tightened, and he leaned forward, shuddering. She could feel his breath on the back of her neck. "I did love him," he said. "But...I think I always saw him for what he was too."

Miri patted his hand.

A quick glance toward Desa revealed that the woman was riding with her eyes on the distant horizon. It was never smart to conclude that Desa Nin Leean wasn't paying attention, but she seemed to be distracted.

It might have something to do with Adele, who practically cuddled up with her cheek on Desa's shoulder. The mayor's niece was certainly content to be sharing a mount with the object of her affections. That would not end well, but it wasn't Miri's business. Best to focus on the battles she could win.

"Sometimes," she began, "Sometimes, it's hard to acknowledge the failings in those we love."

Tommy grunted.

The sound of an approaching rider was followed by Marcus galloping up on his gray and then pulling the beast to a stop in front of them. "The road is empty for at least three miles ahead of us. No ships on the water."

"Thank you, Marcus," Desa said.

Miri tossed her head back and rolled her eyes. Her brother wore the mantle of the watchful protector with such dedication that it was almost a cliché. Sometimes, she wanted to punch his fool face.

"Bendarian is still ahead of us," Adele said. "By twenty miles at least. Maybe more. I can't say."

Tommy growled, and Miri looked back to see the lad gritting his teeth and shaking his head. "We ride from sunup to sundown and the man keeps gaining ground on us," he spat. "How is that possible?"

"Black magic?" Miri suggested.

"It's not magic," Desa said automatically. "But I think you have the right of it, Miri. When we fought in that warehouse, he just disappeared. I thought perhaps the power had consumed him, but it seems he has become capable of instantaneous travel."

"If that's true," Tommy put in, "then why not go directly to his destination. Why waste time with riding...or walking...or whatever he's doing?"

Desa hunched over in the saddle, exhaling forcefully and shaking her head. "I don't know," she lamented. "Perhaps he can't. The Nether seems to be chaos made manifest. It may be that the only way to control it is to restrict the scope of each feat he performs."

They continued on in silence for a while.

Miri found herself wishing that she could be elsewhere, perhaps on a ship headed downriver, far away from Bendarian. She had only been a girl when his experiments with Field Binding had killed a dozen people and driven twice as many mad. Any ambition she might have felt to find the ether for herself had vanished that day.

But if Desa Nin Leean was correct, then the fate of the world itself depended on them stopping Bendarian from doing whatever he intended to do. Well, she would do her part, but she didn't have to like it.

Right then, she was most worried about the young man who shared a saddle with her. Tommy was holding himself together well enough, but it was clear that Sebastian's death had rattled him...and though she couldn't be certain, Miri had a sinking suspicion that Desa was to blame somehow.

It wasn't anything she could pinpoint, but the woman was remarkably tight-lipped whenever the subject came up. If Desa *had* taken the young man's life, it would be best for everyone if she simply told Tommy. Miri didn't want to see what would happen if he found out on his own. She would have to keep his spirits up.

And she could think of several ways she might do that.

TOMMY KNELT in the grass by a steaming pot of chicken stew he had heated with one of Marcus's Infused coins. Preparing it had used up most of their supplies, but they would all eat well tonight. The scent alone was worth it in Tommy's estimation.

The small disk of light that Desa's ring projected over the grass offered very little visibility, but he could make out his four companions all standing around and waiting for a good meal. It was nearly an hour past sundown; they had ridden all day, and they were all very hungry.

Desa was at the edge of the light, tending to Midnight, gently brushing the horse's mane. Even at this distance,

Tommy could hear the soft sounds of her murmurs, but she was too far off for him to make out anything specific.

With his hands shoved into the pockets of his duster, Marcus paced a line back and forth through the grass. The look of concentration on his face made it clear that he did not want to be disturbed.

Then there was Adele.

The mayor's niece sat in the grass with her legs drawn up against her chest, hugging her knees and gazing out upon the river. A light breeze made her long golden hair flutter. Tommy had tried more than once to engage her in conversation, and he had received only scorn for his trouble. In fact, the only one who wanted to talk to him was Miri. Marcus had no love for him, and Desa had been avoiding him since Ofalla.

Closing his eyes, Tommy leaned forward to inhale the aroma of stew. Warm steam caressed his face and left a dampness on his skin. "I think it's ready!" he called out. "We should probably eat."

Marcus was the first one to strut over and extend his hand with all the arrogance of a king who simply expected a servant to fetch his wine. Tommy ladled stew into one of the small pewter bowls that Miri carried in her pack.

Adele came next, and she at least had the decency to mutter thanks before she took her bowl and went off to sit quietly by herself.

"It smells delicious, Tommy," Desa said as she approached.

He looked up at her with a great big grin and let out a trill of nervous laughter. "I certainly hope so, ma'am," he replied. "I learned to make it for my dad back before they put me in a jail cell."

When he filled her bowl, Desa offered a curt nod of thanks, then turned her back on him and made her way down to the riverbank. Perhaps she wanted to be alone as well. Or perhaps she was just trying to avoid Adele. Any fool could see that those two were falling for each other, and Tommy wished they would just hurry up and admit it already. It would do wonders to ease the tension of this long journey westward. He was also hoping that Desa would resume guiding him in his meditations.

Miri came over to sit with him, and when he handed her a bowl, she offered a smile and a pat on his leg. "You did a good job." She lifted a spoonful of chicken to her mouth, then closed her eyes as she savoured the taste.

"Glad you like it."

"I do."

"How are you?"

Tossing his head back, Tommy blinked several times as he pondered the question. "I suppose I'm all right." The fatigue in his voice was surprising even to him. "The more that I think about it, the more I realize Sebastian was destined to come to a bad end."

Miri frowned but nodded slowly as if his answer were a foregone conclusion. "That doesn't make it any easier," she said. "For what it's worth, I'm sorry."

"You didn't kill him."

"No...I didn't."

Something in her tone caught Tommy's attention, and when he looked, he found her staring wistfully toward the river. Now, what was all that about? He knew that Miri had followed Sebastian to Bendarian's townhouse. He knew that she had caught Sebastian in the act of his betrayal, but...she wouldn't have *done* something to him, would she?

Tommy was no fool; he had seen the woman brandish

throwing knives and use them with deadly skill. Might she have harmed Sebastian, and if so, could he really trust her, knowing that she had-

"No, Lommy," she said. "I didn't kill your lover."

Tommy felt his mouth drop open, then shook his head with enough force to make himself dizzy. "How..." He had to resist the urge to scramble backward to get away from her. "Can you read minds?"

"I am Ka'adri," she explained. "We are trained in the art of observation. The Synod sends us out into the world to watch and to report what we see. Aladar is strong, but we are only one small nation. If the others chose to invade..."

"I see...Why are you telling me this?"

Miri shuffled a little closer to him, close enough that her arm touched his, and when she gazed intently into his eyes, Tommy felt very nervous. "Because," she said. "To gain trust, you must offer trust. And I want you to trust me."

"Well...That was something."

HAVING DISCARDED HER COAT, Desa stood by the river in pants and a simple work shirt with the sleeves rolled up. The sound of the Vinrella rushing past was almost soothing. In the last few days, they had seen two ships sail past, both heading eastward toward Ofalla, but at night, the river was always quiet.

The sound of footsteps alerted her to Marcus's arrival. The man was good – only a trained ear would notice his approach – but he had never been able to sneak up on her. She suspected that he kept trying just to prove he could.

"The girl is a liability," he said. "Send her back to Ofalla."

Closing her eyes, Desa breathed in slowly. "You think I

haven't tried?" she asked, spinning around to face him. "Adele is determined to follow us. So, unless you want me to resort to violence..."

With his back to the light cast by her ring, Marcus was just a shadow to her eyes, but she could tell that he was scowling. "Perhaps you should," he replied. "It would drive the message home."

"Blunt as ever," she said, stepping up to him. "I really must admire your singularity of purpose."

"You have feelings for the girl."

"Of course I do," she snapped. "But if you think that's why I allow her to remain, you are sadly mistaken. I know next to nothing about Adele Delarac except that her talent for manipulating the Ether is beyond anything I have seen before. If she is indeed one of Bendarian's agents, I would rather keep an eye on her."

An uncomfortable silence stretched on while Marcus considered what she had said. Had the man always been this difficult? They had learned Field Binding together, though Desa had picked it up faster. She could remember his gruffness, but the truth was that she had spared little thought for Marcus in those days, and – so far as she knew, anyway – he had spared even less for her.

There had never been much in the way of affection between them. They respected each other, but they had never been friends. And the thought of anything beyond that was laughable. Even if Desa had fancied men, she would not have fancied him. "Perhaps you are right," he said at last.

"I'm glad you agree."

He raised a single finger as if to warn her that the consensus between them was quite fragile. "But," he said, "if

I become convinced that she is a threat to us, I will kill her myself."

Hearing that hurt more than Desa would have liked, but she schooled her face and nodded. "I would expect nothing less."

19

The overcast sky was fading from gray to blue when they finally stopped after the end of another long day in the saddle. Across the dark waters of the Vinrella, Desa saw a town of wooden buildings sprawling haphazardly along the opposite shore, and behind it, a forest of conifers that dwarfed every one of the small houses.

The lamps were lit, and she could even make out a few people walking along the street closest to the northern river-bank. A large wooden ferry was moored in the marina, but there was little chance that anyone would be coming across at this hour.

Her little group stood on the southern shore, near a second dock for the ferry, all staring wistfully across the river to the town on the other side. Thrasa was an odd village; cramped between a forest on one side and the Vinrella on the other, it spread out along the shoreline in an almost crescent-shaped pattern.

Adele took a few steps toward the water's edge, inclined her chin and then sniffed disdainfully. "We should continue westward," she said. "I've watched Bendarian through the Ether, and I can promise you that he isn't in that town."

Her suggestion produced a growl from Marcus. The man showed his teeth as he came forward and shook his head. "Fool of a girl," he spat. "And where do you suppose we'll find supplies if we don't stop here?"

Adele coloured and lowered her eyes. Desa felt very little in the way of sympathy. The other woman's suggestion was rather foolish; in fact, it almost seemed *designed* to leave them stranded in the wilderness without food or ammunition. Resisting the urge to glare at Adele took some effort.

Tommy stood a way back from the riverbank with the bridle of his father's horse in hand. A frown betrayed his unease. "How are we supposed to get across?" he asked. "We might have to wait until tomorrow."

"And lose another day," Marcus grumbled.

In answer to the young man's question, Desa raised a closed fist toward the distant town and pulsed the Light-Source in her ring. She let it flicker again and again at full intensity. That should get someone's attention.

Of course, she had to stand there for about ten minutes before she noticed two men standing on the opposite shore and pointing at her. Her arm was getting tired. How long before they sent someone across to investigate?

Tommy chose that moment to step up beside her and frown thoughtfully at her attempt to signal the townsfolk. "That's clever," he said. "Um...Mrs. Kin-Uh...Desa. Do you still intend to teach me Field Binding?"

"I will teach you," she muttered.

"I see."

No doubt he was hoping for some clarification as to why she had been avoiding him since they left Ofalla. How on Earth did she tell him that it was because she was the one who had killed his lover? Another problem that she had hoped to evade for at least a little while longer.

When she didn't offer any further explanation, Tommy turned away and walked back to the horses, muttering to himself. Desa clicked her tongue. She would have to deal with that soon, before she lost every shred of the young man's trust.

At last, she saw a team of men releasing the ferry from its mooring cables. It wasn't long before the large wooden craft was drifting across the river toward them. About time. The last bit of twilight was fading from the sky. Desa kept pulsing her ring. If she stopped now, they might turn back.

Finally, she heard the shouts and grunts of men working the oars as the Ferry pulled up to the dock. A man on the deck approached the railing with a lantern in hand. This one was short and spindly with a wrinkly face and white hair that poked out from underneath his top hat. "What's this then?" he shouted.

Desa approached the dock, craning her neck to squint up at him. "My friends and I would like to request passage across the river," she said. "Do forgive us for our sudden arrival at this late hour."

The boat's captain – at least, that was what she assumed he was – was none too pleased by her answer. He shook his head and then leaned over the railing to glare at her. "And what of that blinking light?"

She lifted her hand and triggered the Source within her ring, causing it to glow with intense light. The captain, though visible to her in the lantern light, now looked as though he were standing under the noonday sun. "The gift of Aladar," Desa said. "Which I will offer to you in exchange for passage. In addition to whatever money we can spare."

"Rings that glow?"

"That and much more." It pleased her to see that he was genuinely curious about Field Binding. True, many people called it witchcraft – and some even went so far as to run her out of town – but there were a few with enough wits to realize that a thing wasn't evil simply because they did not understand it. "Will you give us passage?"

The man bit his lip as he considered it, then nodded slowly. "Very well then," he said at last. In the blink of an eye, he was turning his back on her and barking orders at his crew. "Palmer! Fromm! Get the plank extended! And be quick about it, damn you! I have enough trouble with Elsa as it is, going across at this hour, and the Almighty take me for a liar, I won't have her fretting long into the night just because you louts decided to lollygag!"

A SHORT WHILE LATER, she was standing at the prow of the ship and watching as the orange lights of Thrasa crept closer and closer. The sounds of men grunting and a few muttered curses filled her ears, but she ignored them. Her mind was focused on how to tell Tommy the truth of what she had done...and she had no answer.

Footsteps drew her out of her reverie.

She turned around to find Captain Rufus Sharp – that was what the man called himself – stomping toward her with a grimace that could shatter rocks into sand. "Idiots, the lot of them."

Pursing her lips, Desa studied the man for a long moment. "You don't seem to think much of your crew," she said, her eyebrows climbing. "Forgive me, Captain, but it does not inspire confidence."

The man replied with a mocking smile and a shake of his head. "Confidence," he said, stepping up to the railing.

He braced his hands upon it and bent forward to peer into the darkness. "Half my men wish that I had left you and yours on the riverbank. And the other half think I should have shot you."

Desa spun to stand beside him with her hands clasped behind her back, breathing deeply to soothe her agitation. "I see," she said at last. "Then I suppose I must thank you for your forbearance."

"I am not a fool, woman," he muttered. "Nor am I some sad country bumpkin who never passed beyond the borders of his little village. I have sailed many waters before age humbled me."

He turned his head to regard her with a pinched expression, then nodded once. "I have seen marvels," he went on. "And the inventions of the Aladri were not least among them. I know they are not magic."

"Then you are wiser than most."

"But now I must beg your forgiveness, madam," he said. "And ask that you explain how that ring of yours works."

She felt her lips curl into a small smile, then lowered her eyes to the deck under her feet. "It draws energy from the Ether," she explained. "I can make several for you before we arrive in Thrasa, but you will have to learn to touch the Ether yourself if you wish to replenish them after their energy is expended."

The captain crossed his arms, took one step back and then shook his head. "I don't suppose that this is something you can teach before we reach the northern shore." He must have noticed something in her face because he stifled a grimace and then turned his head to stare out on the water. "No...I thought not."

"It takes years of practice."

"As I suspected."

"But I can teach you the basics," Desa quickly added. If she had her way, she would teach Field Binding to every last man, woman and child on this continent. Sweet Mercy, they might need it if Bendarian unleashed the Nether upon this world."Now, perhaps you should give me the objects you wish to have Infused. I will need a few moments of quiet to complete the task."

A STOUT MATRON with brown hair that she wore pulled back in a bun and spectacles riding a little too low on her freckled nose looked up the instant they walked through the door of her little inn. "Travelers coming in at all hours," she said, maneuvering between the round wooden tables spread across the floor of the saloon.

Marcus stepped forward to meet her, his boots thumping on the wooden floor, and then extended his hand to offer several bank notes. The innkeeper gave them a cursory inspection, then looked up to study his face. "From the Ofallan bank, eh?" she asked. "I suppose they're trustworthy."

Leaning one shoulder against the door-frame, Miri yawned and then stifled it by clamping a hand over her mouth. "Goodness," she murmured, ignoring her brother's sad attempts to haggle over the price of a night's stay. "All the time in the saddle does leave a girl worn out."

Prim and prissy Miss Adele Delarc was waiting just outside the inn with her feet together, toes pointing forward, and her hands clasped in front of herself. She was quite focused on what Marcus was saying. Well, let the fool of a woman fret about it. No doubt she thought she could do better. Perhaps she really could.

Miri turned her back on her brother, pushed past Adele

and then stepped out into the open street. Despite its ever-expanding borders, Thrasa felt very much like a quaint little village. Houses made of wooden logs were spaced almost haphazardly on either side of the road.

Tommy was waiting with his hands shoved into the pockets of his trousers, his eyes downcast – as usual – and his shoulders hunched up. "I could use some sleep," he said in response to her earlier remark. "Suppose I'll be stuck with Marcus again."

"You could stay with me," Miri replied with a devilish grin.

The young man looked up at her, and his eyes widened until it seemed as though they might fall out. "But we-" he stammered. "I mean...Men and women...sharing a room together. It wouldn't be proper."

"Curious," Miri replied. "You shared a room with your lover in Ofalla, and no one thought anything of it. Why should it only be a problem when it's a man and a woman."

"I..."

"Don't tell me you and Sebastian never shared a bed."

Spots of crimson flooded Lommy's cheeks, and he stepped back, pressing a fist to his mouth and clearing his throat forcefully. "We have... I mean..." His cheeks puffed up just before he let out a wheeze. "We have been intimate, yes."

Miri approached him with her hands clasped behind his back, smiling down at her own shoes. "Well, then I don't see why you would see an impropriety in sharing a room with me."

"I-"

"Relax, Tommy."

He swallowed visibly, then squinted at her as if he

couldn't quite believe what he was seeing. "You called me, Tommy," he observed.

Now, it was Miri who blushed. Damn this fool of a boy; it had been years since she had been guilty of that kind of slip. "Yes, I suppose I did," she said. "Well, take whatever satisfaction you can find in it. It won't be happening again."

She patted his cheek.

BENDARIAN EMERGED from his trance to find his body much the same as he had left it, sitting cross-legged in the grass near a solitary oak tree with leaves that sighed in the cool night wind. The small tent that he would sleep in tonight had been erected, and he could hear the crackling of Morley's fire.

Grunting at the pain in his knees – the man's complaints on that subject had been numerous – Morley sat on a boulder with his elbows on his thighs and steepled his fingers as he observed the flames. He said nothing.

A frown tightened Bendarian's mouth as he unconsciously ran a hand over his bald head. There were still a few stray hairs sprouting from his scalp. He would have to see to that, but he was hoping that restoring his youth would alleviate the need.

The Nether beckoned.

It tantalized.

Licking his lips, Bendarian shut his eyes and then let out a shuddering breath. "She is in Thrasa," he said. "And the girl is still with her...If I had known Charles Delarac was harbouring a Sensitive. Well...No matter."

Morley glanced in his direction, a scowl betraying the man's irritation. "And what good does such knowledge do us?" he said. "I'd go back and kill her myself if not for my current...predicament."

Abruptly, the man stood up, grunting from the effort, then twisted around and lifted the boulder as if it weighed no more than a pebble. He threw it with considerable speed, sending it flying at least two hundred feet before it crashed to the ground and shattered on impact. "Strength and frailty at the same time," he muttered. "What have you done to me, Bendarian?"

"No more than what you asked," Bendarian spat. "Show some respect."

"Respect," Morley sneered, making no attempt to hide his disdain. "You promised me life everlasting, but all you've done is hasten my journey to the grave."

With a hand over his mouth, Bendarian shut his eyes and breathed deeply to calm himself. "I have already assured you that I will remedy the situation," he said. "I granted you invulnerability by tethering your life to mine."

"And then you made yourself old."

Bendarian snapped his fingers.

The gesture brought an immediate flash of pain to Morley, who sank to his knees with his fingertips massaging his temples. "Stop," he whimpered. "Stop please...please. I will obey you."

"Your life-force is tethered to mine," Bendarian said. "That grants me certain...Let's just call them privileges."

Ignoring the pain in his knees, Bendarian rose, then exhaled and shook his head. "I expect a modicum of respect henceforth," he said. "Unless you wish your eternity to be a most unpleasant one."

Morley was folded up and clutching his bald scalp with both hands. "Yes! Yes!" he panted. "Whatever you say."

With a dismissive wave of his hand, Bendarian withdrew

the pain from his servent's body, and Morley began to gasp. It was as though the man just couldn't fill his lungs fast enough. "Now, I have work to do," Bendarian said. "You will remain here."

Sinking into a deep trance, he stretched out with his thoughts to commune with the Ether. The world changed before his eyes, solid objects collapsing into violent storms of particles. He soaked in the awareness of everything around him. He knew that there was no one else around for miles, not another soul besides himself and Morley.

Being in communion with the Ether of the Earth, its shape and curvature, he knew the exact distance and direction he would have to travel to reach Thrasa. Of course, he would not be able to make the journey in a single jump.

The Nether pounded on his mind like wind trying to smash through a window. It was getting harder and harder to resist that call. Fortunately, he would not have to do so this time. He severed himself from the Ether and let the Nether consume him.

It was so...different.

There was a new awareness, yes, but not the precise intimate understanding of his surroundings that came from contact with the Ether. He did not see the world as a tempest of particles. It was more an understanding of natural laws.

And how he could break them.

Bendarian grinned as a new idea occurred to him. "You will be pleased, my friend," he said, turning to Morley. The man was still on his knees in the grass, still clutching his head and trying to push past the pain. "I have found a way to regain my youth."

Morley looked up with wonder in his eyes, firelight

casting flickering shadows across his face. "You can?" he stammered. "How...How would you do that?"

"It's really quite simple," Bendarian answered. "All I have to do is reclaim the life-force that I've wasted on you."

He raised a hand, palm up, and crooked his finger. Morley screamed and spasmed as his body shriveled up. His skin turned gray, then crumbled to dust, leaving only a frail skeleton in its place. Seconds later, that too collapsed to ash. All that remained of Morley was a pile of tattered clothes.

Closing his eyes, Bendarian tilted his head back and felt renewed strength wash over him. Silky, blonde hair grew from his scalp, falling to the small of his back. The wrinkles on his face faded away. His muscles no longer ached.

"Now," he said. "To end this."

He drew upon the Nether and ripped his way through the fabric of reality. And rip it did! A crack stretched across the sky from horizon to horizon. The world seemed to blur and split apart like a cracked eggshell, leaving a new world in its place.

He was now standing on the banks of the Vinrella, near the bend where it turned northward toward High Falls. He had traveled a good thirty miles in a matter of seconds. At this rate, he should be in Thrasa by morning.

20

Desa reclined in the copper bathtub, submerged to her shoulders in hot soapy water, her head hung back over the edge. Her eyes were shut as she reveled in the blessed joy of tired muscles unwinding.

Mrs. Collins, the matronly woman who had inherited this small inn from her dead husband, had been more than eager to draw the bath herself. "The least I could do," she said, "for a woman who travels with the likes of him." She had favoured Marcus with a scowl that intensified with every syllable.

Desa almost laugh.

If the woman only knew...

Marcus was the very least of Desa's worries. Between Tommy's gentle but insistent attempts to ferret out why she was avoiding him and Adele's penchant for making herself a nuisance, it was likely that she would go mad before they found Bendarian. That might be for the best. A crazy Desa Kincaid might actually be able to end him once and for all.

She clicked her tongue in annoyance. When exactly did she start thinking of herself as Desa Kincaid? Martin was a good friend, and their sham of a marriage had alleviated certain legal complications, but she had always been Desa Nin Leean.

Then again, perhaps she no longer had a right to that name. She had turned her back on her Aladri heritage not once but twice. And Martin...Dear, sweet Martin Kincaid. The man had known that Desa would never be able to love him – not as a wife should love her husband – and he had married her anyway.

In their years together, she had seen him look at other women, seen him develop an affection for more than one bright-eyed young lass, but no woman would have him while he was tied to her. She had been searching for a way to free Martin from their marriage.

And then Morley had killed him.

Desa sat up, scooping up water with both hands and splashing it over her face. "He will pay for that," she assured herself. "Immortality just means that I get to kill him more than once."

She heard the click of the door opening.

Twisting around in the tub, she saw Adele standing in the candlelight in nothing but a thin white robe, a robe that she unbelted and let slip from her shoulders. Sweet Mercy! Did the woman have to be so beautiful?

Flowing gracefully through the room on bare feet, Adele circled the tub and then smiled for Desa. "I could use a bath myself."

Desa scooted backwards until she was cramped against the wall of the tub with her legs folded up against her chest. "I'm not sure what you think is going to happen here," she said. "But what we shared that night–"

"Was exquisite."

Adele climbed into the tub, sinking to her knees and

crawling forward with an almost predatory gleam in her eyes. Long golden hair hung loose and framed her lovely face. "You can't run from me," she whispered. "No one can run from destiny."

"I can try," Desa insisted. "By the eyes-"

Before she could finish that sentence, Adele leaned forward to kiss her mouth, and Desa melted into the other woman's embrace. Despite her objections, she found herself sliding hands over the woman's bare back, pulling Adele close and then kissing her neck.

Mercy save her fool daughter, she thought as she felt Adele's lips on her collarbone. *I never did have much sense when it came to women.*

STIFLING A YAWN WITH HIS FIST, Tommy stepped into the room he shared with Marcus. He took two steps forward, paused and then shut the door behind him with a loud *thunk.* Almighty, he was exhausted.

The room was much the same as every other one he had seen since leaving Sorla: a cramped space with two beds, one on either side of a square window. One solitary candle on a wooden table provided just enough to see without tripping over his own feet, and the scent of lavender filled the air.

Odd, that...

He had taken the time to wash a week's worth of sweat and grime off his body – it would make sleeping much easier – but he certainly hadn't put on perfume and he didn't think Marcus was the sort of man who ever did so.

The man was already asleep, a lump in the bed on the left. Marcus was a strange contradiction in many ways. The man would spring awake in an instant at any sound that might indicate danger, but he slept like the dead otherwise.

Tommy started forward with his arms hanging limp, his footsteps thumping on the floor. He shook his head. "How did I get mixed up in all this?" he whispered. "Father was right. I really don't have any sense."

The lump in Marcus's bed moved.

But it wasn't Marcus.

Once she was sitting up, it was clear that he was looking at Miri with her long hair unbound to fall over her shoulders. She held the blankets to her chest, and Tommy was fairly certain that she wasn't wearing a stitch of clothing beneath them.

He felt his face heat up, then covered his eyes with one hand. "I am *so* sorry!" he blurted out, stumbling backward. "I must have gotten the rooms mixed up! Sometimes, I really am a fool."

"You didn't get the rooms mixed up."

Tommy stopped retreating when his backside hit the door. He let his arm drop and then blinked at her. "But I..." he stammered. "Marcus told me..."

He thought the embarrassment might kill him, but matters only worsened when Miri got out and confirmed his suspicions. She moved toward him like a cat stalking her prey, her smile setting his blood on fire. "You're not in the wrong room."

"I'm not?"

"I spent an hour at the bar, regaling one of the serving maids with tales of my brother's exploits. He will be spending the night with her. I am quite sure that Desa and Adele will appreciate my absence. So...What do you want to do?"

Tommy swallowed, then forced his eyes shut and gave

his head a shake. "I...don't think it would be wise to say...what I want to do." Keeping his hands stilled required a lot of effort. "It wouldn't be proper to-"

Gently, she took his face in both hands, then stood up on her toes to kiss his lips. It was a soft kiss, but Tommy felt himself responding. He slipped his arms around her and pulled her close.

Miri stepped back, smiled and lowered her eyes almost bashfully. "I've never been one who cared much for what was proper," she said. "So, it's up to you. You can sleep in the other bed, and I won't be offended. Or you can sleep next to me. But if you sleep next to me then you do so *without* clothing."

Well, put that way, the decision was easy.

He kissed Miri again, and she responded with such eagerness that his back thumped against the door. Tommy lifted her up, and she wrapped her legs around his waist as he carried her to the bed.

Her hands clawed at his shirt, pulling it up over his head and tossing it to the floor. Tommy kissed her neck, her ear...He felt a little guilty, almost as if he were betraying Sebastian. Which was asinine since Sebastian had betrayed him. For once, though, he pushed that voice away and just focused on the moment.

ADELE ROLLED Desa onto her back, her soft hands gliding lightly over Desa's belly. The woman sat up, and golden hair spilled over her face. "Still think I'm in league with Bendari-an?" she panted. "Do you still not trust me?"

Desa shut her eyes tight, gasping for breath. "I think you are a fool of a girl." Her hand settled onto the back of

Adele's head, pulling her close so that she could press her lips to the other woman's neck.

"Why is that?"

Desa pulled back, blinking. "Because you have lived your whole life wanting for nothing," she said. "And you walked away from all that to follow some damn fool of a woman on her quest for vengeance."

She gasped when she felt Adele's touch, and it became very hard to think through the haze of lust. She just wanted to push conscious thought aside and lose herself entirely in the other woman's embrace.

But Adele sank her teeth into Desa's neck, then brought her lips to Desa's ear and whispered, "What if I told you it was fate?"

"There's no such thing as fate."

"Oh, I disagree I-"

Unable to finish that sentence, Adele cried out as she writhed under Desa's touch. Desa pushed her down onto her back, then kissed her lips with an almost savage ferocity. If nothing else, that would make the fool girl shut up!

LYING flat on his back with his head sinking into the pillow, Tommy shut his eyes and let Miri take the lead. It almost felt as if she were trying to take care of him, as if she thought she could soothe away his pain and sorrow. And...she wasn't wrong.

She bent low to kiss him, and Tommy rose up to meet her. His hands glided over the soft skin of her back. It surprised him when she bit his ear and then rasped. "You're very good at this."

He froze.

Miri smiled down at him, shaking her head. "Don't lose

heart now, Lommy," she teased. "I meant what I said; you are good at this."

"I've never done this before."

Miri nuzzled his nose and giggled. She gave him a light peck on the cheek. "Didn't you tell me that you were intimate with Sebastian?" she asked. "That counts."

"Well...It was mostly me taking care of him."

"Why am I not surprised."

Overwhelmed by a sudden wave of passion, Tommy threw his arms around Miri and rolled her onto her back. His mouth found hers, and then her fingers were grabbing a fistful of his hair. "Thank you," he whispered.

"You don't have to thank me; I wanted to do this."

"Well...Just the same."

IN TAN PANTS and her sleeveless undershirt, Desa sat on the small table in her room and gazed through the window at the dark night outside. With two fingers, she slipped a toothpick into her mouth and chewed it anxiously.

Adele came over in her thin white robe, seating herself in the only wooden chair the innkeeper had put in this room. "You should be sleeping," she said. "I am quite sure you'll want to cover as much ground as possible tomorrow."

"You needn't worry about me."

A sly smile spread on Adele's face and she laughed. It was sweet, musical laughter that made Desa's heart flutter. "Is that not one of my duties?" the woman asked. "Don't lovers worry about each other?"

Desa sat with her hands gripping the edge of the table, her head hanging as she let out a sigh. "Listen to me, Adele," she began. "I am not the sort of woman you want to court. I will bring you nothing but misery."

To her great frustration, the other woman got out of her chair, leaned forward and kissed her lightly on the forehead. "Something troubles you," Adele said. "Tell me about it, and I will do what I can."

"There is nothing you can do."

Adele's fingers touched the underside of Desa's chin and turned her face up so that she had to look into the other woman's eyes. She found sympathy there. Sympathy and concern. By the eyes of Vengeance, how was it possible that Desa Kincaid had let this pampered rich girl ensnare her?

"What do I worry about?" Desa muttered. "I face a man who wields a power that I cannot even begin to understand. I should think the source of my discomfort would be obvious."

"You will defeat him."

Touching her fingertips to her eyelids, Desa massaged away the beginnings of a headache. "I suppose you're going to tell me that it's destiny," she said. "You will forgive me if I find little comfort in that."

"I'm going to tell you that you are the most talented woman I have ever met." When she looked up to find Adele standing over her, she found nothing but sincerity in the other woman's unflinching stare. "And that you will find a way."

"Perhaps there is a good reason to keep you around." The words were out of her mouth before she even realized what she was saying, but there it was. She was quickly developing a fondness for this woman.

"I like to think so," Adele said. "Now come. Let me help you rest."

. . .

STILL CATCHING HIS BREATH, Tommy rolled over on his side and slipped an arm around Miri's stomach. She snuggled against him, sighing softly, and rested her hand on top of his. Tommy felt relaxed...and a little confused.

Closing his eyes, he nuzzled the back of her neck. "Why?" he murmured. "I'm still a little confused as to why you would want to do this with me.

She twisted around in his arms, facing him, and then gave him a soft kiss on the nose. "Because you're sweet," she answered. "And I enjoy your company. Now, the real question is why you have such a hard time believing that I would want to."

"I was never popular with girls."

"No?"

A smile that Tommy didn't even try to fight came on suddenly. "Now, who's having a hard time accepting the obvious?" he said. "Take a good look at me, Miri. I'm hardly the big strapping man girls dream about."

She pushed him onto his back, and then she was on top of him, waves of dark hair cascading over them both. Miri kissed his lips. "Maybe you don't know women as well as you think you do."

She sat up, flinging that hair back over her shoulder with a quick toss of her head, and then smiled down at him. "You would make a wonderful partner for any woman," she said. "Or any man."

Blushing hard, Tommy shut his eyes and let his head sink into the pillow. "Well, I'm glad you think so," he mumbled. "At least someone does."

She swatted him.

He was about to protest, but before he could get one word out, Miri fell on him and kissed him again. He was suddenly very aware of her warm body. His hands were sliding over her back. "If we keep doing this," he panted. "We won't get any sleep."

"Who cares," she said between kisses. "We'll sleep when we're dead."

BENDARIAN WALKED ALONG THE RIVERBANK. For a moment, he did, anyway. Halfway between one step and the next, he called upon the Nether and ripped his way through the fabric of space and time. The world around him was torn apart to leave another world in its place.

Without breaking stride, he was suddenly in the front yard of a farmhouse, walking toward a quaint little home with a gabled roof and orange lights in its windows. He saw a family through one.

And they saw him.

The farmer, a bald man with a thick beard who wore overalls over his white shirt, turned his head to look out the window. His eyes widened when he saw Bendarian, and he quickly leaped out of his chair.

Bendarian smiled a menacing smile, shaking his head as he approached the house. "Busy little bees," he whispered. "Time to set you to work."

The front door opened, and the farmer stepped out onto his porch with a rifle in his hands. "Who are you, stranger?" he demanded. "What do you mean by showing up at my door in the middle of the night?"

Bendarian reached for the rifle.

It flew out of the farmer's hands, zipped across the yard and slammed hard against Bendarian's outstretched palm. He closed his fingers around the weapon, paused for half a moment to admire it and then tossed it to the ground.

The farmer was gaping at him, blinking slowly as if he

didn't quite believe what he was seeing. "What are you?" he whispered. "What...What kind of devilry is this?"

Bendarian stepped onto the porch.

The other man cringed against the front door, tears welling up as he moved to block Bendarian's way. "Please," he whimpered. "Spare my family. Take me."

Gently, Bendarian touched a single finger to the other man's forehead and watched as the farmer turned gray. Every last spec of colour faded. Not just from the man's skin and beard but from his clothing as well.

His eyes turned black.

Stepping past him, Bendarian found the man's wife cowering with her arms around their son. Both were just inside the house, and both were backing away from the door. "I won't hurt you."

They turned and ran deeper into the house.

Bendarian drew upon the Nether.

The world split apart, and suddenly he was inside this family's small sitting room with both mother and son running toward him. They both stopped short when they saw him in their path.

"Don't be afraid," Bendarian said. "I come to give you purpose."

He touched the mother's forehead, and she turned gray. The boy was next, transforming before his eyes. "Go and join your father," Bendarian said. "We have work to do."

21

Descending the stairs to the saloon on the first floor, Desa set her hat upon her head and nodded once in thanks. "You run a fine establishment," she said, stopping on the final step. "It was the best night's sleep I've had in months."

Mrs. Collins was waiting at the foot of the stairs in a gray dress with long sleeves, her hair pulled back into a bun. The woman sniffed but returned Desa's nod. "I should hope so," she said. "The Wagon Wheel is the finest establishment in all of Thrasa. We have a reputation to maintain."

Desa stepped past the woman into a saloon that was already filled with half a dozen men. One fellow with a large belly and a thick brown beard that stretched from ear to ear was eating a breakfast of eggs and ham. Desa could smell it from here, and it made her painfully aware of her own hunger.

She turned around.

Mrs. Collins was standing there with fists on her hips, a thin smile on her face as she shook her head. "About to rush off without breakfast, were you?" she asked. "Oh, it pains me to admit it, but there are some women with as much sense as the average man."

Seating herself on a barstool, Desa folded her hands in her lap and bowed her head to the innkeeper. "I'll have what he's having," she said. "And some tea if you have it. Any flavour will suffice."

The waiting made her belly rumble, but it gave her time to think. She had spoken to Marcus on her way down; the man intended to purchase new supplies before they set out across the river. Desa was beginning to wonder just how much money he had left. Her own supply was diminishing.

She needed a good bounty. Bring a thief of a murder to the local sheriff's office, and you would walk away with enough cash to keep a grown man fed for at least a month. She had spent the last decade living on whatever funds she and Martin could cobble together from the bounties they brought in. The man had never learned Field Binding in spite of her many attempts to teach him, but he was an excellent tracker. She had learned most of what she knew from him.

When there were no bounties to hunt, she and Martin would sometimes take work as deputies. Any reservation that a magistrate might have about a woman in his employ quickly vanished when he saw what she could do. Assuming, of course, that he didn't cry witch and declare her a wanted fugitive. That had happened more than once.

Perhaps she should visit the sheriff's office; she might see a wanted poster. But that would mean delaying her pursuit of Bendarian, and she didn't think she could afford to do that this time.

Mrs. Collins put a plate of fried eggs and cooked ham in front of her, and Desa wasted no time digging in. She shoved a bit of meat in her mouth, chewed thoroughly and then looked up to say, "Delicious."

The innkeeper sniffed.

Dabbing her mouth with a napkin, Desa shut her eyes and let out a breath. "I was wondering," she began. "Have there been any strangers in town lately? I'm looking for two old men with a talent for making everyone else nervous."

Mrs. Collins folded her arms and backed away until she almost bumped the shelf of liquor bottles behind the bar. "And what would a smart woman like you be wanting with these...malevolent old men?"

"I'm a bounty hunter."

"Oh really?" Mrs. Collins narrowed her eyes as she studied Desa through the lenses of those spectacles. "I haven't heard tell of any wanted men who fit that description. Not that I concern myself with such matters, you understand."

Desa shoveled food into her mouth with the gusto of a starving man. She paused just long enough to say, "They're extremely dangerous. If you see them, do not approach them or do anything to reveal that you recognize them."

"Where are these men from?"

"Downriver," Desa answered. "From Ofalla."

"How typical."

Desa looked up to favour the other woman with a smile. "Thank you for a delicious breakfast." She hopped off the stool, set her hand down upon the bar and pulled it back to reveal several coins. "I wish you good fortune."

With that, she turned to go.

MIRI SHUFFLED through the streets of Thrasa with her hands inside the pockets of her coat, hunching up her shoulders against a cool wind that blew in off the river. Her hair was tied back again, and her hat rested snugly on her head.

All around her, people flowed up the street, most going in the opposite direction: a young mother in a green dress who ushered her son and daughter forward with a hand on each child's shoulder, a man in dungarees and a stained work shirt who followed a wagon full of lumber toward the water's edge.

The morning was bright and clear without a cloud in the sky, and it was getting warmer now that spring was rushing at full speed toward summer. She looked out upon the river to see a wooden ship with large white sails heading eastward.

The sound of footsteps caught her attention.

Grinning down at herself, Miri shook her head. "Right on schedule," she muttered, turning around to meet the man she knew she would see.

Tommy was rushing toward her and breathing hard, his face flushed with just a bit of pink in his cheeks. "Hi there," he said, stumbling to a stop in front of her. "I thought...I thought I should help you get supplies."

"You don't have to do that."

"Well, it's just..."

Miri stepped forward, taking him by the shoulders and forcing him to look up so that she could gaze into those gorgeous blue eyes of his. "Lommy," she said. "I'm happy that you enjoyed last night, but I don't want you to feel like you owe me anything."

His blush deepened, and he lowered his eyes again, reaching up to scrape a knuckle across his brow. "I...I don't," he said. "And you're never gonna stop calling me Lommy, are you?"

She patted his cheek.

Content to let him join her if he was intent on doing so, Miri twirled around to stand beside him and linked arms with him. They strolled toward the water, taking their time. It was a pleasant morning, after all.

"Where are we going?" Tommy asked.

Pressing her lips together, Miri felt her eyebrows climb. "I heard there was good fruit in the markets down by the river," she said. "People buy it on trade ships that come up from the southern coast. Fresh oranges and peaches. You ever had an orange?"

"No, I have not."

Miri rested her head against his shoulder, smiling despite the little voice in the back of her mind. A voice that cautioned her not to push too quickly with a man who had just lost someone he loved. "We have them in Aladar," she said. "They're delicious."

"I'd like to see Aladar one day."

She spun to stand in front of him, stood on her toes and brushed his lips with hers. "Well, you're in luck!" she exclaimed. "I plan to go back there one day. Maybe you could come with me."

Tommy seemed to be drowning in chagrin, but he smiled and nodded just the same. "I'd like that," he said. "Very much. Oh no-"

"What's wrong?"

He didn't speak; he just stepped back and pointed into the distance behind Miri. When she turned and saw what had frightened him, her breath caught in her throat. "Oh no...Not again."

There were three gray people in the crowd: a bald fellow in overalls, a farm-wife with a carving knife and a youth with short hair, all drained of colour from head to toe. And their eyes were black.

Other people were backing away from those three as if the grayness was a disease that might spread. Miri couldn't blame them. The gray family moved with purpose toward her and Tommy.

"Get out of here," Miri hissed.

"I can help!" Tommy protested.

"Please, just go!"

He backed away from her, moving off to stand by one of the houses on the side of the street, but he did not leave. The brave, noble fool. If she got out of this with her skin intact, she was going to have her way with him again.

Mother and Son split off from the group – one going left, the other right – and moved to surround Miri on all sides. That left Father coming straight up the middle with glazed eyes fixed upon her.

She let him get closer...

Closer...

Miri turned her body for an arcing kick that took Father across the chin, breaking his jaw with a devastating *crunch*. She brought her leg down and spun around in time to see the farm wife coming at her, trying to stab her with that knife.

Miri leaned back, one hand coming up to seize the other woman's wrist. She lifted the woman's hand into the air, did a little twirl under it and then twisted around to grab her opponent's arm with both hands.

Forcing Mother to double over was difficult, but once that was done, Miri brought her knee up to smash the woman's face. That produced a groan, and Mother toppled over onto her side.

Movement on her left.

Miri whirled around to find the youth charging in, snarling and practically frothing at the mouth. By the speed of his onslaught, it was clear that he meant to tackle her, and she was fairly certain that she wouldn't be getting up if he managed it. Miri backed away to gain a few extra seconds.

Her hands were a blur, drawing throwing knives from her belt an tossing them up to catch the tip of each blade. She flung one and then the other, each knife landing in one of the gray boy's thighs.

He faltered on his next step, falling flat on his face.

Despite a broken jaw and a dark-gray bruise along his cheek, Father was coming at her again. "Run, Tommy!" she screamed. "Find Desa! Get help!"

Of course, the fool boy ignored her, choosing instead to step out into the middle of the road with his pistol in hand. He extended his hand, squinting as he pointed the gun right at Father.

He fired.

A bullet punched through one side of Father's skull and burst out the other side with a spray of black ichor. The man – if he could still be called a man – fell over, lying dead in the road.

"Come on!" Tommy shouted. "We stand a better chance if we find the others!"

IN A BLUE DRESS with short-sleeves that she must have purchased from a seamstress somewhere in this town, Adele Delarac stood at the side of the street and sniffed disdainfully at the next cart they were to visit. "I don't see why I should have to engage in this task."

Marcus ignored her, walking right past her toward a fishmonger with a thick beard who sold his wares from a cart down by the waterfront. "You will make yourself useful," he said without breaking stride. "And if you cannot do that, then I will be happy to put you on the first ship headed to Ofalla."

"I can't go home," Adele protested.

Marcus turned back to her, inclined his chin and then offered one of the glares that usually made people stop yammering and attend to their duties. "Then you will learn to contribute," he grated. "Even the fool boy can at least cook, but you? You do nothing but cling to Desa's coat-sleeves and complain."

He didn't bother giving her an opportunity to respond. The truth was, he was itching for an excuse to send her home and be done with her once and for all. Turning his back on her, he started toward the fishmonger...

And froze.

There, down by the waterfront, he saw four men with their backs to the river, all gray from head to foot. One man had long, dark hair, and another had thick silver curls. The third man wore a prominent earring, and the last had a scar on his chin. They all saw him and then quickly rushed toward him like a pack of dogs hunting a rabbit.

Marcus reached into his coat pocket and retrieved a bullet that he hadn't loaded into his gun. He tossed it down in the muck about halfway between himself and the oncoming hoard. Then he triggered the Heat-Sink within.

Mud froze with a crackling sound and ice spread out from the bullet in a wave. The four men didn't even seem to notice. They just kept on running. Long-hair slipped, falling hard on his backside. Scar went down next.

Earring managed to keep his footing and continued in a mad dash toward Marcus. The man bared teeth and hissed with every breath.

Drawing his pistol with a flourish, Marcus dropped to a crouch and extended his arm to point the gun. He fired.

A bullet hit Earring's right shin, knocking the man's leg out from under him and forcing him to topple over. He landed with his face in the frozen dirt, groaning from the pain of it.

Curly leaped over his fallen comrade.

That man was fairly large, and he flew through the air with his arms spread wide as if he meant to catch Marcus in a bear hug. Only one thing to do. Marcus stood up, and he triggered the Force-Sink in his pendant.

Curly slowed to a stop, hanging in midair.

Marcus killed the Sink and let him drop to the ground. The man landed with a loud grunt, disoriented and confused. That would do. Instinct kicked in, and Marcus aimed his gun without looking.

He fired a shot straight through Curly's chest, black blood spraying out behind the heavy man as he stumbled backward. Of course, these gray things didn't go down easily. Curly recovered his balance and came at Marcus again.

Marcus shot him a second time.

That threw the man down onto his back with black ichor pooling around his broken body. With Curly down, there was nothing between Marcus and the other two. Long-hair and Scar were both back on their feet.

Marcus spun to face Adele with his teeth clenched, then shook his head as he strode toward her. "Are you just going to stand there?" he bellowed. "Make yourself useful, girl, and *help* me!"

She was terrified, backing away from him with a gaping mouth. Her face was deathly pale. "I can't..." she whimpered. "I'm sorry, but I can't!"

Footsteps in the muck.

Marcus triggered the Gravity-Sinks in his shoes, then jumped and curled his legs as he rose into the air. He let

Long-Hair and Scar rush past beneath him, then dropped to the ground behind the pair of them.

One shot took the back of Long-Hair's thigh, forcing the man down onto his knees. Another did the same to Scar. Marcus would not aim for the centre of mass so long as these gray demons were the only thing between him and half a dozen innocent bystanders. Soft human bodies did not stop bullets.

"Marcus!"

He looked up and saw his sister scrambling down the inclined street that led away from the riverbank. Young Tommy was right behind her with another two of these gray monstrosities on his heels.

"Brilliant..." Marcus grumbled.

STEPPING out of the inn with a sigh, Desa pulled the brim of her hat down to shade her eyes. The street was busy with the onset of mid-morning. People rushed by, going this way and that, some calling greetings to those they passed. Now, where were her friends? She was of a mind to be on her way as soon as possible, but it might take some time to find suitable provisions.

She strolled across the street with her hands folded behind her back, smiling as she shook her head. "Well, you have to give the girl this much credit," Desa mumbled. "She *did* manage to take your mind off your troubles."

Whoosh.

Desa turned at the sound to find Bendarian standing directly under the sign to the Wheel and Wagon. The man had somehow regained his youth. Long blonde hair spilled over his shoulders, and his skin was as vibrant as it had ever been.

She felt her mouth drop open and blinked several times as she took a few shaky steps forward. "How did you..." Suddenly, her mouth was dry. "Radharal, this power you have found will destroy us all."

A grin split Bendarian's face as he shook his head. "You didn't think I would come to meet you, did you?" His laughter sent chills down Desa's spine. "Well, I think it's past time we finished it."

She scanned the street, trying to get a sense of the danger this man posed. There were wooden houses on each side, and any one of them might contain an entire family for all she knew. She saw a man in a long black coat a short way up the road, walking away from them with his back turned.

There were children in the other direction, a group of them playing. Their laughter filled the air as they ducked into the space between two houses. If Bendarian chose to use them as hostages...

"Looking for your friends?"

When she turned her attention back to him, she found Bendarian standing under the hanging sign with a malicious smile. "I'm afraid they won't be coming to your aid, Desa," he mocked. "You see, I've arranged for a little privacy."

She flung her coat aside to expose the gun on her hip, then drew it with lightning speed. Without even thinking, she cocked the hammer. "You want to finish it?" she said. "All right, let's finish it."

She raised her weapon.

Bendarian raised a hand to shield himself.

Desa fired with a ferocious clap of thunder and watched as two bullets jerked to a halt right in front of Bendarian's raised hand. That ring on his third finger...It must have been a Force-Sink.

Bendarian shut his eyes, and when he opened them, they were midnight-black from corner to corner. His grin widened. "I'm afraid that's not going to help you this time, my dear." He flung that hand out toward her.

Desa threw herself down on her belly just in time to hear it when her own bullets whistled past above her. They pounded the front wall of a house with a loud *thunk-thunk*. How was she supposed to kill a man with that much power?

Desa rolled aside.

Mud stained her coat as she tumbled up the roadway. With a growl, she came up on one knee and raised her gun again. Once again, she fired, and once again, her bullet came to an impotent stop a few inches away from Bendarian.

The man threw his head back with a triumphant smile on his face and roared with laughter. "Honestly, Desa!" he exclaimed. "You thought to kill me with a gun?"

Desa angled her gun upward.

CRACK!

Her next round cut the chain that supported the inn's hanging wooden sign, causing it to fall. Bendarian reacted by instinct.

He raised a hand up above his head, and the sign slowed to a stop about two inches above his outstretched fingers. Of course, that meant he was momentarily distracted. Desa adjusted her aim.

CRACK!

A bullet ripped through Bendarian's left thigh with a spray of blood, and he leaped backward with a yelp of pain. Clamping a hand over the wound, he screeched in pain and then vanished before Desa could shoot him again.

Desa stood up slowly, looking this way and that for any sign of her adversary. She saw only wooden houses and frightened people far off in the distance, each one of them gaping at her or shielding their faces as if they expected her bullets to fly their way next.

She took the opportunity to pop open the cylinder of her revolver and load it with four new bullets. It took only a few seconds; over the years, she had learned how to load a pistol in a hurry.

A soft whoosh of air caught her attention, and she spun around to find Bendarian standing about ten paces up the road. His face was red, and there were thick green veins climbing up the sides of his neck. "Your meddling no longer amuses."

The man flung his hand out, and a small ball of fire streaked from his fingertips. It sizzled through the air with a menacing crackle.

Desa fell over backward, catching herself by bracing both hands on the ground. She felt the heat as the fireball passed over her stomach, chest and face and then sped off into the distance behind her.

In a blink, she was upright again.

Bendarian thrust that hand out toward her, his fingers curled into a grasping claw, and she felt something lift her off the ground. Desa was yanked forward with her toes dragging in the dirt. Those invisible fingers were closing around her neck.

She felt tears welling up, felt them spilling over her face. "No," she panted. "No, I won't go out that easy."

She aimed her pistol down at Bendarian's feet and fired bullet after bullet, planting each one in the dirt. When she had the last one right where she wanted it, she triggered the Force-Source that she had Infused into the metal.

Bendarian was hurled backward.

He flew through the air with his legs extended, arms

flailing, and then dropped to land on his backside. Windows on either side of the street shattered as the kinetic force smashed through them.

Bendarian tumbled backward through the muck and then came up in a crouch. His clothes were stained, his hair in a state of disarray. "Oh, clever, clever girl," he said. "You always did like to put up a fight."

Bendarian spread his arms wide as though reaching for something on either side of him. The shards of glass from shattered windows suddenly floated upward. They hovered for a moment and then converged upon Bendarian, swirling around him in a cyclone.

Released from the bonds that had held her, Desa stood in the middle of the street with her gun in one hand, gasping as she tried to catch her breath. What was this man? No human should have this kind of power.

Bendarian shoved his hands forward.

Shards of glass came rushing at her.

Turning her shoulder toward the onrushing storm, Desa raised her forearm up to shield her face and ordered her bracelet to drain kinetic energy. Thin shards stopped dead in mid-air mere inches away from her body.

She felt her bracelet filling itself as more and more shards came. It drank and drank until it had taken all that it could. One sliver of glass sliced a gash in the back of Desa's coat, leaving a cut across her skin.

Another buried itself in her thigh.

She cried out and bent double, hobbling to the side of the street and ducking into the narrow space between two houses. She was going to die. Though she strained to deny it, she knew there was no way out of this.

Letting her shoulder fall against the alley wall, Desa

grimaced and then shook her head. "Not like this," she pleaded, her voice a hoarse whisper. "Please not like this."

The whoosh of displaced air drew her attention, and then Bendarian appeared at the other end of the alley, smiling that dreadful smile, his eyes now pits of darkness. "You put up a good fight," he said. "Really, you should be proud. But it's over now."

With teeth bared, Desa threw her head back to squint at the open sky. "Not just yet, my friend," she whispered. "Not just yet."

She tossed the gun.

Bendarian caught the grip with a chuckle. He took one step forward and then raised the weapon to aim for Desa's chest. "Well, I suppose if you want me to kill you with your own gun, that would be-"

He cut off when Desa triggered the Force-Sink that she had Infused into the pistol itself. Drained of kinetic energy, he was frozen in place, trapped. In fact, he would not even be aware of the passage of time. Every particle in his body was motionless. Which meant that whatever the brain did to generate consciousness was temporarily suspended.

Hissing air through her teeth, Desa shook her head. "Idiot man," she muttered. "It never occurred to you that I might develop some new tricks after our last encounter?"

Of course, she couldn't do anything to him.

This Force-Sink was not refined like the one in her bracelet. It would take kinetic energy from anything that got close enough, including Desa herself. If she tried to rush in and stab him, she would be frozen as well.

But then there were other options.

She drew one of her daggers, tossed it up and caught the tip of the blade. She threw it with every last ounce of strength she had and watched it tumble end over end through the alley.

When her knife got within ten feet of Bendarian, she killed the Force-Sink to let it continue unimpeded. "Acceptable," Bendarian said in the split second before the dagger planted itself in his left eye.

He shrieked and stumbled backward, falling on his ass and dropping her pistol. A second later, he was gone. But Desa could still sense her dagger miles to the west of here. Nine miles and eight hundred twenty-two yards to be precise. A Field Binder would know the exact location of anything she Infused even if someone carried it to the other side of the world. She triggered the Heat-Source in that dagger.

Maybe that would be the end of Bendarian...Maybe not. With any luck, he had not been able to extricate the blade from his flesh before she triggered it. But then there was the distinct possibility that being burned to a crisp was still not enough to kill the man. Not with his new powers.

She killed the Heat-Source before it released its last bit of energy. That way she could still feel the Infusion. If Bendarian was still alive – and if he kept the dagger on his person, perhaps out of some sick desire to taunt her – it would allow her to track him. If he did discard the knife, at least she would be able to recover it.

Hobbling out of the alley, she set off to find the others.

22

"To the saviours of Thrasa!"

The man who said that, a Mr. Todd Finnegan, stood up from his table at the Wagon Wheel, thrust his mug into the air and added, "May they live long, happy lives that never take them far from this town."

Everyone else in the packed room cheered, all raising mugs or glasses of their own, some pounding on the tables with their fists. One man went so far as to stick two fingers in his mouth and whistle. Poor Mrs. Collins was frowning and shaking her head as she maneuvered between the tables. Clearly, she didn't appreciate the ruckus.

Desa sat at one table with her hands resting on her knees, grimacing as she endured yet another round of praise. When she was a girl, her teachers had all warned her against public displays of Field Binding. Non-Aladri would view it as demonic sorcery, they had said. Desa had never cared for that rule.

She wanted *everyone* to learn Field Binding – it was a useful technology – but she would have preferred it if people saw it as a means to improve their living conditions and not as a method for inflicting violence. Lately, most places she visited saw the latter and not the former. She turned to Marcus, who was sitting next to her.

He returned her scowl with one of his own.

She bent forward, set her elbow on the table and pinched the bridge of her nose. "I suppose there's little chance of slipping away quietly," she muttered. "They'll be at this all bloody night."

Seated across from her with booted feet propped up on the table, Miri had her arms folded as she listened to the crowd. "Let them have their moment," she said. "Let us have *our* moment! We've earned it!"

Tommy was beside her with an ear of corn in both hands, and he attacked the thing with an almost savage enthusiasm. "Personally," he said between crunches. "I'm just glad that for once, we *don't* have to flee a town three steps ahead of an angry mob."

Well...Desa couldn't argue with that. In truth, she lacked the energy to argue about anything. Extricating the glass from her leg had required a surgeon's care, and then she had spent an hour in communion with the Ether to accelerate her body's natural healing. It wasn't perfect – she still felt a mild sting when she walked – but it would do for now.

One of the serving girls, a pretty young lass with tanned skin and long brown hair, displayed a little bosom as she bent over to refill Desa's mug. "There you are," she said. "Compliments of the house. You've earned it."

Closing her eyes, Desa nodded.

Adele was between Marcus and Tommy, holding the stem of a wine glass with two delicate fingers and glaring with such intensity that Desa might have thought her eyes could flay the serving maid. "We should continue west," she said. "Bendarian is going that way."

Desa could confirm as much. Or, at the very least, she could *confirm* that *someone* was taking her knife westward...Which almost certainly meant that Bendarian was still alive. The man was a roach; killing him was becoming exceedingly difficult. He had covered about six miles of ground with no sudden jumps that would indicate the use of his new powers. Perhaps he was tired.

"She's right," Desa agreed.

No one argued.

"What I want to know," Miri said, inspecting her nails with idle curiosity. "is why those gray people were a little easier to defeat this time."

"I suspect Bendarian was controlling them," Marcus answered. According to him, the gray demons had all collapsed at the same time, and though Desa could not pinpoint the exact second of their defeat, she was fairly certain that it happened right as she put that knife through Bendarian's eye.

"No, not quite," Desa mused. "I don't think he was controlling their every move. But I do think they were tied to him in some ways. The ones we saw on that farm all died when the intelligence that was controlling them retreated. It would make sense if the same thing happened here."

"So, what now?" Tommy inquired.

Desa set her elbows on the table, laced her fingers and rested her chin on top of them. Slowly, she exhaled. "Now, we enjoy our laurels," she replied. "And then we cross the river first thing tomorrow morning."

Evening was coming on fast and the few miles they might travel before sundown were nothing against one more night in an actual bed and one more morning with a real breakfast. "I think we've all earned a little rest."

"I'll second that," Miri replied.

. . .

THE NEXT MORNING, as she led Midnight off the ferry by his bridle, Desa noted the looming ceiling of gray clouds that stretched from horizon to horizon. What a wonderful day to set out on a journey! She could all but feel the rain about to fall.

With her bracelet replenished and some extra ammunition that the townsfolk had been more than willing to part with, she was ready for whatever Bendarian would throw at her next. As ready as she could be, given the man's new abilities. The thought of what he had done still sent shivers down her spine.

The southern riverbank was much as she remembered it: green grass, the odd tree and a road that ran parallel to the Vinrella. There wasn't much to see, but Captain Rufus Sharp came up to stand beside her anyway.

His mouth was a thin line as he gazed out on the vast expanse of open country. "I'll reckon that you'll be having a hard time of it now," he said. "If your man really has gone west, well..."

"I know," was all Desa could say.

Hooking his thumbs around his belt, the man puffed up his chest and then blew air through puckered lips. "I'd be wanting to leave you with some extra supplies," he said. "It is the least I can offer after what you did yesterday."

Midnight snorted his agreement, then gently nuzzled Desa's shoulder. "All we did was defend ourselves," she said. "And the damage to your town is not insubstantial. You owe us nothing, Captain."

"Blast it, woman, are you really so daft?" She gave him a sidelong glance and saw that the man had favoured her with the same exasperated scowl she had seen on many of her teachers all those years ago. "The man was a demon, and you fought him off, and I'm of no mind to think on what kind of devilry gave life to those gray creatures. If you're off to end this Bendarian, then I can't imagine there's a single man in Thrasa who won't lend you his support. But it was more than that. The boys are abuzz with praise for those light-coins you gave me."

Despite herself, Desa smiled. "I'm pleased to hear that." It was a rare pleasure to find an Eradian who could appreciate the marvel of Field Binding. "Your friendship is much appreciated, Captain. Rest assured that I will visit again if I ever come back this way."

He nodded.

Ten minutes later, the ferry was sailing back across the Vinrella, and they were on their way, headed up the road. Desa could feel her knife in the distance. They had a good thirty miles to cross before they caught up with Bendarian. The man must have performed one of his jumps while she slept. Desa had a hard time believing that even he would be able to press on without rest or food.

She rode with Adele behind her, and the other woman took every opportunity to snuggle up with her cheek on Desa's shoulder. Miri and Tommy shared a dun filly that the people of Thrasa had offered as a gift. She was a young horse with strong legs. Desa was quite certain that she could keep pace with Midnight if push came to shove.

Tommy's gelding was now a pack-horse who carried the considerable supplies they had accepted from the townsfolk. At the very least, they would have enough food to reach Fool's Edge, but what they would after crossing into the desert was anybody's guess.

Marcus, of course, did what he always did, rushing off into the distance and then hurrying back to report that the road was clear. Adele tried, on numerous occasions, to spare him the effort by using her talents as a Sensitive, but Marcus was determined to do the scouting himself, and Desa was content to let him.

It was an uneventful ride until, at some point in the mid-afternoon, a light drizzle began to fall on them. At first, it was a welcome reprieve from the mugginess of a late spring day, but the drizzle soon became a deluge and they were forced to ride on for over an hour before taking refuge in a copse of trees.

There was just enough room to set up the tent Miri had purchased yesterday. No small expense, that, but Desa suspected the shopkeeper had been willing to offer Miri a discount after stories of her exploits had spread.

Desa and Marcus used coins Infused with Heat-Sources to stave off the chill and dry everyone's clothing. With any luck, the storm would pass quickly and they would be able to resume their journey.

BY THE TIME the rain stopped, the deep blue of twilight had settled over the land, and the dampness brought with it a chill that would make traveling very unpleasant. They could go no further tonight.

Desa emerged from the tent to find Adele standing with her back turned between elm trees, gazing out upon the rushing waters of the Vinrella. Her long blonde hair was still damp from the recent downpour. "You seem troubled," Desa said.

Adele hunched up her shoulders, but she did not turn. "We're losing ground," she replied. "You and I both know that we must destroy Bendarian before he looses that force of darkness on this world."

"Have you used your abilities to track him?"

"Not since we stopped for lunch."

Moving cautiously, Desa stepped up beside her and braced one hand against the trunk of a tree. "Perhaps you should do so," she said. "It would behoove us to know it if Bendarian has decided to turn back and finish us off."

Adele's face was barely visible in the dim light, but Desa could see that the woman had closed her eyes. She seemed to be trying to calm her excitement. "So, does that mean you trust me?"

Desa strode forward with a heavy sigh, the grass squishing beneath her feet with every step. "I don't know." It was nothing but the simple truth, but Adele would not like the bitterness in her tone. "But for better or worse, you have made yourself a part of this group; so, I think you should try."

When she turned around, Adele was standing there with a look of concentration on her face. There was a brief pause before Desa felt the resonance that told her someone else was in communion with the Ether. A *very* brief pause. Even with her many years of training, it took several minutes at least for Desa to reach a state of mind that would allow her to manipulate the Ether. That Adele could do it in a matter of seconds... A moment later, the resonance faded away.

"I found him," Adele said. "West of here and a little to the south."

"How far?"

"About forty miles."

Pacing toward the other woman with her arms crossed, Desa stopped in front of her and grunted. "Can you be more specific?" she asked. "I want to know his exact position."

"What does it matter?"

"Humor me."

The other woman collapsed against a tree trunk, groaning as she battled her own fatigue. In seconds, she was touching the Ether once again. "Thirty-nine miles," she said, "two hundred thirteen yards and nine inches."

Her finger seemed to fly out almost of its own volition, pointing westward and ever so slightly to the south. "That way!"

That was all Desa needed to hear. Adele had just stated the precise location of her dagger, which meant that Bendarian was still carrying it on his person. Perhaps he wanted it as a memento of their last encounter. Or perhaps he thought that slaying Desa with her own weapon would be a sick kind of poetic justice.

She turned on her heel and stalked off into the night.

"Where are you going?" Adele called after her.

She didn't respond.

THE THWAP, *thwap* of rain on the tent's roof kept Desa awake long into the night. In the pitch darkness, she was lying flat on her back and staring upward, lost in thought and barely aware of Adele's arm wrapped around her. The other woman slept with her head on Desa's chest, and she sighed contentedly every now and then.

Marcus was next to her, snoring softly, and on the other side of him, Tommy was cuddled up with Miri. That left Desa alone to ponder the questions tumbling through her mind.

An hour after their first attempt, Desa had asked Adele to locate Bendarian, and once again, Adele had reported the precise location of Desa's dagger. That could not be a coincidence.

There was no way that Adele could know about the

dagger. Desa had told no one, which could only mean one thing: Adele was genuine. She really *was* trying to help them find Bendarian.

That made Desa smile. As painful as it was to admit, she really was starting to care for the young woman. Adele seemed to notice her movements because she rose up with waves of hair falling over her face and sighed. "You're still awake," she whispered.

Shutting her eyes, Desa let her head sink deeper into the folded coat and shirt that she used as a pillow. "Just thinking," she replied. "Go back to sleep before you wake up everyone else."

Adele's soft hand caressed her cheek. "What are you thinking about?"

"Nothing of consequence."

"Tell me."

Desa sat up slowly, then scrubbed her hands over her face and ran fingers through her hair. "I'm thinking that I might just be willing to trust you." Getting those words out was not easy. "A little."

Adele slipped her arms around Desa's neck, leaned in close and kissed Desa's lips. It was a soft kiss, but Desa felt her body responding just the same. Every instinct made her want to melt in this woman's arms.

"I WILL RIDE with Desa Nin Leean this afternoon," Miri said.

"Excuse me?" Adele protested.

Desa was down on one knee under the branches of an apple tree, lacing up one of her boots. That caught her attention. The group had just stopped for lunch, and now they were ready to be on their way.

Wincing at the thought of whatever those two were up

to, Desa shook her head. "It never ends," she muttered, getting to her feet. No one else seemed to be paying any mind to the conflict that was about to start.

Adele stood with fists on her hips about two feet in front of Miri, and her cheeks were flushed pink. "I thought you fancied the boy," she said. "If you're thinking to come between me and the woman I love-"

Miri was as calm as you please with her hands clasped in front of herself, her head bowed almost demurely. Her sly smile made it clear that she was not the least bit worried about Adele's threats. "I merely wish to speak with Desa."

"About what?"

"Plans for our journey."

Desa strode toward them at a brisk pace. There were days when she was painfully aware of why she preferred to travel alone. "Children," she said in mocking tones. "Must I separate the two of you?"

Two heads turned, and two sets of eyes fell upon her, both smoldering, though Miri seemed to take control of her anger in a heartbeat. Her glare was replaced with another knowing smile. "I only wish to talk to you."

"And so I have to ride with the boy?" Adele spluttered.

Tommy would not like hearing that, and Desa could not say that she liked hearing it either. Oh yes, there were days when she would rather travel alone, but she would suffer no insult to her companions. "If you are so opposed to traveling with 'the boy,'" she said, "then perhaps you should not have joined our party."

Adele went bone white, stumbling backward as if she had been slapped, and she blinked in confusion. "I meant no offense..." The quiver in her voice almost made Desa regret her words. "I don't like riding with young men. I've yet to meet even one who did not take every opportunity to paw at a woman."

"This one won't," Miri said quickly.

It wasn't long before Desa was riding along with the reins in hand and waiting for the inevitable conflict that would flare up any moment now. Miri had won the argument – due in no small part to Desa's unwillingness to suffer Adele's insolence – and now she rode Midnight as well. "I have to ask," she whispered in Desa's ear. "Are you going to tell him?"

"Tell who what?"

"Are you going to tell Tommy about Sebastian?"

Shutting her eyes tight, Desa trembled as she drew in a breath. "You know." It was not even a question at this point. "*How* do you know?"

"It doesn't matter how I know," Miri insisted. "What matters is that if I could figure it out, so can he. He's much smarter than you give him credit for."

A little ways up the road, Tommy was riding with Adele clinging to him, and it was clear by his posture that he wasn't any happier about the situation than she was. In fact, he looked like Desa's old cat Mittens whenever Desa's mother chased him with a broom.

The clouds had finally parted, leaving nothing but blue sky and warm sunlight that dried damp grass. The river's babbling was exceedingly loud after all that rainfall, which made Desa just a little uneasy. It would be harder to hear approaching horses that way. Well for them that Marcus insisted on performing his scouting duties with the utmost diligence. "He doesn't need to know," Desa said at last. "It would break his spirit."

"That's cowardice, and you know it."

"What I know is that we have enough problems without

adding turmoil within the group," she said. "Perhaps I can tell him after we've dealt with Bendarian, but for now, it's best that I keep silent."

"That's not good enough," Miri replied in a low, dangerous voice. "I will make this simple for you, Desa; either you tell him, or I will."

A knife of fear went through Desa's chest.

This could not end well.

A FEW HOURS LATER, they parted ways with the Vinrella as the river turned northward and their path continued due west through open grasslands with only a few trees dotting the landscape here and there. The horses would have plenty to graze on – for now, at least – and they still had supplies, but it still made Desa a little apprehensive.

The river had been a constant companion since they left Ofalla ten days ago, and its departure meant that they were inching ever closer to the Gatharan Desert. Few people braved that empty expanse to reach the fertile lands on the other side, especially since the final leg of the journey would mean crossing the Molarin Mountains. Most people who reached Eradia's western shore did so by ship.

Adele was with Desa again, hugging her close, nuzzling her shoulder. "What did Miri want to talk about?" she inquired in a sweet voice that hinted it was nothing more than an idle curiosity to her.

Pinching the brim of her hat with thumb and forefinger, Desa tugged it down over her eyes to block the glare of sunlight. "It was nothing serious," she replied. "She only wanted to discuss our route."

"She couldn't have done that while we were eating lunch?"

A grin spread on Desa's face, and she shook her head slowly. "Jealous, Adele?" she inquired. "You needn't be. Miri only fancies men."

"That doesn't mean you don't fancy her."

"My, you *are* jealous."

That earned Desa a slap on the back and a sniff of derision. "Trifling with a young woman's affections is exactly the sort of thing a man would do." It was said with a hint of a levity, but Desa could sense a little desperation as well.

Marcus spared her from having to think up something to soothe Adele's worries by riding up on his gray and grimacing as he took in the sight of them. No doubt he thought they were all lollygagging while he tried to press on in haste. "There are a few farms up ahead," he said. "Might be an opportunity to purchase some more vegetables."

"Can we spare the money?"

"I have a bit left yet," he answered. "The Synod gave me a substantial allowance. They were quite eager to have you back. And I have earned a bit of money here and there since leaving Aladar."

Desa felt her eyebrows rise. She would be very interested to hear exactly what he had done to earn that money, but she said nothing. Marcus could keep his secrets. It had only taken a few weeks for Desa to learn that Aladri dogmas didn't always work outside of Aladar's borders. She had never imagined that she would trade Field Binding for food, but she had done so with surprisingly little reluctance in those first few months on her own. Whatever Marcus had done, she was in no position to judge.

"Let's go then," she said. "We're wasting daylight."

. . .

THE DAYS WORE on with little to see except grass and trees and the occasional farm. There was little to do except ride and talk, and by their third morning in the saddle, Desa felt as though they had run out of things to say. Adele took every opportunity to cuddle, which was actually becoming something of a nuisance.

Marcus scouted ahead and came back to report nothing in their path. Sometimes, they stopped to rest the horses, which gave Desa many opportunities to commune with the Ether. She took solace in that. If nothing else, it soothed the pain of long hours in the saddle. Sometimes they walked and spread the pack-horse's burdens out among the other animals.

Every day was very much like the one that had come before it: they started with a hearty breakfast and then rode – or walked – until well past midday. When hunger finally got the best of them, they paused for a quick lunch and then pressed on until diminishing sunlight made it impossible to go any further. Sometimes it rained, but otherwise the weather remained pleasant. At first, Miri insisted on setting up the tent every night, but she gave that up when fatigue and clear skies made the call of her bedroll too tempting to resist.

On their fourth day out from Thrasa, the road just stopped. Green fields of rolling hills stretched on toward the distant horizon, but the road had decided that it would go no further. From that point onward, they had to march across an open countryside.

There were no more farms and no indications of civilization. Trees became so rare that catching sight of one was almost cause for celebration. Almost. Their supplies were dwindling, and without a road to guide them, it was all too possible that they might miss Fool's Edge by a dozen miles or more and find themselves lost in the desert.

Fortunately, they had Bendarian to set their path. Adele was able to keep an eye on him through the use of her talents, and though she told no one about it, Desa could sense his movements as well. Whether or not that would do any good was anyone's guess. For all she knew, Bendarian no longer required food or water, which meant that there was no guarantee they would find supplies by following his path.

Bit by bit, the grass changed from green to yellow, and by the sixth day, it was crunching under the horses' hooves. By the eighth day, there was no grass except for the odd patch that sprouted here and there from an endless expanse of reddish soil that scuffed like sand beneath their boots. They were in a vast scrubland of thin plants with small leaves, bushes and even the odd cactus here and there. For a while, Desa worried that they would bypass Fool's Edge entirely and wander aimlessly through the desert.

If only fate were that kind.

23

The scrubland stretched on from horizon to horizon, unbroken in all directions except for one thing: a small town of white stone buildings constructed near the edge of a lake that Desa could swim across in about ten minutes.

The instant they got within shouting distance, a man who waited on the roof of one of the outer buildings turned and vanished from sight. Moments later, doors opened and men came spilling out into the main street with rifles.

They formed a line at the edge of town, lifted their guns and pointed them directly at Desa's group. "That's far enough!" one shouted. "We want no strangers here! Ye'll be turnin' back if ye know what's good for ye!"

Sitting atop Midnight with her hands raised defensively, Desa felt her jaw drop. She shook her head in confusion. "We mean no harm!" she replied. "We just want to purchase supplies and then be on our way."

She urged Midnight forward.

The six men in the street all choked up on their rifles. One even worked the bolt to emphasize that he *would* fire if they got any closer. The sight of it made Adele cling a little harder to Desa.

Shutting her eyes tight, Desa scraped a knuckle across her forehead. "Of course..." Why should she have expected anything else? With the exception of Thrasa, she had been greeted with hostility almost everywhere she went since forming this little group.

Marcus decided to escalate the situation by rushing forward on his gray with a hand on his holstered pistol. "Try to bar our path," he said. "And you will face a power such as you have never seen before."

Desa covered her face with one hand, rubbing her eyelids with the tips of her fingers. "Trust a man to make things worse." The fool only saw one solution to any problem, and it was going to get them killed.

"Why are you barring our path?" Miri asked.

One of the townsfolk, a spindly man in overalls with a broken strap and a straw hat that had seen better days, stepped forward and spat on the ground. "The man in black told us ye'd be coming. Said to stop you."

"Man in black?"

"Scary fellow with green veins on his face."

Bendarian.

Grunting as he gestured with his rifle, the spindly man stared them down as if he thought force of will alone could bar their path. "We've already faced a power such as we have never seen before," he said. "Man in black killed three people when he came through. He said he'd kill more if we let you pass."

Desa retrieved an Infused coin from her pocket, triggered it and nearly flinched at the powerful glow. It seemed as though she held a tiny star in her hand. She lifted it up above her head, and several of the townsfolk gasped. "We have a power too!" she said. "But we won't kill you! I will teach you to wield this power!"

Several of the townsfolk murmured.

Others looked as if they might fire those rifles.

Miri urged the filly forward. She was holding the reins with Tommy behind her, and the lad was very pale. Young as he was, he had learned the difference between men who shouted and blustered in the hopes that you would back down and men who would make good on their threats. "Perhaps we could speak to the sheriff," Miri suggested. "Or make an appeal directly to the Village Council."

The spindly man spat another gob of phlegm onto the ground. "Lady, yer talkin' to the mayor. And he says ye ain't passin' through."

"Enough of this." Marcus booted his horse forward.

Desa reacted by instinct, urging Midnight to keep pace with the gray and lifting her left hand to shield herself with her bracelet. Thunder cracked as rifles let loose a storm of bullets, each one coming to an abrupt halt in front of Desa or Marcus, then falling to the ground as they passed.

The riflemen saw that their weapons were useless and began retreating through the street. "No!" some shouted. "Demon!"

"Marcus!" Desa growled.

The fire in her voice urged him to pull on the reins and bring his mount to an abrupt halt. He looked over his shoulder, snarling at her. "We gave them a chance to show good sense," he said. "They refused."

Scowling at the thought of what he might do, Desa shook her head. "I will not kill these people," she said. "I swore that I meant them no harm, and I have every intention of making good on that promise."

"We must stop Bendarian!"

"There are other ways."

Without waiting for a response, Desa turned Midnight around and urged him back to the spot where the others waited. Miri and Tommy looked very uneasy as they watched the whole scene play out. And the pack-horse had been spooked by the noise.

"Come," she said. "Let's put some distance between us and them."

THE GLOW of Desa's ring sitting on top of a pile of rocks illuminated their campsite. The five of them sat in a tight circle around those rocks, though no one was talking. No one wanted to address the question that had been hanging over them like a shadow since Desa had turned away from Fool's Edge earlier that afternoon.

What did they do now?

Pursuing Bendarian into the desert without supplies was a death sentence. Oh, they might survive for a few days, but they were already low on food, and there would be no water. Worse yet, the five of them together were too slow to catch Bendarian anyway. It irked Desa to no end.

She might be able to make a run for it on Midnight. The two of them alone at a fast gallop might just give her enough speed to overtake Bendarian. But would the others let her? Adele, in particular, would insist on coming along.

Desa squatted over the glowing ring with hands on her knees, her head hanging with fatigue. "We're wasting time," she said. "If we want to have any hope of catching Bendarian, we *must* leave now."

Marcus sat on the dusty ground with his legs stretched out, chewing on a piece of meat as he considered their options. "We would almost certainly die in the attempt," he countered. "I say we take Fool's Edge."

"No."

It was one flat word, delivered in a hoarse voice, but Desa meant it with all of her heart. Those people were only trying to stay alive. She could imagine what Bendarian had done to intimidate them. She would not do the same.

Sliding a toothpick into his mouth with two fingers, Marcus chewed on that instead, and it waggled around as he spoke. "We need supplies," he said. "They have supplies. It's fairly simple, if you ask me."

Tommy was lying flat on his back, gazing up at the night sky with his hands folded over his chest. "Simple," he said. "If you're willing to kill a few of them. You must know they'll leave you no option."

"The fate of the world may depend upon us stopping Bendarian," Marcus replied. "I will not hesitate to do what is necessary."

"We're not killing them," Desa insisted.

She stood up, turned away from the light and stalked off into the empty wilderness. Sliding her hands into the pockets of her duster, she blew out a breath. There was only one solution to their problem. She knew it.

The sound of approaching footsteps was no surprise to her. By the gait alone, she could tell who had come to speak with her, and when she turned around, she saw exactly what she expected to see.

Adele was standing just a few feet away, silhouetted by the light from the campsite, only a shadow to Desa's eyes. "I know that you won't want to hear this," she began. "But Marcus is right. We must-"

Tilting her head to one side, Desa raised one eyebrow, and that alone was enough to forestall the other woman.

"You think we should attack frightened people?" she asked. "If we did, would we be any better than Bendarian?"

The silhouette shook its head, and the ground scuffed beneath Adele's shoes as she strode forward. "I don't want to do it!" she exclaimed. "You should know me better than that...But Bendarian *must* be stopped."

"On that, we agree."

"Well then..."

Desa stepped up to the woman that she had grown to care for, craned her neck and stared unflinchingly into Adele's eyes. "There is a solution," she said. "But I am certain that you won't like it."

An instant later, she was striding back to the campsite and steeling herself for what she knew would be a painful conversation. The others were gathered around her glowing ring. Three heads turned at the sound of her approach.

"I'm going alone," she announced.

The toothpick fell out of Marcus's mouth as he looked up in slack-jawed confusion. He remained dumbstruck for a moment, then blinked and regained his wits. "You cannot be serious. There is no way you could survive the trip."

"That is irrelevant."

"No, it's not," Tommy insisted with more backbone than she would have expected from him. "You're our friend. We're not leaving you to die."

"The boy speaks wisdom," Marcus added.

"It's a welcome change from the other men in this group," Miri put in. She stood up to face Desa on the other side of the glowing rocks, then nodded. Perhaps in respect. Or perhaps in assent to Desa's plan. "If you must go, I will not try to stop you. But I feel this is a decision that should be made by the group."

Adele strode back into the light and paused beside Desa,

the wind teasing flyaway strands of her golden hair. "And the group has decided that you are not going alone," she said. "We set off on this quest together; we will finish it together."

"Enough! All of you!" Desa shouted. "Every second that I linger here only lowers my odds of success. Midnight and I can cover more ground when we aren't hindered by the four of you and your animals. I can find him by morning...and then I will end this."

"You're not going alone!" Tommy growled. "And that's-"

"This is not a debate!" Desa had learned, over the years, how to stand tall with her shoulders square. It was a little thing but absolutely necessary when you were shorter than everyone else. "I am going. My love to all of you."

"You wish to leave now?" Marcus protested. "Your horse will break a leg running headlong through the dark."

"Midnight is no ordinary horse."

She didn't give them an opportunity to argue; she just turned away and paced over to the spot where Midnight waited just beyond the edge of the light. In the darkness, she could still make out his shadowy form. The horse was watching her. She felt a resonance from him and she knew that he had been watching the entire argument.

Closing her eyes, Desa nodded to him. "You don't have to come with me," she said, reaching out to lay a hand on Midnight's long face. "You've been a loyal companion, but I won't condemn you to death in the desert."

He licked her fingers.

Warmth flooded Desa's cheeks, but she breathed in slowly and then took control of herself. "All right then," she whispered. "As long as you're willing."

"Desa!"

Unexpectedly, she found Tommy coming toward her,

and though it was too dark to make out his features, she was certain he wore a snarl that could frighten off an angry wolf. "You are *not* going into the desert alone."

"Tommy-"

"No! I won't listen to any more talk about your duty or the danger that Bendarian poses or any other hair-brained explanation for why you think you must ride off to your untimely death. You saved my life, Desa. And though he came to a bad end, you saved Sebastian as well. Do you think I'm just going to let you-"

"Tommy-"

"I owe you my life and a whole lot more than that," he pressed on. She could see his silhouette, standing a few feet away and glowering at her. At least, she assumed he was glowering. "You saved me from the whims of backward townsfolk. You gave me a sense of purpose. You saved the man I love-"

"I killed the man you love."

That brought him up short. In fact, he actually recoiled from her, stumbling away as if she had suddenly become a demon. "What...What did you say?" The stammer in his voice had returned.

Desa felt a single tear on her cheek, felt it run down all the way to her jawline and then drip to land on her shirt. "He was with Bendarian," she whispered. "He betrayed us all. I knew I couldn't trust him, so-"

"He was with Bendarian," Tommy murmured. "You mean he attacked you?"

"No."

"He was trying to kill you."

She forced herself to look up, forced herself to meet Tommy's gaze even though he would not be able to see her. "No." One syllable, and yet forcing that word through her lips was agony. "Sebastian was in league with Bendarian. Two weeks of feeling that boy's hateful stare on me everywhere we went, and then he allied himself with Bendarian even after seeing the abominations on that farm, even knowing that Bendarian was a creature of unparalleled evil.

"I looked at your lover, Tommy. I saw his snide little grin, and I reacted without a second's hesitation. It was over in an instant. Before I even knew it, I had my smoking gun pointed at Sebastian's chest. I watched him fall backward, watched him die on the floor. And I didn't feel guilty. Not even for an instant. Not until I thought about what it would do to you."

"How..." Tommy shuddered. "How did you feel...when you shot him?"

"Righteous."

It hurt more than she would have expected when Tommy turned away from her and shuffled back to the campsite. She saw Miri standing in the light and watching the whole scene play out with a pained expression.

Bendarian was forty-miles southwest of here and stationary for the moment. Most likely he had stopped for the night. Midnight could cover that distance before sunup if he pushed himself. Unless she missed her guess, Bendarian would have no way to sense her approach until she was right on top of him. It was time to end this at long last.

Desa climbed into Midnight's saddle, making no effort to stem the tide of tears that flowed over her face. She sniffled. "Come on," she whispered. "You only have to endure until morning. After that, what happens to us won't matter."

They took off into the night.

24

Desa fled into the desert.

She rode atop Midnight as he barreled across the sandy plains, his hooves kicking up dust, his tail streaming out behind him in the wind. She was no longer aware of the ache in her thighs from long hours in the saddle, no longer aware of the gnawing hunger or the sting of leather reins on her palms.

Morning had come, and the sky was now a fierce blue without a single cloud to be seen. There was nothing but an endless expanse of dusty red clay. Even the sparse plants of the scrubland near Fool's Edge were gone.

She leaned forward in the saddle.

Clenching her teeth, Desa hissed as the wind assaulted her. "Just a little longer," she whispered for the hundredth time. "We're almost on him."

They were; she could feel the presence of her Infused knife within about two miles of here. In less than an hour, they would be on top of Bendarian. In less than an hour, this quest that had consumed the last ten years of her life would be over. One way or another.

Midnight slowed to a stop, and Desa felt the resonance as he communed with the Ether. In seconds, he would know the terrain for miles around this spot. It was rare for an animal to achieve Communion, but doing so enhanced their cognition considerably. He would be able to remember every hill, every pit, every bump in the ground.

Before Desa could even catch her breath, the stallion took off again, racing up a gentle slope and then down the other side. She would have liked to have seen *something:* a cactus, an outcropping of rocks, maybe a small oasis. But of course, there was just more empty land.

They ran on.

As the sun climbed halfway to its zenith, the air became uncomfortably warm. Desa wanted to take off her coat, but there was nowhere to put it. Except for her saddlebags, and that would require a lot of finagling. More time than she wanted to waste on comfort.

They pressed on...and on...Soon, they would find Bendarian. Soon-

The knife shifted.

Desa felt her jaw drop, creases lining her brow as she shook her head. "No," she whispered. "Please...Not now!"

The knife was now just over ten miles away. Bendarian must have used his strange powers to traverse the distance in a matter of seconds. Which meant that Midnight had to keep running even further.

Desa pulled him to a stop.

She sat up, covering her face with both hands, and then let out a shuddering breath. "I can't ask you to go further." It was a hoarse whisper that passed through her lips. Her throat felt like it had been coated with sand.

When she let her hands drop, Midnight had turned his head to give her a sidelong glance. She knew what he was thinking. Staying here would be just as bad as collapsing from exhaustion. There was no water, no food. And it was unlikely that Midnight would have the strength to run back to Fool's Edge. Less likely that they would find respite there even if they tried.

Desa let her head sink, then reached up to pinch the brim of her hat. She removed it and felt the sun beat down on her. "All right," she said. "You're stronger than any horse I have ever seen. If you can carry me the rest of the way."

Midnight was galloping again before she even realized it. The surprise nearly threw her out of the saddle, but she steadied herself, set the hat back on her head and tried her best to ignore the fatigue...and the thirst.

It wasn't long before she saw something on the southern horizon. A glimmer. As if the sun were glinting off something. But she couldn't make out what it was. In the end, it didn't really matter. Bendarian was there; she knew that much.

Midnight ran, and the glimmer became sharper, clearer, more distinct to her eyes. Within an hour, she was certain that it was a man-made structure. In fact, those big gray lumps surrounding it weren't hills or boulders. They were the remains of buildings that had crumbled centuries ago.

There were towns in the desert, all of which were located near wellsprings formed by underground streams that flowed down from the Molaran Mountains. The largest was Dry Gultch, but it was nowhere near here. And its buildings would not be in ruins.

Something about this felt ominous.

As they got closer, Desa realized that it wasn't a town so much as it was a collection of ruined buildings around something that sparkled. She strained to identify it, but all she saw was the gleam.

Onward Midnight ran over rugged terrain, pausing only briefly to commune with the Ether and get a sense of his surroundings. Within an hour, they were close enough to see the glittering substance.

It was a crystal.

A crystal as big as a house, shaped like a teardrop and set upon what looked like the base of a stone pyramid. It seemed to hum in Desa's mind, which was ludicrous, except that she was quite sure she could feel the Ether.

Shutting her eyes, Desa concentrated and felt a single bead of sweat rolling down her forehead. "Yes," she murmured. "You feel it too, don't you?"

Midnight whinnied.

The Ether was...pulsing...There was just no other word for it. On a good night, she would only have to meditate for a few minutes to commune with the Ether. Sometimes it took longer. But here, it seemed to cry out for attention.

Desa reached out tentatively, and the world changed before her eyes, solid objects breaking apart into swarms of dancing particles. She went limp and nearly fell out of the saddle before she forced her consciousness back into her body. It was so easy. It should not have been that easy.

Bringing Midnight to a stop, she tried again and found the Ether with almost no effort. Desa floated in its soothing embrace, sensing the world around her. The buildings, the parched landscape, the countless molecules of hot, dry air. She felt Bendarian inside the pyramid. Was he aware of her? He must have communed with the Ether himself and sensed her approach. Or had he lost the ability to do so after embracing his new powers? Something else occurred to her.

She Infused one of the bullets in her belt pouch, creating a Force-Sink – it was the first thing that came to mind – and nearly gasped in surprise. The lattice seemed to snap into place. It was so easy.

Normally, it would take several minutes to create a Sink that could take in enough kinetic energy to be useful, but she had accomplished the task in seconds! What was this place? Did the crystal amplify the Ether?

Yes...

She could feel the pulses radiating from the crystal like waves washing over her. It was this place. Someone had created technology that would allow Field Binders to work at an incredible pace. And she had never heard of it. Not once before today.

Desa came back to reality, patted Midnight's neck and urged him onward. They had less than half a mile to go, and she wanted it over with. Bendarian would not flee. Not this time. He had chosen this place as the venue for his last stand. It wasn't long before they reached the edge of the small town...or whatever it was.

Midnight ran between two ruined buildings.

With a tight frown, Desa turned her head and felt her eyebrows rise. "I don't think I like this place," she whispered. "I almost feel..."

Some of the structures were still standing – or parts of them were, in some cases – but the windows had been shattered, leaving holes in stone walls. Other homes had been reduced to piles of rubble. And yet, Desa had the strangest feeling...An itch between her shoulder-blades. The feeling of unseen eyes upon her.

Desa hopped off Midnight.

She landed with a scuff of dust, then straightened and removed her hat. The wind blew at her short brown hair. "What is this place?" she muttered. "Who built it? Were my people unaware of it, or did they just not tell me?"

Midnight snorted and nuzzled her shoulder. He had no more answers than she did. Well, if they had to die out here, in the desert, at least they had seen something marvelous before the end.

She fell to one knee.

Craning her neck, Desa squinted at the crystal and ignored the assault of hot wind on her face. "It does not make sense," she whispered. "If this technology were possible, the Aladri would have discovered it."

Midnight snorted again.

Grunting from the pain in her legs, Desa stood up and dusted her hands. "You're right," she said. "That *is* arrogant. But we'll learn nothing out here. We have to-"

She was about to suggest that they press on toward the pyramid, but her sharp ears caught a sound she would not have expected to hear in the middle of the desert. The soft babble of running water.

"Let's go!"

It wasn't hard to follow the sound; it came from a structure in the inner circle. Four stone walls surrounded what might once have been a garden. At least, that was what Desa assumed since one of those walls was pressed against the side of a small hut. Of course, there was little chance of finding any food. This town had been abandoned for centuries. Perhaps longer.

Stepping through the arch-shaped entrance disabused her of any cynicism she may have felt. Inside those four walls, she found a small orchard of peach trees in full bloom, with ripe fruit hanging from every branch. Lush green grass stretched from corner to corner, in defiance of the cloudless sky.

In the centre of the orchard, a copper pole so wide she could not have wrapped her arms around it stood two stories high. There was a cylindrical tube on top with a grated face turned toward a crystal, and copper pipes spread out from it like tentacles, each one draining water into a metal bucket.

It was the strangest thing Desa had ever seen, but that thought lasted for only the briefest instant before her thirst overpowered her curiosity. Abandoning caution, Desa ran toward the towering contraption and stuck her head under one of those pipes. The water was ice cold!

Of course, the chill was a welcome relief from the scorching heat, and before Desa could stop herself, she was lifting up one of those buckets and spilling half of its contents over her shirt while she drank the rest. She didn't care about bacteria. She would suffer the consequences if she had to. For now, all she wanted to do was drink.

She turned to find Midnight following her through the arch and pausing to marvel at the bounty this strange place had provided. The horse wasted no time; he bent low and started feasting on the grass.

Desa brought one of the buckets over to him which caused him to pause just long enough to stick his head inside and lap up the water. The poor dear. She should not have taken him on this fool's mission.

Wiping moisture off her brow with the back of one fist, Desa squinted against the glare of the sun. "This place just gets stranger and stranger," she whispered. "Who built that thing?"

She turned back to the strange tower.

It was still functioning, though two of those copper pipes were now releasing water directly onto the grass. How could such a device exist? It almost seemed to defy the laws of nature. There were water pumps back in Aladar, but this thing didn't just move water from one place to another. It *created* water. Or at least, that was how it seemed. She saw no indication of a reservoir that it could use as a source. It was almost magical.

Except...No, it wasn't.

Somehow – perhaps through the deeper communion with the Ether brought on by proximity to that crystal – she was able to understand how this watering device worked. Air flowed through the grate, into the large copper tube atop the tower, where Force and low-level Gravity Sources compressed it. Each one was crafted with exquisite precision, much like Desa's bracelet that would only take kinetic energy from objects that were coming toward her.

Heat-Sinks then lowered the air's temperature until the water vapor condensed and flowed through the pipes into the buckets. It was an ingenious device. An exemplar of truly inspired Field Binding. But...Who was Infusing all those Sinks and Sources with fresh connections to the Ether? A device like this should not have been able to run on its own for days – much less centuries – without a Field Binder to maintain it. Suddenly, Desa was painfully aware of those unseen eyes.

She shrugged out of her coat, letting it fall to the ground behind her, and then paced through the orchard. "It's amazing," she said softly. "That anyone could conceive of such a device...If only the Synod could see it."

Her stomach rumbled.

With a sigh, she walked over to the nearest tree, snatched a peach from one of the branches and took a bite. It was juicy and delicious. Desa gobbled up the entire thing in less than a minute, then tossed the core to the ground.

Turning back to Midnight, she laced fingers over the back of her head as she strode toward him. "Think about it..." Desa stood up on her toes, groaning as she stretched her back. "A little scrap of paradise in this wasteland."

Midnight was too busy grazing to respond, but his ear flicked toward her, and she knew that he understood. Something here wasn't right.

She noticed another arch-shaped doorway in the wall that connected to the hut, but there was nothing but gloom in there, and she had no desire to go exploring. They would have to face Bendarian soon, but it was best to eat and drink for now. Fighting for her life while dehydrated would not end well.

Desa plopped herself down in the grass, curled up her legs and hugged them. She exhaled. "Who do you think they were?" she asked. "Scholars? Philosophers? Engineers? Or were they a warlike people?"

Midnight looked up briefly.

Blushing under the horse's scrutiny, Desa closed her eyes and nodded. "Yes...I take your point," she said. "There's no way we can know."

Midnight returned his attention to the bucket of water, making no effort to hide his slurping as he drank. At least they wouldn't die here. Not from thirst, anyway. Depending on how frequently that tower made water, it was entirely possible that they might be able to gather enough supplies for a return to Fool's Edge. They might actually survive this trip. Assuming, of course, that she would actually manage to kill Bendarian. Desa had to admit that his new powers were formidable.

She fell backward, lying flat on her back and blinking as she felt the hot sun on her skin. "Whoever they were," she mumbled, "I suppose we owe them our thanks. Do you think that any of them would have imagined, when they planted these trees, that this little orchard might have made the difference in a fool woman's quest to save the world?"

Midnight snorted.

Desa sat up just long enough to stick out her tongue, then flopped back down again. "Shows what you know," she grumbled. "Mercy takes care of her children."

Another snort set Desa's teeth on edge.

"It's true," she insisted. "You need only look around if you want proof. We ran off on a fool's quest, headlong into the desert with nothing to eat or drink. We were prepared to die here, and yet Mercy has provided us with water and grass...and fruit."

That last one made Desa's blood run cold. That niggling feeling in the back of her mind, the sense of wrongness that had been haunting her from the moment she had first set foot in this strange town, suddenly made perfect sense.

The tower provided water, but that alone could not have accounted for the existence of this orchard. She saw no mechanism for delivering that water to the trees. So, who was tending to them?

It dawned on her that the buckets had been perfectly arranged underneath the pipes. And while they might have been left in that state when the last inhabitants of this town departed, several hundred years was a long time. And it had to be at least several hundred years for so many buildings to have collapsed.

Was it really plausible that, in all that time, a strong wind had never knocked at least one bucket over? Not even once? Did it not strain credulity to think that a buzzard had never swooped down to sate his thirst, disturbing one of the buckets in the process? The more she thought about it, the more she felt an irresistible urge to run.

Something in the corner of her eye.

Desa turned her head in time to catch a glimpse of a hooded figure standing in the door to the hut. A slender figure in unrelieved black with her face hidden in the depths of her cowl. Only an instant, and then the stranger ducked back inside.

In a heartbeat, Desa was on her feet and drawing her pistol. She cocked the hammer and moved cautiously to the door. "Whoever you are!" she bellowed. "You should know that you face a Field Binder of Aladar!"

Would that even mean anything to this spectre?

Despite her growing trepidation, she forced herself to go into the hut and triggered the Light-Source in her ring... There was nothing. Just four stone walls and barely enough space to fit six people.

Worse yet, there was no exit except for the one directly behind her. The stranger could not have escaped without her knowing it, and yet, there was no one else here. Cold sweat ran down her face in rivers.

Stepping back into the light, she slammed her pistol back into its holster and shook her head as she marched through the grass. Midnight was waiting, watching her with his ears slanted back. "I must have imagined it," she told him.

A shrill neigh was the stallion's reply, and then he stamped a hoof for good measure. "You saw her as well?" Midnight came forward to nuzzle Desa's forehead. The poor dear was frightened, and Desa couldn't blame him.

"Come," she said. "We've disturbed the dead long enough."

25

At the base of the pyramid, Desa brought Midnight to a stop. Ten stone steps led up to the main entrance, a dark tunnel that left her with a sense of foreboding. Her encounter with that hooded apparition certainly wasn't helping matters.

The entire structure was no more than a few stories tall, as if someone had hacked off the top of the pyramid, leaving only the base. But the huge crystal on top seemed to caress the sky. It was beautiful to look at, almost majestic. Every edge and surface caught the light of the afternoon sun, and she could *feel* the Ether calling her.

She dismounted.

Facing her horse with her arms folded, Desa shook her head. "This is as far as you go, my friend." The next words hurt, but she forced herself to say them. "Run. Get as far away from here as you can."

Midnight stamped a hoof and then gave her a glare that called her an idiot. Then he nuzzled Desa's forehead.

She closed her eyes, giggling softly under his touch. It tickled. "No, you can't stay here," she insisted. "One way or another, this will be over soon. If Bendarian wins, I don't want him to find you."

Without another word, she turned her back on the most loyal friend she'd ever had and began climbing the steps. Halfway up, she reached out to the Ether and accepted its warm embrace. The world changed before her, but she paid little attention to the violent tempest of particles, choosing instead to Infuse several bullets with fresh connections to the Ether. A Force-Source, a Heat-Sink, a Gravity-Source. Any one of them might give her an edge in a desperate moment.

As she completed her work, Desa sensed something new. A fourth presence nearby, not herself or Midnight or Bendarian but someone else. Adele was riding hard toward this abandoned town. She was still a few miles away – which should have placed her well beyond the outer limits of what Desa could sense through the Ether; that crystal was enhancing Desa's talents in more ways than one – but at such a breakneck pace, Adele would be here in less than an hour. She must have slipped away from the group on the filly they had acquired in Thrasa.

Breaking her connection to the Ether, Desa opened her eyes, breathed in slowly and then shook her head. "Fool of a girl," she muttered. "This goes well beyond loyalty."

She would have to dispatch Bendarian with haste. There was no way she was letting that man anywhere near Adele.

At the top of the steps, Desa removed her duster, leaving herself in a sleeveless tan shirt and exposing the weapons that she carried. Her holstered pistol on her right hip, her dagger on the left, a pouch of spare ammunition between them.

Desa drew the revolver, thumbed the hammer and lifted the weapon up in front of her face, its barrel pointed skyward. "Mercy, guide your foolish daughter," she whispered. "Let my aim be true."

She stepped into the tunnel.

The gloom seemed unusually oppressive, which was surely a consequence of what she had seen in that orchard. Was the hooded figure here? Would she attack? Desa hadn't sensed anyone else when she communed with the Ether, but could you sense a ghost that way? For that matter, *was* that thing a ghost? Until today, she would have scoffed at the idea of vengeful spirits. The dead were dead, and that was all there was to it.

The tunnel sloped gently downward, and Desa followed its path with her gun thrust out in front of herself. She didn't bother with her Light-Source. There was enough natural light ahead to see clearly.

At last, the tunnel opened into a massive room with a hole in the ceiling, allowing sunlight to filter in through the base of the crystal. It cast sparkling patterns on the stone walls, each one unique and magnificent.

In the centre of the room, a raised floor that stood only a hair's breadth taller than Desa herself was positioned directly under the crystal. There were unlit torches at all four corners; so, it was an altar of some kind.

Bendarian stood there with hands clasped behind himself, smiling down at her as he watched her approach. It *was* Bendarian – she knew that without a doubt – but he looked nothing like the man she remembered.

Those green veins covered almost every inch of his now bald head. His left eye was gone, replaced by rough scar tissue. "Welcome," he said. "It's been a long road, hasn't it? A road that led us both to this place."

Desa climbed the steps to the raised floor.

Thrusting out her chin, she narrowed her eyes as she

studied him. "Why have you brought us here?" Though she didn't intend it, her words were a contemptuous sneer. "Is it the crystal? Is that part of your plan?"

Bendarian smiled, shaking his head as he began pacing a circle around the raised floor. "You know, separating you from the others required considerable effort." He spun on his heel, facing Desa with a chuckle that made her skin crawl.

Then he brought one hand out from behind his back, revealing the dagger that had wounded him clutched tightly in a vein-covered fist. "Fortunately, you made that a little easier," he went on. "I do hope you appreciated the surprise I left for you in Fool's Edge. I went to great lengths to make sure those people were sufficiently motivated."

"What did you do to them?"

"Oh, nothing much," he said. "Just a few nightmares. An illusion here or there."

"Why?"

Throwing his head back, Bendarian cackled. His laughter echoed off the walls and sent chills down Desa's spine. "Why?" he exclaimed. "You ask me why? I should think it would be obvious!"

His gaze snapped down to her, and Desa nearly jumped backward. By the eyes of Vengeance, the man had her on edge. "I've been trying to kill you for years," Bendarian said. "And each time, I was met with failure. Your stubborn refusal to die haunted me until I thought I might go mad. Was I doomed to live out this cycle forever, battling you over and over and yet never achieving victory?"

"You have a very grandiose opinion of yourself."

"But then, at long last, I understood," Bendarian continued as if she hadn't even spoken. "I couldn't kill you before because I wasn't meant to kill you then. Because you were meant to die here."

Turning her head to survey her surroundings, Desa felt her brow furrow. "I suppose there are worse places to spend eternity," she muttered. "One of us won't be leaving here; that much is certain."

Bendarian raised a single finger, waggling it at her as he strode forward. "You see, it all made sense to me when I finally grasped the true nature of the Nether," he said. "You wounded me in Ofalla, and in that moment, my power increased tenfold."

Bendarian spread his arms wide, and then he floated upward. In seconds, he was hovering above the raised floor, directly in the sunlight that came in through the hole in the ceiling. "Emotion, Desa!" he exclaimed. "After Thrasa, I understood. You wounded me, and I hated you for it!"

Slowly, he descended to land on his toes, and his grin widened into a sickening rictus. "That hatred made me powerful enough to pull myself back from the brink of death. The Nether responds to raw, unbridled emotion. It was the only thing that saved me."

Desa aimed her gun with a steady hand, cocked her head to one side and sniffed disdainfully. "Can it save you this time?"

"It won't just save me," Bendarian declared. "It will elevate me to godhood. I found this place years ago when I was still searching for a way to Infuse the Ether directly into living tissue. Our abilities are amplified here. We can manipulate the Ether with greater dexterity. So, when I kill you here, I will be strong enough to rip a hole in the Ether. The Nether will flood into this world, and I will remake it in my own-"

CRACK!

Bendarian's hand shot up to close around something. A moment later, his fingers uncurled to reveal a bullet in his palm.

Desa stood with her gun pointed straight at his chest, a thin trail of smoke rising from the barrel. "I have no patience for speeches," she said. "If we're going to fight, let's be done with it already."

She triggered the Heat-Source in the bullet.

Bendarian screeched as his hand became a blackened mass of scorched flesh. He tossed the bullet aside and then vanished with the slight whoosh of air filling the space he had vacated.

Every sensation was heightened as Desa ran across the raised floor and leaped from the edge. Triggering her Gravity-Sink allowed her to fly up to the second level, where a doorway in the wall led to a tunnel.

She ducked inside, spun around and pressed her back to the stone wall, gasping for breath. Sweat rolled over her face. "Come on, you ugly bastard," she whispered. "Show yourself!"

No sense in staying put.

Desa hurried up the narrow passageway with her pistol held in both hands. It wasn't all that long before she came to an opening the wall on her right, and when she went around the corner, she found a corridor identical to the one she had just left. A corridor that was illuminated by stones that gave off a soft, orange glow. Light-Sources.

No sooner did she take that first step than Bendarian appeared twenty paces in front of her with a fireball balanced above his upturned palm. He sent it flying toward Desa with a flick of his wrist.

Desa spun around the corner.

Pressing her back to the stone, she watched as the fireball hit the wall across from her with enough force to send chunks of rock flying. Some of them grazed her, and one left a gash across her bare shoulder.

Squeezing her eyes shut, Desa trembled as she drew in a breath. "Mercy shield your daughter from harm," she whispered. "This I pray as one who has served you from birth, as one who will serve you until the moment of her death."

She fired around the corner.

Bendarian danced backward in the adjoining corridor, his hands flying up to snatch her bullets out of the air. Soft laughter echoed off the walls as he retreated. Desa followed him in, advancing as he backed away.

Suddenly he vanished.

Her last shot hit the wall, shattering one of the glowing stones. Its fragments fell to the floor, but they still gave off faint orange light. An Infused object was still Infused even if you bludgeoned it into a hundred pieces. The Infusion was woven into every molecule.

Desa continued forward. If Bendarian could appear anywhere at will, there was no point in trying to get away from him. And if she could keep him away from the crystal, so much the better.

A whoosh of air behind her.

Twisting on the spot, Desa fired the last bullet in her gun without even bothering to look at her target. When she turned around, she saw Bendarian backing up with his fists closed around several of the slugs she had loosed.

He hit the scorched wall, then bared his teeth and gave his head a shake. "You are becoming quite the nuisance," he snarled.

He threw the bullets back at her.

By instinct, Desa raised her left hand to shield herself. Four smoking slugs came to an abrupt halt right in front of her. They all fell to the floor when she let her arm drop, but Bendarian wasn't done with her.

He stretched a hand out toward her, and his face contorted into an inhuman mask of rage and malice. Desa was lifted off the floor, pulled toward Bendarian like a fish caught on a line. There was no way to stop it. The man had her in his grip, and he knew it.

Discarding her empty pistol, Desa made a fist and triggered the Light-Source in her ring. The harsh glare hit Bendarian's face, forcing him to shut his eyes tight. In that brief moment of distraction, Desa drew her knife.

She collided with Bendarian, wrapping her legs around his waist, and then drove the blade of her dagger into his throat. His eyes flew open, and he let out a gurgling sound as dark blood spilled from his gaping mouth.

He vanished again.

Desa landed, bent double with a hand over her chest, shaking her head as she tried to get her bearings. "It's not that easy," she whispered. "Mercy protect your foolish child, it can't be that easy."

She straightened and rubbed her eyes with the back of one fist. Then she recovered her lost pistol. Popping open the cylinder, she loaded six more rounds.

That done, she went back around the corner and ran for the central chamber. She was only two steps away from the ledge when Bendarian appeared just beyond the opening, floating in the open air on nothing at all.

He was snarling, with green veins growing over his face, and there was a scar on his neck where her knife had pierced his flesh. "Die!" he screamed, flinging one hand out toward her.

Jagged cracks appeared in the ceiling, deep chasms in the stone, and then chunks of rubble were falling on Desa.

Shielding herself with her left hand, she triggered the Force-Sink in her bracelet.

Large rocks floated right above her head, suspended in midair. That gave her time enough to run at full speed and leap from the ledge.

She slammed into Bendarian, and her momentum propelled them both down onto the raised floor. They hit hard and rolled apart, grunting from the impact.

Skidding to a stop, Desa got up on one knee and looked over her shoulder toward Bendarian, a line of blood dripping from the corner of her mouth. "You were right," she panted. "We are destined to do this...Forever."

"No!"

He stood up, facing her and shaking his head in disgust. "No! I will not be bound to you!" His trembling hands came up, and a ball of fire coalesced between them, growing larger and larger until it was the size of Desa's head.

She opened the cylinder of her gun and spun it to select the bullet she wanted. Then she slapped it back into place and took aim.

Bendarian was standing with the growing fireball between his palms, his face alight with devilish glee. His laughter echoed through the pyramid. For half a second, he let his gaze linger on Desa...and then he sent that monstrosity hurtling toward her.

Desa fired, triggering the Heat-Sink.

Perhaps it was her increased awareness of the Ether, but everything seemed to slow down. The bullet came spiraling out of her pistol, trailed by a line of smoke. It flew lazily toward the oncoming fireball, and when it passed through the flames, they winked away in an instant, their heat consumed.

Onward, the bullet flew toward Bendarian, who stood

with his gaping mouth frozen in a silent scream. It pierced his body, just below the chest, and frost spread over him in a wave, stretching to the souls of his shoes, to the tips of his fingers and the top of his head. There was a crackling sound as flesh stiffened and moisture crystalized over his eyes.

He was dead.

It was over.

Pressing her fingertips to her forehead, Desa shut her eyes as she struggled to catch her breath. "It's over," she whispered. "Sweet Mercy, it's over."

She stood up and became instantly aware of her aching muscles. The effort nearly knocked her back down again. Of course, she could just...The Ether seemed to wash over her almost of its own accord, and the pains throughout her body began to fade. Slowly, but they did fade.

When she looked at the collection of particles that made up Bendarian's body, she gasped in fright. There was a darkness between them, linking every molecule to each of its neighbours and straining to burst forth from his skin. The Nether. He was its conduit into this world, and it wanted out. Which could only mean one thing.

Bendarian was still alive.

She released the Ether and watched in horror as the frost that covered Bendarian from head to toe melted away. His lips parted in a smile. "You simply refuse to learn, don't you?" he said. "How many times must I tell you, Desa? You can't hurt me."

He spread his arms wide, striding toward her and tittering like a madman. "Do you not see?" he bellowed. "I am connected to a force far older than this universe, a force that will remake the cosmos. I am immortal! Unbreakable! You cannot hurt me!"

CRACK!

Bendarian stumbled as a bullet went through his left side and burst out his right. *CRACK! CRACK! CRACK!* He staggered with every step forward, squealing as hot lead pierced his flesh. Finally, he collapsed to his knees.

Adele stood on the edge of the raised floor in a tattered dress, her long golden hair braided and wrapped around her neck, a pistol in her outstretched hand. "Maybe not," she said. "But I can!"

26

Desa rushed into her lover's arms, abandoning any thought of lecturing the other woman for foolishly following her into the desert. She stood on her toes, taking Adele's face in both hands and kissing her lips.

Closing her eyes, Desa let her head sink with the weight of her exhaustion. "I love you," she whispered. "Thank you."

A blush coloured Adele's cheeks, but her fond smile was one of the most beautiful things Desa had ever seen. "What are soulmates for?" she asked. "But we must be quick. He will be on his feet again shortly."

"I'll finish him."

Wincing as if the thought of it brought her pain, Adele shook her head. "You can't kill him, Desa," she said. "He was right about that much at least. The Nether will sustain him through any damage you inflict."

Desa took a shaky step backward, her pistol in one hand and pointed at the floor. She drew in a shuddering breath. "Then what do we do?" she rasped. "I can think of no other way to subdue him."

Adele looked upward, blinking as she took in the sight of

the massive crystal in the ceiling. "He needs that to release the Nether," she said. "If I can destroy it, it won't matter if we kill him."

"*Can* you destroy it?"

An impish grin was Adele's reply. She bent forward to kiss Desa's forehead. "I don't know who created that thing," she said. "But it amplifies our abilities. In this place, I can guide the Ether with a precision I would have never thought possible. It's a simple matter of creating a feedback loop."

A feedback loop? Turn the pulses back on their source. Yes...Desa could see how that might shatter the crystal. But it would require Adele to enter a trance-like state. She would be vulnerable.

The other woman seemed to realize the implications because she turned her back and rushed down the stairs, running for the tunnel that led back outside. "Just keep him off me for a few minutes," she said. "This won't take long."

A few minutes? Something about that felt off. Even with enhanced control of the Ether, it should have taken longer to crack a crystal like that. But then, Adele had always displayed abilities beyond anything that should have been possible. Perhaps it was fate. Perhaps she was here because Desa needed her. Either way, Desa didn't argue.

When she turned, Bendarian was getting to his feet, and his face was...demonic. His skin was a sickly shade of green with veins that seemed to pulse. His one remaining eye was red. It seemed that every time he used the Nether to heal himself, he lost a little more of his humanity. "The girl is a fool," he spat. "She cannot shatter that crystal. Certainly not with only a few minutes of effort."

His lips parted in what might have been a smile, and Desa gasped at the sight of two large fangs protruding from his mouth. "I will dispose of you," he said. "And then I will deal with the girl."

He threw a small fireball.

Desa jumped, triggering her Gravity-Sink, and back-flipped as the sizzling ball of flame passed by beneath her. She uncurled, killed the Sink and dropped to land upon the edge of the raised floor.

Her head came up; she breathed slowly through her nose, and then her eyes flicked open. "You simply refuse to learn," she said. "You cannot kill me."

With a snarl, Bendarian flew up toward the crystal.

He floated in the air, spreading his arms wide, lightning flashing from the tips of his fingers. Damn it, Marcus was right! If only Desa had bothered to make an Electric-Sink. Then again...

The Ether came to her with no effort at all, and Desa worked by instinct. She chose her two earrings, laying down a lattice that would draw electrical energy from anything coming toward her, but not from her own body.

She broke her connection to the Ether.

Bendarian hovered under the bottom the crystal with a ball of lightning crackling between his palms. He screamed, thrust his arms forward, and Desa triggered the Sinks.

A jagged silver lance tried to stab her, tried to obliterate her, tried to scour her to ash, but it winked away before it got within an inch of Desa's body. Even still, the light was so fierce that even behind her eyelids, her eyes were smarting. "Why won't you die?" Bendarian moaned. "Why won't you die?"

He began a quick descent toward her.

Desa ordered her belt buckle to drain gravitational energy.

She jumped when Bendarian drew near, turned belly-up

and brought her feet up to smash the underside of his chin. Flipping over, she flew backwards until her feet hit the wall. Then she compressed like a spring and pushed off.

A dazed Bendarian was still floating in the air before her, black blood dripping from his mouth, running over his chin. Desa slammed into him, propelling them both across the room until his back hit the wall.

She punched his face once, twice, three times. Each blow elicited a snarl from his monstrous throat. Two claw-like hands grabbed Desa's shirt and shoved her away.

EVEN FACTORING in its low height, climbing to the top of the pyramid was not easy. No, not the least bit easy. A woman of means should not have to subject herself to this, but Adele stifled her complaints.

She had work to do.

On her knees at the edge of the pyramid's flat top, Adele panted and wiped sweat off her brow with the back of one hand. "Focus..." Her eyes flew open. "Just a few more minutes. You can do this."

She looked back over her shoulder.

Midnight was waiting at the base of the pyramid, watching her with apprehension on his face. If a horse could display apprehension in his gaze, that was. This one certainly managed a reasonable facsimile of it, anyway. This wasn't the first time Adele had caught him staring, and she hated it.

Getting to her feet was difficult, but she did it and then stumbled forward to lay her hand on the crystal. It was warm to the touch, and the Ether's pulses seemed to intensify when she made contact.

Only a few minutes more.

If Desa could keep Bendarian busy just a few minutes longer, Adele could do what had to be done. She set to work.

DESA HIT the raised floor and rolled like a log across its surface. Flopping over onto her belly, she groaned and then tried to push herself up on extended arms. Her head was ringing like a struck gong.

Through blurry vision, she saw Bendarian descending toward her. Only one thing to do. Drawing her pistol from its holster, she extended her arm and pointed it at the wall. A wall would do well enough.

She fired.

Once her bullet embedded itself in the stone, she triggered the Gravity-Source that she had Infused into it along with the Sink in her belt. Bendarian was yanked backward until he crashed into the wall. And with him pinned, she had a moment to get up.

Desa rose, lifted her gun in one hand and fired again and again. Each slug that ripped through his body caused Bendarian to writhe and spasm against the wall. He shrieked and hurled fire at her.

A blazing stream of it.

Desa threw herself off the raised floor to land in the narrow space between it and the wall. No time for standing still. She ran for cover.

LOST in the task Adele focused. The world around her was a sea of particles all colliding and jostling each other. She ignored them. This deep in the Ether's embrace, she was barely aware of her own body.

She did feel it, however, when something pulled her

downward and sideways, leaving her sprawled out on the pyramid's rooftop. Would that fool woman never tire of her trinkets? Manipulating gravity with all the subtlety of a charging bull. Desa Kincaid had a pretty face and hands that could work magic on any woman, but damn it, she could be a trial. Adele put that aside.

Just a little longer.

She felt the Ether quivering.

Just a little longer.

BENDARIAN STOOD on the edge of the raised floor with a fire-ball in each hand, his face now hideously twisted with snake-like features, his eyes red with a single slit. A forked tongue lashed out from his mouth.

Standing with the pistol held in her extended hand, its barrel pointed straight at her enemy, Desa squinted at him. "How it must frustrate you," she said. "All your power, and you still can't kill one woman."

Bendarian spread his arms, throwing his head back to howl in impotent rage. Dust rose off the floor and swirled around him in a cyclone, a pillar of sand that stretched all the way up to the ceiling. And suddenly, the pillar was coming for Desa.

She fired.

An instant later – less than a fraction of a second – she triggered the Force-Sink that she had Infused into the bullet and watched the swirling winds of that cyclone come to a sudden stop, every particle frozen in place. It was still close enough to Bendarian that he might have been frozen as well.

Pacing to the corner of the raised floor, Desa saw that her suspicions were indeed correct. Bendarian was a statue with scaly hands stretched toward the cyclone, a look of murderous glee on his serpentine face.

"Didn't think I'd put one in a bullet, did you?"

Twirling her gun around her index finger, Desa caught the grip and then extended her hand to take aim. She lined up the perfect shot, waited just a moment and then ordered her bullet to stop draining kinetic energy.

The cyclone lurched forward.

Desa fired.

A hole appeared in the side of Bendarian's head. The man dropped to his knees and then fell flat on his face. His cyclone collapsed into a pile of dust that spread throughout the room.

Pressing a fist to her mouth, Desa coughed several times before the wave of dust finally settled. "By the eyes of Vengeance," she squeaked. "Let that be the end of it."

She holstered her weapon.

Approaching Bendarian took a little more courage than she would have expected. A part of her was still expecting him to leap back to his feet and start hurling death at her all over again. But Bendarian remained still.

He was stretched out on his belly, black blood pooling around his body. Maybe it really was over. Maybe Adele was wrong. Perhaps death had taken him before he could use his dark magics to restore himself.

Any hope she had of that died when the whole world changed. It was the change that she experienced every time she communed with the Ether – she didn't see solid objects as collections of particles – but it *was* a change.

Everything looked red, as if the sun itself had dimmed. When Desa examined the crystal above her, she saw that the light passing through it had a distinctly crimson tint. It was unnerving, to say the least.

Kneeling down next to Bendarian's corpse, Desa hugged herself and then shook her head. "What is it now?" she wondered aloud. "Vengeance carve me up for dog meat, can't a woman get any peace?"

She drew her revolver and watched aghast as the barrel melted. Well-forged steel just dissolved into a metallic goop that made a sickening sound as it dribbled to the floor. Desa patted her body to make sure she was still whole. Everything seemed in order. Still, she was frightened.

"My, word...What did you do to Benny?"

Desa was on her feet in an instant.

The speaker's voice had a distinct twang that was unfamiliar to her, but when she turned around, she saw Adele emerging from the tunnel that led to the surface. Or rather an apparition that looked like Adele.

Instead of a tattered dress, this woman wore a flowing white gown of impeccable cut. Her long hair was still braided, but there were no more flyaway strands. Instead, it was silky smooth, and it seemed to catch the light somehow.

And her eyes.

Her eyes were pure white from corner to corner, and the smile that blossomed on her lovely face was nothing short of bone-chilling. "I simply abhor wasted potential," she said. "On your feet, Benny."

Adele snapped her fingers

The wound in Bendarian's head closed itself, and he groaned as life returned to his twisted body. He stood up slowly, rubbing his face with a scaly hand. "What happened? Where am I?"

He turned his red-eyed stare upon Desa, and his lips parted to show two monstrous fangs. "You!" he hissed. "Will I never be rid of you?"

He thrust a hand toward Desa.

She jumped back instinctively, reaching for a pistol that wasn't there, but nothing happened. In fact, Bendarian seemed to be as confused as she was. He flung his hand out several more times, but when the gesture failed to produce a fireball or lightning bolt or whatever it was he had intended, he threw his head back and wailed.

"Now, now," Adele said. "Ain't no cause for cryin'."

She vanished from sight and then suddenly reappeared atop the raised floor, never breaking. "You always did have a penchant for theatrics, didn't you, Benny?" she cooed. "It does get a might wearisome, I'm afraid."

Gaping at the other woman, Desa blinked several times and then gave her head a shake. "Adele...What did you do?" She was fairly certain that she knew the answer, but a part of her still clung to hope.

Adele twirled on the spot, the skirt of her gown flaring, and then faced Desa with her hands on her hips. "Oh, honey," she said. "Do I really gotta spell it out for y'all? I do prefer a woman with brains, but if you insist."

Adele puffed up her chest as she drew in a breath, and when she spoke again, her voice changed. It wasn't the voice that Desa remembered, the clipped speech patterns that were common to the people of Ofalla. Nor was it the twangy accent that she had adopted for some reason. No, it was a voice Desa had heard only once before.

The voice of the entity that had been controlling those people on the farm. "Adele is no more," it said. "We are one now."

Adele sat primly on nothing at all, folding her hands in her lap and tilting her head to one side as she examined Desa. "Of course, we aren't exactly the Nether either." The twangy accent had returned. "Suppose we'll have to take a new name."

"What did you do to her?" Desa growled.

"Do to her?" the other woman exclaimed. "Oh, Sweetie, you mean you still don't understand?" She vanished, and when she reappeared, she was lying face-down on a bed of nothing but air.

With her chin balanced on the backs of folded hands, she floated at eye-level with Desa. "She welcomed this," the twangy voice purred. Rolling onto her back, the entity giggled and kicked her feet. "Oh, Benny, you look so crestfallen."

The serpent-man that had once been Radharal Bendarian scowled and looked down at the floor. "You promised yourself to me," he mumbled. It was just a statement of fact, delivered without anger or venom.

Adele sat up, drumming her fingers on the invisible surface that supported her as she studied him. "Yes," she agreed. "But honestly, hon, you bore me. All those grandiose speeches...And how do I put this?"

She hopped down off her invisible ledge and glided to Bendarian, her hips swaying with every step. She reached up to lay a hand on his scaly cheek, and he tried to turn his face away. "You're...Well, I don't want to say 'used up.'"

Bendarian flinched at her words.

"And this one," Adele went on. "Such a clever girl. Did you know she watched you with her talents, deduced your plans and then...Well, she was just a little quicker on the draw, now wasn't she? And you!"

The other woman spun around to face Desa, grinning from ear to ear as she strode forward. "The sweet little things she whispered in your ear." A fit of giggles made Adele double over. "You...You *actually* believed she was your soulmate!"

Desa felt her jaw drop, then grimaced and forced herself

to put aside the pain of that barbed comment. "The light," she said. "What did you do? Why is everything red? Why did my gun melt?"

"Oh that," Adele scoffed. "Ain't nothing to worry about, sweetheart. You see, my presence distorts what you might call the natural order, creating...Well,you might call it a glitch in the rules that govern this universe."

Adele stood under the crystal with fists on her hips, craning her neck to stare up at the red light coming in front above. "In this case, a slight red shift in the local light waves and a loss of molecular cohesion among metals. You might want to have a gander at your pants, my love."

Desa did as she was bid and found that her belt buckle had melted, creating a stain of brassy goo on her pants. All metals? Even her bullets? Her ring? The clips that secured Midnight's saddle and bridle?

She touched her earlobes and found that her earrings had indeed melted. And when she pulled the ring off her finger, it left a sticky residue behind and then squished in the palm of her hand. "By the eyes of Vengeance!"

Curiosity got the better of her, and she triggered the Light-Source that had been Infused into that ring. The puddle in her hand began to glow with a somber yellow light. An Infused object was still an Infused object even if you broke it into a hundred pieces.

"Be glad the effects were mostly harmless," Adele said. "If my arrival had altered the cosmic speed limit, for instance."

"Cosmic speed limit?" Desa mumbled.

Adele gave her a sympathetic look. "Right, of course," she said. "Your people are right on the verge of discovering that little nugget. My sisters did create an interesting little playground for y'all."

Desa's mouth worked silently, and she shook her head in disbelief. "Your sisters," she mumbled at last. "Mercy and Vengeance."

"My my, the girl does have some brains!" Adele covered her mouth with one hand as she giggled. "Yes, I do suppose that *is* what you would call them, though neither term encapsulates the totality of them."

As Desa took in the horror of it all, the enormity of what she faced, Adele sauntered over to Bendarian and patted him gently on the cheek. "Come on then, Benny," she said. "I do believe it's time we were on our way."

A god.

This creature was a god, and Desa had facilitated its arrival by allowing Adele to travel with her party. By trusting her heart over the instincts that told her Adele Delarac was no good. She had been so fixated on Bendarian, so single-minded in her pursuit of him that she had turned a blind eye to the treachery right under her nose.

Rage lit a fire in her belly, turned her blood to acid and set her mind racing. Maybe there was still away. The creature was dependent on Adele's body. If Desa could destroy it, maybe the entity would lose its hold on this world.

But how?

Her weapons were gone.

Except...An Infused object was still Infused even if you shattered it into a thousand pieces. The leather pouch that carried her melted bullets. Some of them were Sources and Sinks.

She pulled the pouch of her belt – it wasn't hard with the buckle gone – opened it and tried to splash some of the goo onto Adele.

The other woman had her back turned, but she raised a hand dismissively, and the goo stopped in midair. "Now, I like you, Desa," she began. "I wasn't lyin' all those times I said so. But so help me, you start chasin' me, houndin' me or tryin' to stick me with pointy objects, and I swear on my sweet mama's grave, I will slap the taste outta your mouth. Come, Benny."

Adele snapped her fingers.

And they were both gone.

27

At the end of the tunnel that led out of the pyramid, Desa saw a crimson landscape and a cloudless pink sky. The sight of it filled her with despair. This was the cost of her arrogance. By the eyes of Vengeance, she should never have let Adele Delarac into her bed. Much less into her heart.

Desa stepped into the sunlight with her arms hanging limp, her eyes fixed on the ground. Down the steps she went to where Midnight waited patiently like the loyal friend that he was.

It shocked Desa to realize that she had half expected to find him gone. Why would he stay after Desa's failure had damned the world? But the horse didn't judge her; he just came forward and nuzzled her shoulder.

Desa shut her eyes tight, tears leaking from them to stream over her cheeks. A fit of sobs forced her down onto her knees, and she shuddered with every breath. "Why did I not see her for what she was?"

Midnight bent low to lick her forehead.

"Stop!"

Wiping tears away with the back of her hand, Desa sniffled. "Stop," she said again in a softer voice. "I appreciate your efforts, old friend, but I fear I have proven unworthy of your kindness."

Midnight snorted.

She stood up and took the stallion's bridle in hand. Of course, the whole thing fell apart when its metal fasteners melted. That almost had her down on the ground again, but she took control of herself and led Midnight away from the pyramid.

Just before they reached the first ring of ruined buildings, the world changed. The sky brightened from a somber pink to a vibrant shade of blue. The sun was once again a brilliant white disk only a short way past its zenith.

Desa stepped forward, shielding her eyes with one hand and staring hard into the distance. "What happened?" She turned to Midnight and sighed with relief when she saw that he was his proper shade of black.

Turning around, she expected to find the pyramid bathed in a thick haze of red, but it looked normal. The stones were a proper sandy brown. The massive crystal sparkled in the sunlight, and the sky was still blue. Perhaps the world had righted itself. The laws of nature had reasserted themselves somehow.

Three quick strides toward the pyramid put paid to that notion. The sky reddened, and the pyramid and everything else in sight. Even though he stood just outside the borders of this phenomenon, Midnight appeared to be a deep, dark red to her eyes.

So, the effect was localized.

Desa strode back into the natural light, shaking her head. "I don't know what Adele did," she began. "But we can thank Mercy it didn't spread very far."

There was no point in remaining here, but another flight

across the desert could kill them if they didn't take time to eat and drink, and the only source of water she knew of was in that haunted orchard.

At first, she thought she would have been hesitant to return there, but it pleased her to realize that her fear was greatly diminished. Desa had tangled with a god; what could a vengeful spirit do to her.

When they returned to the small orchard, they found the copper tower still standing, which only made sense. It had not been in the area of effect of whatever Adele had done to the pyramid. But all of the Sinks and Sources were depleted.

Desa reached out to the Ether and found that it came as easily as it had the moment she arrived in this town. The crystal was still doing its job...somehow. Desa had no desire to question her good fortune in that regard.

She scanned the water condenser with her mind, Reinfused all of the Sources and Sinks and set them to work creating water. It wasn't long before she had several buckets full. She gave one to Midnight and let him drink until he was sated.

After that, he started grazing on the grass while Desa ate peaches to fill her belly. Not the most satisfying meal she could have imagined, but it was better than nothing. If nothing else, it would improve her chances of survival.

Standing before Midnight, Desa laid a hand on his long face, and he leaned into her touch. "I suppose we'll have to choose our destination," she said. "I don't think we'll find much of a welcome at Fool's Edge."

Midnight's ears slanted back at the mention of the town.

"We could press on to Dry Gulch," she said. "Though I'm not sure I know the way, and I have no map. We're likely to find ourselves stranded in the desert with no food or water."

It was quite the conundrum; if they raced back to Fool's Edge, they would find it hard to procure supplies. And it would be several days of trudging through inhospitable wilderness before they reached the fertile lands of the Vinrella. Could they hold out that long without food? Or water? Desa carried a water skin that she had filled, but that would only take her so far. And Dry Gulch...Well, they might not even be able to find Dry Gulch. Quite the conundrum.

Clamping her mouth shut, Desa felt creases in her brow. "Of course, there might be another option," she murmured. "You could try communing with the Ether. Think about it! If that crystal extended the range of my senses, it will surely do the same for you."

If Midnight was able to sense Dry Gulch's location, even across dozens of miles, he would know which way to go. He seemed to think it worth the effort because Desa soon felt a resonance from him. His eyes took on the vacant stare of someone who was lost in the Ether's embrace. Several minutes later, Midnight came back to the waking world, and then he did something Desa had never seen before.

He nodded.

A grin stretched across Desa's face, and her cheeks grew uncomfortably warm. "All right, then," she said. "It seems your senses are more attuned than my own. I assume this means you know the way."

Midnight turned and walked out of the orchard.

Desa shrugged and followed.

AT THE EDGE OF TOWN, they found the poor filly standing with her ears flicking this way and that. The girl had been spooked by what she saw at the pyramid. She must have run off. Midnight, dutiful steed that he was, had remained.

Desa approached the young horse with one hand extended, careful to avoid doing anything that might agitate her further. "Easy girl," she whispered. "Everything's all right now. We're your friends."

The horse retreated further, dancing backward.

Shutting her eyes, Desa trembled as she drew in a breath. "We might have to leave her here," she whispered. "The poor thing is too spooked."

Midnight trotted past her and went right up to the filly, who seemed quite willing to tolerate his presence. Something passed between them, something that Desa couldn't even hope to understand, but when it was over, Midnight simply turned and started off into the desert, and the filly followed him without complaint.

Desa had to jog to keep up, and as she fell in beside her horse, she shook her head ruefully. "You old charmer," she teased. "If I didn't know any better, I'd say you fancied the poor girl."

Midnight gave her a look that said it was none of her business.

Once they had put a little distance between themselves and the abandoned town, Midnight slowed down long enough to let her mount up. Unfortunately, Desa had to ride bareback; Midnight's saddle was useless with all of its buckles melted. It was going to be a very long and uncomfortable journey.

The air was still warm with the onset of evening, but the sun was sinking slowly toward the western horizon, and Desa was happy to be free of its glare. Soon, the chill of night would be making her huddle up in her coat – which no longer had buttons – but for now, she was thankful for the drop in temperature.

She wasn't sure what made her do it – curiosity, she

suspected – but she ventured a glance back over her shoulder. She knew what she would find, but she forced herself to look anyway.

The abandoned town was as silent as a tomb, its buildings cloaked in the gloom of lengthening shadows. And there between the rubble of two houses, a figure in unrelieved black watched them go, a hooded figure who seemed to make the very air grow cold.

Desa peeled her gaze off the spectre and rubbed her forehead with the back of one hand. "Let's hurry," she urged Midnight. "I have a distinct impression that we do *not* want to be here when the sun sets."

She risked another glance.

The hooded figure was gone, of course. She saw nothing but broken buildings and the faint glint of evening sunlight on the distant crystal. Despite herself, she shivered. The dead could have their town. Now that she had failed in her task, she had no further need of it.

Midnight did not bother to look back, but she could tell by his stiffness that he had sensed whatever that thing was. Perhaps it left a kind of reverberation in the Ether. And maybe that was how Desa could feel its eyes on her back.

They carried on in silence.

WHEN THE LAST traces of daylight were gone, they were miles away from the town, and the night's chill was making Desa huddle up in a coat that lacked buttons. The wind threatened to whip the hat off her head.

Stifling a yawn with one hand, Desa shut her eyes. "Maybe it would be best to stop for a while," she murmured. "We are in no hurry, and even with the Ether to guide your steps, riding at night is unwise."

The filly could not duplicate Midnight's feat of mapping the terrain with his mind and using that knowledge to avoid danger. Of course, their gentle pace made it unlikely that they would have to worry about one of the horses suffering an injury. A fierce gallop through the dark – the kind of mad dash they had employed in their pursuit of Bendarian – was inadvisable, to say the least, but horses could carry on in low light. Still, Desa would take any excuse to stop and sleep.

Midnight, however, seemed determined to press on. He didn't even acknowledge Desa's suggestion; he just continued on his steady pace forward with the filly eyeing him from time to time.

Scrubbing a hand over her face, Desa moaned her displeasure. "Yes...I suppose you have the right of it," she mumbled. "Better to cover more ground before the sun scorches us again."

She was about ready to nod off, and the difficulty of keeping her balance without a saddle only made things worse. Thankfully, there didn't seem to be anyone else out here. If they ran afoul of bandits, she would have a very hard time of it without guns, knives or Infused weapons.

Suddenly, Midnight stopped.

Desa felt him communing with the Ether, and then his ears twitched. Before she could say one word, the stallion took off like an arrow loosed from a bow. In the wrong direction! As far as Desa could tell, they had turned northeast but Dry Gulch was about forty to fifty miles northwest of the abandoned town. "Where are we going?" she asked.

Midnight didn't answer; he just galloped.

The filly whinnied as she struggled to keep up, and Desa felt a moment of panic. She was likely to hurt herself, running at that pace through the darkness. Desa hoped her horse knew that the terrain was level.

They had traveled for at least fifteen minutes, maybe longer, when Desa decided that enough was enough. She was about to insist that they stop this foolishness and turn back toward Dry Gulch, but a light in the distance caught her eye. It seemed clear that that was Midnight's destination.

But what was it?

Not a fire. The light was too even for that. And the glow had more of a white tinge than the fierce orange of flames. In fact, the only thing outside of an electric bulb that could emit that kind of light was an Infused object.

Grinning like a fool who had drunk himself stupid, Desa shook her head. "Why you glorious bastard," she shouted, patting the stallion's neck. "You could sense them even in this endless wilderness?"

The light drew near, and she saw people standing up to face her with guns in hand. No doubt they had been roused by the sound of Midnight's galloping. Tommy projected a bravery she would not have expected from him, moving to bar her path with grim resolve on his face.

Miri was at his side, of course, but she seemed more confused than focused. And the fact that Desa couldn't see Marcus meant she would have bullets flying her way any second now. "Don't shoot!" she hollered. "It's me!"

Tommy lowered his weapon.

Miri sighed visibly and immediately sank back down to sit with her legs curled up. Even at this distance, Desa could see that the poor woman was exhausted. Had they been riding all day to catch her?

Midnight slowed to a trot as they approached the light, and then a gruff voice from the darkness made Desa flinch.

"What happened?" Marcus demanded. "Did you kill him? And where is Adele?"

"Bendarian is no longer a threat." Desa replied.

"And Adele?"

She dismounted and told them everything: her frantic scramble through the desert, the abandoned town, the crystal and the strange orchard that ran on self-renewing Infused technology. She told them of her fight with Bendarian, of Adele's betrayal and possession by the entity they had encountered on that farm.

Marcus stood at the edge of the light with teeth bared, shaking his head in disgust. "I knew that girl was no good," he growled. "We should have been done with her a long time ago."

"She would have followed us anyway," Desa lamented.

Tommy, she noticed, was unwilling to look at her. His face was turned away, bathed in light from glowing coins that Marcus had set on a large flat rock. It pained Desa to see that, but she offered no complaint.

She was on her knees in the dust, head hanging as she exhaled. "Somehow, Adele learned of Bendarian's plan in Ofalla," she went on. "She made up all that nonsense about soul mates and destiny so that we would take her with us."

Desa did not state the painfully obvious: that it was she herself who had been taken in by Adele's lies. Now, the world itself was in danger, and she did not know what to do. "We were headed for Dry Gulch," she added faintly.

Marcus paced a circle at the edge of the light, tapping his thigh with one hand. "It seems as good a plan as any," he said at last. "We'll find no welcome at Fool's Edge, and we lack the supplies to travel back to the wetlands."

"After that, I don't know what to do next."

To her surprise, Miri rose, came forward with the

caution of a man approaching a feral tiger and then knelt beside Desa. "You needn't decide that on your own," she said, clapping a hand on Desa's shoulder. "We will face this challenge together."

Closing her eyes, Desa felt tears on her cheeks, but she nodded anyway. "Thank you," she whispered. "But I fear it won't be that easy."

"One problem at a time," Tommy said without looking at her. "First we get out of this wilderness, and then we decide what to do about Adele."

Desa couldn't argue with that. She wasn't entirely sure how Adele's new powers worked, but she suspected that the woman could travel great distances in a single hop. It would do no good trying to chase her. Their first priority was to secure food and supplies. That meant a trip to Dry Gulch.

"Sleep well," Marcus grumbled. "We ride hard come morning."

28

Dry Gulch was a village of white stone buildings with flat roofs, tucked away inside a ravine between two rock walls. The town was built upon the bed of a river that had dried up long ago. And yet the people were thriving. Tommy wondered how they found water in this wasteland.

He saw people in ponchos and wide-brimmed hats as they shuffled through the streets, the men in tan pants or dungarees, the women in thin dresses with short sleeves.

One lovely young lady with copper skin and black hair that she wore tied up in a bun eyed them as she carried a basket of laundry down the street. A short little man with a bushy mustache smiled at them from the saddle of his horse.

Tommy led his father's horse by the reins, frowning as he glanced this way and that. He kept expecting Adele to suddenly appear in the middle of the street and rain lightning down on him. That would be just like her; the woman had been insufferable *before* she had taken up with a demon.

Tommy shut his eyes, his head hanging with fatigue, and

then he slid the knuckle of one fist across his forehead. "So, this is what our journey comes to," he mumbled. "Stuck out here in the middle of nowhere."

Miri was at his side, walking casually, but the way her gaze settled on everyone that passed told him there was nothing casual about it. From what he had come to understand about the Ka'adri, she was one of Aladar's greatest assassins. "Only a brief stop on a very long journey, my love," she assured him.

In a way, she had been his saving grace these last few days. Marcus had been in a fit from the very moment that Desa rode off into the night, and Tommy had feared that his inexperience would ruin everything. Every time he wanted to lament the burden that he was to the rest of the group, Miri just smiled and told him that everything would be all right. He was growing to care for her.

Desa walked beside Midnight, but the stallion had neither saddle nor bridle, and for that matter, Desa's gun and knives were conspicuously absent. He was dying to ask why she had removed the buttons from her coat, but doing that would require him to confront a storm of emotion that he was more than happy to ignore for the time being.

Desa had killed Sebastian.

It bothered him that she had done so – that she *could* do so without hesitation – but what bothered him even more was the fact that he wasn't even mad about it. Oh, there had been anger, but it quickly faded into a kind of somber resignation. The sad truth was that, sooner or later, Sebastian would have forced Desa's hand. There was just no getting around that sad reality.

A woman in a brown hat suddenly rode her dun mare into the middle of the street, barring their path. Tommy could see that she wore a sheriff's star on her tan vest.

"Whoa there now," she said. "What brings the lot of ya to our fair city."

It wasn't much of a city. Not compared to Ofalla, anyway, but Tommy had enough sense to keep that observation to himself. "We need supplies," Marcus said gruffly. "We don't intend to stay long. Is it common for the sheriff to greet new arrivals?"

The woman dismounted with a scuff of dirt, and when she stood up straight, he saw that she wasn't much taller than Desa. Her face was lovely with a delicate nose and tilted eyes. "It is after the sort of strangers we've had comin' through here," she answered. "A few days back, we had a fella with green veins on his face come round and start harassin' everybody, threatenin' them."

"That man won't trouble you again," Desa said.

The Sheriff put fists on her hips, drew herself up to full height and strode forward with a smile on her face. "That a fact?" she asked. "How would you be knowin' that?"

Marcus stepped forward to meet her. Tommy could only see the back of the other man's head, but he was well acquainted with Marcus's scowl. "What matters is that we do not intend to stay."

"Just the same, I think it'd be wise if I had a word with y'all," she said. "My name's Sheriff Kalia Troval. Right this way, if you please."

SHERIFF TROVAL'S office was exactly what Desa would have expected: walls of white plaster, a simple wooden desk with an unlit lantern on top, windows that looked out upon the street and allowed sunlight through. There were a pair of pistols hung up on the wall with their barrels crossed. An interesting sight, that.

Desa seated herself with hands on the armrests of her chair, frowning as she studied the other woman. "Is this really necessary?" she asked, raising one eyebrow. "We've told you our intentions."

The sheriff rounded the desk and leaned forward with her hands braced upon its surface. The intensity of her scrutiny almost made Desa flinch. Almost. "That you did," she admitted. "But I want to know what you know about the man with veins on his face."

Shutting her eyes, Desa took a deep breath before responding. "All I can tell you is that he's gone," she said. "And he will never trouble you again."

"Why should I take your word for that?"

Desa sat back with her arms folded, nodding once in respect. "Perhaps you should not," she answered. "But I've told you all I can."

A sigh exploded from the sheriff as she removed her hat and tossed it aside to land on an empty chair by the window. The woman was quite lovely. Long brown hair framed a face that belonged on a statue. "You'll forgive a country lass for her trouble keeping up. We are a bit thick-headed."

"I said nothing of the sort."

"No...But you seem to take me for an idiot." Kalia Troval dropped into her chair, propped her feet up on the desk and crossed them at the ankle. "You come into my town. You say you know the man who terrorized some of my people, but you refuse to tell me anything specific, and then you expect that I'll let you be on your way."

"His name was Radharal Bendarian."

"See? Now, we're getting somewhere."

With her mouth agape, Desa blinked several times as she considered exactly how much she could tell this woman.

"What do you know of Field Binding?" she said. "The secret of Aladar."

To her shock, Kalia Troval actually laughed and shook her head. "Now who's the idiot?" she exclaimed. "You've got a lot to learn if you think Field Binding belongs only to the Aladri."

That was like a splash of cold water in the face. In all her travels, Desa had never encountered anyone beyond Aladar's borders who had learned the arts of Field Binding. But then, she had never ventured this far away from the eastern coast. Was it possible the people of Dry Gulch had been using the talent themselves? Perhaps to grow food in the desert? She was suddenly reminded of that strange orchard.

"Well then," Desa began, "Since you know of Field Binding, that will make things easier. Bendarian was a student in Aladar, the son of a foreigner, but he had a remarkable talent when it came to Infusing items. He came to believe that people could be Infused with the power of the Ether. His experiments never worked, of course, until one day, he tried something different.

"No one knows what he did, but every one of his subjects died. The Synod ordered his arrest. Bendarian fled the city, and I pursued him. I have continued that pursuit for ten long years."

"Quite the story," Kalia replied. "But it doesn't explain how you ended up in these parts. Would y'all mind skipping to that?"

Desa shoved her reservations down into the pit of her stomach. Given a choice, she would have preferred to avoid discussing the pyramid and the abandoned town, but it was clear the sheriff would accept nothing less than the whole tale. "I pursued Bendarian to a town southeast of here, an abandoned city with-"

Kalia Troval shot out of her chair and practically leaped over the desk. Perching on top of it, she leaned forward until she was almost nose to nose with Desa. "You went into the Nameless City?" Her breath stank of whiskey.

Blinking in confusion, Desa recoiled from the other woman. "Yes," she replied. "It was necessary to prevent Bendarian from-"

"You went into the Nameless City."

"As I told you-"

The sheriff sat on the edge of her desk with hands on her knees, her eyes fixed upon the floorboards. "Well, isn't that just dandy?" she muttered angrily. "Tell me true now, did you see it?"

"See what?"

"The thing that lurks there!" Kalia blustered. "The thing that watches anyone stupid enough to venture into that graveyard."

Desa felt sweat on her brow, and yet, at the same time, she was cold from head to toe. Her first breath was a frigid shudder. "Yes, I saw it," she whispered. "Watching me from the shadows. What is that thing? And who built that city?"

"She asks me who built the city?" Kalia grumbled. "We don't know who built it! It was here when our ancestors settled these parts two hundred years ago. Some folks went in looking for treasure. And some found it, you might say. They studied the devices there and learned what you call Field Binding.

"But the Watcher was always there. Everyone who came out of that place spoke of feeling eyes on them everywhere they went. Some claimed to have seen the Watcher, but no two could agree on exactly what it was they saw. Some folks who went in there didn't come out quite right. And some didn't come out at all. After a while, we stopped sending expeditions. Best to let the dead sleep undisturbed."

Desa shivered, huddling up in her coat. Her head sank, and she reached up to rake fingers through her hair. "I had to go," she said. "Bendarian wanted to use the crystal on that pyramid to unleash something horrible into this world."

Kalia rose to stand over her, clicking her tongue in annoyance. "I can promise you this much," she said. "That place isn't through with you yet. No one who goes in there is ever truly free of it."

A SMALL WOODEN porch outside the sheriff's office sat in the shade of an overhanging roof, and the tiny bit of relief it offered from the heat was enough to make Tommy bless his good fortune. The town was busy with people milling this way and that on the sandy road, all hurrying about their business under a cloudless blue sky.

Miri was leaning against the wall with one foot propped against the wooden boards, watching the people go by. "You have to tell her how you feel," she said at last. "Best not to let these things fester."

Tommy sat on the edge of the porch with his elbows on his thighs, his chin cradled in both hands. His eyebrows rose at the suggestion. "And say what?" he demanded. "Gee, Desa, I sure am mad you killed my lover."

The soft thumping of Miri's footsteps made him twist around. She knelt beside him, grimacing at that last remark. "You have every right to be angry."

"I know."

"Then tell Desa how you feel."

Wincing, he touched fingertips to his eyelids and

massaged away a dull throb. "Just what makes you think she cares how I feel?" he mumbled. "Desa does as she pleases with little regard for what the rest of us think."

He stiffened momentarily when Miri slipped her arms around him and kissed him on the cheek. "Tell her," she urged. "You'll never trust her if you can't work this out."

"Does it matter if I trust her?"

Miri actually froze at that.

Tommy stood up, his feet scuffing in the sand as he paced away from the porch. He turned abruptly and faced her with hands on his hips. "We could go," he suggested. "It's not like Desa has much use for us. Maybe Sebastian was right. Maybe we should just be done with her."

It frightened him to realize that he was echoing his dead lover's sentiments. It was a hatred for Desa that led Sebastian down a path that ultimately brought him to a bad end. Would Tommy suffer the same fate if he let anger dictate his decisions?

Miri was on her knees at the edge of the porch, her head bowed as she sighed. "Oh, believe me, Lommy," she began. "Desa may not be able to admit it, but she does need us. Now more than ever, I think. I fear that Adele's betrayal will send her down a dark path."

Tommy wanted to reply that Desa was already on a dark path, that her whole damn life seemed to be a long road into the very heart of the Abyss, but that sounded a bit too much like something Sebastian would say; so, he swallowed his objections and let Miri have the last word. A wise man had to know when it was time to let others take the lead.

Still, there were thoughts tumbling around in his head, and though he would have buried them under a mask of taciturn diffidence not so long ago, he was starting to realize that once you got into the habit of speaking your mind, it was hard to stop. "Maybe your brother's right," he said. "Maybe caring only makes you weak."

That put a bit of colour in Miri's cheeks, and when she looked up, Tommy wanted to back away from the intensity of her stare. "My brother is a fool," she said. "A fool who thinks that being callous is the same as being strong."

"But-"

"A fool, Tommy."

It made him pause when Miri called him by his real name. She only did that when she was deadly serious. Perhaps she was right. Perhaps Marcus and Desa both shared a stubborn refusal to be vulnerable, and perhaps that was why both of them made foolish decision after foolish decision. He very much wanted to be away from here.

"If you ask me, you're all fools."

That voice...

Tommy felt the hair stand on the back of his neck.

When he turned, he found Adele standing in the middle of the road in an elegant white gown that left her arms and shoulders bare. She stood in the shade of a thin parasol that she held with delicate fingers. "Hello, Thomas," she said. "Don't suppose you'd be so kind as to help a girl find her soulmate?"

29

Miri was on her feet in an instant, flinging open her duster to draw her throwing knives. She tossed them up, caught the tips of each blade and flung them at Adele one at a time. Sunlight glinted off each blade as they tumbled through the air.

Adele snapped her fingers.

Both knives became water and splashed against the ground at her feet, soaking into the sand. The sight of it sent chills down Tommy's spine. He had seen what Desa could do, but her power seemed predictable. Orderly. This was something else entirely. "Now then," Adele said, gliding forward like a debutante at her first ball. "Maybe y'all could help a girl out."

Miri bared her teeth, snarling like an angry rottweiler, and then broke into a sprint. She ran at full speed as if she meant to mow the other woman down.

"Sigh..." Adele mumbled.

In the very instant that Miri got within arm's reach of her, she vanished and then reappeared on the roof of a building across the street. She stood with one hand on her hip and the other holding the parasol over her head. "You know, I sometimes wondered why I had such a hard time bonding with y'all."

She stepped off the ledge and, to Tommy's shock, she didn't fall fifty feet and break her neck. Instead, she descended a set of invisible stairs, moving gracefully and giggling with every step. "And suddenly, it's clear as day. Y'all are savages."

Gaping at the woman, Tommy felt sweat on his brow. "Desa!" he called out when he recovered his wits. "Help!"

The door to the sheriff's office flew open, and Desa came hurrying out, shaking her head. "What is it, Tommy?" she grumbled. "We were in the middle of a very important-"

She froze when she saw Adele, the colour draining out of her face. "No..." Sheriff Kalia Troval emerged a second later, and before the woman could so much as blink, Desa rounded on her and shoved her into the wall.

"What in blazes-"

Desa stole the sheriff's pistol, cocked the hammer and whirled around to point the gun at Adele. She didn't hesitate. She just marched forward, squeezing the trigger again and again, filling the air with the crackle of thunder.

Bullets transformed into little puffs of smoke in front of Adele, who just stood in the middle of the road with a smile on her face. "Are we finished then?" she asked when Desa had fired all six rounds.

Tommy swallowed.

Adele seated herself on nothing at all, crossing one leg over the other and folding her hands in her lap. Her grin broadened as she took in the sight of them. "So...Now that you've gotten that out of your system, I thought we could talk."

"Who is this woman?" Sheriff Troval demanded.

"A demon," Desa whispered. "She took the dark power that Bendarian was trying to loose on our world."

Staring slack-jawed with a hand over her chest, Adele scoffed. "A demon indeed!" she said. "Desa, I thought you of all people would be capable of showin' a modicum of respect."

With the initial shock of Adele's arrival fading, Tommy tried to think. There had to be a way to overcome her powers. Obviously, she couldn't just do whatever she wanted – remake the world as she saw fit – or she would have done it by now. Well...He certainly hoped that was the case, anyway.

"What do you want?" Desa spat.

"Oh, no, no, no," Adele replied. "This isn't right. You should all be here for this. Where is Marcus?"

As if summoned by the sound of his own name, Marcus appeared from around the corner of a neighbouring street and stopped short when he saw Adele. His mouth twisted into a sneer of contempt.

"Oh good," Adele said, rising from her invisible chair. She flowed toward him with a smile that would set any man's blood on fire. "There he is."

Marcus drew his pistol with lightning speed, raised the weapon and fired without a moment's hesitation.

Like the others, his bullet transformed into a puff of smoke about two inches away from Adele's chest, but the instant it did, she was thrown backward, hurled as if by some violent tempest.

Adele screamed as she flew across the street, the parasol flying out of her grip. She crashed into a wooden pillar that supported the roof above a porch, cracking it on impact, then bounced off and landed flat on her face.

Desa watched the whole thing with her lips pursed, nodding with satisfaction. "A Force-Source?" she asked.

Marcus didn't bother answering.

He moved cautiously into the middle of the road with both hands clutching the grip of his pistol, his aim never wavering, not even for a moment. Tommy suspected that the only reason he hadn't fired again was that he wasn't sure if it would do a lick of good.

Adele looked up at him with strands of hair falling over her face, her teeth clenched as she hissed. "Now, that was just rude." Slowly, she got to her feet. "I do hope you'll like spendin' the rest of your days as a slimy frog."

She snapped her fingers.

Marcus looked down at himself with a frown, then patted his chest several times as if to make sure that he was still there. When it became clear that Adele's magic had failed, he continued his forward march.

For the first time since her sudden appearance, Adele looked genuinely concerned. She stepped back, nearly bumping into the cracked pillar. "I said I hope you like spendin' your days as a frog."

She snapped her fingers again.

Nothing happened.

Adele's eyebrows shot up, and then she shook her head. "Well, how 'bout that?" she said. "Seems I can't transubstantiate you. Bullets, knives, but not you. What makes you so special, Marcus?"

She stretched a hand toward him.

Marcus was lifted off the ground and then dragged toward her. Her fingers closed around his neck. "I can still pull you," she snarled. "Reckon I could snap your neck with only a flick of my wrist; so, why can't I transubstantiate you?"

Marcus had an answer for her, an answer in the form of a quick punch to the face that made Adele release him and stumble back. She raised a hand to her bloody nose. "I suddenly find myself very uninterested in why I can't change you."

Tommy braced himself for the sight of his friend's painful death. His friend...When had he come to think of Marcus as a friend? It didn't matter; he knew then and there that he did not want the other man to die.

"Adele!" Desa shouted, striding out into the street, distracting the other woman from her murderous intent. "He's not the one you want."

Clearly, she had the right of it because Adele turned her gaze away from Marcus and settled those icy blue eyes of hers on Desa instead. "I told you, honey, I'm not Adele anymore."

"Whoever you are," Desa countered. "You came here for a reason. You sought me out for a reason. So, tell me...What do you want?"

"See, that's what I like about you, Desa. You always cut right to the point." Adele cleared her throat and went to meet Desa in the middle of the road. "You know, startin' a religion is hard work. I was thinkin' about all the miracles I'd have to start performin' just to get some attention, and then it occurred to me. What I really need is an emissary. And you, little girl, are it."

"No."

"No?"

Tommy could only see the back of Desa's head, but he knew from the way she put her hands on her hips that she was giving the other woman a withering glare. "No, I will not be your emissary."

"Well, ain't that a shame?"

"So, might I suggest you be on your way?"

"Oh no, darlin'," Adele said. "'Fraid it's not that simple." She flowed around Desa and moved toward the sheriff's office. Her gaze lingered on Kalia Troval for a very long moment. "I see y'all found someone to take my place. Well, the more the merrier, I say. But this really isn't the venue for a negotiation."

Adele snapped her fingers.

Tommy stepped back and felt his shoulders bump up against a stone wall. He was in a building of some kind, a building with a vaulted ceiling and stained-glass windows that depicted scenes of a woman in blue robes pouring water on flowers.

There was a huge golden sun painted on the floor, and Adele stood right on top of it, smiling as she took in the sight of their new surroundings. Desa was right behind her, and Marcus was leaning against the opposite wall.

Everyone seemed to maintain the same relative position they'd had before Adele transported them. Tommy was relieved to find Miri at his side, though the way she gaped at everything she saw made him uneasy.

He gave a start when he saw that Sheriff Troval had made the journey with them. The poor woman looked very much like a frightened rabbit. "May the Almighty protect me," she whispered. "I've gone mad."

It was only then that Tommy noticed the light fixtures. Glass devices that hung from the ceiling, each one glowing with more light than any paraffin lantern could emit. Was this Field Binding at work?

"Now," Adele said. "This is more like it."

Desa stood behind her, scowling at the other woman's back. "Play all the tricks you want," she said. "It won't change my mind."

"Well, maybe you just need some time to think it over," Adele said. "Reckon you'll have plenty of that once you meet our hosts. So, I'll leave you to it then and check back in once you've had some time to cool off."

She vanished.

Pressing his back to the wall, Tommy hunched over and rubbed his forehead with the back of one hand. "Where are we?" he said at last. His voice was hoarse. "Where did she take us?"

Miri strode out into the middle of the room, pausing on top of the golden sun on the floor. "The Temple of Mercy," she mumbled. "This is-"

"Aladar," Desa cut in.

Rubbing his neck with one hand and grimacing from the pain, Marcus grunted as he went to join the two women. "So, we're home at last," he said. "I suppose we will just have to leave again."

"Why bother?" Desa countered. "It seems Adele can go anywhere, traverse almost any distance in a matter of seconds. We could chase her for months...or years...and we would never catch her."

Tommy shut his eyes tight, breathing in slowly. "Then the quest was a failure." He slumped against the wall until his bottom hit the floor. "Well, I suppose if I was going to witness the end of the world, I'd like to do it in Aladar."

"Excuse me."

Everyone had forgotten Sheriff Troval, but when the woman spoke, all eyes turned to her. Kalia wore a scowl that could make a hungry wolf retreat. "I don't know anything about this quest of yours," she began. "And I'm not sure how I feel about Aladar, but I do have to get back to Dry Gulch."

"I suppose I can help with that," Desa said. "I-"

A pair of wooden doors burst open to admit half a dozen

men and women in blue uniforms. They filed into the room, drawing pistols, making space for the leader, a portly man with tasseled epaulettes on his shoulders.

He had a distinguished face of olive skin, a thick dark mustache with flecks of gray and dark hair with wings of silver over his ears. "Just as the woman said," he barked. "A disturbance in the temple."

"Yes, but who caused it?"

That was a woman's voice.

Seconds later, a reed-slender woman in flowing blue robes followed the deputies into the temple. She had a sharp face with a long nose and gray hair that she wore pulled back in a clip.

Her expression changed when she saw them, creases forming in her brow. "Can it be?" she asked. "Desa Nin Leean, home at last?"

"Apologies, Prelate," Desa replied. "But I cannot stay. I-"

"Arrest them," the Prelate spat.

The deputies were in motion before the last syllable left her mouth. Tommy didn't resist when one – a young man with bright red hair – turned him around and fastened a metal device to his wrists. Two rings linked by a chain. No doubt it was intended to keep him from using his hands.

"We'll start with charges of high treason," the prelate went on. "Desa, Marcus and Miri at least have that much to answer for. I don't know who these other two are, but if they have abetted Desa's crime, the punishment is the same. Take them to the stockade. I will have many questions for them in the days to come."

30

The Weaver felt reality shift around her, her view of the temple blurring until it split apart. Like watching an egg crack from the inside. When the two halves of the old reality fell away, she was standing in a lush green field under a blue sky,

Her white gown was still pristine, her golden hair still braided with not one single strand out of place. "Well, now," she said, placing hands on her hips. "I'm pleased to see you didn't try to run this time."

She turned.

Benny was kneeling in the tall grass, his snake-like features set in an expression of resignation. He looked up at her with yellow eyes that glowed, each with a vertical slit as its pupil. "What good would it do?" His voice rasped as he spoke. "You hunt me down every time."

The Weaver smiled down at him. "We're friends, Benny." She reached out to lay a hand on his scaly head. "After all we've been through, do you really think I'm gonna just let you go off by your lonesome self?"

"What do you want with me?"

Touching her fingertips to the underside of his chin, the Weaver turned his face up to her. She bent over to kiss his forehead. "I told you, darlin'," she said. "Every god needs an adversary. That's how it works."

Benny was even more crestfallen upon hearing that.

"Now," the Weaver added, ignoring his despair. "What say you take out some of your frustration by terrorizin' some country bumpkins. I know the cutest little village just a few miles over yonder."

She snapped her fingers.

Once again, the world split apart around her, a crack stretching across the sky from horizon to horizon, and when the two halves fell away, she was standing in a small grove of trees with Benny still on his knees before her.

"Best to wait until nightfall," she cautioned. "We don't want them gettin' too good a look at you."

"What are you going to do?"

The Weaver shrugged her shoulders, tilted her head back and smiled up at the deep blue sky. "Oh, I don't know," she said. "I'm a god, remember? I reckon I'll go and be god-like."

Once again, the world split apart, and this time she found herself in the middle of a dirt road that ran between two lines of brick houses with tiled roofs. There were at least two dozen people milling about: men in work clothes, women in modest dresses. A horse and buggy came up the road toward her.

Everyone paused to look at the woman in the spotless evening gown who had just appeared out of thin air. The Weaver didn't give them much time to gawk. Emotion had drawn her hear. Pain.

She found the source of it with no difficulty.

A man in a top hat and a long black coat emerged from one of the nearby houses, followed closely by a crying woman who clutched her baby to her breast. "Please!" she wailed. "He's burning up!"

The doctor stopped short, but he did not turn. Instead, he just grimaced and shook his head. "There is nothing I can do," he said in a gruff voice. "Your son will either fight off the infection, or it will claim him. I'm sorry."

"Please!"

Gliding toward the pair with a smile, the Weaver stretched out a hand. "Let me help him," she pleaded. "I can soothe his pain."

The mother clutched her baby closer and pulled away as if the Weaver's touch were poison. That look of wary skepticism was one the Weaver had seen before. She had seen it on the faces of her father's friends and business associates when she told of her ability to sense the world through the Ether. She had learned, painfully, that silence was wisest in the company of men who feared what they did not understand. "Please," she said again in soothing tones. "I can help him."

The doctor harrumphed. "Madam," he intoned. "I am a trained physician, and yet I am unable to treat this child. What could you possibly hope to accomplish?"

"Have faith, good sir."

The mother's face softened. Tears streamed over her cheeks as she sniffled. "If you can help him," she squeaked. "Then please..."

Gently, the Weaver took the infant in her arms. "Shh...Shh...Shh..." she whispered as she touched two fingers to his forehead. Within seconds, the child's shivering stopped; his eyes drooped shut, and he settled into a peaceful sleep. "Here."

The mother took her child from the Weaver's embrace, and when she backed away, her eyes widened. "His temperature dropped!" she exclaimed. "What did you do?"

The doctor was squinting as he studied her through thin spectacles. "Yes...What *did* you do?" he demanded. "I won't abide charlatans in my town!"

"You, sir!" the Weaver shouted, pointing to a spindly old man who walked with a wooden cane. "Come here!"

The old fool hesitated.

"Yes, you!"

With excruciating slowness, he hobbled over to her, his face scrunched up from the pain in his leg. "Thank you, Miss..." he said in a breathy voice. "But I don't see what you can do for-"

The Weaver laid a hand on his shoulder, and he shuddered at her touch. His cane dropped to the ground, but it didn't matter. A grin spread on the old man's face. "By the Almighty!"

He flexed his leg and then laughed as he ran back to his family, who quickly rushed over to marvel at his new-found mobility. A young woman with curly blonde hair – most likely his granddaughter – actually covered her mouth with both hands and gasped.

By this point, a crowd had formed around the Weaver, and the people all muttered nervously to one another. One man – a handsome fellow in his middle years with dark skin and flecks of gray in his neatly-trimmed beard – stepped forward to speak with her. "How are you doing this?" he mumbled.

Grinning beatifically, the Weaver shut her eyes and shook her head. "People," she said. "Fear not. I come not to judge you but to redeem you. Step into my embrace, for I am the light and the way."

Her flock did as they were bid, each man, woman and child coming forward for her to lay hands upon, most speaking in hushed whispers. She accepted their adulation. When she was done, every last person in this world would drop to their knees and marvel at her glory.

ABOUT THE AUTHOR

Richard S. Penney is a science-fiction author and futurist from Southern Ontario. He graduated from McMaster University with a degree in mathematics and statistics. Rich knew that he wanted to be a writer ever since he was a child, when he would act out complex stories with his action figures.

He has worked in a number of different fields, including banking, teaching and software QA.

In 2014, Rich published his first novel, *Symbiosis,* the first volume of the Justice Keepers Saga. The story was one that he had been planning to write ever since he was a teenager. The Desa Kincaid novels grew out of a tandem story that Rich started on Theoryland.com, a Wheel of Time discussion site.

Rich has been an environmental activist since his early twenties, and he has given talks on sustainability in Greece and Australia.

BOOKS BY THE AUTHOR

Symbiosis (Justice Keepers Saga I)

Friction (Justice Keepers Saga II)

Entanglement (Justice Keepers Saga III)

Relativity (Justice Keepers Saga IV)

Evolution (Justice Keepers Saga V)

Dirty Mirror (Justice Keepers Saga VI)

Dark Designs

Desa Kincaid – Bounty Hunter

Lightning Source UK Ltd.
Milton Keynes UK
UKHW021954231020
372136UK00003B/224

9 781715 647391